CW00621516

# THE ALIGNMENT

THE ALIGNMENT

# THE ALIGNMENT

## CONNOR S. LYNDON

Connor S. Lyndon Pub

*In the face of mere difference,*
*we can all be* heroes.

# THE
# ÆLIGNMENT

THE
ALIGNMENT

# Chapter 1

The Dream of Orange Plains & Ungodly Pain

*Raven*

His eyes closed yet felt peeled, exposed to Eyldia's brutal elements. Pure darkness, slamming open to a bright red drop, straining against the twirling hues and the binding treelines. His eyes threw from side to side within his skull. A dreamer's soul fell, dancing on the ribbons of life. The past, the present, the future, all as one within dreams. Moments in time ripped up and stuck into countless possibilities. Raven's lean body remained softly twirled into his old feather mattress, yet the walls of reality crumbled upon a dreamer's mind, throwing his soul through the sky's thinned clouds with ungodly force, bracing, begging for a clear landing. Raven peered up to an orange tainted world, observing the environment as he struggled to his feet. The tinted plains waved, staining the air in a thick, charred-oak scent. The metallic taste rang through his taste buds, causing him to wince upon the possibility of another dream he found himself stuck within, begging for any understanding of what's being told.

A mighty storm brewed with unnatural haste, with wind spiralling, wrapping its force around his torso, roping his joints in mid-air like an elemental restraint with all-consuming strength. An ink black horse rode by a hooded figure, raced up the plains, grating its foot, tossing the gravel into the thick, dusty air. The voice echoed across the grassland, pushing against the grass blades, passing an old stone wall with a sign dropping to a slight slant between the stones' cracking foundations. The horse and its rider rode into the blood orange fog.

"Forwei" Raven murmured.

The orange tinted world crumbled at his feet as if the magic itself pulled at the soil. He descended into the abyss. A view of clustering patches of soil and grass dropped into ribbons of pure life flew, burning his eyes. Absent of warmth and its sun. The ribbons weaved swiftly, pushing memories once old or ready to become new across his vision. Babies born or yet to be. Grandparents dipped into graceful death. Wars fought and battles lost. Raven couldn't control his descent, kicking his legs into the hues of ink black. His arms waved through the thick abyss, pleading for his bony arms to grip the bursting beams of ribboning light.

A ribbon shined at his left, staring. It wanted him; it grabbed with eternal force, wrapping its burning strands around his skull, causing a scream. One lasting plea. The smell of thick dripping blood filled his nostrils in a rushing moment of relief, straining himself up from the layers of thick, trampled sludge. Soldiers screamed, bleeding out of every freshly slashed wound. Some cried, knowing their organs in their hands would be their last moment of grace under Eyldia's gifting sun. Suits of armour, running through him as if he was truly dead. The never-ending battlefield of men and women. roared, pushed, begged, and smashed into one another in primal anger. Yet one stood firmly upon a meadow's hill, radiating a sense of beauty wrapped in unfiltered anger and ink black runes climbing his muscular arms. One lone, mighty strike from his sword upon the blood-soaked muck caused the ground to quiver. The purple hues whispered like an ancient song between two old friends. It knotted the sword and man truly as one. As if they communicated on their next strike mere seconds before.

The man glanced up at him with a soulless expression. "Dreamer." Its head whipped to the left, observing him. "This is one possible outcome of what will come. Ones you love or come to love. Falling in grace to greet an unknown fate." The man's whispers scratched at his ears.

The silence swept away, filled by a soldier running at the soulless man. Metal wrapped in anger charged up the meadows as he spoke. One strike. His head rolled down the meadows, dripping the warm blood across the trampled grass. Eyes once bold with meaning, faded to nothing. The last flicker of life, of a stranger, yet he sobbed, kneeling in his blood, staring into each detail of his black tunic and protective leathers.

A never-ending wave of souls, piling upon the plains as the air pierced the land, collapsing under the pressure of mere whispers.

"*Two souls ribboned as one*". The air purred.

"*Two souls ribboned as one.*" The elements chuckled.

"*Two souls ribboned as one.*" The air screamed with all the might magic could muster.

He dropped to his knees next to a pile of dead soldiers. "Stop. Please." Pleading to the air, begging for the whispers to stop. It did. Not even the wind graced his face with a smoothly icy breeze.

The world transformed around his feet once more. Colours and ribbons twirled, interlocking, connecting as one entity. It was incredibly beautiful. His heart filled with wonder as the sky filled with colour. Reds, purples, oranges, and greens. They danced in harmony. Four magical elements as old as time itself. At least that's the story each Eyldian told their Young. Power that picked you, like a soul picking another to love.

The sky ground to a halt. The four ribbons raced as they reached Raven, wrapping its raw power around his bony frame, pushing and pulling, throwing him across the four lands. Each kingdom and queendom being different in culture, density, and structure. Raven's head pulsed in pain. The pressure, it felt as it would pop in the very next click. Raven landed in a place unknown to him. A mountain range with the purest snow, never touched, not one footprint upon its ranges. Peaks and waterways dancing against the landscape. Stones pulled, groaning and grating open, revealing people in leathers. Purple sewing lanced up the shoulder padding. The snow reflected the purple across the mountain. People trained, yelled, and worked together in an army-like structure.

Raven walked as curiosity took over him. What is this place? The whispers of the air started once more...

*"Two souls ribboned as one".* The air purred again.

The air grabbed him. It also grabbed another man from within the mountain. Raven didn't know him; the taint blurred his features to nothing Raven could analyse. The air dragged both men to come eye to eye. No soul laid inside the human vessel.

"Who is this?" Raven questioned the air in annoyance.

*"War, chaos, peace, love."* The air breathed into Raven.

Golden ribbon of power flew through both men's veins as the air squealed the words again and again and again.

*"The Four will fall as the crow screams and Sun's Peak mourns."* The air screamed as if it was in pain.

*"Two souls ribboned as one. War, chaos, peace, love. The Four will fall as the crow screams and Sun's Peak mourns."* The air let out a piercing scream as it dissipated.

The golden power pushed, plucked at them both. At their existence. It pulled at their souls. The golden power grew within them. It raged out of every vein. It threw them both to the ground. Raven eyes bled out; blood replaced water as red tears fell to the soil. The abyss felt like a warm welcome compared to the golden power. Raven blinked as blood filled his eyes. The black abyss waved to welcome him back. It whispered to him once more.

*"Alignment."* The void stared.

# Chapter 2

Raven's Farwell

Raven clenched his heart as he woke, looking down to his boned-textured torso, lines of dried blood crusted onto his stomach. He shot up, racing to clean himself, bashing his shoulder at every sharp angle. His heart felt like the golden rage still consumed him, leaving an everlasting burn coating his veins. Looking at himself in the mirror, flicking his blood-stained curls out of his eyeline, filling his palms with water, dashing it harshly into his pale features. Staring into a reflection in a mirror, him, blinking, a movement, a change, begging to be seen, to be observed. Flickers of orange and gold, pulsing against his sea blue colouration within his iris, battling to be at the forefront.

Raven stared at himself as time stood still. "Two souls ribboned as one." He whispered to his reflection.

Thoughts echoed through his body. "War, chaos, peace, love."

"The Four will fall as the crow screams and Sun's Peak mourns." His eyes flickered.

Raven dropped to the floor. The dream could be false; Raven spat to himself. Not all dreams were true. The future often spoke in riddles through rumours and dreams. All the thoughts pierced through him. Who was that hooded guy on the battlefield? Where was that mountain range?

His mind couldn't locate any sort of mountain range to that scope of beauty. It must not sit within Drossor's borders. The riddles of words played in Raven's mind: Alignment. What things could line up? Nothing made sense.

Raven pulled a thought from the back of his mind, placing it on his dry tongue. "Forwei...". The town was a half rotation walk from there. He pulled himself off the floor. His essence twirled, humming his words.

-

Raven closed the rustic cottage door for what felt like the last time. He consumed a big breath of air before turning around to reach the streets of Elcoo. His travel bag normally used for Peaks Solstice came into use, ramming as much stuff as he could think of into it. Food, water, clothing, and an unused travelling pot Eben gifted him on his eighth birthday, trying to get him to embrace the wild elements. He threw it on his back and started his walk in the frozen mud. The ancient cottage sang behind him, whistling a last farewell.

A goodbye to the settlement of mud, buildings left to sink, rot and blend into the terrain. The vibrance of nature refused to pass Elcoo's borders. He often heard the hums of trees begging to be ripped out of the dead ground.

-

The smell of fresh bread filled the air as he struggled against the rocky path. He edged near the bakery door, Ms Moori's. What would he say to her? Raven shook off his thoughts as he pushed open the rounded red door. The bakery felt like one of Raven's dreams. The air ribboned with happiness and passion. Small circular tables for indulging in one's cravings.

He couldn't help but let his eyes trace over the walls, mostly covered with handmade glass jars of spices, sugars, powders, flours, milk, cloths, and materials for packaging. Ms Moori surely put all her love into this, Raven's cheeks raised. Between these four walls, he could let go of the pressure on his narrow chest. Echoes swam in the air in perfect harmony as Ms Moori sang and whistled upon her runic orb. She never used her runic power to harm or to get an advantage over any of the village people, lighting up her palm with a faultless, upbeat whisper. It sounded so angelic, lingering, like a memory of a forgotten, distant era. She could've lured any man into her trap if she was ill-hearted. Raven's heart pulsed at her power, or maybe it was the everlasting scent of freshly baked breads. Ms Moori took as a statue of grace, a rune whisperer of old with hues of black, painted like it had been drawn into her mature skin mere days ago. Spell symbols upon her palm and arms, proud of all their years of service.

Raven placed a hand on the kitchen counter, giving a soft warning of his arrival. She beamed from ear to ear at his presence, slapping the layers of flower off her hands as she wrapped her arms around his torso for a brief yet warming embrace. Raven's nose filled with spices left on Ms Moori's apron, allowing the spices to consume him. "My dear, how sweet of you to visit." She smiled, "I'm making a cake using butter, all the way from Dualia." Her craft gave her unfiltered love and excitement, living a simple, yet loving life, serving the miners and branching their idle chatter.

He mirrored her beaming smile. "Is Dualia's butter better than Drossor's?"

"Dualia has the most beautiful fields graced with unsullied nature." She paused, like she forced her smile to keep firmly in place. "It's the one thing the Four haven't poisoned. The Dual Mountains produced the freshest waters."

"I'm sorry." He stood still, offering limited comfort.

"There's no need. I haven't been back to Dualia since King Alonn took our lands." Ms Moori struggled out a laugh, dusting off the flower from Raven's side. He nodded in understanding.

"I've got to go meet up with some friends in Dreaka." The guilt, the lies, it punched Raven's heart in two.

"Go, dear, have fun." A smile grew as her eyes widened. Raven simply nodded once again. He knew if he replied verbally, he would choke on the goodbye that came next. She seemed to understand, nodding back with an added wink, returning to her runic orb. He had to be dishonest. He couldn't open his thoughts to her, as the path forward remained clouded.

–

The roars of trading counts continued through the frozen market street, straining their voices for any chance to barter away their goods. Raven browsed through new cloaks, admiring the stitch work and the vibrant colour details down the seam. One cloak especially remained to rob his focus each time he gathered the confidence to pander the overwhelming voices, but a hollow expression always followed it, spreading like fresh butter from Ms Moori's shop. A cloak only a slim amount of Elcoo could afford.

Raven's feet flew from under him, as a force small yet forceful launched his bony frame forward, gliding onto his right cheek. Glancing up from the frozen stone and dirt. He didn't know if to laugh or cry from such a gliding drop from grace.

"STOP HER!" the market trader pleaded. The child's clothing looked like it had two seasons of dirt gripped into its fabric. Rips that climbed their way up to the child's face from all angles. Raven peered up at the child's face as she prepared for her escape. His thoughts distracted by the child's hair, appearing to have been in a fight against a bush and lost completely.

She glared at the traders' eyes with complete distrust, as if she had been raised by Gnomes. Before Raven produced his next blink, she dashed through the market. Stall by stall, she jumped onto tables, pushing people as she skated side to side. The trader tried to rush after her, but he didn't have a chance. She was gone. Leaving only trampled goods in her wake.

Raven pulled himself up with support from the market stall. He investigated the ground around him and all the damage that the frozen dirt now claimed as its own. His heart pulsed as thoughts of that little girl, abandoned, cold, brimming with sorrow, filled his head. Did no one care for this child? No one to brush her hair as she prepped for slumber.

Being invisible to the people of Elcoo became second nature to Raven as he dipped through the shoulder-to-shoulder miners at the tavern's bar front. The Old Mace, what a rotted dump, but it was home for as long as he could remember. Running through the tavern as a child, marking the walls to watch the paint slowly peel as a source of entertainment. A slight grin climbed his sharp features, noting the success of the paint markings that ran down the bar. He still didn't know if he kept the markings for fondness or for the lack of counts.

"Anyone seen Eben?" Directing his query to the barman, serving the late rotation rush. The barman glanced over, wiping away with an emotionless brow lift.

The barrel storage door opened with a roaring force. "--Don't be rude, Ewa." Eben squeezed his sleeves, wringing the water with an effortless huff. "Raven, how's the library?"

"Fewer books returned from this season's collection." Eben's eyes widened vaguely, like words had left him hollow. "Eben, I've got to go for a while. Travelling with friends." Raven lied through his teeth again, darting his eyes to Eben, waiting, scanning his face for any sign of suspicion.

"Friends? Paying for their company doesn't make them friends." Eben laughed as he glanced at his workers behind the bar.

Raven forced his lips up to form a smile for Eben. "You're never funny."

"You'll always have this place when you return." Eben smiled, while tossing a withering rag over his broad shoulder.

Raven saw that crackle, that Eben coated his features in such laughter, masking an unknown sadness that he could never breach. He knew Eben kept secrets but never could get anything out of him through his teenage hood. Raven once camped behind the bar in a pathetic attempt of protest. Never worked on Eben, though. Nothing did. The tavern carried on as it always did. Raven pushed the door open, not knowing if he would return.

–

Raven walked through the streets of Elcoo after a long day at the tavern, his arms clamped at his ribs. He pushed against the seasons' might as he glanced down the alley between a furniture store and an abandoned storage hut. A little girl sat on the cracked stone and oak foundation. Quietly shaking upon the battering winds. It was her. Raven could point out that battlefield hair from a village away.

He paused, took a huge breath that filled his lungs. Smoothly gliding his hand that pulled down his hood for what felt like a whole rotation. Step by step, he lowered to her eye level. His heart climbed up to his mouth, scanning over the shades of brown coating her. He couldn't help but jerk back slightly, the mix of dirt and bruises piling upon the girl's face like a book of her unfortunate events.

"Don't be afraid... Are you okay?" Raven whispered with care filled expressions. The girl blinked rapidly.

"Don't run." Raven raced out calmly before she calculated her escape. He slowed his movements as he pulled at the knots, keeping the cloak's fabric wrapped around his torso. Sleeve by sleeve, he pulled, freeing his withered warmth. "There, have this." His breath slowed, placing the old, muddied cloak over the girl. Her eyes darted with clear disbelief. "It's okay."

"W—why?" The girl breathed.

"I don't need it." He beamed a grin, hoping it would allow her some comfort. "I know a wonderful lady, Ms Moori, say I sent you—" He held back his tearful choke. "She'll give you the late rotation of baked goods no one wants."

The girl brushed her clumped hair from her eye, letting a slight orange hue highlight her bruised cheek bones. "I see so much, it hurts. I see you, so much pain." Her tears dropped into the layers of dirt upon her cheek. "How do I control it?"

"I don't know. There's not much knowledge written on our power, but if I find anything, I promise I'll share it with you." Raven climbed to his feet, wiping the dry mud from his knees.

-

The wind sang to Raven in the slowest tune, like a monster in the shadows. It teased his hair as he walked to Elcoo's exit. He had lied to the two people that cared for him. His heart let out a sob, pleading for his eyes to follow.

Raven didn't know much about travelling alone. Every solstice he would travel with a group of people from Elcoo to keep safe from the creatures that lurked in the shadows. He strutted through the plains northwards. He admired the nature he didn't often see being in Elcoo. The green life grew, spread and sang. Deer sprinted across the plains with freedom in their leaps. Did the entire realm feel this way under the Four?

-

Raven ate food Ms Moori secretly packed in a container in his travel bag. Camping didn't strike Raven as an activity he would enjoy, but he found himself being consumed by the peace of nature. Alone under the moonlight, even if it still held a brisk from the freezing's seasonal might.

He pulled his travel bag close as he grabbed the sleeping bag that held on for dear life to the side of the bag. He didn't know he had one before he packed. Maybe it came from one of the market's roaring sales. The sleeping bag felt like the Old Mace oak flooring. At least the stars filled the night sky to keep him company. Raven sighed, turning into a curled-up position, allowing fatigue to blossom.

The tree line barked at Raven, begging for him to wake. The shadows moved in the night's glow. Green tinted eyes peered through the bushes; they observed the human as he slept alone. Fingers flew in the air as a signal from the group's leader. Grunts, moans, and yells speared Raven's mind.

Raven pushed himself from the ground, one, two, four... eight, panic raced over his face as he froze still. *Goblins.* He'd never seen them with his own eyes till now. Their flaky skin peeled as they licked their lips. They monitored every reflex, every twitch, and every breath. Time stilled as Raven scanned them back. Their poison-stained eyes that were supported by at least 3 dark circles. They looked to be at least 4 feet tall. Raven had his height on his side, but that didn't ease his panic. He knew their keen five-inch razor tusks would cut his mission short lived. The goblins started to form a circle around Raven before he realised it. This first night hadn't gone according to plan. All he wanted was peace, alone under the starlight.

The stars beamed down onto Raven's face. It sang, teased him once more. *"Alignment"*

Raven groaned in confusion. What did that mean? He didn't know what the air meant. His power within him did. The goblin's heads tilted slightly as Raven's eye filled with golden embers. Roars echoed into the meadows; their feet dug into the ground as they charged Raven in full force, one by one. Their stained tusks shone in the starlight, but so did Raven's golden eyes.

Raven never had training in Elcoo but somehow, the panic left him; his arm raised from his side. The golden ribbon of pure force flew from his veins into the first goblin that charged. The golden twirls lit the meadows in a rich golden tint.

One by one, they dropped to the soil. Their blood and their bodies were now a gift to nature. The goblin leader launched with rage filled tusks, aimed at Raven's head. Raven's eyes began to flicker back to blue. The panic climbed his body once again. His legs went to jelly as he stumbled to the campsite floor, hoping to assess his belongings. Raven's eyes popped as he saw one of Eben's old daggers that teased out of the clean travel pack. His knees groaned and bled as he dragged his aching body across the dirt. One arm begged to reach for the dagger. Pleaded to his soul. The goblin landed at his side; grief dripped from his tusks, begging to swim in hues of thick red.

Time didn't stop as Raven begged his bones to move further. Blood covered Raven in one mighty slice. The head rolled as it accompanied Raven's travel pack. He shook, he didn't grab the dagger in time. His blue eyes peeled themselves from the flaky goblin head to a hooded figure. His eyes raced over the figure's mighty broadsword that now hugged the goblin's blood. Raven's lip moved, but nothing came out.

The figure grabbed their hood and pulled at it back. The sun shone down, gliding down the figure's blooded broadsword as it caressed his neck. "Get up." The tone struck deep, yet felt familiar to him, leaving his eye glowing bright like hues of the sun and blooming meadows.

# Chapter 3

The Temple, Its Thieves & The Moon

*Astrid*

Wind twirled, wrapping around the thick stone pillars, whistling against Astrid's sweat-dripping biceps. The sparring floor vibrated as swords clashed and groaned at one another. Astrid flew into the air as he whispered into the air itself. Violet power whipped from his palm, launching to his opponent's broadsword.

"That a new spell?" Pazima gracefully winked, fluttering her full eyelashes. Astrid dropped to the ground in full force. Dust layered in motion, filling the sparring floor. Strike after strike, they teased their swords together. A dance of metal and knowledge.

Astrid smirked. "Anything for you."

Pazima's eyes teased a flicker of rose red, twirling her power within, battling against her amber irises. Her sable skin consumed by a thick red mist, the only thing that would remain was her essence, manipulating her knowledge of creatures, holding every flake of her skin, every fibre of her being, reforming to what she wanted as the red mist bowed to her will. All that remained was a mighty golem made of sand and mossy stone. Seven feet tall, a creature now stood in her place. She charged at Astrid with primal shifter force, roaring into his sharp cheekbones.

Astrid smiled at the golem, accompanying a playful curl of his sword to avoid a critical, direct strike. He whispered, unable to hold in his slight grin. His body became one with the air and stones, unable to be observed. All but his footsteps left to the naked eye.

"Smart ass." She broadcasted into the empty space. Astrid took that reply as confirmation to finish the spar. His ribbon of power pulsed him into the air. He was not only a thief of Moonsong anymore, but one with everything, the air, the drips of moisture from the cave's stalactites, every crack and scratch upon the temple's foundations, slamming himself into her golem's head in one swift jolt.

"I won!" Astrid's celebration written across his face. Pazima's red mist returned around her golem form. The mist bent to her will. Every flake, every piece of hair, all at her control within the mist cloud's free-forming boundary. Pazima waved her hands in a curling motion at the mist, forming and moulding the mist at its base, cutting, and holding its shape as if only her imagination could stop her will. Its shape morphed into an impossible ghost-like staircase, guiding her to land on the sparring floor in angelic grace.

"I let you win." Pazima's half smirk danced on her face. Astrid didn't know if she meant it. All he knew was he enjoyed being around her. She held life within her angelic features. As if her shoulders were the foundations of the temple itself. The red mist removed itself from the room with one commanding glance from Pazima. She prided herself on the definition of self-control and discipline within the guild and everyday routine. Every time the Commander came to spectate, she would drop Astrid to his ass in a mighty chomp. Astrid dragged his fingers through his wet thick, ink-black hair, dropping it back into its natural short middle parting, free-forming into rogue strands in-front of his eyeline.

The guild's home cleared of dust as they chatted in its centre. Astrid glanced at the four stone pillars that held the cave in place. Magic whistled through the caves as water dropped into the rivers in the corners of the structure. Stories drawn into the stone walls; carvings of the originals of Eyldia. Their history, culture, and love, written and kept safe within its hidden structure.

The sparring floor stood at its core, for mission briefs, speeches, calling upon their moon, asking for guidance, for balance to be restored upon the four continents. Stone stairs chiselled its way up the three outer layers, which they now used to observe fights, learn techniques, and teach classes to their Young. The guild accepted the beauty of nature, its flora growth, drooping from the cave's stalactites. The outer centre rings split into three long hallways, for sleeping quarters, weapons storage and eating quarters. They slept in rooms of two unless you had rank within the guild. The shifters some-times desired to form into bats to hang off the cave ceilings, engrossed by the moss. The ancient hall could house a grand feast for all Dualia's people if they tried. Astrid loved what the guild was and how they made him a part of their family when he was truly alone.

"Astrid... Tris, you alive" Pazima grinned at him as she sharp-ened her broadsword.

"Stone-cold dead." Astrid laughed while he snatched the sword from her hand, following his feet's natural path, launch-ing down the eating quarter's hall.

-

The sun dropped behind the mountain's peaks; Astrid would often find himself consumed by his thoughts while staring into the dimming sunlight of orange luminescence, highlight-ing Fellow's Gap. The fire crackled, animating Astrid's sharp facial features. He waited for sun's fall each rotation, waiting to see a dreamer about his conflicted mind. The ribbon of his soul echoed loneliness without him knowing why, ever since the lone, brisk night that bit at his feet, as a Young one, left alone and abandoned. At least that was all he could remember. This feeling of emptiness stuck out like a ghost in a corner of a room. Sensing it, seeing it, being consumed by it like an object he couldn't grab, even with a primal outburst of fury.

Fee stepped into the campsite that was a short walk up from the temple's entrance, on the edge within Fellow's Gap's beautiful valley of towering trees. Her cloak flicked as she perched onto a wet oak stump on the opposite side of the campfire, greeting one another with a simple nod and an added smile.

"I saw your spar with the Commander's daughter today. How's that going?" Fee's smile, slightly covered by her straight, lone strand's of her ink-black hair.

Astrid's smirk raised slightly as memories of the spar flashed by. "I won"

"That isn't what I meant," Fee stated with a wide glance.

"It can't happen." The word wrapped itself around his mind. Astrid loved her since she welcomed him into Moonsong. She helped him get accustomed to their ways, even as a Young one, she stood proud and powerful, all for justice, and mighty in her ways. Astrid admired each light, every flaw, and every creature that had her amber eyes.

"You don't want to love her, hold her." The dusk's breeze waved her off-white fabrics, revealing scars of old upon her left arm. "To protect her?"

"She doesn't see me that way. I won't push." Astrid stood, anchoring his footing into the gravel, turning to stare into the mountain's silhouettes. Why take her focus? She trained her whole life to be her father's successor, to lead the guild into something more. The thoughts tackled his mind every time he stared into Pazima's glowing umber skin, or her tight ash-brown springy coils, kept just above her shoulders.

"You won't... or can't? Fee questioned.

"Aren't you meant to help me?"

"Everything I say will help you in the end." Astrid was used to Fee's often riddle-like speech. Her knowledge of the mind was one of mystery. She could dig through minds to pull out the greatest of poisons someone could muster, then came a young Astrid. A child placed in the care of the guild by Pazima's elder sister, left with a torn letter. No one knew where she got him, or how he came into her care. All they got was a child and a plea to keep him safe at all costs. The mystery child, haunted by nightmares at every rotation. Fee, tasked to care for his mental state since his arrival, always unable to reach the entity that lured in his nightmares.

"You could be faster about getting there." Astrid laughed.

"Has the feeling been around today?" Fee lifted herself up from the support of her Katana. Astrid loved her choice of weaponry, her unique swordsmanship within the guild's ranks. Most carried around two daggers, swords, and powders that supported their power. Not Fee, she commanded missions with only her Katana attached to her back.

"I haven't noticed."

"You still look away from me when you lie." Fee now sat next to Astrid.

Astrid glanced into the fire as Fee placed her hand on his head. She glided her fingers to his temple.

"Ready?" Fee asked. She knew an answer wouldn't greet her.

–

Her eyes closed yet felt open to every sense in the realm. She found herself in the guild's home, on the sparring floor. The air didn't accompany her, neither did the cave's whistles. Nature didn't live in this place. The ground quaked from under her. Black mist filled the temple, filled her lungs and her veins. She struggled to keep the connection to Astrid's self-consciousness that lived deep within his essence. The black smoke cleared to accommodate the entity that stood at the centre of the floor. Fee's senses pulled at her, her very essence screamed at the entity, almost fearing its energy. She'd never been able to reach it. It teased her with no visible expression, all with the thickening air clawing at her neck. Her imbued Katana glided, twirling effortlessly between her fingers. Yellow ribbons of power swirled around the bond between weapon and user, the dreamer's yellow glow proud, yet refused to glow against the entity.

She launched and danced against the black ribbons of power. The entity simply vanished and reappeared on the other side of the sparring floor, using the thickening smoke as a tool against her. She pushed as hard as her power allowed. The entity followed like a mirror, copying, teasing her with each poetic swing. Each swing screamed at her, as if it grew bored with her visit. The black smoke consumed her, removing her soul with remorse, grinding her teeth against the sandy sparring floor.

Her eyes bled, it dripped onto her snow-white kimono; her fingers collapsed from Astrid's temple. Fee failed to fix him once again. Astrid tried his hardest to not show his disappointment. That also failed every time.

"We'll try again tomorrow." She wiped the blood from her eyes.

"Fee." Astrid murmurs across the campfire. "You'll get it."

The short walk up to the guild's entrance was always silent, only accepting the crushing push of the snow under their boots.

The morning air filled the main temple structure as Astrid and Commander Sakhile sparred. The child that landed in his lap one brisk night. He always spared a morning whenever he could for Astrid. Members of the guild stood and watched as they launched at each other. The Commander's eyes glistened a bright green. His connection to the realm through creatures and the circle of life. He was a rider. One of the best riders in the guild, him and his Quetzalcoatl, Ambe.

"Lazy on your feet today, soldier." The Commander loved to tease his opponents, get into their heads. To open a pathway for his victories. Astrid's lips simply grinned. He loved it. Astrid whispered into the air. His eyes rippled to a vibrant purple as runic magic obeyed his words. Ribbons of power collected at his fingertips, knotting into an energy ball, one of the runic whispers laying in his arsenal.

Commander Sakhile seemed impressed by the new whisper; a proud laugh echoed through the sparring floor. Astrid's energy ball listened to his essence, what he commanded of him. The ribboned connection built as they admired each other. The energy knew what to do as it flew to the Commander's footing, launching the settled dust upon the sparring floor into disarray. Nothing but a dust cloud in its wake. Astrid grinned. His whisper breached, launching sparking balls of energy into Sakhile's sides. Command Sakhile scoffed, highlighting the dust in a pale green hue. An out-worldly force pushed through the wall of dust and sand. The crystallised, sparking figure slashed, revealing the spirit of green that coated the Commander. A rider's strongest ability, to summon animal spirits of great power. A rare yet loving power from the soil below. Ribbons twirled and interlocked, forming a bear that now hung over Astrid.

"You can't always win, soldier," he stated through the dust. Astrid climbed to his feet. He graced the Commander with no reply as he walked out of the dust cloud.

Laughter and noise of cutlery meeting their plates filled the room, but Astrid sat with nothing to say. He circled his spoon

through a bowl of fresh rabbit stew. His soul sat in a place unknown as the room moved on through time. He now sat alone;
hours passed that felt like seconds.

"Astrid," The Commander entered the room and sat next
to him.

"Yes, Commander?" Astrid jumped back into reality as he
realised time had run off without him.

"I have a mission for you and Pazima," he stated with no
emotion. "You must go to Charr and observe. Sources suggest
some questionable wrong doings to its people by their high
magistrates." The Commander said with a glance of worry.
"Whatever you do, don't get caught. Especially with my daughter. I don't want to kill you. I've invested nearly ten years
into you." Astrid investigated Commander Sakhile's eyes, but
they didn't offer any answers. They ran cold, as if the Fellow's
mountains' freezing climate held in his stare.

"I understand, sir."

"One more thing. Don't dwell on the loss of battles, engross
yourself in how to be better the next time battle offers you to
dance. Learn to dance Astrid."

The Commander didn't allow a reply to enter the room.
Astrid sat with his cold rabbit spew in silence once more.

Astrid walked the temple's long corridors when he couldn't
sleep. He would often find his feet being lured to the levels
below the temple. Rooms, structures left as frozen frames of
time passed. Grass cracking through the stone floor, climbing
up the ancient furniture. The narrow staircase connected to
the great hall was one only some were allowed to access. A
place their riders kept their partners. Stone level foundations
descended, cracking, filled with living quarters and bedrooms
abandoned, leaving lone oak bed frames accompanied by vines
and ever-growing moss. The guild respected that slow decay
of an old era, offering the respect of peace, left frozen and

untouched. The only place left in an era before The Four. They kept to the cave that sat on the edge of the mountain's cliff face, a moist, yet warm cave that Ambe and other mystics called home. No human could enter that way on foot. The mountain wouldn't allow it. Only people with eyes tinted by poisonous ivy could push through the mountain's runic protective illusions of old.

Myths and rumours echoed through the soil of the realm. Stories of creatures, the hisses echoing through the clouds. Riders would spend their young life at sea, consumed by the waves and the little islands that remained untouched. Stories of Commander Sakhile and Ambe had many versions. One would state he found her hurt on a stone plain shore, about to be consumed by the sea. Another suggested he saved her from an abusive leader in Sun's Peak. No one would dare to ask which is true.

Astrid silently stepped his way down the narrow staircase, keeping hold of his breath as he gripped the mossy stone railings. He wasn't a rider, but he loved to glance at the myths below. He felt a relatability to them. Something inside he couldn't tell nor understand. The room sang to the myths as they lay in the moonlight; the wind bellowing through the crack, rippling throughout the cave's formations, as if the realm hummed in a beautiful melody. Astrid sat up against Ambe. He never understood why the myths would allow him to do so. Ever since he arrived nearly ten years ago. Astrid heard the myths in his dreams. A feeling that desired to be itched. Astrid slept against Ambe's feathered wing as it wrapped its serpent body smoothly against him, trapping the surrounding warmth.

# Chapter 4

## Hoods & Crows

### *Raven*

Come with him...

A stranger. His reasoning remained unknown. Lies could loom as carefully crafted bait. He looked back at the path to Elcoo. His feet begged for the way back to normality. The brutality of miners, the cooking of Ms Moori and the love that sang from his petite ancient cottage. He missed that rustic red door a little too much, pleading to feel the radiating warmth from jolting the door's lock ajar.

Raven and the man monitored each other as they walked through Iron Forest. Rumours told of this forest and how it had creatures born of chaos, waiting, watching the outer settlements for an easy meal. A short, commanding threat from a broad man with a blooded broadsword, removing any choice in the matter. The man decided on the Iron route for a quicker route to Forwei. Raven's mind raced like a pulsing pain at his left temple. The desire to seek answers had become his downfall. The dreams, the sleepless nights, all the questions that remained unresolved. Every fibre of his soul begged to run, but his heart pushed forward, demanding to find the answers.

24

The men's eyes brushed over to greet Raven's; he choked at the confidence as the man captured his stare. "I'm Sevar." He spoke plainly.

"Raven," He forced out the single word he could.

"Crow," Sevar murmured to himself. Raven glanced at Sevar, admiring the striking beauty, as if his features dared him to stare longingly. The shadows of the forest cast over them, refusing to cast over Sevar's glowing umber skin. His muscles pulsed as he took each step in the gravel path, pushing a radiating hum through his veins. Sevar's structure towered over Raven by six inches. Heat gripped Raven's cheeks as Sevar surveyed him. The air remained thick with fog and dust from the nearby iron mines. The taste of iron climbed to his tongue, shaking off the primal thoughts. He crossed his arms while forcing every step. Raven didn't know what he expected from the flashes of Sevar in his dreams, but it wasn't this.

–

"Why save me?" Raven looked away, forcing his view to the left treeline.

Sevar glided his eyes to Raven, but his lips remained closed. Sweat started to form under Raven's blood covered hair, turning back, spotting a runic symbol drawn into Sevar's hand. "Why threaten my life if you saved me?"

"I'm doing what I need to do."

Raven's feet stopped, begging to leave. He couldn't when this man had him with no knowledge of how to leave the woods. The trails circled and twisted upon themselves. Darkness, oak trees, and paths that moved were all that laid in his view.

"Who would task you to save me?" Raven almost snorted. "I'm a barkeep, not a person with heritage, no self-made fortune. I'm just... me." Raven's head scanned the tree line out of boredom.

Sevar brushed the rune with his fingertips. "I have a task to protect you. Even if I need to threaten you to do so."

"I don't need a guard." Raven's ribboning energy quivered at the thought. Being stuck to the other, letting anyone in, a risk, one he couldn't take. The bargain of knowledge, Raven had begged for answers to so many parts of his life, not knowing anything about his childhood. All memories clouded like the fog they now crept through. Dancing trees upon the wind, following the elements with pure grace. The air split against the silence, punching them with a growing monstrous growl. Footsteps stomped from the left of the path. They froze in their step; Peeled at where the noise radiated from. One big ruby eye flung open in a parting of oak trees. Stones groaned, crashed, and interlocked to form a beast.

"A cyclops." Sevar stated to Raven. Sevar didn't give him time to think, moving himself in front swiftly, like being a shield was mere instinct. He began to whisper into his arm. The dreamer went to talk, but Sevar clamped his mouth closed with his hand, wrapping the damp warmth of his breath within his palm. Sevar slowly pointed to the cyclops, returning his pointing gesture to his ears and nose in a slow motion.

Sevar kept a connection between them as they crouched to the small clearing, smoothly sliding a dagger from his hilt. Their breath slowed. Their footsteps silenced. The dagger was ready to kill, almost winking in the light in response, waiting for Sevar to command its next move. Raven observed this man at work, like he had done so millions of times before. The same man, repeating, folding, screaming, riding that damned horse across the meadows. It had to mean something. Sevar let out a long-focused breath before he jumped into the air. The cyclops threw its head towards them, letting out a low whistle from its stone's cracks, slamming its stone arm into the dagger's side.

Sevar was left unconscious on the other side of the parting. The cyclops groaned, pushing its stone feet into the ground, running for Sevar's lifeless body. The dagger remained in the middle of the clearing, partly hidden by the swaying blades of grass. Raven flung himself without any thought, aiming for the cyclops' eye like Sevar displayed moments earlier. He took that as a trustworthy fact at that moment. It meant life or death for them both. His ears began to pierce, ripping by an ungodly noise, a pressure that could pop him into pieces in seconds. He shook, pleading for it to stop, and it listened, forcing him to glance at the dragger that glowed a golden tint. He stared into his reflection within it. His eyes, the golden ember hues, it burned yet felt freezing to the touch, sending chills down every bone within his spine. Raven hadn't seen it before; he didn't have time to question what unleashed inside of him. He jumped onto the cyclops' back as it roared. It smashed the ground, pushed and threw itself at him one stone at a time. Their lives hung in the balance, he climbed. His body groaned and yelled for him to stop. Raven's hand wrapped around the beast's boulder head. He took a long breath as he swung to the front side of the cyclops. Before Raven could launch the dagger into the cyclops' eye, it smashed its head into the dagger's side, whipping Raven into the nearby treeline. It was lost. The forest shadows had the only weapon he had; panic ran through his veins. The cyclops sniffed the air and the golden power that simmered from inside of him; it flickered in his eyes. An emotion filled the cyclops' eye, almost scanning him like he now became the predator. It roared, throwing him across the parting. The force of the cyclops' stone feet echoed through Raven's ribboning essence. He froze. Death tried to consume him. The wind whistled, accompanied by purple light and whispers that twirled in the wind. Pure power forced out of the whisperer's veins; The beam carved through the cyclops' stone torso, screams and cries pierced their ears. The trees in the clearing quaked at the force. All that remained now laid in a crumbled pile of stones next to his frozen body.

"Get up," Sevar commanded.

It had been two rotations since they entered the forest, facing a beast of stone. They didn't talk the rest of the way to Forwei. Raven refused to collect his thoughts. Two attacks in one day were enough, almost turning his mind to mush. Sevar walked close, brushing his shoulder. He blushed as his stomach pleaded with him. Raven shook off that feeling. He didn't want to be saved by him. He didn't need to be saved.

They arrived at Forwei by sunfall. Their feet pulsed as they peered over the river line, their thinning breathes filled the air between them. Forwei. The city of lumber and craftsmanship. Walls of granite held the river into place as it groaned at the water's current. Three bridges accompanied by neighbouring watch towers came into view from the north, south and west. Sevar pointed at the southern gate, directing Raven to the right path.

The town's noise flew in the wind like a peaceful grace. Towering walls of thick oak foundations with granite bricks layered perfectly between the oak beams. A wall an army would find hard to crack. He wondered how much raw granite the workers carted and mined from the nearest mountain range. Raven and Sevar glanced at the guard posted outside the city walls. Sevar glanced, pulling his thumb and pinkie finger up. The guard's eyes stared, pondering. The distrust grew in his mind. Sevar nodded with no emotion as they carried on through the Forwei's southern gate.

He couldn't ingore the pressurising feeling of Sevar staring into his features. "What was that, back in the parting?" Sevar investigated, staring into his eyes for a long moment. "You're a dreamer..." The whisperer walked close to Raven, like a layer of caution weighed upon him.

"I don't know. That's the first time outside of the... dreams of war."

"You need to tell me everything." Raven stared at Sevar for a moment, trying to calculate how much he may know of this possible approaching war.

Raven looked away, ignoring his command.

They walked from the southern gate through the city, streets full of people doing their daily chores. Alleyways carried the wind through the busy streets, washed clothing sprung from building to building by a piece of thick string. The streets felt like a maze of communities packed into themselves. Sevar walked in front of Raven, silently directing their movements. The noise grew thick in the wind as they reached the city's main square. The hub of Forwei brimmed with life. It stood as the primary activity of the lumber trade in the two kingdoms: Drossor and Dualia. Many people came here to plan their buildings, compare pricing, and prepare for transportation of goods. Rave froze, weighing if the overflowing noise and movement came with mere awe or flooding anxiety.

"Crow." Sevar sighed at Raven.

Raven caught up to Sevar as they walked along the river that cut through the square. The buildings moulded themselves to form a beautiful structure of brick, wood and a carefully crafted ruby tainted slate roofs. It was gorgeous. Full of colours that Raven couldn't completely take in. He had been to Rale within Dreaka's borders and its famous seaport, but that didn't live up to the colour of Forwei's structures. Children played in the streets; grins plastered to their faces. Raven's awe slipped; the little girl he gave his cloak to. If she was born in Forwei, she could have been happy. Why did this city have happiness when his home didn't?

-

They dropped their travel packs onto the floor as they groaned into the inn's freshly made beds. The wood beaming dipped in and out of the room, supporting the entire building with might. Candles dropped from the steep ceiling like magic.

Most definitely whisperer magic. Pure blue washed the walls, sourced from the sea's rich blue weeds of the southern coast. A colour not yet tainted by history and blood. The mattresses dipped in perfectly to their body's shapes, filling them with undisturbed pleasure.

When morning came the sun slowly rose, pulling at the curtained windows. The silent room graced with his sleepful groans, looking to his right. Sevar wasn't in his bed. His bed looked clean, like he had never touched the room. Raven questioned if to run while the whisperer was nowhere to be seen, but he knew he wouldn't get as far as the southern gates. Sevar seemed too skilled to be outsmarted by him - a barkeep, he thought to myself as he glanced around the room's fundamental details. Symbols of axes seemed to be drawn into every centre point within each piece of furniture. He forced his focus back to his flooding queries. Why drag him to Forwei, just to abandon him in an inn? Raven sat, glancing at the mirror that laid against the nearby wall. His hand glided up his shirt with accompanying sighs, revealing his torso. His fingers ran across his skin, slightly dropping into the indents of his rib bones. As his eyes cut at his body, his mind jumped to the delights of Ms Moori's meals. Her warmth, the bakery's stuffed sounds attacking him at every moment. That feeling of emptiness filled the room. His arms dangled at his sides, nothing but skin and bone. A long breath withdrew from his lungs, dropping his shirt back over his torso.

# Chapter 5

## Cruelty of Men

### *Astrid*

Ambe's feathers waved delicately in the calm wind. Astrid opened his eyes, suprised by a monstrous lick. What time was it? He climbed up from Ambe's never-ending serpent body. The sun had silently risen upon the mountain's creases, complimenting Astrid's hazel eyes. In these moments, Astrid felt an essence of peace he couldn't get from other guild members. Fee tried to her best abilities to support him, but he always had the ghostly figure at the side of his eye. In the corner of every room where the noise of others kept absent, it giggled at him. Sneaking and observing, it would never let Astrid feel complete.

"My feathered friend," Astrid softly glided his fingers through Ambe's feathers towards his face. "In another world, we would have been brilliant partners." Ambe's eyes wondered over his face as he let out a playful hiss. Ambe's body slithered comfortably against the dungeon floor. His scales vibrated at Astrid's company. The contrast of feathers and scales left any living thing at awe. Its neck coated vibrant hues of red and orange, cutting its coat short, touching its scales of blood red and dark hues of brown.

He pulled his tunic down fully to conceal his chiselled torso. His last breath of air from the myth's dungeon felt like an entity. Step by step, carefully finding his way through the ancient stairwell.

–

Pazima cleaned her weapons, as she always did in the morning before a sparring session. "Have you bathed?" She raised her arm, teasingly covering her nose and her half-risen grin.

"Come smell and find out." Astrid smirked proudly as he tied his leather boots up tight.

"Pig." Pazima slid her sword into her holster. "Have you packed essentials? She pulled her travel pack from the ground.

"I don't need anything more than my sword and my charm."

"Charr is a rotation worth of travelling away. I'm not sharing. You'll end up leaving me with the scraps again." Pazima's brow lifted, waiting for answers.

No answer came out. A long sigh escaped his mouth as he walked to the entrance of the temple.

The Commander walked past at a hasty speed, tossing a bag in his direction. "Cover your tracks." He didn't stop walking down the halls, allowing for his footsteps to echo throughout the temple's foundations. "Good luck!"

–

"Why does my father adore you so much? You have the temperament of a Youngling." Pazima walked off down the path that connected to the stables halfway down to the snowy plains.

"I'm the strongest?" Astrid grinned. It wasn't a question.

Astrid and Pazima walked side by side down the mountain's pathway. "Have you got the Commander's permission to use the horses?" Astrid pushed Pazima slightly with his shoulder.

"I asked him last night, in his study." Pazima said with a blank expression. "As I'm the only one that'll sign off the missions for the both of us."

"And I'm grateful for it." He launched up upon a white horse, offering his hand to support Pazima to hers.

She glanced for a moment, deciding to place her sword into his icy-cold hand. "Thank you." Effortlessly, she launched onto her horse and held out her hand. Astrid's cheeks glowed a slight rosy red, smoothly placing her sword back into her palm.

-

The horses trotted against the gravel path, allowing the sound of the water stream to consume their thoughts. It whirled in the bitter air, pushing for the freezing season to end. The smell of change, cracking through the realm's natural essence. Its grass, its trees. All waiting to reach another long brightening. Astrid loved to see the change in the air. Maybe then his hand wouldn't threaten to drop to the gravel pathways below his feet.

"What things do you think their high magistrate is doing?" Pazima placed her hand on her hilt.

Astrid stroked his horse with praise for the long journey. "What does the mission sign off say?"

"Word of abuse and control. At least that's what the source says." Pazima folded the mission papers back into her pocket. "Let's hope force isn't necessary."

"Aw, don't say that. I was looking forward to an actual fight." Astrid felt Pazima's sharp glance pierce his cheek.

-

The gravel path ended at a bridge that angled up to a crossroads, bridging to multiple houses around the water stream. The white stone buried itself into the wet stones of Charr. Stone complimented by red stained wood structures. A town most far north in the whole of Eyldia, but no snow seemed to drop onto its land. No sign of the freezing rage or the dropping's decay. The trees stood proud and tall, almost frozen to time and rogue gushes, towering over the houses with their thick leaves. The river cascaded through the hills and into the creases of the land. It kept all the plains perfect for crops and resources for all Dualia. The air had a smell to it, lacing each Eyldian's tongue with an ever-lasting metallic tang. Astrid scanned the land to see any drawn runes upon its structures, but nothing peered out to his sharp view.

Pazima and Astrid gripped their horse's leads, tying them both to the hitching post outside the town's bridge entrance. Both kept a steady hand on their hilts, ready to strike at any moment. No noise, no talking, not even a whisper. They walked into Charr smoothly while they observed the layouts and structures of the town. The scent remained, even growing as they crept into the town's centre. Astrid kept his eyes out for any signs of runic activity. His eye scanned the biggest home on the left of the river's stream. A tint of purple light shined at him. A runic symbol drawn on the third-floor wall of the home. Astrid's right brow raised ever so slightly at the symbol's shape, letting a sigh of annoyance escape through his lips. He'd never seen a rune like this, at least not in the tomes from Moonsong's library.

Astrid's face filled with frustration as he looked at Pazima. "I've never seen that symbol in our books. Must be something more powerful, a less known spell."

He knew what that meant. Knowledge of rune spells was everything to a rune whisperer. Knowledge to remember a spell others hadn't obtained. A whisper, a connection to magic, to the realm and its history.

"What is it with whisperers and their secrets..." Pazima rolled her eyes as she scanned the paths for activity.

Sudden fury gripped him, leashing against Pazima's words. "Knowledge is power to a rune whisperer. You're not one, you wouldn't know. Learning a rune no one else has is everything. A move no one may expect. A true power advantage in battle."

"Calm down Tris. We were told not to be spotted. I'll see if anything's happening in the fields." Before Astrid would have objected, she twirled her hands, commanded her red mist. It transformed her into a simple orange cat. One that wouldn't make anyone blink an eye.

He stared at the rune; his finger tracing through the purple dust left behind. He admired the way it stained the wall with its runic power. What did it mean? The frustration bubbled up in him. Why did this other whisperer know more, consume more, connect more with the earth? His eyes overflowed with purple rage.

"The high magistrate seems to be shouting at figures in the fields. Let's go check it out." The red mist consumed her essence as she stood in her original form next to Astrid.

He gave a nod in agreement.

–

The fields were filled with grown carrots, potatoes, and tomatoes. Maybe more if he took the time to observe the different shapes and colours that consumed the farmland. Astrid and Pazima used some lone trees to keep cover from the town officials. They were tasked to observe the ongoings of Charr, told to keep out of sight. Astrid's eyes carried his rage for him. He had orders but he didn't care at this very moment.

"Pazima, their children. They couldn't be more than eleven years old." The anger spoke for him as he watched. The high magistrate stood proudly over the children that struggled to keep their bodies up from the farmland. Whispers left the high magistrate's lips. The children screamed, dropping to the moist soil below, as if they hoped the ground would swallow them whole.

She itched at her hilt. "Ready to stop this?"

"I thought you would never ask." Astrid already had his sword gripped to his side.

Pleads and sobs poisoned the air and their ears. The shifter's sword reflected the sun's glare as she twirled it around in her hand. Astrid loved when she did that. A playful twirl, a connection to their weapons they both could agree on. They snuck their way through crops, trees, and bushes to make their way to the cries from the children of Charr.

Astrid and Pazima nodded to each other. splitting between two approaches into the opening. Astrid snuck to the left, pulling his aim to the high magistrate. He looked back to see Pazima as she lined herself up to help the children. She was so kind, yet powerful. For that second, his rage calmed.

Astrid's whispers filled the surrounding air, pushing through, dancing upon each piece of wheat. Hues of purples, stalking its prey as commanded. Once a cocky smile peered upon the high magistrate's ageing folds, whipped by one mere whisper, throwing the high magistrate across the fields. Now this was the fight he craved.

Astrid found him in the dirt with half-baked whispers choking its way out of his lips. "How could you do that to the town? To the children." His rage boiled, pushing the contents of his stomach to bubble up his throat. "What book did you learn this from? Was it another whisperer?" He grabbed the man by his coat, searched his pockets to find nothing but a broken watch and a bag of counts. His cheeks brightened to a flaming red, as if he embodied the rage of the fallen Old Ones. "Tell me!"

"Astrid. Stop." Pazima pleaded from her heart as she held eight children behind her, clutching her moss-stained cloak.

His eyes flickered, tempering the drowning anger. "He knows things. I need..." His hand refused to let go, as if the emotion controlled the blazing runic essence, flowing, suffocating him.

"You don't." Her words stayed calm, like a song. A tale they would tell the Young ones when the dark came to their dreams, stalking their innocence, claiming it as their own.

"How do you know what I need? Your power remains at your disposal. You shift to anything at will. No limitations."

"Tris... we need to get these kids out." Pazima's face looked at Astrid as if his eyes were ones of a stranger.

Astrid looked at the high magistrate, kneeling with his remaining grip. He whispered into his ear. "Come back here and I'll rip your limbs from your torso, plant them for beasts to enjoy, turn this field into your own personal nightmare." Astrid's words spat venomously, as the high magistrate's neck bobbed, faintly swallowing his blood. "I wonder how long it would take for The Four to realise you're dead?" He didn't wait for an expression from Charr's official. He turned around to head up to the town houses with Pazima and the children, smiling as he flicked the bag of counts playfully into the air.

-

"Get the kids to pack some stuff up they want to keep." The command flung out as he walked off into the far-left house.

Interiors of red, oak, and white mixtures. Clearly influenced by the building's outer structures. The red stained wood seemed the fashion inside Charr. All the houses shared the same uniformed furniture. Most likely crafted by the same person, he thought. Nothing of power called out to him, nothing of runic scent. Astrid scanned from the kitchen area, noticing wind teased the corner of a rug.

"Always the secret room." Astrid muttered to himself in a humourful tone, kicking the carpet to the left.

He jumped down completely, ignoring the ladder that stood in front of his feet. The room smelt of runic power, threatening to buckle him to his knees. A scent of spells he never smelled before, completely virgin to this consuming power of old. His hands glided the edge of the old, stained work desk, scanning the contents of the room, but there was nothing besides a desk with a damp chair. The desk, cramped with old, dusty papers, books, and maps. One noticeable thing was an entire map of Eyldia that hung above the desk, pinned with notes of noticeable towns, cities, and trade ports. Why have a map of Eyldia? The three Kingdoms and the Queendom highlighted with importance and care.

"Meetings with The Four?" He read out the readable notes, scanning across the old running ink, reading through the damp layers of papers, pinned into place. Some remained fresh and detailed with petite angled ink quill tips.

"Control over the seaports."

"Sun's Peak threats." His finger touched the words carefully, refusing to skip a single letter. "Rising rebellion." Fuck was the only word his lips allowed to escape his tensed jaw.

Astrid's head darted from side to side as he scanned the map and the surrounding papers. The knowledge twirled in the air. Whispering, calling for him. Astrid reached his hand out but the sense of unknown screamed. Pleading? A test? He pulled with all his might, opening the desk's rustic drawer. *"The Book of Untold"* His breath was lost as his purple eyes flickered in excitement. His veins, his essence, it craved this. All rune whisperers would.

The book now laid upon his hands, floating, supported by the twirling hues of joyful, ribboning purple that streamed from his very essence. Its power layering his own, teasing his palms. Tickling him as it remained closed. The power whispered, almost like it mocked him.

*Open me.*

He smiled. His whispers twirled around the book, turning it invisible for any other living being but him. He placed it softly into the inner lining of his cloak, folding its magic like the space between him and the book's contents were his to control.

"The kids are ready to go."Pazima cast her voice across Charr's village square. He stepped from the inside of the house, greeting the kids with a warm smile.

Pazima helped pack the important items of the Charr kids, soft animal toys, puppets and notes from their parents.

"Are you all okay?" His words softened its way to the children's ears.

"Yes, sir." Eight voices rippled slowly towards him.

"Let's go."

"Where are we going? This is all we know." The kid's lone tear dropped to the compressed dirt ground.

Astrid dropped to one knee, forming the children into a circle around him. "I know it's scary. These people kept you to do work for them for nothing but a roof in return. We are people who can help. Give you something more. A place where you can be more." Astrid choked faintly. "A place to call home."

Most of the kids nodded in reply. Scared but knew in their hearts it was better than this. Pazima, the children, and Astrid carried on through the crossroads of bridges, towards Charr's entrance. One child kept to Astrid's hip.

"What happened to all the adults?" Astrid mustered the calmest tone.

"Our parents gatherED each week to drink, to talk. They went and never came back. " Astrid turned his face in disbelief.

His eyes scanned over the firepit that laid in the middle of the homes, a pile of ash. It sparkled white. "You'll be okay now, kid."

The kid looked up at Astrid with a realm worth of curiosity. "What power do you have?" Surely, he would have seen him and his purple eyes when he attacked the high magistrate.

"I'm a rune whisperer. Were you not educated on Eyldian magic?" He pulled his eyes down for the kid to see.

"Yes, sir." It remained unclear to Astrid if the child's features were clouding with fear or in awe. "But your eyes... The golden angel came to save us."

# Chapter 6

## Trouble in Forwei

### *Raven*

The door's handle jolted as Sevar walked into the room. "You're up."

"Where did you go?" Raven turned his head, peering inside from the balcony.

"Just a walk."

No reply left Raven's lips. He returned to the noise of the city, adoring the layout of the land, how it branched and formed off into many streets, like a maze of lives and its own history. The shapes the houses made, sitting against the pathways. How the market square sized up compared to the city's homes. Chops and swings echoed through the air like a soothing tale, staining the air by its accompanied smell. Flakes of wood chipping twirled through the pathway's creases, played with by nature's gushes. It was another rotation for Forwei and its lumber trade. Why had this place been happy, at peace? While Elcoo sat in sorrow, slowly accepting its push to death. That empty feeling creeped its way through him, causing a tear to shed.

"What's the matter with you?" Sevar raised his brow slightly, watching Raven walk back through the balcony door frame.

"Nothing." He said, with no desire to display true emotion. "So, what's your plan? Keep me here, in this Inn? For what?"

"My task is to keep you safe till you're ready for what's next"

"What's next? You tell me!" Raven's voice climbed to a casting yell. Bubbling with frustration, of queries unclear in his mind.

Sevar looked away, grabbing his sword's holster, ripping it around his broad chest. "Let's get some breakfast. I'll explain shortly." Raven's eyes

-

Raven pulled a cloak from the market stall, allowing his face to glisten, feeling its details. The colour that displayed the city's cultures. Red stringed through the fabric of most of the clothing. He loved the cloak, the warmth, the comfort away from the outside world and its people. It made him feel truly invisible.

"That's not food." Sevar looked over his shoulder, his lip lifted ever so slightly.

"I know, I just..." His face scanned the wide range of cloaks. "I gave mine away."

"How heroic." Sevar whispered to him. Raven eyes darted up towards Sevar.

They walked on through multiple different market areas, exposing himself to several trades and interactions. Sevar scanned through weapon stalls, like its contents were the only thing that piqued his interest, till they landed in front of a dark old shop on the corner of the square's western entrance. The red stained oak darkened by time and unkept cleaning routines. Its brown-washed exterior slowly lightening to a pale shade, discoloured by time, leaving the only inviting feature to be the ancient windows, covered in burning light and count-less layers of dirt.

"In there?" Worry raised up his throat.

"Indeed, you'll learn from travelling around Eyldia. The dirtier the shop, the better the craftsmanship." Sevar seemed to grin at him as he spoke about his knowledge of the realm. Raven followed his lead, entering with a slight quiver at his ankles.

–

The lights tinted the surrounding air. A thick layer of sawdust twirled within the light, dancing with the smell of numerous oil stains. How did this place make the mess look magical? The light floated above the display countertops, inviting the customers to adore its light and its products. Embers swirled, encased by a ribboning field of near translucent energy. Raven's eyes scanned the weapons on the handcrafted display tables. Daggers of unique designs laid down on top of a reused red sheet of fabric. Raven had never looked at a weapon in awe till now. His eyes landed on a pair of daggers that shined in the ember's light. An engraved symbol of a crow with its wings expanded with pride. The wingspan launched out into small but mighty cross guards. Its hilt allowed the blade to curve slightly, crafted to rip out any internal organs that came within its reach.

"Daggers engraved with a crow." Raven could feel Sevar's eyes beam into his back, his neck, and his essence.

Raven's fingers slid down the hilt. "It's beautiful, but I've got no training, well apart from fighting my father with a stick when I couldn't sleep."

"You'll need to learn. Even with my skills, I may not be with you to stop what may come around each corner."

Raven turned around to give Sevar eye contact. "I still don't know why you think I need protecting."

No reply filled the dusty air. Raven sighed, staring at the daggers. Before he could grace his next blink, Sevar scooped up the daggers, swiftly turning, greeting the shop owner like he had known him for a lifetime. This man saved him, threatened his life and now gifted him weaponry. Who was this man, and what did he want?

"Take them." Sevar held the daggers and a new belt that had two sheaths accompanying it. Raven stood with an unreadable face as time slowed around him. He didn't know if to accept or to crumble into his own essence.

He looked up, staring at the whisperer's stubble. "Thank you."

Sevar softly placed his stance close to Raven, looking into his eyes. "Can I?" Raven nodded slightly. Sevar's hand wrapped around his waist, attaching the belt to his body. He slid the daggers into their rightful place.

The daggers were perfectly balanced in their holders at Raven's sides. It felt unnatural to his narrow torso. Sevar pulled his head away from Raven's new belt as shouting and runic scents filled the streets, attacking his nostrils. The people of Forwei gathered into a crowd, covering the noise with curiosity and worry. People murmured between themselves as more people poured into the square.

Raven darted to Sevar's side as they walked together into the crowd. "What's happening?"

"I don't know. It doesn't smell good."

"The runic scent is powerful." Raven noted. "Is it always so strong?"

"You get used to the scent" Sevar slowly sighed as he scanned the crowd. Soldiers dragged a woman and two young men onto a platform in front of the crowd, dropping them below long pieces of knotted rope that swung slightly with the wind. Raven followed Sevar's tense expression for a moment, realising the events that they were about to witness. A sentence of tension, of rebellion.

"Today we stand as proud people of Forwei. As people of the crown! We will not accept any form of rebellion, of this disrespect!" A polished axe dragged against the hardwood foundations. The noise of the steel as it scraped against the wood was like poison to their ears. "The Four till Death!" Soldiers screamed, their presence projected across the whole of the market square, the river quivered at the tension.

"Put their heads on the blocks." Commands flew between the soldiers. "Put the boy in the rope."

"Any last words?" The soldier's Commander smirked with pride, plastering his narrow, pale face.

The men cried, pleaded, and prayed to the land. To any gods they may believe in, they begged for any last hope.

"Choke on the King's cock." The woman spat at the axe, grinning towards the soldiers, as if her grin was a final stand against the royals.

Blood dripped from the axe's head, screams and groans leashed the wind to a standstill. Raven looked up to Sevar to see tears stream down his cheek. Before he thought of what to do, his hand interlocked with the whisperer's, Sevar's hand grabbed back instantly. Raven pulled as hard as he could, using the cobbled floor as support.

"Sevar, come on." Raven stared up into his eyes. He guided his body to a nearby street, away from the noise that echoed through the air. Sevar's soul jumped back into his eyes, filling his mouth with shock. He choked up, unsure of what to say. What would bring comfort to a man that remained a stranger to him? The man protected him when he could have ran.

His legs lowered him to the ground. "Sorry."

"Don't be. I understand the feeling. How the thoughts drag you down into yourself. Feelings that hunt you down from the corner of your eye." Raven's stomach dropped; his heart raced as he placed his hand on Sevar's stubble. This feeling echoed through Raven's essence, a want, a desire.

"I dream of things that would drive people to madness. Death, desire—" He choked upon his words, almost gagging at the emotions. "Grief of future loves, dying in my arms." A singular tear slowly rolled. "You have kindness, I can see it, behind all..." Raven's pale fingers glided smoothly across Sevar's stubble, reaching his chin. "Tell me everything." He dropped to a mere whisper.

# Chapter 7

## Like clockwork

Down busy streets, around corners, into a street that seemed to be forgotten in the city. A block of houses with flickering embers in its window panes, raggy clothing left, hung from the building's connecting wire lines, abandoned to the weather's temperament. Nothing but silence in the air. "Down there." Sevar directed towards Raven.

"An old clock shop?" The building stood detached on its left, letting way to a narrow alleyway which the front door accompanied with discarded boxes by its steps. The solitary shop was the only one he had seen with its door facing the alley. It seemed odd to Raven, but he didn't have a choice but to follow Sevar up the cracking steps.

"Indeed, it is." He spoke with a vaguely gloating tone. Sevar pushed the door, a bell connected to the door rang to greet them.

The shop was truly a museum of clock craftsmanship. Grandfather clocks towered on the sides of the room. The walls were littered with clock arrows. Each of Raven's foot-steps greeted with a groan from the ancient miss-matched, wood flooring. The noise of this place would be overwhelming to anyone, noises of hundreds of clocks that slowly ticked away, accompanied by the flooring's groans. The essence of the room felt different from any shop he ever stepped into. It felt magical. Each clock felt different, each tick, each detail to the numbering. The displays of the rotation number. It all rubbed against Raven's soul, adoring all the different clocks and their woven connections to ancient magic. Magic greeted him as he greeted it. A connection he only just began to accept.

"How can I hel—oh." A blonde-haired woman walked off, back through the shop's counters. The ticking spiralled, grating against the humming of whisperer magic. Sevar's face lifted at the sight. Before Raven could enquire about anything within the shop's interior, a grandfather clock slid to its right, groaning against the wooden foundations, revealing a narrow staircase that carried on into pure darkness.

"What is this place?" Raven whispered.

His words bounced off the newly revealed staircase walls. "Clockwork Base Drossor."

Raven walked behind Sevar as closely as he could. The thought of reaching out to grab his shoulder for support raised through his mind. Even though this man threatened his life. He saved it too, twice, without a lingering doubt. Maybe he could trust him, if he told him the full truth about why he desired this journey. His heart raced at the thought of companionship, causing his throat to tense, building knots of pressure.

Light and clock machinery noise flirted in the air. The staircase stopped suddenly as their feet graced a big meeting room, supported by naked foundations and clock machines covering the walls. Hues of colour littering the wall with hazardous beauty. Something felt different when he looked at the clock structures. Even though he wasn't a rune whisperer, he still felt its runic imbuement wrapping around his bones, wrapping the entire building's structure. The walls remained like a timeline of Eyldia's history, a littered collection of clocks, cogs, and stripped wood foundations. Golden arrows with green wood framings, to red stained grandfather clocks that moulded together from time's might. A tiny gasp escaped Raven's lips.

"This is the clockwork Forwei safe house." People glanced up. Why was a stranger in their operations? Internal hisses flew like a primal scent. Telling Raven to keep to himself, to keep to Sevar's side.

"A safehouse? You're all criminals for hire?" Raven raised his right brow, trying to control the waves of worry.

"Mostly, but this is the life we got given to us, most didn't get a choice. It was this or die." Raven looked over his features, like memories stained with sorrow over, even Sevar's thick beard couldn't mask.

"So, why hide in safehouses?" He had to know. Too many questions lay in front of him.

"We don't hide, its quarters for us to regroup, get missions. Sleep in a warm bed. Clockmaster Horo also kept the safehouse network for precaution, protection." Sevar's voice dropped to a soft tone. "The answer is, I'm a mercenary. Paid to fight, kill. Rescue..."

Raven's eyes looked up to Sevar as he spoke about being a mercenary. He knew he didn't tell him anything detailed, . This had to be linked to why he needed to protect him. Did someone hire him? Impossible, no one cared for him that much that would want him protected. The question bounced around in his mind as he read Sevar's lips.

"Why are you showing me this?"

They scanned over the long table. Scraps of old clocks, odd cogs, and abandoned palettes of wood were used to craft the clockwork's belongings. The long table branched across the meeting room, covered by piles of paper titled in a blood red stain. Mission plans, placements of clockwork informants around Forwei and main officials' identities. Folders left open, tossed across the meeting table. "I was briefed on a mission to save some people from Forwei soldiers. That's why I wasn't around when you woke up. As you saw earlier, I didn't get to survey the situation in time. King Plu Kan and his men got to them first."

Curiosity waved over Raven, softly flicking through the folders. He could feel the stalking stares pierce through his curls, threatening without muttering a single word. "Sevar, look at this. A second woman was spotted in the lumber stripping area with the others, according to this record."

Sevar grabbed the papers from Raven's grasp. "A second woman? I would have known." He flicked through with an obvious annoyance plastered over his broad, sharp jawline. "There are no characteristics, no age, no way to identify this woman. Only one account of her talking to the other rebels."

A figure glided in smoothly, like his feet didn't touch the wooden foundations, sitting at the far side of the table, flicking a lone arrow into the air. "You're a dreamer. You find her." The arrow landed perfectly on his finger, flicking into the air like a pet he had trained for endless rotations.

Sevar rose his head sharply as the flicking stopped. The fellow clockwork mercenary put his hands in the air for a moment, displaying a humourful laugh. "Only a suggestion, Sev, didn't know you wanted to fuck him." His feet glided towards the corridor to the sleeping chambers. "You should bring more dreamers around. They are so convenient. Well... if they haven't lost too many cogs" He tapped the side of his head, three times in a mocking tone. "Oh, he definitely understands." He left with a parting wink.

"I don't want to fu — I" Sevar broadcasted only to be greeted by a laugh from far down the hall. "Sorry about Bastian." Sevar's eyes remained on the paper.

"It's okay." He murmured. Raven walked off to the nearest chair that accompanied the meeting table. Focus filled his essence, echoed to his ribbon. Raven did not know how to use his dreamer powers well, but he would try. For this woman who fought for a better life for herself.

"You don't need to. Bastian's just a bastard. You don't know how to control your visions yet." Sevar pulled up a chair next to the dreamer.

Raven let out a claiming breath. "Let me try." His eyes closed but felt carved by a knife.

The street's shadow stared at Raven as he scanned the orange tinted world. Screams filled the alleyways that connected to the street. He didn't let the anxiety consume him, forcing his feet to plant against the ground as he ran towards the bellowing screams.

The air echoed, pushing against his ear. Sevar's voice groaned. "Raven, what do you see?"

"The streets are covered by shadows. I'm trying to find her." Raven's eyes bounced around in his skull.

The alleyway dripped at Raven's feet; the screams grew louder than his feet pushed from the ground. Soldiers ran through, past the alleyway's opening. They yelled and roared at the cloaked woman. That must be her. It had to be. Raven ran after them, scanning the street signs and any possible hints of where he was. A soldier gripped his feet on the floor, turning to tackle him. His sword flew, ready to cut his head in two. Raven's legs collapsed from under him. His eyes were blinded by the hues of orange rays bouncing off the sword's blade. The water climbed his clothing, gripping at its fabric like an unfiltered god.

*"The crow shall scream. You shall die so we can live."* The shadows laughed, climbing each granite block with ease.

The bitter cold flooded his essence as the sword flew down upon him.

His eyes jolted open, jumping from his chair, his breath rapid, his heart pulsed against his rib bones.

"Raven, you're okay, you're here, I'm here!" Sevar pleaded to him.

His legs forced him back into the chair. He had to focus on the vision. What did he see? What hints did his power offer to him? "I saw her run away from soldiers in the dead of night. It was wet, dark, and the street felt abandoned."

"Did you get a street name?" Sevar questioned, leaving no room for mistakes.

"I don't know." He rubbed his eyes. He hissed at the throbbing pain in his temples. The power was overwhelming. He had never used his power purposely before. A raw power. Understanding the little things seen and unseen. Infinite probabilities within time, straining, holding time within his grasp like two ropes burning at his palms, screaming to remember what he loves and who he is, spotting the errors within boundless probabilities.

He closed his eyes, pulling himself to the street she ran in. It had a big sign for a library, but it seemed like it had been closed for years. "There was an old library in the corner of my eye."

Sevar walked to the nearby bookshelf, hovering his fingers across multiple book spines till he grabbed out an ancient dusty book. "This is a copy of the city's architecture from one hundred years ago. Maybe this will point out where the library is."

"In this whole city? Surely it has more than one library for its people." The curiosity calmed him, masking the pulsing pain.

"It's a lumber crafting hub and planning community. Not many of the workers read in their spare time. Not many carried on their studies after the age of fourteen," Sevar spoke like it was a fact. "The Four also took most knowledge books from all the power groups in Eyldia. Runic books, dreamer guides, Shifter knowledge books and rider journals, all taken and locked away. Only some books are found in old places that haven't been searched. Or off the royal's scope. Some people keep books secret if they're brave enough."

"They also did the same to Elcoo, even though most of our books were sold by the village leader for counts." Raven sighed to himself. "Knowledge is power."

"Indeed. Come on, let's give her assistance." Sevar tossed down the folder, placing his hand on his hilt.

"Thought you wanted me safe?" Raven's confidence teased out.

"You're safer with me. It's not a suggestion." Sevar stepped up to the staircase. "Now, Raven."

The dreamer's blazing pain still throbbed against his skull, drowning in his nerves. He didn't know how to fight, especially against trained soldiers. "Now, Raven." He muttered mockingly from behind. He couldn't tell if he found it humourful, unable to see his facial expression.

"Real mature..." Sevar replied bluntly.

–

Rain shot down from the clouds, layering the surrounding streets. Raven's hair dripped in front of his face, draining his skin of any remaining colour or warmth. Soldier's yells echoed down the alleyways. Each alley, every street, similar, yet completely different. Signs swinging violently within the storm's rage. Their stomps, their eyes darted to all the signs that dangled in the streets, begging to themselves to land upon the library's engravings.

"Get her!" The soldiers yelled into the street. The woman came into their line of sight with the soldiers on her tail. Her cloak weighing her down like stones dropping upon the fabric. This was different from his vision. He and Sevar were on the top of the street, where each possibility seen within his mind had placed her death. Her lifeless body abandoned, drowning in rain and her own pooling blood. They had a chance, but only one. Raven tensed, knowing this wasn't a dream. He couldn't jolt from his bed, blanked by the comfort of possibilities. This was real. Right now, but that's all they needed. Sevar's eyes sparked with purpose. The mission of keeping one soul out of the King's reach, Raven could see it in his eyes. They begged for this to work; he needed it to work.

Sevar's runic whispers slid past Raven's ears, layering the grey street in hues of purple. The energy twirled around his left arm, solidifying its ribbing form into an ever-fluxing energy shield. A stream of draining power for protection. The rain smashed against his stubble, dripping to the ground drop by drop. Raven's eyes couldn't leave Sevar's essence. His might blazed from his energy shield, highlighting his stance.

The woman tracked her own footing and the soldier's reach. Side to side, she threw herself, dodging the runic blasts. Her eyes caught Sevar's stance. She looked truly terrified. Had they looked like a king's brute? Sevar saw the terror fill her veins. "Assistance, my lady?" A smirk raised.

"Do you flirt with everyone?" Raven spat out from Sevar's side.

"Only the pretty ones." Sevar's smirk stayed. He looked in his element. Posture of proficiency, skills that looked second nature to the dripping whisperer.

"I'm not in a situation to say no," She breathed.

Raven's head rattled as he calculated how much time they had before the fight came to their feet. When the woman joined them, they would have ten clicks to form up. Then to strike down on the soldiers with all their fury.

"Raven, time to use your daggers. Use your abilities to see the probabilities of their next move. If you can't, then aim for the neck." Sevar turned for just a moment to stare at Raven. "If it gets bad. You run till you get to Dualia."

"Dualia?" Raven's eyes flittered.

"No time for questions, little crow. Daggers out." Sevar commanded, stepping back into his strike position.

The woman's feet turned as she lined up with Sevar. "Who are you?" The guards roared, commanding the arrest of the rebel. One by one they pulled at their hilts.

"Ask me again if we survive." Sevar flicked up his sword, placing it side to side with his energy shield.

Ten clicks felt like a rotation, but now it had ended. The fight came at their feet. Raven's panic flooded him. He couldn't fight an old miner in a tavern. How could he fight against Royally trained soldiers? People that protected and serviced the King of Drossor, people who had control over their power. His daggers quaked in his hands as panic ran through his veins.

The woman's movements had such grace, her body moved with the air itself. She dodged all the weaponry while maintaining eye contact with him. Her essence scanned over him as she slid her way to his side. "Fear will get you killed." Words couldn't form in Raven's mouth.

Sevar's sword sliced through the air accompanied by his twirls of power, one soldier gutted open on his right as another got blocked by his left. A soldier groaned as Sevar's sword met his stomach. "Your form." The soldier choked, drowning in his blood.

"Raven, behind you!" Sevar broadcasted through the street.

Raven and the rebel lifted their weapons into the air, aiming to block the attacks. Metal grinded against metal, as brute power clashed between their weapons. He groaned, pleading his knees wouldn't buckle under the pressure. The rain upon the soldier's face highlighted pure gold, causing his expression to crack. A jolting force pushed both Raven and the rebel back, bracing their footing to a stable stance. The rebel roared, pushing her remaining power of control into a stream of mist. The soldier saw that as a moment to strike, grinning at them.

His sword swung at a left side motion, slicing at the two with prideful rage.

Their bodies dropped to the floor as the street ran red.

# Chapter 8

## Blood from The Vein

Raven's vision blurred; the metal felt like poison, biting, ripping at every flake, every dent and angle upon his skin. Forever burning. The pain. It was nothing like he had ever experienced before, an uncontrollable cry burned through his essence. This wasn't what he had seen in his visions, or how he desired to leave the world. Death as a rebel. How did he come to this? From Elcoo to the visions, curiosity and emptiness consumed him, only to be greeted by a sword to the throat. Forwei as his deathbed.

He never got to know the whole story. What had Sevar been holding from him? Information about why he believed it right to keep him at his side for protection. What linked Sevar and the visions? Was he the man on the battlefield? The emptiness that poisoned the realm, the emptiness that consumed him. Death came telling with a simple left-swinging motion.

The poor woman too. Hope given to her only to be slaughtered in the cold, empty back streets. That rebel could have been a catalyst to change in Eyldia. Question the very brutality of the Four continents, their officials, and their royals. Even if she saved one child, it would have been a moment for good. A new connection to the soil, for happiness. Raven's dreamer powers bubbled in his veins. Raw power, like it lived within him, calling him to listen. The knowledge of its own, layered within his essence. He just had to listen.

His eyes shot open, drowning in a grief unknown to him. Sadness that threatened to crack his skull. The warmth was like he was wrapped in layers of muscle, blood running through his veins like a warrior. The rain poured upon his stubble, dripping. It wasn't his body. It was the pure rage of a bellowing mercenary.

Sevar's worry fuelled his fight and his sword. The soldiers were nothing more than goblins to him now. Ready for slaughter. No mercy. Raven felt every emotion that consumed Sevar. His sadness fuelled him, too. Grief pulled, threatened to rip him in half entirely. He wouldn't allow that.

The rain cleaned the blood from his sword between each gliding strike in the air. Soldiers cried out, running towards the mercenary. Energy raged from his shield, wrapping around a nearby soldier's head. His skulls cracked at the pressure, screaming, grabbing at the blazing purple ribboning energy, hoping he could escape. There was no escape. The corner of his lips curled, forcing his power to squash the soldier's skull into a burned pile of mush. Screams of death echoed against his shield. Sevar didn't give the soldier one glance. Knowing his death meant nothing to him. The quicker they died, the better.

Only one stood at the very edge of the street, one left between him and saving them. Sevar glanced at his sword. His power echoed in agreement to his plan. His power wrapped effortlessly around the sword's hilt, launching towards him with all his force. Sevar didn't care about a fair fight as he stood upon a pool of bodies. All his might flew through the ribboning power as it launched through the air. The sword pierced through the soldier's forehead in one brutal aerial strike, drop-ping his body into the puddling street.

Raven's power couldn't keep intertwined with Sevar's any longer. Raven dropped into the abyss of dreamers. Endless possibilities of how life could have been or would be.

–

Light pushed against Raven's eyes, forcing him to open them. The pain held him down in the bed he now found him-self in. "Don't move." Sevar pleaded on his bedside.

He focused his eyes slowly, scanning the room. How did they survive that attack? His eyes wandered over Sevar's shoulders. His burning eyes focused on the bed frame. Its frames burned together with clock hands. He brought them back to the clock-work safe house. Worry dropped out of his body. slamming back into the abyss.

–

"Oh, he's awake." The woman called out.

Saver stepped into the sleeping quarter with haste. "Raven. Are you okay? You've been out all night."

Raven's body groaned. "The pain."

"You'll heal." Sevar claimed to him, lowering himself to Raven's level.

"I want to go home." He breathed.

"The realm needs you." Sevar seemed to scan over his body, assessing him." You need your rest for everything. The prophecy--"

"What do you know of the prophecy?" Raven climbed up, hissing as he grabbed the metal bed frame, cutting off Sevar's stringing sentences. His voice had a sudden change, like his privacy had been ripped away. Had he known about the dreams this whole time they travelled to Forwei? Sevar stayed silent as he walked away from his room. "I told you of war, of blood, nothing of the prophecy. Sevar, tell me!" Raven yelled down the hallway, the command echoed through the whole of the safe house.

Sevar walked to the main meeting room. "Little crow, calm down—"

Raven struggled his way across the hallway, gripping to the clocks on the wall for support. "You can't keep me here with you for a mystery mission forever." Raven pushed against Sevar, abusing the withered amount of strength left in his body.

"I need you." Sevar choked slightly.

Raven's body raised slightly, no longer in pain. Gold light shined through his blood-stained bandages. "Let me go." The gleaming warmth wrapped around him, spiking his emotion. Unfiltered and unseen, till now, to these mercenaries.

"Don't be an idiot." Sevar scanned the glow that radiated off Raven's torso.

He couldn't handle this anymore. The brutality of royalty, the death, the smell of blood stained every sharp breath. The interlocking hues of gleaming gold and brightening yellow radiated, using his emotions like fuel. He threw himself to Sevar with golden twirls of power bursting from his fists. The chairs flew to the ground by outbursts of golden power.

Sevar's nose broke into two, his broad body dropped to the floor as shock paralysed him. "Raven, I don't know about your dreams." Yells filled the main room.

"What do you know?" Raven climbed on top of Sevar, his hand quaked with golden power ribboning around his essence. His shakes showed his lack of control over any of his raw golden power. How his instincts had full control of his body. Consumed by emptiness, sorrow, and brutality.

"I was tasked with a mission to murder a dreamer that knew too much information about the high magistrate of Kresa, in Enguria. I found the woman cloaked with ancient magic. She sat down in the woods, waiting for me to arrive. I don't know how she knew, but she did. I arrived, sword in hand. She knew my name, my families' names. So, I listened to her. What she had to say. She put her fingers to my head and showed me a prophecy." Blood slowly dripped from his broken nose. "of you, crow... How you will bring my family back, how you'll save the realm. If I get you to Dualia. She told me to *protect the crow till he flew on his own.*"

Raven's tears dropped down onto Sevar's chest. "You're protecting me because you're trying to get your family back or to save the realm?" His eyes scanned Sevar, waiting for the truth.

"Both can be true." He whispered, wiping the blood from his nose. "I haven't seen my mother since I was Young. I don't know if she's alive." A tear rolled from Sevar's face to the old floor foundations.

The golden ribbons pulled back, retreating to his essence within. Raven grabbed control of his emotions, pulling himself off Sevar. "I'm not a hero. I'm no warrior." He pulled back further, closer to the narrow staircase. "I can't breathe." He gasped, running up the staircase.

–

Raven sat at the front entrance of the clock shop. He went through the prophecy countless times, but the connection to Sevar had him in a knot. What were the connections between all the people and the possibility of war?

"Little crow." Sevar spoke calmly behind him. Before he continued his sentence, he dropped to Raven's side. "I need your help, if what is said is true." Sevar placed his hand into his palm, angling slightly, looking into Raven's petite features. "You had a dream of me?"

"It felt like death came to claim me in the night. The tears, the never-ending screams. I still hear it if I think hard enough." Raven turned his face to come eye to eye with Sevar. "The dream showed me you, riding a horse into Forwei, like a knight that knew his death awaited him. The burning. I had to see if it was true."

"It seems we both kept our motives hidden." Sevar forced a slight smile.

"Sorry about your mother." Their sights remained locked between them.

Sevar scanned over him once more. "You share my loss?"

"I don't remember anything before Elcoo. My Young life, it's just black. Nothing but an abyss, staring back at me. Teasing me."

"We can help each other; I'll help you find the answers you seek." Sevar placed his hand upon Raven's thigh. Will you come with me, little crow?"

"A barkeep and a mercenary. Armies would tremble." He stood, smirking proudly at Sevar.

Sevar jumped up, mirroring his movements, laughing as he launched off the shop's steps. "Golden boy could take on any army."

Raven ran down the street, refusing to be caught. "Touch me with those dense fingers and I'll burn them!" Their laughter bellowed.

# Chapter 9

## Children of Charr

### *Astrid*

The brightening teased him, slamming Dualia's sharp gushes throughout the forests. Astrid forced his feet to move forward across the gravel path, drawing his bow as far as he could, ignoring his exhaustion, pleading to his fingers to keep in place. He closed his eyes for a moment, for a glimpse of peace within the blankets of snow. His mind remained in one place, to get the remaining children of Charr back to Moonsong, back to some scrap of normality.

A lone deer glided through the maze of frostbitten oak, leaving its prints in the layers of unmarred snow. Astrid laid behind a thick group of blueberry bushes. Using it as cover; an advantage point in the tree line, glaring at anything that caused motion in his eyeline. He needed to feed and protect the children. They both did.

Astrid pushed the thoughts of Pazima and the children out of his mind. For that moment, he needed to be a hunter. One of strength, of stealth. To use what he learnt from his elders, from the Commander, from Fee. To be their protector and provider for their travels back to the temple.

His fingers pulled the bowstring with all his focused might, aiming with every ounce of his mind's muster. The arrow sliced through as if it were bending its way between the frosted, narrow oaks. Sliding its way through nature itself, entering the deer's skull in a mere click. An instant death for the wandering deer, Astrid couldn't bear to see the beautiful creature suffer. He sighed, letting out a cloud of cold air.

The deer dropped as its life drained from its body. The arrow did its job, its purpose to feed the group. Astrid threw the bow over his shoulder, jumping to assess their next meal.

Astrid knelt to the deer's body and whispered as he placed his hand on the arrow. "Thank you for your service." The body weighed down on Astrid's back muscles as he lifted it from the ground. He pushed through the trees and the thick snow, sinking several inches with each step. The deer's warm fur brushed against his neck.

–

The mountain range always left Astrid at peace. The fields shone, graced by the sunset's limited light. Astrid had one hand on his horse, as it had the deer tied around her with thick binding rope. He kept petting the horse as they walked, thanking her effort. The view of Dualia's mountain range had to be the most beautiful in Eyldia. Astrid felt it as a fact, which no other soul could prove wrong. The fields' flowers, branching out for a new cycle of life and death. The never-ending circle of embracing warmth and freezing decay. Beauty upon the realm's rotation. He smiled, accepting the feeling of happiness, even for just a short moment, while a cold breeze brushed his rosy cheeks. The figure that never left the corner of his mind, wiped away for a mere click within nature.

–

"Come here, you" Pazima chased the children around the field, their laughs echoing along the mountain's sides. Astrid allowed happiness to climb onto his face. Seeing Pazima laugh, playing with the children, keeping them joyful after all they experienced.

"Tris. How was the hunt?" Pazima called out, dropping to the ground as the children jumped on her back, some wrapping their joints tightly around her ankles. Their giggles had the power to heal the realm of its most evil traits.

He pointed to the rope that wrapped around his horse. "This should keep us sustained till we get home."

Pazima Smiled as she untied the deer from the horse. "I'll prepare it. You go entertain the little charr demons."

"Can I... hit them with sticks?" Astrid's face beamed.

Pazima looked up at him with a daring glare. Before she could respond, Astrid ran across the plains with sticks in his hands. "Break their skin, I'll break your nose, Mr Talo."

—

The chatter of the children glided through the fields as the campfire flickered at their feet. Astrid's mind dipped in and out, staring at the campfire and the meat that laid above it. At least that's what he aimed for, yet the treelines' shadows stared at him, like a dare in the night. To see what stalked in the corner of his mind. He kept thinking about what the child said to him in Charr. Golden eyes. It's not a colour of Eyldian magic. The four powers, balancing the realm upon a thin-pointed needle. The shifters of primal red mists, infinite possibilities of the dreamers, dropping through time and tales coated in orange hues, the caring green tamers and their unbreakable bonds, hues of purple glowing from the skin of runic whisperers through the realm, branching history and runic knowledge. If another colour kept dormant had been coursing through his veins... Worry bubbled at the thought. Could he keep Moonsong safe with an unknown, dangerous power?

—

The moon's grace left them in awe, smiling with the camp's embers highlighting their cheeks. He pushed a pillow out from his travel bag, glaring at Pazima. "Don't." He spat out with a bursting attitude. "It's comfortable."

"My lips are sealed..." She glared, placing down the remaining thin blanket, giving the other to the children. "I refuse to believe that gives you a full night's res—"

His heart pulsed, pushing against his ribs. A roaring pain bubbling into fear, dropping to the bottom of his stomach. He stared at the hooded figures that now circled their camp, placing a blunt weapon that refused to reflect the moon's grace.

Pazima's lips kept open, forcing her breath to a sudden stop, calculating each click of time like it was under her complete control. He could read her like she laid down upon a desk within Moonsong's library, inviting, full of information. She told him all he needed to know within a mere click, gliding her eyes to her left, to the children and to the horses. He refused to let a response paint across his face, leaving his features plain, emotionless. "Cut a single hair upon her or the children's heads, i'll gut you, sell every organ for a couple spare counts." He smiled, his menacing expression stood proud, like the sword didn't snuggle comfortably between his shoulder blades.

"Your horses, your weapons, the children. They are now ours." The raspy voice creeped across the campfire.

Pazima forced her way to her feet. Her mist, teasing and waiting for her signal. "The children aren't yours. They are now free." Her fingers tensed, holding ropes of mist at her palm. "We already warned you once." Ropes of mist now flung at their arms, wrapping around the blunt knife that grated at her neck.

"Another flicker of that mist, shifter. He'll die." The commanding voice broadcasted from behind Astrid. Pazima's mist retreated as her gaze stalked each person of their group. Her features cracked slightly as moans layered the campsite. The children began to wake like they had heard their old high magistrate's grunting disdain.

"Pazima? What's happening?" The eldest Charr child called out.

"Macur, It's okay." Pazima replied, focusing her voice on a calmer tone. The air stood still, only their quickening breaths filled the void between them. Three figures marched, clad in old, missmatched leathers, towards the tied up horses.

"You know what, I'll take dear Macur and we'll call it a deal." The raspy man's yellow teeth gleamed. He laughed, jumping towards the children. "With me, boy." He spat, itching his grey-ing beard.

Astrid grabbed the sword, spinning to the person behind him, taking advantage of the moment without hesitation. "You know what, my pockets are feeling horridly empty." Without time to process what words left his lips, he plunged the sword into her stomach, grating it across for every moment of pain possible. He turned without a flicker of indecision, whispering as he lunged to Pazima's side. The air filled with the runic me-tallic tang, ribboning in a gleaming force, balling into multiple shots of blazing energy towards the grouping thieves.

Astrid let out a groan. "Paz, mist please!" He called out. She had already circled the group, gliding across the meadow in a mere click. The mist clouding above like the sky had opened to an entirely new world. Red and full of burning rage. She pulled it, wrapping the mist around her or now whichever creature that stalked within. Its own environment to roam, to hunt down its prey. A ready-made enclosed battle force. Astrid kept his warrior-like stance, lunging across the mist's thick, unbreakable boundaries. A roar, primal as any other, crept its way across the closing environment. Click after click, the mist dragged across the meadows, pushing at their feet.

The group threw orders across the closing boundary, launch-ing half-baked energy beams towards Astrid. Their own shifter remained in the centre of the boundary. Waiting? Astrid peered out, wondering what it meant.

A figure on all fours covered in a thick coat of red and brown fur, pulsing out mist from its facial features. Pazima was now completely a beast. Its teeth grated across each thief's spine, ripping it from their flesh like freshly cooked meat. It moaned, almost mockingly, using the bones to pick meat out of its teeth.

"Please!" The raspy voice begged, lunging to his knees. The creature's roar didn't stop. It climbed, running towards the begging man.

Astrid knew if he didn't stop her now, she may lose all control within its form. Left for rotations at a time in a shifting maze within her own mind. His brain always called back to when he broke her favourite bow. She shifted to a Moonfox, unable to return to her own body for eight rotations. "Paz, it's time to come back." He called out calmly.

The creature remained digging its feet into the ground, roaring into its next meal.

"Pazima." His voice climbed, fighting against the slapping sounds of the thick mist.

It peered its head, looking at him as to consider if he would be next. "The children, they need you." He refused to cut contact from its glare. The mist called out rapidly, folding on itself in ease. Pushing and pulling against the creature's groans. It wrapped Pazima, moulding her back to her Eyldian form. Every loose coil as she had left it moments before.

Pazima peered down to the other shifter, remaining motionless. She wasn't waiting. Astrid's face filled with confusion and wonder. This shifter saw Pazima as stronger, respecting her power, as if she stood still in terror, wrapped in complete awe. "What's your name?" Pazima stood tall, peering down with a primal mist that swirled within her irises.

Astrid ran to the children, keeping his focus on both the Young and his friend.

"Agie. Agatha." The shifter coughed out.

"Go, be something better, do something worth more than a couple counts." She ordered plainly, as if she would never see her face again.

Astrid's brows clamped together. Puzzled. "You're letting them go?"

She smiled, "Her, yes." She refused to give the raspy old man any form of communication, flicking one of Astrid's throwing knives into the base of his skull. "He threatened a child."

Astrid guided the children to the path, folding his arm around Pazima's shoulder. "You're one scary creature."

"Don't forget that." She laughed, looking at the abandoned bodies with ease, knowing they had saved the children's lives. People that could bring more to Moonsong, to Dualia, maybe to Eyldia's future. A longing hope in a bitter world.

-

The thick air and snow welcomed them back, the cold mountainous air of the temple's little plains shocked the children's systems. "Where are we?" Lucar looked at Pazima.

His innocent eyes could've thrown any soulless being to their knees. Pazima looked into the children's eyes with care. "The temple of Moonsong. It used to be a home of the old ones. A place of education and discovery. You'll be welcome here. Make friends and train to protect yourself. Be whatever you want to be."

Astrid looked at Pazima as she spoke to the children. She cared passionately about the next generation, how she wanted to make positive changes. Lead and protect Moonsong with her last breath. "Let's get into the warmth." The carpet of snow gleamed a light hue of purple, exposed to the whispers of a smirking man. The stone moved with grace, groaning slightly against the stone's framings. "Welcome to Moonsong."

-

The children gathered at the first stone railing that over-looked the descending layers of observation levels and the sparring floor, some using their toes to peer over the thick stone railings. Each of them stared at the ancient pillars that held the temple together. Magic ran through them like energy cells, humming, singing away to ancient tunes only some may hear.

"This is the main sparring area." Astrid waved his hand from left to right, panning around the temple's main entrance, signalling to each hallway, branching off into mazes of history and clear-cut smooth stones.

Yells echoed through the halls. "What happened out there?" Commander Sakhile's deep voice shook through Astrid's body.

Pazima's body tensed. "Commander. We'll debrief you away from the children."

"Every detail." The Commander spat out.

Pazima turned to tell the children to go into the sparring mat to play. Laughter had been a rare thing within the temple for many years. The Commander's ears cringed slightly at the sound. The three of them marched down the hall in silence, till they reached the old spruce double doors that laid at the end of the left main hallway. Each hallway stood tall at scale to the centre room of the temple. Smaller ancient pillars that held rooms and other halls together. Arching with carved detailing, stories of old, some lost within context. Stories of murder, of love, all written in this temple. The sleeping quarters split off into many other halls and private bedrooms. It often felt like its halls carried on infinitely, as if a dreamer imbued their magic into the temple's structure.

The Commander pushed the old spruce doors open as they entered his study. "What happened?" Commander Sakhile walked behind his desk, pulling the chair to him.

"The mission was an enormous success." Astrid beamed with a smirk. His playful expression dropped in a mere click as the blazing glare from Pazima told a million words.

Pazima held her hands behind her back, pushing her back up tall. "We observed the outgoings like you ordered. Charr's high magistrate had runic spells drawn on the house's exteriors. We couldn't tell what the spell did." Astrid's eyes pulled away from Pazima while she debriefed the mystery of the Charr runes. He kept the book a secret, scanning through the collection of spells before leaving the Charr's official's house. The rune was a seasonal control spell. Using structures and areas of land to control the seasons within its boundaries. This spell had to be powerful enough to manipulate nature itself, twisting storms around the user's fingers at will.

Pazima continued, "We spotted the Charr officials using children for labour. They slaughtered the adults for being rebels." Silence filled the room, waiting for the Commander to cast his discontent.

"You bring those children here. To our home. They are not ours to protect." He spoke plainly.

"We should protect the people that need it. Especially the Young that are abused by our royals and officials."

"We don't risk our home for anyone. We help people from under our cloaks, singing our song in the shadows. Not from the rooftops. We take to help the unfortunate. When we can."

"We should protect the children of Eyldia. I believe we can be a group for bravery. Using our abilities to make change." Pazima slammed her hand upon Commander Sakhile's desk, swirling the paper into the air.

The Commander rose from his chair. "Enough! We do what we do to keep us all alive. The children can stay. Be one of our Young." A slow sigh left his lips. "But you'll be in charge of their training. If any of them step out of line, it'll be on you both." Sakhile's eyes directed that threat towards Astrid. "You're both dismissed." Commander Sakhile waved his hand as if it would brush the issue away.

Pazima and Astrid gave a nod and turned to the spruce doors. The doors slammed closed, leaving the two alone in the hallway. Pazima continued walking towards the sparring room.

"Looks like we have children to settle in." She spoke with a charge upon her step.

—

He softly pressed against the old wooden door imprinted by ancient vines. The air waved, stuffing his nose with hints of vanilla, layering in staleness. An unwelcome pressure pushed upon his chest, parting him from the cave's fresh winds.

The library's layout spread out, branching into rings of bookshelves, layering narrow walkways like a maze of dense paper, preserving history within its pages. Every section was labelled and lit by encased embers. All cast and maintained by the keepers of knowledge and history, giving their lives to preserve all that's written. He pushed himself, slowly stepping onto the diamond-shaped carved flooring.

His eyes glanced up, looking into the rocky stone that held coloured glass into place. The glass was the only thing that looked cleared, daily touched over. Cleaned to accept the moon's glow upon their written history, highlighting in blue hues as if the ocean crashed into the mountain's peaks.

The taste of old paper, the flakes of turning pages folded in his eyeline, letting out a low breath.

The section of magic history. His fingers traced the words on the book's spines. Murmuring into each book. "Our Young and magic." His eyes rolled, gifting the silent library with a radiant chuckle.

"The Connection of Riders." His eyes stuck, only for a moment. His mind flickered to Ambe. He softly shook it off, kicking the ladder gently across the section.

His annoyance painted upon his brow, tracing the words of another subsection.

"Dreaming." His thoughts jumped, thinking of Fee. He hovered over the book, flicking through its contents. "Dreamers throughout history often broke upon the pressures of time and possibilities." He breathed. A feeling of sorrow cast over him. Fee held his issues and her own pressures without complaint. He sighed as he slid the book into its original placement.

Each section darker than the last, he walked like the library folded into itself, pulling the ladder with him as he read each spine with evident contraints on his patience. His finger hooked onto a book with a dull, aged black hue, causing him to jump back into focus. "The Origin by Dola." He walked with the book in hand, heading to the nearest enclosed reading space. He kept to the farthest layer of the library, hoping no one would question his odd movements.

The book opened, slopping to both sides. His eyes danced upon the text. Carefully, he flicked through each page. Sections about dreamers, whisperers, riders, and shifters. Absent of the knowledge he desired. Nothing but the lone last page.

His throat convulsed, he had to swallow back his last meal that nearly covered the reading space. "The Aligners."

Each chapter seemed to have notes slotted into the margins. Handwriting so clean, like nothing could've interfered with the reader's thoughts.

His fingers traced every letter, reading it in his mind. "The Aligners, wielders of gold. *The time of Alignment.*" Each letter erupted within his mind, like a key pressed into a hidden lock. "Quested, an oath to keep Eyldia at balance. Weapons of peace, unity. When difference aligns. Knotting the ribbon of fate."

A note dropped from between the pages as he held up the book, pulling his focus. "The golden power passed through bloodlines, like all other magical properties?" He folded the note, pressing it into his trouser pocket.

# Chapter 10

## To Dualia

### *Raven*

How would they get to Dualia? What would he need to do there? The questions floated around in Raven's head. The light shone through the inn's red stained panes. His eyes peeled at the harsh morning rays. Rolling to his right, accepting the desire to drop back into the sleeping abyss. His eyes dared him to look over at the unconscious mercenary, spreading his thoughts over his bulky, hairy chest.

Sevar's lips moved, shock spread over Raven. "Do you always watch me sleep?" A laugh teased out of the mercenary's lips.

"No. I... Was watching the windows." The most half-minded lie he could muster up. Sevar pulled his pillow closer to his head, giving Raven a drowsy smile.

It's been eight rotations since he met Clockwork and helped the mystery woman. Well, Sevar did. Before they left, Clockwork had accepted her as one of their own, refusing to let go of her skill sets. One more person, one more helpful soul in the realm aiming to do good. Raven nuzzled into his pillow, thinking of what was to come. The mystery of adventure, lighting an ember within, a yearning for more.

"Little crow." A whisper caressed Raven's ear.

"What?" He murmured with his face squashed into the feathered creases.

"Get your little head out of that pillow. I've got our plan." Sevar ripped the blanket off, walking carelessly across the room with his broad chest bare to the elements. He stepped around Raven's bed to the wardrobe. Raven's eyes peeked out to see Sevar's exposed upper frame. A longing clawed away at him, fuelling the flame that brewed within his mind and his heart. No. Desire would complicate things, ruining their mission before any notable progress arised. Raven had to keep his eyes on their goal, rather than Sevar's broad chest.

Sevar pulled fresh clothing from his bag. "We'll travel to Sreset and get the next cargo ship to Dualia." He pulled a clean, worn-out tunic out, hooking it around his arm muscles with ease. "Hopefully we'll get there before word has spread about our brief fight with his majesty's pricks."

"How will we know what we are looking for, when we are in Dualia?" Raven pushed his body up to a sitting position next to Sevar.

"I don't know. The dreamer never said." A vague frown peered over his sharp stubble. "Just to wait for you to fly on your own," Sevar's smirk bounced back as he pushed him off the bed. "Guess you're stuck with me."

"You're a bastard." Shock and laughter filled their room. "After this is over, we won't be friends." He launched a rogue pillow, crashing it into Sevar's cheek.

-

Raven and Sevar packed up their bags, sneaking out of the inn without notice from the other visitors. The soldiers marched through the streets, waving their commands around like weapons. Anyone that had any facial similarities to them, they pulled over, crashing them into the ground for investigation—for interrogation. The laughter that layered the streets now stomped out by their magistrate's.

"Want to have some fun?" Sevar whispers to Raven as they hid in an alleyway outside the Inn. Raven's body leant against the granite as Sevar hovered over him.

Anxiety bobbed in Raven's throat. "What do you have planned?"

He smiled down at him. No reply came, only a laugh that echoed down the alleyway. They both ran through the busy streets, keeping within the creases and shadows until they reached an old, small stable. Its contents being rusted locks and foundations of granite and climbing moss.

Sevar opened the stable gate while scanning the lone horse. His hand waved smoothly through its thick black hair. "Quick jump on."

"But there's only one" His cheeks shone a rosy hue.

"No time for that. Officials could spot us any moment." Sevar launched Raven up by his waist. Raven's stomach knotted by the powerful grip, hooking himself to the horse's frame. The horse groaned at Sevar's brute weight as he pulled himself up, slotting his body in front of Raven. The control of the reins was given to Sevar, a mercenary that Raven guessed would have exceptional skills on a horse. He guessed right. The horse accepted his comforting power with a glum huff, racing out into the streets of Forwei.

The mountainous terrain between the two cities of Drossor kept their cultures apart. From the red stained oak, lumber craftsmanship of Forwei, past the north of the mountains where the city of smoke laid upon the ocean side. A city washed of colour within its borders.

Raven's body bobbed at the horse's trots, rubbing against Sevar's tunic. "Those mountains, they are massive." His gaze never left the peak's shapes. Elcoo had never before possessed such beauty within its nature.

"There's more to Eyldia than Drossor's southern mud land." Sevar spoke into Raven's ear.

"The mud land kept me safe." He reminded himself.

"It also kept you isolated. Do you not want to see beauty like this?" Sevar questioned.

His golden essence flickered at him, at the anxiety that stabbed him from within. "There's nothing wrong with a peaceful life."

They trotted through the mountains, watching the snow-melt from the valleys. Dusk creeped over the mountains' peaks as they entered an old campground. Raven's body stiffened, gripping his senses firmly. A taste in the air attacked his nose. Sevar pulled the horse to a slow trot. The central fire stomped upon, packing down the dust and burned wood logs with brute force.

Sevar dropped from the horse. The scene's scent stained every breath. Blood. The smell of blood and runic power lingered at Sevar. Even Raven identified the magic's tang. "Stay close." Sevar snapped.

He pushed himself to Sevar's side, his right hand hovered over his left dagger as Sevar had instructed. Thick circles of red pooled at the campfires sitting, dripping throughout the campground. "Blood everywhere. Officials? bandits?"

Sevar didn't reply, moving slowly towards a damaged wagon. Parked? Left? Its wagon remained close to the camp's edge. Blood ran up its sides, with sword indents at every corner. White-stained wood chipped, attacked like rage fogged the attacker's vision. Sevar and Raven kept their hands on their daggers as Sevar teased the wagon door open.

A rotten scent flew, escaping the enclosed wagon. A pressurised grave, swimming in blood. "Fuck." Sevar cursed under his breath.

Raven's body froze, disbelief held his body and his eyes upon the massacre that laid in front of them. Tears flooded his eyes, fogging his vision, his mind. Two bodies of two young men laying together, they couldn't have been older than sixteen. The bodies of the boys lay strewn, stomped, sliced, bloodied, leaving only their hair as the sole defining characteristic remaining. Dried blood soaked into their interlocked hands, firmly connected in their final moment.

Sevar pushed the wagon. "I'll murder whoever did this." Anger written evidently over his umber skin. "Hatred never ran this deep before the Four. Before they wiped everything from the old world, slowly but surely, removing the old officials that ruled over them till nothing but them remained on top. They control everything from their castle."

Raven sat on the edge of the campsite, as far as he could get from the smell of blood. "We can't stop them. They have the power, the influence."

Sevar stood still next to him. "Maybe they do, for now. Clockwork, and other people share the same mission. Maybe we'll join that path."

Raven's breath cut short, focusing Sevar's words into his mind. "Imagine the life's that'll be taken. I can't. I won't be on that battlefield. I felt every death on that field, crying out. It felt like I had died inside. Replaying over and over." He rubbed his cheek, flicking a tear away. "I don't know if I can watch that again. I just miss my home."

Their eyes looked up into the mountain's curves, sitting away from the wagon. Sevar turned, pulling his head up to Raven. "Your cottage is quite cute, but it's a pebble upon a sea of stones. I've seen the awe on your face in Forwei. You loved it."

"How long were you watching me?" His eyes refused to move from observing the mountain range.

"I kept an eye on you for two years. Watched you serve ale to dusty old bastards. Saw you give your cloak to a little girl in need." Sevar smiled warmly. "Don't wave the subject amiss, crow. What are you scared of?"

A tear teased its way from Raven's face. "I — I feel like a shell of myself most of the time. Like I've missed most of my life." The words slowly turned to a whisper. "All that's left of me is fear and dreams. I don't know if I can do what you need me to. Just look at them in the wagon." He felt a powerful embrace around his side. Sevar held him in his arms, pushing all the thoughts from his mind. Nothing but the feeling of Sevar's embrace enveloped his heart. One rogue thought placed against his skull. He could do it with Sevar at his side.

–

Sevar's muscles reflected the dawn's light as he dug away at the dirt. They both agreed to bury the couple together at the river's edge next to the campsite. Raven searched through the wagon, bringing any personal belongings to their resting place.

The couple laid together in peace within the soil. Back with magic and nature. No one could find them slaughtered in the back of a wagon in the middle of nowhere anymore. They both let out a sigh, letting out a wish for magic to treat them well in the next world they may end up in, together.

–

Sevar and Raven cleaned up the campsite of the blood and the rumble. "We'll get justice for them." Sevar spoke as he launched him onto the horse, launching Raven behind. "Hold on tighter. Don't need any tumbling accidents." Sevar's words beamed as Raven firmly gripped around his torso. The sound of horses' hooves lifting the loose gravel path filled the rest of their journey through the valleys, racing, slicing through the mild air in haste.

# Chapter 11

## Tunnels of the Dreamer

Sreset, the city of smoke. Black stones stained by thick soot and coal dust, its walls towered over the landscape, forcing the hills to feel insignificant in comparison. His neck stiffened, looking up at the wall's faded peak. "How in all the realms are we getting into that place?"

They peered from the treeline a couple fields away from the city's entrance. One that looked impenetrable to most living things. The walls dug into the soil, moulding itself firmly to the realm. The gate to the city appeared unimportant, living without fear of damage, dismissing any of the brutality roaming outside their borders. A black metal gate, wide enough to comfortably accommodate the clear passage of ten soldiers side by side without crowding, shoulder to shoulder. Heavily guarded by armed Officials with black crossbows and spears. Sevar observed their movements for an entire shift, mentally noting around fifty guards and two golem brutes.

"We'll need to find another way." Sevar sighed against the old oak.

Raven scanned the wall, looking for any abnormalities, any cracks that could've shown to a crook's keen eye. The wall stood proudly, like nothing questioned its strength. Outer pillars of black metal pierced through the ground, supporting the structure. Nothing but greys, blacks and metal stood in front of them.

"Like Forwei, this place was built by advanced architects and academics from the time of the Old Ones." Sevar whispered.

The sound of water drifted out from a small stream, cutting through the treeline as if it was a fresh channel, dug out by design. "The water channel." Raven pointed towards the circle grate at the end of the man-made stream. A water system, pushing their water supply back into the sea, an never-ending stream of refreshments. That had to be a way in without getting spotted.

The thickness of oak and its shadows protected them from detection. Guards circled, idle as if their routine allowed their thoughts to wonder in disarray. The golems were a whole different story. Sevar whispered into the air, sliding his hand into Raven's. The purple ribbons curled their way discreetly, folding around their every joint. It burned deep and true, without a notable mark upon their skin. The magic stained their senses, tinting their vision with a gleam of purple hues. Invisibility, a rune with a high price for anyone that dared its effects. Only Runic Whisperers with trained senses could hold on to its power for a productive length of time, being unseen in the meadows, as if they hid their bodies behind lone blades of grass.

The golems stomped to the edge of the riverbank, scanning its edges. Nothing. It groaned vaguely, stepping back into its given path. Step by step, the tint of purple creeped through their veins, straining their sight. Magic always claimed balance. He knew Sevar struggled with the balance with his magic, but this. It felt vengeful, like magic demanded its price, without compassion to its user. The feeling of erasing their bodies from the realm's view, pushing their senses to the brink. Balance. Sight for sight, claiming it with haste. Sweat clammed between their palms. The spell choked them, bit by bit, for what they consumed. Sevar's grip tightened as he glanced down, giving him a reassuring look. Even the water at their feet refused to notice their existence, not one ripple caused by their steps. Sevar's face dropped at the scent of metal and sweat, the strongest protection spell staining his nostrils. Much more powerful than the Clockwork safe house ever could. Magic fought back against their veiling senses. Sevar's face filled with worry. The golem creeped closer with every click that passed. Raven had never seen the mercenary's face crack like it did in front of the grate. His free arm pulled at the metal grate, begging for it to crack under the pressure. The rune's protection pushed him back harder, fighting against his pleads. Tints of purple bloomed, fogging their vision completely. The golem's stomps quaked, casting shocked ripples to their feet. The power of the magic attacked them from all sides, knotting at their joints, as if it would have snapped their bones like a twig. They couldn't hold the power at bay. Their grip dropped as they pushed at the grate, accepting the defeat of magic's will upon them. "Brute strength isn't going to open it." Sevar groaned, wiping his eyes. Raven mirrored his pleads, rubbing the fog away from his eyes.

The golem scanned at the movement in the water. Their vision remained blurred. Raven stood still, pulling at his essence, at his power. Sevar groaned as the metal sliced through his palms. Blood dripped slowly into the stream's ripples. Raven's eyes flickered, planting his hands on Sevar and the grate as impulse claimed control. His essence pushed against the protection spell. He could feel Sevar's knowledge, the echo of his experiences, rubbing against his mind. The whispers of the protection spell roared, fighting against the gold that brewed deep within. His hand felt the force push against him, against everything he had ever known. Their power shone through the metal, cracking the foundations of the ancient spell. The golem's stomp quickened, almost breathing on their neck hairs. They jumped into the damp tunnel system, grinding their knees upon the ancient metal structure. "Come on," Raven groaned as the golden hues withered. Sevar slammed the grate with a brutal crash. His sweat dripped upon his cheek, slowly, as time felt trivial. His heart bounced against his ribs, causing his breath to rasp. The golem stood still on the grate's exterior, unable to collect their unprotected scent.

Their boots submerged in the system's water, accepting the slow current that slid around their ankles, filling the layers of socks he kept on, hoping the charitable amount of fabric could've kept him warm. The tunnels split, cutting in two directions. Left and right. "Which way?" Raven whispered. Sevar whispered in his hand, casting a low light into the tunnel. Each tunnel branched off into more directions. Too many for them to check. Ten tunnels? A hundred? A million? The realisation of becoming lost within water tunnels, dying with an ancient metal tube as their tomb. Stop. He pushed the command to his racing thoughts.

"This'll take forever." They both sighed at the unlimited outcomes.

Sevar turned to Raven, grabbing his arm. "I've seen dreamers utilise the dark, able of the best tracking skills through their probability power. You can do it."

"Controlling it?" He sighed, gathering his thoughts, hoping the anxiety of his dreamer powers wouldn't buckle him completely. Raven knew he had to try, giving into the limited options. "Do you know how they utilised the possibility?" He questioned plainly.

His eyes radiated orange, asking for its help. Endless shadows flew through the tunnels, but only through his dreamer's eyes. A lens into everything and nothing, all in one. The tunnel of black metals transformed by echoes of orange tints, blurs, and shadows. Figures of where they may go, where they have already gone before. Time folded by murmuring figures.

The probability power struck at his head like a blunt axe. "I can't see the way. There's too many of them."

Sevar forced Raven's focus up to him. "Focus on one at a time, explore that one ribbon of probability. You'll get the right one."

Raven's eyes darted around the tunnels, and the shadows called for him. Whispering at him. *"This way."*

*"Raven, the guards!"* The warnings of a deadly possibility loomed.

*"Dead end..."*

He searched, scanned each blur, each figure one by one. Tossing his instincts into the air for any of the blurs to consume.

A whisper teased against his right side, *"Follow me."* That was it. He felt its purity, an energy he couldn't grasp, forced to accept its offering. "This way, I'll take the lead." Raven spoke with success proudly written across his face. Sevar shared that grin as they followed the whispers of probability, guided by Raven's glowing rays of orange.

–

Their feet groaned, begging for them not to take another step. Tunnels that felt infinite, endless halls of darkness and slow running water at their feet. Raven struggled to hold on to the murmuring purity. The more steps they took, the quieter the voice became. His ears begged for them to roar, to scream at his ears till it bled. Tunnel after tunnel, no sign of life, just accompanied by black metal, stone, and darkness.

Raven's steps stopped. "I can't hear it anymore. I can't hold on to it." The frustration crunched his fingers, forming a fist. "This power is uncontrollable. I don't know how any dreamers do it." He slumped down, sitting against the metal wall. "I would rather be one of you."

Sevar stopped next to him. "You get to see what most deem impossible. You get it all. All the abilities and possibilities, all the knowledge from within, calling at you like a ring of a bell." Sevar placed his hand on Raven's cheek, exposing purple runic symbols drawn into his palm, the newest spell learnt, tattooed to their palm like a stamp of honour. "We don't get that. The runic power doesn't call to us, doesn't care about us. To control a spell, we must learn its symbol, learn its origins. Use dust from the rarest flower in Enguria to stain it upon our skin. Even then, the balance strains us even more." Sevar's words felt emotional, wrapped in a pleading call for him to accept his power. To accept himself. "You are a dreamer, Raven. Accept the dreams as what it is. A dream, a tool. It's a part of you..."

He raised a small, pure smile to Sevar. "Thank you."

Light creeped at the edge of the tunnel. Teasing itself to the men's eye line. "That way." Sevar jumped up, clawing the wall for support. "See! You knew the way." He claimed, clawing against the narrow tunnels in a hurried longing for natural light.

---

The dimmed light attacked their eyes. The metal grate opened by a simple push; no protection spell held the inner systems. Metal and magic played in partnership within this building. The unadorned structure's barenaked foundations, with its metal beams completely exposed to the naked eye. Even Elcoo had better interiors. Nothing but a shell for a system run by Officials. Keeping water clean and safe for those who lived within their borders. Raven had never seen such systems in place, not at that scale. Elcoo used wells and old systems. Forwei had a limited water cleaning system, used by only officials and main water posts. This place had to be the home of a royal.

"Never seen one so complex." Raven broke the silence.

"Only the main cities of the Four have such spells. Keep them clean, happy." Sevar's face stood still, emotionless. "Keeping the knowledge to themselves. Creating the divide, with them on top of the food chain. Laughing with full bellies."

He poked Sevar in the arm. "Let's go."

# Chapter 12

## To the Sea

The streets of Sreset stood proudly on stone, high above the realm's natural terrain. Homes, buildings, towering high and dense, all tucked into the thick wall's boundaries. Section by section, the steep polished stone staircases spiralled, cramming between the slender creases of the building's structures, like an afterthought. Only branched freely for one wide grand staircase for the masses, a never-ending descent to the city's bustling seaport. A city of stone and metal that shined in the dim light. Smoke billowed into the sky from the smelting furnaces, heating mined ore materials, extracting every vein, clanging of smiths moulding the iron into useful materials and weaponry filled the air. Bashing sparks into the sea breeze.

The lack of any colour quivered his skin. After many rotations surrounded by red stained oak and bright granite, this seemed an external force sucked happiness out.

"It's cosy." Sevar spoke into his ear.

He whispered back. "Is this where positivity comes to rot?" Grins pasted over their faces but cut short by the ever-teeming push in many directions. They walked through the streets, hoping no one would notice their confusion. Raven pulled to the left, down the steep, never-ending staircases. Fear threatened his stable footing, as if one mighty gust of wind would've caused them to tumble down thousands of polished, yet abused, black stone steps, each step fueling a burn between his joints.

Raven's heart raced, gasping for a longing breath. His glance pulled, catching Sevar's racing thoughts glued to his features. "Where's the dock?" He teased Sevar with a worried glance. The enjoyment of Sevar's face, he smirked proudly at his side.

"Didn't realise you were funny." His reply was accompanied with a playful push, launching Raven's shocked body down the last two steps upon the next section of streets, full of gleeful businesses. Shock peered from his eyes and greeted Sevar when he returned his glance to his travelling partner. Sevar carried on before Raven mustered up between his crisp lips. The streets remained packed with residents, the shop owners yelled, greeting possible customers at their doors. The scent of fresh fish and rich assortments of baked goods teased its way through the busy walkways.

Sevar's face stood still. "Look at these people with no knowledge of what goes on outside their walls. Stories in settlements like mine talk of times before the Four's separation" His words withered to a whisper. "They look down at us now, like we didn't live as one."

"No one can change that now, the time of the old ones passed long ago." Raven walked ahead. Shaking off the words that pierced at him.

Sevar placed himself against an alleyway, hidden into the creases between the structure's shadows, between two different shops, one closed, seemingly condemned several rotations before, and the other, selling rich collections of weapons, all branded with the Four's embossment. "Don't you feel the burn? The pain in the pit of my stomach. Like we don't belong?"

Questions forced him to think, stopping him in his stead. "Maybe that's the balance we're forced to bear."

"You don't believe that, crow." Sevar guided him into the alley's shadows. "We both know we deserve more..." He choked on an emotion, something new Raven couldn't read on his features. Rage? "They don't care about us." Raven knew deep within, it was a raw sorrow that peered through, like a memory flooded back.

"Were you one of them?" He questioned, already knowing the answer.

"Feels like a life ago now." Sevar cracked.

"Sev—" He breathed, but Sevar wiped his tears away, choking on "We'll miss the next boat."

Every section of the huge city shared the same structures, the same metals that held them all together. The range of polished black stone stained by the dimmed sun. The whole city smelled of runic power. Invisible waves of purple magic ribboned through the city, the power masked, leaving nothing but the lingering smells within its walls. With each breath he took, it stained his nose.

Their feet pulsed, begging not to descend another stone staircase. He stopped counting the number of them by the time he reached seventy-four. "If I force another step, I'll vomit." Sevar choked on his laughter as they took their last step to the seaport.

Glancing up at the city's ascend caused Raven's neck to ache. He wondered what Sevar had said, what had he seen?

Raven and Sevar arrived at the seaport of Sreset. Their feet throbbed against the final step that branched onto the seaport's foundations. The building hung off the edge of the city, folding into themselves, clinging to the stone of the city sea wall. The foundations were mixed with black metal and colourless wood, stained by the sea's currents.

He scanned over the foundations of stone and metal. Cracks and burn marks scarred into the seaport's history. How the Four took everything from the old ones two hundred years ago, forging the realm into their image. The land burned in the months after the Four's siege, mighty unrest as Elydia shifted upon its axis. That's what Eben had told him as a young man. A story passed down generations, whispering its horrors at dusk, hoping no soul had curious personalities.

Voices echoed against the current as ships docked into the busy seaport. "King Dreaka needs this shipment by dusk." A woman's voice commanded the dockers with haste. A hollow tone remained barking through the old port. Her boots stamped upon the old wooden foundations, grabbing the bustling seaport atmosphere into her grasp.

Sevar grabbed Raven's arm, pushing his body behind one of the seaport's storage buildings. "We can't use the port."

His face dropped, scanning Sevar's emotion. "Why? Do you know her?"

Sevar spied through the building's cracks. "She is a mercenary, like me... but she's loyal to King Dreaka. I've seen her slaughter whole settlements after a single command. She's unattached from any ounce of remorse."

Raven pulled Sevar to his eye line. "We'll find another way."

The voices from the seaport dockers silenced as the ships left the seaport. Sevar's face recoiled at the thought of her stalking around Sreset, being close to him. That observation came clear to Raven, glancing at Sevar's arm hair that kept sprung up high. The worry waved over him. How this woman unnerved him, peeling his stone, warrior mask from him, exposing a worrisome expression, with widen eyes and sweat filling his short coily hair.

Raven and Sevar found themselves creeping in the shadows of Sreset, brimming with soldiers for another rotation. Echoes of soldier's disapproval for the woman's arrival, following the echoes through the cracks and alleyways of the city. Sevar pulled his hand out, stopping Raven in his tracks. Their eyes beamed to the end of the long main street, widening swiftly to calm embers, highlighting a polished building proudly, detailed by myths and twirls, sculpted into its black stone pillars. The white embers reflected against the woman's movements. "She's heading for that building." Sevar pushed through the stream of passers-by.

"I'll scale the buildings. Stay here, out of sight." Sevar's voice dropped to a commanding, plain tone. Raven nodded at the command, never letting his eyes leave Sevar's ghost-like moments. Sevar's feet pushed his body up the metal braces of the nearby building, placing his body at the peak of Sreset. His cloak flew in the air, gliding from building to building. Raven's instincts got the better of him, pleading for Sevar's figure to keep in his eye-line. He ran through the street, keeping to the shadows, reaching the corner of the street where the main city building stood proudly. White embers flickered at its pillars and its grand doorway. His eyes bounced back to the cloaked Sevar. His figure launched into the air, landing himself upon the tiled roofing, hoping his landing allowed no sound.

–

Sevar pulled himself off the roof, returning to the streets below. "I told you not to move." His voice remained cold. His hand glided up to remove the hood from his face.

"I had to." His voice cracked, looking up at Sevar's face. Emotion pulled at his features. He waited for a stiff reply, but nothing came. Only greeted by a grip on his hand, folding their fingers into one another.

–

The moon shined down onto Sreset, casting dim light to the streets. guards circled the streets section by section. Sevar stood on the roof of a petite inn, observing Raven's amateur abilities. "If you're going to train, we'll start with some climbing and movement exercises."

His cheeks stuffed with air, pushing at the stone at his feet. Begged for it to push him up, to bear his limited strength.

A small echo of laughter bounced down in his ears. "Physical abilities are nothing like magic. Use your own strength. The stone can't help you."

He pushed his words while he gripped the roof's edge. "Are you going to tell me the plan?"

"Seems to be a gateway within that building." He threw his hood over his face, covering everything except his smirk. "When you catch me, little crow, I'll tell you the plan. You won't like it."

"What's a gate... way" Raven called out. No response echoed back as Sevar's cloak glided in the moonlight, like it did in the dreams many rotations ago. He refused to let him have the last laugh, pushing himself to a sprint. With each step, he swallowed his bobbing anxiety, wrapping it in his saliva. Leaping across the building's gaps with horror painted over his acute features. Every gap he hoped it wouldn't grab his feet, dragging him into the alley's abyss. The possibility of his teeth grating and smashing against the narrow black stones caused his stomach to drop. Raven wouldn't let Sevar win. His sprint collected into a focused, stable footing. He smiled, truly, like nothing had burdened his mind. He could jump on rooftops with Sevar till his hair thinned, go entirely grey, withering into an old dreamer of an era far gone by.

Sevar's smile beamed in the moonlight, his lips being the only thing visible under his hood. His soft lips, never cracking under the freezing season's might. Silky... Fuck, that thought threatened to plunge him into the building's creases. He kept up behind Sevar's movements, jumping from rooftop to rooftop. Sevar jumped up cracks of stone, reaching a balcony at the very top edge of the metal city. Raven pushed himself, forcing his bony torso to grate against the stone. Sevar reached his hand down, but he refused it, groaning against the metal railings. His feet slowly pushed up to the balcony, tethering to the last strands of core strength. "How do you d—" Raven groaned. Sevar beamed as Raven pushed his joints onto the balcony.

They both dangled their feet over the edge, peering over the hundreds of faded embers from settlements off in the distance, coated by meadows of grains, flora, and uncut grass. "Where are you from, really?" He pulled his eyes to Sevar. The moon sparkled onto Raven's cheekbones.

Acid bobbed in Sevar's throat. "Quarria, the Queendom of Engoria's capital. It's quartz buildings. I still see it when I close my eyes. Halls of polished white, like a never-ending blooming."

He pulled his sight to the dock, admiring the crashing waves. "I've never been that far west. Any plans to return?"

"I can't—Let's just go through the plan." He wanted to grab him. Help him with his emotions, but how could Sevar express that when he didn't offer his in return? Raven nodded, waiting for the plan to unfold from Sevar's tongue. "You'll use your dreamer abilities to map out a way through. When we have that, we'll go into the building with my invisibility spell. From our limited view, it'll be dangerous."

Raven's body jerked at the involvement of invisibility. The feeling of giving up sight jolted every nerve in his body. "You're positive we'll make it to the gateway with our sight?"

Sevar placed his eyes on Raven's. "Now that depends on your dreams. If you can get us the fastest way through without alerting the guards."

"I'll try my best." He looked at the ocean once again before closing his eyes to an orange flickering glow.

# Chapter 13

## The Golden Angel

### Astrid

The trees waved in the winds, absorbing the melting snow, climbing closer to the first rotation of the brightening season. Astrid pulled and groaned as the old circle of targets ripped at his palm. Preparing environmental targets through their hills, treelines, and pathways. Rabbits raced between the tree lines, jumping across bushes, running from roars that simmered in the sky, looking up to see the blurred outline of a Quetzalcoatl above the thinning clouds.

The blurred myth's wingspan sliced the cloud in two, its dimmed violet scales rippled the skyline. Astrid stood still, respecting the myth's gliding thrusts through the mountain range. Its force thrusted the air, like a display of its power, causing the snow to quiver.

Training in real environments, possibilities of planting your face, eating a rocky mouthful of soil, anything nature could muster. He placed down a bag of arrows, sorting through the weapons and the precautions he had to remember to recite to the Young. His sigh accompanied the wind in the treelines.

"Damn children." He murmured, grating against the thought of training tumultuous young ones.

Step by step, his feet pulsed, whispering a charm, a tale as old as time.

*"When the Moon falls, glistening alone in the skies of old. We love, we guide, just as it does for us."*

The song of the original Moonsinger, like a beautiful wave of harmony, opened the entrance of the temple with grace. His footsteps echoed against the temple's pillars, teasing up the ancient drawings within its stone. He never expected to be a mentor to a group of Young, but what's commanded must be followed.

Astrid peered over the top railing, where Pazima stood in a commanding position. The Young of Charr all held wooden staffs, beaming their eyes down to the floor, while focusing on their stances. "Position one, Viali!" She commanded in a low tone.

He stepped down through the two observing rings, entering the training circle. "How's the session?" His voice flickered with amusement. Pazima's sharp glance answered all the questions he had for her about their progress.

"Always trust your instincts. Remember, your weapon is an extension of you. Keep your eye on your opponent. Them and their weapon as one." He positioned himself next to Pazima.

"For Pazima, she, her staff, and her mist. All as one, you must keep yourself ready for all possible strikes." Astrid grabbed a staff from the floor, striking against Pazima's staff.

Pazima grinned. "Get into pairs, carry on with your positions."

The children's chatter layered the sparring floor. Their cheeky remarks and the clashes of the wooden staffs pushed a smile to Astrid's face. "How are you feeling?"

Pazima sat on the middle layer's stone railing. "I'm good. The Commander is demanding progress reports in seven rotations. We need to push out more sessions."

He sat close next to Pazima. "I have the environmental training ready." Looking into her facial expressions, it struggled to hide the importance of this being a success. "We'll prove bringing them to the temple was the right thing."

The children's chatter flamed to a groan towards Astrid. "Sir, can we be dismissed to the grand hall?" He nodded with a coated scent of warning. Pazima and Astrid followed behind the children, rushing to get their meals.

-

The Young ones ate, consuming the scent of freshly cooked chicken, vegetables, and stews. Astrid pulled his eye to one of the Young boys. "Where did you get a golden angel from, on the bridge?" The questions filled his mind for too many rotations.

"My dreams, a saviour with golden essence, came down to save us. It had your eyes." Macur spoke with wonder in his eyes. Looking at gold that wasn't there. He could see what others couldn't.

Astrid's words played on his tongue. He roughed his hands through Macur's hair, messing with his styled curls. "Dreamers and their stories." Playing it off to the Young.

Astrid and Pazima sat with full plates, slowly going cold, planning the next seven rotations one session at a time. As ink touched paper, the only thought consumed his mind. How will he care for all these young, and his own trainee – Caelan. Fuck, he missed countless sessions with him, choosing to hide in the lower chambers with the mystics.

-

The brightening season air pushed at his cloak; flowers began to push through the layer of mountain snow. Fee's hair refused to move with the wind as she sat down on the log opposite. "Your Young group seems to be the talk of the grand hall." She spoke.

"It's been a hard change, but it had to be done." Astrid's face tinted by the flame's orange glow.

"Is that because of how you became a Young one of Moonsong." The question peered through the fire as a fact.

"I couldn't leave the children alone, scared like I was." Astrid's emotions reeled.

"Yet you still appear to reel at the corner of your eye." Fee's face pushed forward.

"Nothing we have done has changed that." Astrid pulled himself up, turning hastily.

Fee stood up faster than he had ever seen before, placing her hand onto his temple. "My dreams are plagued by your past, your future." Pushing remained futile as Fee's grip blazed with orange hues, connecting to his temper, his shadow, all pushing through her brutally. Fee's body shook, quivering against his skull. "What you will do, what that figure will do. All the darkness." The horrors of his mind dripped into her. Her nails tensed at the pressure, drawing drips of blood to trickle upon his cheek. "Screaming, the never-ending cries." A tear rolled down her bony cheek.

"No more sessions." He spoke with rage on his tongue, ripping her finger's connection to every inch of his essence. The feeling of being completely exposed flashed over him, like he stood naked, bearing nothing but his fearful expression.

"It's a crow." She wiped away the blood from her nose. "The figure shaped itself into a crow."

# Chapter 14

## Memories & Patterns

### *Raven*

The black stone pillars tinted orange, stained, changed, melded by power. His feet stepped slowly up to the main double door. There stood two guards, dressed in the royal symbol and their stitching patterns. Each blinding, knotted their patterns, changing the possibilities of the most futile differences. Raven rubbed his eyelids, forcing his mind to focus. Grunts escaped their clammed lips as the doors slid open.

The building's structure stood proud; pillar foundations held up the upper floor above. Two staircases climbed up to the next floor, circling into each other at the top level. Raven's eyes peeled over the first level. Two soldiers stood upon the ivory flooring, they observed the plain doors that stood at the left and the right. Raven closed his eyes, listening, feeling the room. Voices teased against his ear. The soldier's conversations continued, wrapped in foot movements of their timetable changes.

His hands shook, grappling at all the patterns and possibilities. Taking it all in his hands, picking at them one by one. Offices drowned in building plans, meeting rooms and furniture filled the first floor. Soldiers' yells echoed from below, pressing a painful pressure against his temples. Raven's jolted down the staircase, whipping to the main hall. A staircase of cracked stone and wrapping moss appeared. Ancient, like one made by the old ones, or era's unwritten in Eyldian history. Blink after blink, the ground opened, groaning into cracked stone steps. Each step he took, the orange twirled, quaking in his veins.

The room was open and brisk, sending a freezing chill down his bony spine. Blackstone columns held the room together, detailing the ancient structure. Raven glanced down, tossing his confused glare at the painting, covering most of the polished stone floor. The shape of Eyldia... Names of the continents, carved bluntly into the stone flooring, seemingly a bladed weapon used to crack the polished stone.

"Dualia, Drossor, Engoria and Dreaka." Raven knelt to the carving of Dreaka. Cracks of letter changes, a name written over another. His fingers ran around the cracks, lines, and shapes, reading each letter from the trace of his touch.

*His lips breathed, tracing the letterforms of old. "Rivora..."*

His mind stopped the questions that rattled within his skull, returning to his investigative glance across the room for a body count and shift patterns. The struggle of splitting the voices buckled his knees. The tint of orange swallowed his mind, pulsing against his senses.

Nine different runic doorways sculpted to the stone floor, standing in their expected places on the floor's map. All active, imbued with ancient runes carved into its stone. The ribboning energy twirled within each doorway, a mirroring image of the gateway's destination, coated in an eternal hum.

A force gripped Raven's feet as he walked towards the nearby gateway. Screams of death crashed through every gateway, every sorrowing voice echoing their experiences. His veins pulsed out of his pale skin, filling with the brutal memories of every living being.

Voices that scratched at his essence echoed at him alone, like a target within a clear meadow. "Kill her," a deep, emotionless voice commanded. Four mighty voices ripped through him with tense words, like their commands deemed respect, entitled to it from every being. Cries filled his mind, a face he didn't recognise. Her death consumed his mind. A tear dropped, soaking the old stone.

His quaking hands supported his bucked legs, placing him upon the painting. His face creased upon Dreaka's shape, using it as a cold pillow. "I hear you. I hear you all. I can't help you." Raven's voice cracked. His sight blurred, opening to an empty freezing room, nothing of value, no bed, no chairs. All but a mouldy blanket in its corner. A woman's scream cracked the walls, begging for the pain to stop. Begging for her son.

The woman curled up on the bed, her finger's skin peeled, cornered in dirt and ice. Her dead eyes pulled him into her grip. "My son. The Alignment." She called out, standing from the mouldy bed. She begged death to come for her.

The next blink slowed, consumed by the woman's cries, opening to the view of the Sreset. "Raven, you're okay." Sevar pulled him close, placing Raven's head onto his chest.

His eyes blinked, returning to the blue skies, collecting the warmth from Sevar's torso. "I think I saw your mother." A tear slid from his cheek onto Sevar's arm.

# Chapter 15

## Gateways of the Unknown

The morning light rose its way upon Sevar's arm, making its way to their faces. The city's streets woke, smoke crawled its way out of the black metal structures, layering its sky in man-made clouds.

He woke in Sevar's arms, an embrace he had never felt before. His heartbeat quickened as his eyes scanned Sevar's muscles, wrapped around him, warm like a comforting thick blanket. The warmth encased his bony frame; it creeped at his essence, fighting against that hollow emptiness of time far gone.

"Feeling up to telling me what you saw?" Sevar spoke calmly into his direction.

"There are nine gateways. The main cities and Kullor Island, with two guards posted at each entrance."

Sevar looked down to his lips, absorbing every word. "Visions broke through, like one was more powerful, casting over the other. Took over. Showing me a future of death. A vision of a woman too."

Sevar pushed himself up, leaning them both against the tower wall. "Show me. Pull your hand to my head. Show me the vision. I need to know."

"I've never shown a dream before." His face dropped to a timid glare. "Is that possible?"

"You underestimate your Dreamer power." Sevar pulled closer. "Only if you're comfortable, can I show you at least what I've seen done before."

He let out a long breath, readying his fingers against Sevar's temple. "Push against my power if it gets too much." His power twirled through his veins, travelling to his fingertips.

Their eyes were closed, yet magic screamed through Sevar's temple, connected as one. The walls leaked, dripping grey water drop by drop next to the tattered blanket. Knotted long black hair flicked to reveal the woman's bruised face.

"Mother?" Sevar breathed in disbelief.

Her scratched feet rushed its way across the rough floor. "Son, the King. He knows where he is. Help him." Screams quaked the stone, ringing, ripping through her pores. She cried, as if it was the end for her, using her final breath to plead her case. "Help him. Help him." She gripped Sevar's shirt. "He needs us." Her voice cracked entirely, as if the voice of an old god had abused their power.

"Raven!" Sevar pleaded. The floor crumbled, throwing him into the black abyss. Dropping through twirling hues of purple, gleaming, fighting against the shadows of Raven's mind. It stared.

His eyes threw open, back to the city of smoke.

Sevar pulled him into a long embrace. "Does it always feel like that?" Raven blushed, absorbing every click of Sevar's exposed warmth.

He smiled against Sevar's shoulder. "It takes everything." He pulled away slowly. "But I'm learning." Raven smiled as his heart felt warm, safe with Sevar's company.

They climbed their way down into the back alleys, nearing the murmurs of the crowded streets. "Your mother, what she said."

Sevar didn't allow him to finish. Throwing his bag over his back. "I don't know. I was Young when she was caught—"

"—For rebelling?" Raven kept his voice to a strict mutter.

"Her last words to me were, '*I had to save my friend.*'" Sevar's face soured with questions, glaring into the alleys sidestep.

He stepped closer, closing the gap between them. "She's alive." At least to what the dreams alluded. He couldn't be entirely sure of that, no dream could, but to Raven's luck, Sevar held to that hope like it kept him from crumbling into the black stone streets.

Sevar smiled, returning to their walk through the narrow alleyways, travelling through the city by backdoors, forgotten paths, and shadows of the city's narrow buildings. A rotation where they couldn't let on to their intentions. Waiting till dusk, striking the guards in the shadows.

The embers twirled against the pillars, lighting the doorway and the guards protecting it. Raven's hand swiped over the dusty window, looking out to the magistrate building. An advantage point to confirm the two exterior guards' movements. He paced away from his position, glancing over at Sevar, prepping his runic words. Purposely silent mutters from the mercenary, practising his knowledge of the spoken, runic language. It sent Raven into awe, seeing Sevar's love for who he was, of his power, his birthright. He brought a slight smile to his features. For Sevar, the man he began to adore.

"Practising? You already know the spell." Looking at the invisibility rune. A star symbol covered with power and twirls. A star living alone, closed into a black abyss.

Sevar looked up with a warm glance. "The better the pro-nunciation, the better the spell connects to us. It respects the words, our love, to their knowledge."

"It's beautiful." Raven whispered. He looked down to Sevar, his eyes scanned every pore, every crease, every little imper-fection. His little path of stubble which refused to grow. The sleepless circles that hung from his brown eyes. His eyes, rich like spruce, absorbed the sun's vibrant tint.

"Yes. You are." Sevar's voice shook his nerves, his essence naked for examination. His heart quickened, scared of it all, every extra spark that quaked inside. His fondness of the mer-cenary fought against the fear, but it remained a losing battle. His knees quivered at the thought of intimacy. The hollowness pulled, forcing him to talk. "We need to go, before they start to change positions."

Sevar's face examined him, as if he asked his heart for permission. He slid closer, using one hand on his lower back. "Does this scare you?"

"Yes." He spoke, glancing up at Sevar's face. Their lips danced in the confined space between them.

He grabbed Sevar's hand, guiding it into his own shaking palm. "Please."

Sevar's eyes flickered with sadness and understanding. "Let's get to the gateway." Sevar placed his hand on his cheek, a gesture, a moment of trust from the mercenary.

He smiled at the embrace.

-

The guards handled their hilts like they were rotted food, expressing nothing but distaste for their posts. Raven grinned at their unhidden sorrow. The invisibility spell wrapped around them, through them, affected as one. Step by step, embers ignored their presence. The black stone, absent to greet their steps. No noise, no shadow, no scent.

Sevar pulled his dagger from his left, pulling a second from Raven's belt. The spell infused, twirled around the weapons. Sevar groaned at the extra strain, readying his stance. Their bodies as one, their stares kept to the guards, gliding through their narrow gaps between them. Raven tensed, fighting for a rasping breath. Sevar branched his hand out, his glowing palm warm and inviting. He accepted it without a thought, allowing Sevar to slide Raven through. The guards' tea-stained breath accompanied them.

He pushed the door open, keeping Sevar's eyes on the entrance. "Downstairs." He whispered. Their sight, withering, fading away. Sevar's hand tensed around his bony fingers. Raven groaned, biting his lip to cover the pain. He loosened a moment later, rubbing Raven's palm.

The main hall, empty. No guards at the ancient doorway. The room felt thick, felt completely wrong, like a trap. "We need to leave." Sevar breathed.

"But how could they—"

Rising mist replaced the surrounding air with haste. Sevar pulled his right hand over to him, gifting him with his second dagger. "A shifter! Keep them up." He hadn't seen the mercenary in a panicked state before, his eyes dragging across the thick mist, begging for it to reveal itself.

They ran down the ancient stone steps. Sevar pulled at his back, sliding out his claymore, a hilt crafted with gears and reused clock metal, forming a uniquely imbued partner. Whispers between the mercenary and his weapon, teasing down his veins. Twirls of purple ribboned tightly around Sevar's claymore.

The sword glided, sliding clean across the first three guards. Blood, mist and red hues coated the magistrate's polished floor. Slowly it dripped down the ancient stone, towards the painting of Eyldia. Guards whispered; balls of energy flew into

Sevar's claymore. The force quaked against the imbuement, imploding its energy with all its might.

"Sevar." He called out, gaining his footing. A shine of a sword swung down towards him, throwing himself back. The sword stroked the stone ground, red eyes shone walking towards him. The dust filled room consumed by red mist. A wolf with a full black fur coat launched, unleashing primal groans against its teeth. The mist had its prey. It wanted the crow for its feast.

His hands shook to his daggers, pulling them up. His breath slowed, focusing on his grip, on the wolf that intended to rip him into shreds, pushing down on the air, trapped in his lungs, all his force pushed, throwing the dagger through the mist. Slides and groans filled the mist. Heads rolled around the blooded floor, swimming in cries, the map carved into the stone, stained with their blood. The mist cleared, revealing the dead wolf with the crow dagger in his ribcage. Raven's lips quivered as his mind crashed, murdering another. No wonder a shifter is in its prime form. Sevar's glare glued to him, pulling his arm out. A tear hovered, like it refused to confirm what he had done.

"You killed—" Sevar words rasped out, with no air left in his lungs.

Raven stared into his hands, highlighted in gleaming hues of gold and orange, like a partnership had grown within him. "The possibilities. I pleaded at it, it listened." The shock passed over him. Bodies littered the magistrate building like time had slammed to a stop, but one official stood proudly, smiling at Sevar. His face raised from the dead shifter. A red cloak waved in the stained air above her slaughtered soldiers. Her left hand glided to her side, revealing a sword stamped by the royal design. "Nice to see you again. Time to finish what I started." It was the woman from the docks. Sevar's expression peeled entirely, like an inner-child, of pure innocence cracked, horrified by the mere sight of her.

"This one!" Sevar called out, throwing them both through the nearest gateway. The magic consumed their essence, knotting, circling the realm, its air. Between magic, life and death. The gateway held them in its grip, tossing them into the freezing glacial city of Jinos.

# Chapter 16

## Icy Thieves in Rich Robes

### *Astrid*

The islands floated with a quiet yet piercing hum, radiating from its cores, held by strings of ancient magic, ribboned through its hovering rocks. Water swirled from the island's rivers, dropping from great heights. Its force echoed into the forest borders. No connection to the realm's soil except a grand, expanding staircase. Each step detailed in lapis blue twirls, waves free, forming its way to the island's arching entry. Caelan stared plainly, like the magic holding the city together in the air spent him in complete awe and confusion. The sun peered at the edge of the island's silhouette, causing his rich, bronze skin to glow freely.

"Carry me up?" Astrid grinned, glancing from Pazima's emotionless glare and back to the marble staircase.

He continued, taking the first step of hundreds. "Keep up Caelan, we don't need a reenactment of the last mission." The juggling of the young ones and Caelan's training weighed against his temple.

His voice was layered in youthful excitement. "I won't let you down," Caelan walked alongside the two skilled thieves, weaving his small knife between his fingers.

-

"The royal food storage building is across the city, in the private complex on the furthest island out to sea. They locked the building with an imbuement lock after the guild's last mission here. Pazima and I will get into the complex, find the key." He spoke towards Caelan.

"And what of me, Keep?" Caelan looked excited yet trembled slightly, holding his fingers between his hilt and his trouser line. Astrid's face soured vaguely, twirling his lip at the title given to him. A Keep, as Caelan loved to call out. A title granted as a Moonkeeper, partnering them up with the Moonsong's trainees, linking to them through the calling of their Moon. In its last night of each year, magic and the Moon's gleam grace down as one, linking two into partnership. A routine of connection and knowledge.

Pazima spoke up. "You need to make sure no guards are around the storage building when we come back with the spell key. Clear it of officials." A confident nod came from Caelan.

-

Pazima pulled to the side, stalking a tailor's shop, nestled into the first island's main street. Polished stones washed in hues of blue and off-white, like the ocean had waved over the islands with grace. Did someone raise these islands from the ocean? The thought danced on Astrid's mind, wondering about how this place came to be, and the magic's origins, one of control and flight? He shook it off sharply, facing Pazima, who had three cream robes hanging loosely off her arm.

Hlinos, a city of wide streets filled with residents, all dressed in the same cream robes, layered in lapis embroideries. The dressing was like a statement to their wealth and felt completely wrong on his skin. Caelan peered up, like their mission had washed away. Buildings towered high into the clouds, sprouting from the islands, waving with the air's force. Every small stone floated, almost frozen to time, refusing to follow nature's rules. Hlinos sang, humming through its rivers, ponds, and waterfalls. A hum of peace and power.

Astrid pulled Caelan close, grabbing his arm. "If you keep staring, they'll spot you and I won't save you." Caelan's eyes widened, keeping them pasted to the polished street floor. "They won't hesitate to behead us."

Pazima's eyes rolled slightly, whispering in his direction. "Never-ending cycle..."

The complex building stood ahead. The gate into the royal complex was coated in lapis. A gate made for nothing but a display of wealth, their greed. A commanding nod from him was all Caelan needed, gliding into the shadows, waiting, prepping for his mission.

"Moon's gleaming." Caelan spoke softly.

Astrid nodded with a slight pride. Astrid and Pazima replied as one. "Down upon us."

-

"What did you mean?" He looked at Pazima as they crept behind thick racks of clothing, hiding in the repetitive, idle talk of the Hlinos residents.

Pazima cut at his next breath. "We need to find another way in. We can't get through the guards undetected." Turning away, jumping at the nearest climbable wall. The robe coated her within the streets' thin corners.

The islands pushed, changing its city layout slowly throughout the seasons. He always thought King Alonn ordered the island's movements for a better view of the snow-capped Fellow's Mount, following down the Mount's silhouette, adoring Fellow's Gap for its gleaming beauty. Yet he knew wholeheartedly, King Alonn couldn't love the Moon's gleam between the Mount's Gap, not like them. The island's movements jolted slightly, causing his knees to buckle against the polished stone. Astrid shook it off quickly, glaring at the main street for a brief click. No guards. He jumped with a mouthful of groans, choking on his knee's throbbing pain.

Pazima's feet graced the tiling like feathers, peering to the edge. The air kept her gliding across the rocky drop, climbing to the grassy cliff edge. "I won't be shifting if you fall." Pazima sat smiling with amusement, with her legs dangled over, kicking lone rocks, listening to the hisses of ancient magic.

He smiled, prepping his path with an inviting whisper, the force pushing against the tiling. Step by step, his power flew through his footing, launching from the last tile, stretching his arms. His muscles begged to clamp the stone ahead. The stone quaked, losing his left hand.

"Astrid." Pazima pleaded quietly.

His bicep veins throbbed at the struggle, forcing his way to the grassy edge. "Wouldn't catch me? I'm truly offended." He coughed out, forcing a long breath into his lungs.

Arches, curves, and bends weaved, framing pathways, overhead balconies, and ivy drapes. Truly a maze of blue washed, polished stone and hues of white glass, reflecting the sun's warmth across Pazima's cheek. Guards wandered through doorways, pushing their swords that sat comfortably on their sides.

A whisper sparkled upon his skin, flaring a fresh symbol in bright hues of purple, highlighting a rune virgin to him, drawn just rotations ago. The dust melted into his pores, linking itself to his essence. His smirk raised, sending the whispers towards the wandering guards, twirling its power through their dry lips. A mere suggestion, influencing their brains with simple words and power, sending them stumbling into the soil. A forced slumber within the radiant flowerbeds.

Pazima's shock peered plainly to his side, frowning, questioning him. "How did you do that? As far as the Moonsong library, we don't have that knowledge."

"The Commander has a private knowledge book. He shared the sleeping spell with me." The lie lingered, pulling at his heart. "How would you know, anyway? You're not a whisperer." The rage bubbled slightly, threatening to overflow.

"I think searching the old libraries for runes with you at age fifteen would demonstrate my understanding, Astrid." Pazima scuffed, rejecting his blunt response.

Fuck, he thought. The regret stabbed at him, forcing the memories of their youth, of the endless dusks and dawns within random libraries they could locate within Hlinos, even branching to Jinos if they could sneak away for a whole rotation with enough counts for bargaining their way onto any small supply shipment boats.

They stepped through the gardens, Pazima hovered her ear next to the door's lock, listening carefully to its hums, twirling, stuffing her mist into the keyhole. Her lips remained firmly shut, like her mist screamed at him, an energy radiated from her like a primal roar, like the knowledge of creatures under her Eyldian skin begged to come out, offering to rip his sharp cheekbones from his face.

Astrid dragged the sleeping bodies, fighting against the sleep rune's sharp power. His hands burned slightly, dragging one body at a time by their ankles. The flower pits, that'll be a wonderful natural bed, He smiled, entirely amused by the thought.

The door slid open. They both began to stand cautiously, bringing their palms above their weapons' hilts. Ready for anything. A building that lacked any personality, except wealth. Walls of white arches with lapis blue trims, sharp turns on all sides with no signs in sight. Ordinary offices, storage rooms, useless chatter echoed in the halls ahead. They creeped through each arch, using the columns and doorways as cover. With each step, they slowed their breaths, looking into every office, communicating simple messages through their eyes, when to stop, when to go.

Pazima glanced at his side, a burning nod upon his cheek. She had found something, hopefully the key they needed, pleading the Moon for it to be. He couldn't handle the weight of another disappointing expression from Commander Sakhile.

This office looked different to the rest, layered in riches, items plastered over the walls. Cerulean wood from Verglas Forest, cut and professionally crafted into rich furniture of glossed over hues of blue, yet piles of abused paper stacked up to his waist.

Pazima peered over, scanning the Cerulean blue desk, softly pushing the chair from its centre. "A map." Her lips muttered while tracing the map's drawings with her index finger. Notes, layering its writing, ruled and underlined in a polished sense, yet outbursts of scribbles coated it, as if time had withered the users' need for clarity in their words. A map of outgoings. Rebel actions, food storage amounts throughout Dualia. Her finger placed itself upon the mountain range.

"Possible rebel guild location." Pazima murmurs, pulling his attention. His heart pulsed against every letter. It was not impossible. The temple had ancient protections.

"How?" Pazima said, fuelled, consumed by anger.

"They can't be onto us. They would've attacked." He pulled himself to the desk, scanning the messy notes. "We need to tell your father."

A word echoed through the floor, nearing the closed door. "And I haven't seen anyone have such venom." The voices boomed.

Pazima dropped, folding herself under the desk as Astrid pulled himself behind the lapis blue drapes that hung to the floor, clumping at his boots.

The door slid open; the voices of two men pierced their ears. "I don't know how King Alonn has patience for King Dreaka. His mind isn't what it was." The second voice added.

Seeing nothing but thick lapis drapes, all he could do was hope, while gripping firmly onto the nearest weapon upon his side.

The first voice whispered back. "He did murder his second Queen Consort." Drawers opened and closed; noises of paper crumpling itched at his ears. One extra step till Astrid's warm breath would tease the official's neck.

"Don't." The voice faded, closing the door with a careless jolt.

His breath gasped, pushing away from the drapes, branching out his hand for Pazima. She climbed up from under the desk, leaving his hand hanging in the air. Her eyes rolled, searching the last drawer that sat under a pile of dusty books. "Here. Let's go, Caelan's waiting." She said, walking to the exit.

Walking past the sleeping guards, covered by the dense flora. "Something's troubling you, Pazima?" He questioned.

Pazima carried on walking to the edge of the island, finding her footing for the leap downwards. "You. You're great, you get new spells, you get private moments, you're allowed to treat your trainee like shit." Red hues filled her irises. "Even though you're a raging, arrogant bastard. We used to be soul mates. Your cocky, belittling comments have soured it." Pazima turned her head away from him. "Yet my father still keeps you as number one, the next Commander in his mind, why?" Why... One word that cautioned her voice to crack vaguely.

He placed his hand on her shoulder, resulting in a hasty jolt of refusal. "I'm sorry." Astrid's voice became soft, almost choking on deep regret, bubbling up his throat like a burning acid. Pazima turned slightly, seeing his emotion from a slim angle. "The guild is my home, thanks to you on that freezing night, which I'm forever grateful for." He let out a quivering breath. "But a shadow haunts me since, like a poisonous itch upon my body, in the deepest curves of me, it teases, smiling with my forgotten memories in its palms." Astrid didn't know where to place his hands, rubbing his cheek and jaw in a natural anxious action. "I don't know what's me and what's it anymore, only anger to fill the void."

Pazima's eyes remained firm, refusing to disconnect from his gaze. "I'm here, Astrid, always have been, but Caelan and the others deserve more,"

"I know, but I can't ask that of you." His voice raised slightly, as anger held his heart.

"Why?" Her voice carried years of emotion.

"You can't fill both my essence and my heart." His eyes flickered. Pazima pulled his hand, moving his face down to hers, embracing his broad shoulders, folding her body against his. Her mist crawled, pulling at his broad back, wrapping him in a warmth crafted at her will.

"Astrid, your eyes." Pazima's face filled with shock. "They're gold."

"It's been happening since our mission to Charr." He began to blink and rub against his eyes and hoped it would change its hue. "It feels unlike anything I've ever felt."

"We'll figure it out." Pazima smiled at him. "Come on, you bastard."

"I don't want to be next in line." He spoke closely. Pazima leaped to the island below.

—

He and Pazima creeped through the streets, roaming towards Caelan's position. "Caelan, ready?"

Caelan grinned. "Yes, sir." He placed his and Caelan's hands onto the lock, placing the spell paper between them. The whispering filled their ears, carving at their skin. The paper flamed, shocking them away. "Impossible." He murmured.

"Oh, it's very much possible." A raspy voice spoke. "The real spell key is in my possession, as a precaution from your last visit to our city." The man's voice mirrored one from the office just moments before, raspy and cold, yet this felt different, like he was controlling his voice to be something unconnected to his gossiping purrs. "You can see why we must stop your foolish escapades across our lands, like in Charr." Astrid's expression widened slightly, hoping it wouldn't show as a sign of weakness. Word travelled fast for the Four, faster by the season as more soldiers trolled every trodden path. "A new magistrate stands in the spoils of Charr, all of them homes and fields of full crop. King Alonn was pleased to take it back, swiftly, of course." The magistrate licked his lips, as if he dared at a fresh piece of meat over a roaring fire. "Moonsong's efforts do nothing, saves no one—"

"We feed the people you and your king deem obsolete to the continent, my dear high magistrate." He smirked, leaning into a sarcastic bow. Pazima pushed Caelan behind her, guiding her fingers around her sword's hilt. Caelan placed his footing firmly next to Pazima, following her every move.

"No need, boy, leave your insulting gestures for the King." The high magistrate waved his hand effortlessly. Guards charged the streets from every corner, filling the back streets in mere clicks, their metal armour smashed against their bones, echoing through the stones below.

Caelan and Pazima pulled their swords. "Caelan, in front. We run to the exit. kill them If they get too close. I won't allow you to die." A look of worry waved across Caelan's inexperienced face.

He looked to Pazima, twirling his sword's hilt with his palm. "With me?"

She radiated a sense of calm and reason, smiling up to Astrid's calculating, caring expression. "Till death, Tris."

Residents screamed, throwing themselves to the pathways, into the building's doorways. The three Moonsinger's pushed their feet off the stone ground, running through the market squares and housing streets. The soldier's commands roared from both ends of the street.

"Caelan, energy spell." He commanded.

They carried on running at full speed. Caelan whispered, forming an energy ball in his hand. The energy ball flew, crashing into the soldiers. Debris launched in every direction, filling the air with smoke and stone fragments. The soldier's whispers groaned, throwing beams of energy through the settling debris.

Island after island, they smashed, slashed, and punched the formations of soldiers, pushing their strength and their guild training to its limits. Daily spars for a polished fighting style, keeping a clear mind about what could come through the shadows. Metal, blood, roars. Anything.

"The stairs." He gasped for a long breath. Pazima ran forward, scanning the polished stones that lead to the stairs down to the mainland. A red mist, dark and cold, raged towards Pazima, sensing its similarities. The small corner island, consumed by their mists. Roars of golems, the screams of gnomes, the quakes of Quetzalcoatl's. Calls of creatures, weaving through thick mists of red, all different in hues. The connection to the mythical realms. The power that made Pazima one with beasts.

"Pazima!" He pleaded, pulling Caelan close.

The mist pushed away. "Sword to sword." She broadcasted across the polished stone. Both the shifters pulled their swords, wrapping their mist around them tightly. The guards stopped, staring at the shifters, as if a cub had called to fight an alpha for its throne.

Pazima winked at the fellow shifter, grating her blade against hers. The metal smashed against one another, sending red sparks jolting into the air. The mist roared at the connection between the blades, coating her umber skin in hues of red. Pazima pulled back, jumping onto the right side, waiting for the other shifter to strike, like a mouse to a serpent.

Rage glowed upon her enemy's features, gleaming in her red irises, piling upon her blade. The small blonde's strike was messy and inexperienced. Pazima smiled slightly, launching herself into the air, placing her footing behind the blonde shifter. She gripped her sword, twirling her mist in one mighty slice, ripping deep into her back leg muscles, forcing her to crumble to the polished stone floor. The remaining shifter screamed, seemingly a clear expression of grief for a loved one. Pazima pulled her gaze and her focus from the bleeding woman, running through the blood-soaked polished stone. "Quick!" She shrieked. Every fibre of Astrid's body called to him to grab her, use his body as a shield, even to keep her alive for a few clicks more. Astrid knew she was evidently the most combat trained, better than most in their guild, better than him. He knew that as a fact, but an intense, sharp pain pulled at his heart, begging for him to rip her away from any possible dangers.

Astrid looked at Pazima's face, reading her simple instructions. Quick, Follow. He grabbed Caelan, throwing them both off the edge of the hovering island. Pazima swiftly followed their descent, dropping with grace to a quick descent to death.

# Chapter 17

## Warning from the Left

They floated above the water, pulled together by Pazima's mist, tying around their plunging descent. Nothing but hope is all he had. Hope the mist had a powerful grip upon their lives. Groans burst out, rolling with them across the brisk sands and sharp stony shore line.

"Thanks for the save." Astrid spoke while brushing sand off his cheeks, touching his face, feeling the fresh cuts. Pazima was alive. Caelan, where was Caelan? His focus now laid on locating his trainee. Caelan laid in the sand, no movements, no painful expressions. Astrid ran, kicking rocks into the air. Consumed by deep, dire sorrow, dropping to his ripped, dirty leather trousers. Purple hues fogged by tears upon his eyes, Flicking Caelan to his front, blood dripped through his thick black locks. "Come on, don't you dare." A tear slipped into his cuts.

Purple flickered, choking up a painful laugh from Caelan's lips. "That was—fun."

"Let's go." He sighed, grasping the relief. The guards roared from the grand staircase. Astrid and Pazima hung Caelan between them, pulling their way through the frosty forest.

-

The brightening teased the snowy mountain peaks, whistling the royal songs of the south. The doors of the temple hummed; stone slid open for the bruised Moonsingers. Astrid supported Caelan down the stone halls, dragging his footing across the ancient stone floor.

He pushed through into the healing arc; the scent of flowers stuffed his nose. Healers rushed around, scanning, laying Caelan down onto one of the empty medic beds. "What happened?" The elder healer questioned, wearing a clean beige tunic with a clear symbol of energy, ribboning around a pair of hands - The symbol of Quarria's healer school. The only place any Eyldian goes to be an official healer of the realm.

His vision blurred, the questions twirled, throbbing against his forehead. "We dropped from Hlinos, Elder Rose." The words spat out. Pazima stood next to Caelan, a commanding stance accompanied with polite words towards another healer.

The healing arcs were carved out of stone; bed bays sat privately between each archway. The nature of the temple blossomed, especially in the healing arcs. Moonflowers sprouted out of the cracks of the ceiling, giving scents of sweet berries and freshwater vapour. The flowers of their guild, only found in the cracks of their mountain's cliffs, filled with powerful properties, healing wounds faster than any Eyldian's natural healing processes.

"Astrid, I expect you to come into the Arc, broken into four pieces, but your trainee? Elder Rose sighed while directing her training healers to Caelan's bay.

"Descending from the islands was the only escape, Elder Rose." Pazima jumped in, hooking her sentence in Elder Rose's brewing response.

"Very well, Leave him to rest, he'll be okay by sun fall." Elder Rose commanded calmly.

"Will he survive?"

Elder Rose looked up from her notes, breathing sharply, nodding towards Astrid. "He will." Astrid nodded in return, pushing himself up, walking out of the healing arc. His mind raced, questioning what he did on this mission. Caelan, his trainee, could have died because of him. His fingers clenched, slamming against a hallway stone pillar, causing sharp pain to scream, rippling through his skin, crumbling him to the floor in a piercing groan.

The anger bubbled as he curled against the brisk stone wall. The figure stared at him, always at the corner of his eye, in every room. "What are you?" He murmured into his hands, pushing his body up the stone.

Nothing but cold air passed through the halls. No reply graced his ears. Pazima slid down next to him, placing her hand on his leg. "I know it's hard, all this. But you'll deal with it." She spoke with care, pulling his hands from his face. Her fingers smoothly graced his cheek, wiping a lone tear. "Tell anyone I did that, and I'll gut you on the sparring floor."

He smiled, looking up slowly. "I could have lost my trainee. I haven't trained him. Vaguely remembered his name this morning, Paz." Astrid's voice deepened to a sharp whisper. "The figure in my thoughts, it's an all-consuming force."

"The name – Caelan, shall remain scorched into your thoughts after this rotation." A laugh bobbed. She continued. "Don't look at it like a mission. You're his mentor, blessed by the Moon, guide him, and maybe learn something about him. Take an interest, Astrid."

He pulled up, using the stone walls for support, planting a stable footing with Pazima. "You have it easy; your trainee doesn't talk."

A sharp, narrow glare drawn upon Pazima's face. "She has loss of hearing, she's not stupid." Her face softened, rising to a clear, proud smile. "Certainly knows more than most, don't discredit her. She even educated me in the visual language of the old ones. So, me and her can talk, train together."

He nodded. "Apologies, I wasn't aware. Maybe she can teach me too." Pazima linked her arm with his, walking down the hall.

"In my many, many years of being your friend, I have never seen you learn something so—" Pazima chuckled under her breath. "Academical"

"I can learn new tricks, Paz." Astrid unhooked his arm from hers, dramatically speeding his movements down the temple's long hallways.

"Idiot!" Pazima yelled, smiling with a warming glow.

—

Astrid pushed against the weight of the Commander's office door, scanning the mood of the room and any physical details of the Commander's idle stance, sitting with piles of papers in his company.

The Commander's head shot up. "Astrid, how was Hlinos."

His brows weighed down with moisture. Leaving the temple and its humid climate always slapped him after a long mission in the freezing mountain conditions. "We were ambushed. They knew we would come back for their food storage." A deep sigh hit him.

The Commander dropped his pen onto his desk. "Let's keep away from Hlinos till it calms."

He walked closer, closing the door behind him. "Sir, we also found something alarming." Commander Sakhile formed a half nod, raising his head, observing Astrid's roaming thoughts. "We found a map in the high magistrate's office. It pinned out areas of interest. They are close to finding the temple's location. Labelling us as a clear threat."

Commander Sakhile forced his face to freeze over. "Thank you, you're dismissed." He nodded sharply, refusing to expand the conversation.

~

A new rotation dawned on Astrid's frosty, sharp features, highlighting the melting snow. He spent the night laying at the bottom of the mountain's valley, watching the ripples within the river, observing the fish and the duskfoxes that ran into their burrows.

"This river, it's gorgeous, isn't it?" A female voice caused Astrid to snap back into reality.

He crooked his head, seeing Fee moving to sit next to him, placing her cream-white staff into the shore's bitter-cold grass. "I know you said no more sessions, but I had to see you."

He smiled, looking into his reflection on the river water. "I told her." His breathing released. "I told Pazima that she fills my heart." His eyes sparkled, reflecting the dawn's growing shine.

"What made you disclose your love?" Fee questioned with a vague smile.

"She did, in some ways." Astrid smiled. "Could you help me control my anger?"

"Always." Fee's mature face filled with a sense of purpose.

~

"You can do better than that." Fee spoke, swinging a wooden staff at his legs, dropping him to the river rocks.

"I'm trying." He huffed slightly. "No dreamer power for this lesson?" He spat out.

Fee held her staff, guiding her thoughts into her weapon. The ultimate control between her and the world. She grinned, swirling her staff. The dawn's rays beamed down upon her staff's carved symbolic details, moons, stars, and twirls of power, ribboning around her handcrafted weapon. "Your mind, use it. You control your form with training. Use that in a mental form. Control your thoughts, the magic, the rage, the love. It all goes through us. We all have raw emotions, just in different forms. Our essence is ours to learn, to control." She pulled her staff, hooking his right leg as he balanced on his left. The river rocks crumbled under his foot, pulling his focus vaguely, yet that was all Fee needed, dropping him once more.

His face steamed. "I need to go check on Caelan. I'll carry on trying Fee, thank you." He launched back to his feet, joining back to the dirt pathway.

"Think of what you love most when your anger threatens to consume you." She raised her voice marginally.

–

Commander Sakhile and Fee leaned over the sparring room's furthest stone railing, observing the training floor from a fair distance. Pazima and Daj threw themselves into their positions, lunging, flanking one another, throwing their training into focus. Astrid sat on the stone steps entering the sparring ground, offering insight where he could, but this was Pazima's speciality. Weaponry of all masses, shapes, sharpness, and materials. She knew them all. In their youth, the Commander gave assignments to survive the Fellow's Valley. A test, fighting the wild with whichever weapon Commander Sakhile flung to their sides. Once bolting a duskfox to a tree's root by age twelve with a rustic crossbow, while Astrid would always favour a weighted sword. Pazima found herself accustomed to any tool, especially with her moonstone staff.

She waved it in a motion of pure connection, displaying different positioning and techniques. She pressed it into each Young's hands, teaching them how to control their footing, how to bond with their weapon. What it means to be one with the moonstone, with the metal at your fingertips.

A detailed moonstone staff, imbued, bonded to her mist alone, carvings within its foundations for her power to weave through, strike her enemies in ways only she could know. Its blood red marks ran up, swirling to a sharp blade edge, a staff, deadly and efficient to block multiple strikes in mere clicks.

Daj stood spiralling her hammer into new stances, showing her specialism for heavy weaponry. Moving like Pazima, she trained her as a leader, as a power, crystallised and refined. Her movements sparked the memories of being Young. The joy and innocence of their youth.

The Commander stood by the staircase on the upper level, holding the sparring room's glances and its lurking specta-tors. "Astrid, come." Commander Sakhile commanded. Pazima paused, nodding to her trainee. Daj pushed her hammer to the side, tossing herself completely into the Young's lesson, enjoying every click with a clear smile.

He stepped up the layers of spectating rings, meeting the Commander and Fee. "Yes, Commander?" His eyes glued to Commander Sakhile, placing his footing into a firm stance. Pazima placed herself against the pillar next to them.

"We got a high alert from our Moonsingers in Jinos. No more missions to the cities till further notice." His voice deepened, forcing the command out.

"What if they need assistance, Commander?" Astrid ques-tioned.

Sakhile stepped forward, hovering over his ear. "We ignore it for now." The Commander turned, passing Fee with a glance. His footsteps echoed across the cold stone, sending chills down Astrid's spine.

Fee stood still, seemingly waiting for Astrid to crack. "How are you feeling?"

He angled his face in her direction. "I'm working on that." He forced a smile to form.

The sleeping quarters whistled, carrying unconscious mur-murs down the endless halls. Astrid rolled over, flicking his flat pillow to the colder side, letting out a groan of annoyance as his heart began to ache. The darkness of the stone walls collapsing in, pulling, ripping, reflecting his essence like a mirror. Gasps choked upon his throat, begging for the temple's air to greet him. He whispered into his palm, igniting the candles at his bedside in a hasty click. The room absorbed the warm purple light, exposing its scars. History burdened the ancient stone walls, with teeth and nail marks scraping down the bedside wall, accompanied by countless sword slashes throughout the back walls. Nothing could cover that history, the pain of the temple's predecessors. Restlessness kept him in this cage. Four stone walls of darkness, of memories of old. He lifted himself from the bed, covered only by his cotton blanket. He stared, running his fingers through the nail indents. "I wish I knew what happened to you. Use that knowledge to protect this place." He whispered to the stone, laying on the cold floor, accepting the blanket's warmth fleeing from his body. "I hope you are at peace now."

Astrid pulled himself up, throwing his old black tunic over his muscular chest, cringing sharply at the rabbit stew he had dropped on his tunic earlier during that rotation. Fuck, he cussed with a sharp mutter. He hated eating rabbit strew with its overbearing number of sliced carrots.

His thoughts pulled, asking him to go down, back to the myths below. The warmth of their feathers, their vibrant scales reflecting the moonlight. He placed his hand down on the door handle, accepting his desire.

Yet the doorway suddenly filled with an Eyldian silhouette. Pazima pushed against the handle, finding herself against him, standing in the cracking door frame. "What my father said, we need to go. We should see if someone needs our help." She muttered, refusing to let it echo down the sleeping quarters.

"He commanded me Al. I can't disobey that." He pulled her into the room, closing the door behind them.

"He's wrong, he thinks he's protecting Moonsong, but he's ignoring Eyldia and the pressure it's under." Her red silk nightdress trailed behind her. "You know it too. We will not survive in hiding much longer, neither will the whole realm."

"What commands us to be its heroes?" He slid down the nearby wall, feeling the nail marks against his back.

Pazima stepped closer, sliding down next to him. "It's who we are." Pazima pulled his chest close, folding her arms around him. His face softened into her silk nightdress as Pazima's fingers ran down through his hair, collecting all the lone, sweaty strands. Astrid peered up, absorbing his view. Her every freckle, her beautifully silk-wrapped, thick, ebony curls, her eyes glimmered a rich summer oak.

Pazima's fingers traced his textured imperfections, smiling at every indentation, every little scar upon his jawline and cheekbones. "Remember how you got these?" She breathed.

Astrid chuckled slightly, accepting a big grin to grow upon his face. "You pushed me into a thornbush, which also had a duskfox burrow below it, if I recall."

"That duskfox wasn't pleased." She laughed, running her fingers across the scars. "With my life, I'll protect you." Pazima whispered.

"You always have." He spoke truthfully, without need of a facade.

"We protect each other till death, remember?" A tear dropped from her cheek. Their eyes locked for a longing moment, accepting what they always knew. Their love was strong like the freezing gushes of their home's Valleys.

Astrid looked into her soft lips, "Can I?"

She smiled, running her hand down his left cheek. "Yes." Their lips pressed like silk, softly interlocking, accepting the connection between souls, and their love.

Astrid's hand pulled Pazima up, wrapping her legs around his muscular waist, lowering Pazima to his bed. Nothing but a red silk nightdress and under-garnets between them. A room full of history and scars, now coated in warmth and love.

# Chapter 18

## Chaos in the Castle Walls

### *Raven*

Ice, wind, mist. The sharp air scratched Raven's throat, parting his messy curls. Their feet throbbed against their fleeing sprints. Raven and Sevar weaved around the sharp castle corners, grating against the huge, polished stones coated in thin layers of ice upon its corners.

Guards, soldiers, and the blonde mercenary roared in their tracks. "Close this castle now." She raged.

"It's a dead end." Sevar's thoughts poured freely over his face. Worry, unfiltered emotion, furrowed from his brow, bunching with dripping sweat, his lips muttered, tracing plausible ideas. "This way."

Halls of polished stone, frost-bitten with a faint ice blue tint. His eyes darted around each sharp corner. The roars of soldier's crashed into the nearby wall, followed by a dark mist, consuming the halls entirely. Creature-like arms swung, wrapping around their throats.

"Sev." Raven pleaded. His lungs clawed, grasping the last strand of oxygen. Sevar's energy beamed from his palm, crumbling the icy stones behind the shifter's warping form. Their

130

sight fogged with debris and icy mist, yet growing sounds of bashing metal crashed through the thick mist, forming around Sevar.

Raven's mind begged to flee, but his heart pulsed in a raw refusal. He could feel it, a growing pressure upon him, being next to Sevar, his anchor to bravery, even as death knocked, coated in ice and mist, he felt warm.

Sevar's broadsword radiated runic power, twirling, twisting, slicing their flesh, pulling at their guts. The mercenary groaned, full of anger. Her sword sliced through the mist, clipping his ear to the frost-kissed stone. "Bitch." Sevar screeched, ripping the sword from his bleeding ear with a venomous hiss.

Raven's palm quivered, clenching his daggers. His thoughts waved through his weapons, pushing through every crease in the metal carvings. His right hand broke into the air, dashing his daggers towards her.

The death in her eyes. Black, like darkness, bowed down to her will. "I'll make you suffer, as you did her." Her voice, engrossed. Her blood-soaked leathers trampled the bodies littered over the halls, her sword teased, glowing a thick, burned red.

Her? Raven's mind ran through every word, every singular letter of her drowning hatred. She knew something, and it consumed her entirely, yet Raven knew nothing of her reasoning, of her clear lashing emotion.

Her pace jolted to a dash, placing her sword pointing towards his torso. Sevar's brute arms gripped Raven's shoulders, slinging him across the hallway. Sevar's sword clashed against hers, sparking purple and red hues sparring in the bitter air. She pasted a proud grin, slicing downwards, plunging a small dagger from her leg hilt, striking its clean blade into Sevar's stomach. Blood, all he saw was blood, and Sevar's jolt, twirling into the pain. Blood dripped, sponged by his beige tunic. A wave of soldiers hurled into the hall. "Sevar!" His body screamed, trembling upon the polished stone arches, running from the consuming darkness, from her. Commands between Offical's echoed against the ice. Pain. Blood. He threw him away, to protect him from harm. Tears streamed down his pale cheeks, absorbed by his loose curls.

-

The winds were brutal, bashing against his thin tunic. The city's residents cowered, staring through their white-stained panes. Tears ran, cutting Raven's cheek sharp as blades. A city coated by the glitters of snowfall, bashing the freezing gushes against his cracking lips. Ice towers spiralled above, reflecting against the sun, as if they stood tall, like beacons to a better place, a better way of living. The Four, showing what they hold, their power in their grasp. Ice towers held the castle, piercing through its walls. The coldness cracked into his mind, freezing his thoughts entirely. From everything this adventure with Sevar had taught him, it had to be magic, power strong enough to keep a firm grip of the seasons, causing this island to live in an eternal snowfall.

-

Running through the wide streets, homes that wrapped around the castle's lower exteriors. Raven ran, step by step, his leg muscles throbbed, pulsing his blood through his brittle frame. Nothing but one dagger left to defend himself. The circular streets twisted, no corners, no ending, all streets weaving into each other. Layers of homes filled with laughing kids, kicking their boots into the side paths. Pathways cut through every circular street, ever expanding the labyrinth of ice and snow.

Soldiers' voices swarmed the streets, climbing closer. No way out of the maze of ice and stone. Raven's heart raced. Asking for help but not for himself, but from his friend, the man in his dreams. Footsteps pressed down onto the clean snow paths behind, wrapping their arms around his neck, tossing him to the hard ground. The pain radiated through every bone. His scream cut off within his throat, clinging to hope for Sevar's survival.

His face pressed into layers of snow and frozen mud, yet the cold burned upon his eyes, like a blazing divine source of power, completely raw, powerful and unpredictable. Hues of searing gold burst out from his veins, pouring out from his palms into the soldiers that held him. The gold power swirled, dipping through the soldier's pooling blood. Raven's instincts begged for him to flee, but he stood, frozen. Soaked in a pool of blood.

"Sevar, I—" His voice cracked, staring into the blurring vision of red and white hues.

Silhouettes and alarming rings crashed into the side street. "Get up." A sharp, deep voice commanded.

# Chapter 19

## The Dead & The Wounded

### *Astrid*

The mountains sang, wrapping its pitch around Ambe's wingspan. "Don't tell your father."

Ambe's wings sliced through the clouds. The wind graced their features, pushing through the brisk wind. "How are you doing this?" Pazima yelled into his ear, battling the wind's brute force.

They both knew the knowledge of riders and their bonds to their Quetzalcoatl, a mythical creature ingrained into their essence, like a bond to a father, brother, daughter, a soul mate. A connection ruptured only by death. "The gold in my veins. It seems to connect me to them." Ambe edged to a smooth glide, keeping his wings along the air's current. "I can feel him. His emotion radiates off him like a sequence of noises." Astrid brushed his hand across Ambe's feathers.

Pazima tightened her grip around his waist. Her fingers folded into the depths of his abs. "We need to research this gold power."

His brows creased. The thought of wandering the land for the golden mystery weighed on him. He peered back slightly,

134

smiling, admiring her long battle-ready braided hair, neat rows along her scalp leading to braid tails, wrapped with a diamond-patterned fabric at its core. Her eye line connected to his, sharing a warm glance. "You look beautiful." He spoke. Pazima smiled, pressing a kiss to his crisp cheek.

Ambe folded in his wings, twirling his serpent body, descending to the circular ice city. A mountainous smile grew upon his face, like a child discovering sweet cake, a true sparkling glee. A laugh bellowed, echoing from his torso's depths. Their legs gripped Ambe's form, battling the knots in their stomachs.

-

Screams, yells, death sang in the wind. The ice swam in warm red. The castle of snow and ice, ever stained by repulse. Ambe slithered his body around the castle's tower, angling Pazima and Astrid to a nearby window. Astrid ran his fingers through Ambe's feathers before dismounting the beautiful violet Quetzalcoatl. A mythical creature of unknown origin, only found flying at sea, or resting at untouched aisles in the northwest, along Storm's Way, the enteral storm, told as a tale of revenge, one Fee had said to keep him in his sleeping quarters as a rebellious Young.

-

Pazima kept the lead with her moonstone staff in hand. Halls, pathways, staircases. They moved as one, together. A nod at each entrance, every position traced by one another. Following their footing, keeping her back safe from behind. Soldiers marched, stomping the fresh bodies under their boots. Pazima's power wrapped around her staff. Her power, her creature's power, wrapping around her hand and her weapon. A mighty roar bellowed through her, through her staff like a beacon, throwing a hall of soldiers to the ground in one mighty burst of power.

He grinned, holding his sword in a ready position. "That was... impressive."

"See. I let you win." Pazima turned, giving him a wink.

Pazima's boots were soaked in blood. She pressed down her moonstone staff on the piled bodies, a natural precaution, Astrid observed, mirroring her. "The trail seems to go outside." Her eyes darted across the bodies, as if she read the blood splatter patterns with ease.

Metals clashed, echoing through the castle's main entrance. A man's deep-toned voice groaned, fighting a woman's rageful force. The man's left hand gripped his bloodied tunic, latching onto his open wound. His struggling expression broke through, leaving a cracked man with nothing left but his broadsword, pushing her strikes with withering strength. The blonde lunged, throwing her body across the cobbled entrance, as if this fight was personal.

Astrid flung his daggers back into his holders, grabbing his sword into both hands. They acknowledged each other with a simple nod. A thousand words passed through a plain symbol, an agreement to save a life. Even if it was only one, it could change the entire realm. They pushed forward, running from the castle's entrance. Soldiers glared, raising their blood-soaked weapons. Pazima twirled her staff, lunging, stabbing the soldier's vital organs with the sharp embedded blade while blocking another soldier with the blunt stone detailing at its other end.

Astrid supported his partner, pushing close to her back. A soldier dashed, pulling at her braid, a desperate charge for a miniature upper hand in a losing battle. Astrid's teeth grated, "Pulling a woman's hair, well, that's not gentleman-like." Before he finished his sentence, his blade cleaved the soldier's arm, snapping his bone like brittle bark, causing him to drop, screaming into the red snow.

"Choke on your nobleness, Lorstorm." The woman launched down her sword, full with venom upon her words.

"You first." The man spat a mouthful of blood into the blonde's weathered coat, causing her to jolt back slightly. Pazima lunged into the woman's shock, taking this opportunity to save a life.

A man covered in layers of blood, coating his clean beard in dripping red, murmured. His umber skin flushed, drained completely of any energy, his muscles crumbled, dropping to the cobbled ground. "I need to find him."

He ran to his side, kneeling with the man. "Who?" Astrid scanned the state of his wounds.

"My—" He choked, "Friend, we got split up." The pain remained clear upon the man's features, yet not from the wound, but from deep emotion, collecting within his forming tears. Astrid folded his arm under the man's arm, supporting him on his side. The man's brawny structure tested his endurance.

"What's your name?" His thighs burned, looking up to mist entanglement ahead.

"Sevar." He groaned.

Pazima swung her staff, full of mist ribboning around her weapon, pushing it towards the woman's heart, but she twirled her own dark mist around Pazima's staff, launching it from her grip.

Soldier's commands began to echo throughout the tightening stone's, moving to each exit point. Astrid's head tossed from side to side, the mist, the soldiers, the wounded man. The juggle of life and death weighed on his shoulders. Was this worth one life, risking his own love for another's?

Mist of bright and dark hues exploded, consuming the castle entrance and its connected ice towers. The men pushed against the mist's force, hoping their grip on the cobble ground remained stable. An almighty roar vibrated the ice, casting a rhyme of whining, shifting ice. The mist twirled, shooting into the air, cleared by Ambe's wingspan.

The shifters lunged, roaring through their fangs, both forming into Moonwolves, coloured in patches of red and white fur, both similar but completely different. One full of rage and fury, and another with full brown irises, angling its long head as if it calculated its mist and how to use it against the trained shifter. The soldiers gathered from the main streets gate, glancing at the snow wolves of huge proportions, their fangs angled, slowly dripping acid into the cobbles, sending burning hisses into the air. Their growls creeped under Astrid's and Sevar's skin, their eyes glued to their flared nostrils.

Astrid pushed, launching Sevar into Ambe's saddle, placing his hand on Ambe's side, pushing his thoughts into the mythic creature's mind. Ambe's head bared down, blowing a playful breath through his hair.

He ran, lunging himself across the cobblestones, pulling out his daggers. Ready to jump. Ready to support his partner, to launch his daggers into the enemy's skull but his direct dash was smashed by a powerful jolt, throwing his body into the cracked cobblestones, bashing his head upon an icy tree. Astrid's vision blurred faintly, looking into a man's eyes, his thin beard, refusing to connect to his stingy moustache, his metal armour covered by a thick cloak, detailed in gold and the royal symbol sewed to his right.

"Rebellion means death." The royal spoke.

The wolves circled, launching into each other's necks. Painful groans flared. "Sorry, I'm not stopping your majesty," Astrid spat. He looked through his rogue strands of hair, glancing at the shifter's animalistic brawl. He murmured under his tongue. "Come on, Pazima."

Ambe's face creased, twirling his body in front of Astrid, a shield of red and blue scales. He roared, blowing the royals cloak into the air, throwing his footing against the polished, cracked stone. Hundreds of soldiers swamped, filling the castle's entrance and the connected streets, forming a line of swords and shields, all branded with the royal symbol. A primal cry flew as acid dripped onto Pazima's side. A monster of mist thinned, twirling to her human form, as a smile curled on the woman's face, holding Pazima's limp wolf body by the back of her neck.

Astrid froze completely, as if his heart forgot to pulse blood through his veins. The icy sharp air, cutting deep and raw, kissing his rosy cheek. His cheeks burned, almost scorching by touch. Anger, pure emotion, pushing into the darkness of his soul. Astrid snapped, screaming from his dead, sharp features.

Ambe's wings pulsed, twirling the wind as an elemental weapon, tossing the horde of soldiers a couple of steps back. The mystic creature roared, shaking the ice towers at its deepest foundation, threatening to topple the entire city of ice and stone. Astrid's muscles refused to follow Ambe's command. He couldn't leave her.

Astrid lunged with overflowing purple in his veins, whispering with pure venom overflowing in every letter pouring off his tongue. The mythic serpent wrapped him tight in his wing, tossing Astrid onto his saddle, roaring, launching into the skies.

# Chapter 20

## Walls of Ice & Sorrow

### *Raven*

The walls dripped of cold, rustic water; cracks revealed thick ice foundations. Magic hummed through the layers of ice, leaving a pulsing ache gripping at his ears. A never-ending hum, growing like an illness under his skin. The magic whispered against the cell door, teasing him to struggle at the handle. Locked, freezing sharp upon his gentle, pale skin.

Stomps bashed against his cell door; The metal imbued to the wall with narrow bars to see through, gifting a petite angle of deficient sunlight. A woman with braided coils, dripping blood and lime puss to the cracked stone floor, leaving a lingering smell of death, souring the nearby freezing air.

The moon's light reflected through the small cracks, shining through the runic ice foundations. The ever-consuming scent of deep runes leaked through the stones, filling the marks of tortures of old. How many people died in this cell? Lost and alone, in sharp pain, taken by the bitter cold.

His body crumbled, laying on the wet cold floor. The walls pulled at him, tapping on his shoulder, whispering, rendering his dreaming abilities void. His mind cried. The power of the runes held him in the boundaries of stone and ice. Nothing but the noise of dripping water, screams that followed the horrid scent of charred skin.

-

The night leaked through, touching his wet cheek. His eyelids flared, fighting the darkness of his cell. He dragged his limbs across the stone, laying on top of the thin ripped blanket, tracing the cracks, the indents in the floor. Raven's focus pulled to the knuckle indents on the side of the dripping wall. He traced around the marks, the angles of the stone, carving a face into the stone above his dirty, withered pillow. The face of his friend. His eyelids jittered, dragging down from exhaustion, closing with the traced face as his only comfort.

-

The morning climbed through the ice, casting a ghostly white light across his crusted chin. Raven's fingers lifted from the rough stone. He lifted his torso, revealing blood on the thin blanket. Worry cast over his features, scanning his skin. His fingers ran across every inch of his body, a groan gasped at his lips. His fingers laid over many cuts from the sharp stone floor.

Footsteps echoed, nearing his cell door. His feet pulsed; he threw himself up to an unstable footing. The rune groaned, shifted, as the handle pulled downwards. "This is the one?" The man commanded. The brute nodded plainly, keeping a hand firmly on his sword's hilt.

"You storm through my gateway, kill my people." His voice kept low, wrapped in a venomous tang.

His tongue whipped at every word, looking into Raven's cracking skin. The door slammed closed, leaving the King of Dualia in front of him. "I killed your pitiful companions." King

Alonn stepped closer, placing his lips at Raven's left ear. His tongue flickered with each letter. "Their heads lay on ice pikes at the castle entrance, my gift to you." The words sparked a smirk to rise from the King's flat lip.

He glared up through his brows, lunging at the King, tossing his cut body into the royal's ample body, climbing, clawing, punching with any stored strength he had left. The guards slammed in, throwing him into the far wall. The slam knocked him clean into darkness. The King's voice consumed it. "Make his execution public. A message must be made."

—

The moon shone, peeling open his throbbing eyelids. Pain pulsed with every slight movement. Raven hovered his fingertips over his ribs, feeling the fresh swelling, gently gasping at the pain. He tilted his head, biting down on his tongue.

The brisk air, the darkness, chipping away at his bones, ripping little by little. His adventure to help his friend, to find his mother, was short-lived. The prophecy repeated in his mind, forever a page left, a page unturned.

The details bounced from ear to ear. "Two souls ribboned as one." He whispered.

His lips uttered the words till the sunlight raised through the cracks of ice.

# Chapter 21

Connected Strangers

*Astrid*

Ambe's wing plummeted; his roars quaked through his scales. Astrid gripped Sevar, struggling to staple himself into Ambe's saddle. Slicing through the clouds, Sevar's blood stained his hand. Ambe pulled up, slamming into a shoreline.

Astrid struggled for breath, gasping while scanning the area, pulling at Sevar a safe distance from the ocean's crashing waves. Ambe's body stretched through the shore, digging into the sand.

His thoughts raced. This wasn't his shoreline, a strange new plain. His fingers slipped, dropping Sevar into the sand next to the Ambe.

Astrid placed his fingers on the scales, sifting through the connection. "Ambe, where are we?" He whispered against his scales. Ambe's feathers stuttered, pushing up a black-bloodied wound. Ambe hissed into him; a flash of blinding light radiated through his shut lids.

"Ambe!" He pleaded, dropping to his knees. The blinding light cleared, the roars of birthing Quetzalcoatl's, bright colours and hues, serpents of all sizes, personalities and vibrance.

Some flew in pride with a broad span. Others held back, holding their quakes under their scales. Flying free through Eyldia, the sea, the isle as their home.

He shot up. "Is this isle your home?" Ambe stared with a sparkle in his slit irises.

A voice climbed through the plains, Sevar held his wound, dragging himself behind Ambe.

Astrid's foot ran to the voice. The thoughts of having Ambe taken, rushed, cast in each corner of his mind. The burning in his palms, the raw energy of pure gold, pulsed once more. He traced each person, their weapons, their clothing. Each individual, personalised, pieces of coloured fabrics, feathers and jewels. What could their weaknesses be?

Their sable skin absorbed the light, filling their features with a rich tint. "Stranger." An old voice echoed through the group of people, holding a calm, yet commanding tone. "Let us help you with your mythic." Her silk red dress gracefully glided in the wind, accompanied by a more vibrant cloak, detailed in feathers around its trim lines. The cloak looked different, no hood, nothing in the way of hiding their identity. No secrecy. She walked with pure a clear astuteness with her head held high, graced by the sea breeze, throwing her grey braids to the side. Her braids dropped from her scalp, pink and red beads styled throughout, perfectly clean, like each bead and jewel had its own purpose, its own story to tell.

"Who are you?" Astrid spoke cautiously.

"I'm Elder Noxolo." All their heads stood high, stood united. "We are the Ophidians. We care for the mythic creatures."

He stood still, clenching burning gold energy within his palm. "How can I trust you?" He broadcasted.

The Elder stepped closer. "You tell me, your eyes glow purple, yet you ride." She glanced at his hand. "Your hands burn golden." Her eyes darted up, scanning over his features. Elder Noxolo's observations were absent of any negative emotion, beaming with a smile. She placed her hand over his, pushing against the flickering energy. "Trust me."

Her touch, her words. It clenched Astrid's head. Their presence, their connection, the unity, it radiated with pride. He nodded, taking in her wrinkled hand.

They stepped in unity, placing their group across the shoreline. The elder woman placed her hand against Ambe's wide nostrils.

Elder Noxolo's features dropped to a frown. A sadness like a memory jumped to the forefront of her mind. "Ambe."

His head shook. "You know Ambe?"

She climbed back to her feet, throwing a glance towards her nearest people. Her hand raised, flicking in the air. They moved, placing their hand under Ambe. Many men and women placed their feet into the sand, groaning at Ambe's heavy weight. Noxolo's left hand waved towards Sevar as two of her people threw him over their shoulders.

Her glance directed back towards Astrid, gracing him again with a warming smile. "We need to go back to the cove, save Ambe and your friend." The calm yet chilling tone felt similar. Felt like home.

"You know Commander Sakhile." He stated.

She carried her walk, Astrid pushed forward to her side. "Sakhile is mine. My son."

Astrid's mind raced, trying to connect any information he had known of his friend. His partner. "You're Pazima's grandmother?"

Her foot stopped dead in the grass. "I haven't seen my son in thirty years. Pazima, what is she like?" The sorrow dipped in each word that came out.

His smile raised. "She's the moon itself, the anchor of us all. She's everything." The memory of Pazima, broken and bitten, forcing sadness to wash over his features.

–

Rain smashed down onto the cove, blocking any far views, all but small boats rocking on the sea current, anchored by thick ropes to the rocky wall shores. The elder and her people held Ambe high. Her hands waved in the air, commanding the doors to be opened. The building stood tall, space for many creatures to be housed, healed, and kept safe. It reminded Astrid of the temple's lower levels, the high cave ceilings of rock and history. This building, held by thick cream wood and thick pale blue ropes, tying together the wood proudly, holding the landscape above with ease.

The air slammed against the shut doors, the saltiness of the cove leaking through the seams and cracks, jumping for his foreign nostrils. Healers walked in, draped in white robes, detailed in mixes of red and blue bearings, like Elder Noxolo, but it felt different, as if the colours displayed roles in this community. They mumbled between them, each analysing different parts of Ambe's massive body.

"How's Sevar?" Astrid pulled himself from spacing into the overpowering, salty tang.

"He's lost a substantial amount of blood, but he'll be up after a strong tonic." Elder Noxolo spoke on behalf of the healers. "Rest in the houses on the other side of the cove. No one will spot you there."

His stance turned back to the elder. "You're their leader, their elder? Why would I need to be hidden?" His fingers itched for his weapons.

"The Four placed their officials in our homes, killed many of the ancestors. Planted themselves as the leaders, overseeing our care for the Quetzalcoatl's. Observing if our way is negative to their rule." She spoke with anger, layering her tongue.

"How long have they been here?" He questioned.

"Since the Four's uprising, two centuries ago... Slowly taking more over time. First mentoring us, looking from afar, then taking very little, then taking half our grain. Now, they control everything."

She turned her head, scanning the windows. "They'll be checking on this building soon." She turned back, raising her hand, cupping Astrid's firmly.

"Go. Rest." She commanded.

He nodded, guessing another questioning push would drive her and her people away. Pazima's family. Astrid walked out of the building, stepping into the puddles of water at his feet.

The rain slowed, drizzling as he walked through the cove's edge. Homes ringed the cove, fires and candles burned from each one. No magical embers in sight, no scent of runic magic staining the air. Sea salt was all that roamed its borders.

The clouds opened, moving to a clear night. The scent of crushed flowers, raised from outdoor overhangs. Tables, chairs, and old stumps. All littered with paper, paints, and clothing materials. Campfires tucked under the naturally formed rocky cliff face. The hill's edge was covered in paintings, the mastered care, the unity of all in their shapes and expression.

The story of the Ophidians, possibly.

He stood by the rocky edge of the cove, looking out to isles of trees and landmass. Low groans echoed along the ocean's waves, teasing his ears. More mythics? Astrid wondered how long it had been since they helped the creatures, exploring the Mythic Isles under The Four's sharp glare.

Astrid slid open the door, breathing slowly with no energy left. A little girl in the main room stood with a key in hand. "Are you the whisperer?" She smiled with obvious excitement. "Almost two hundred years, and no one has come to the cove, well except the Legions."

"Your elder, Noxolo, helped me out, just here to heal, before going back to an important task." Astrid forced an innocent smile, "Thank you."

The home stood proud, like its people; the smell of fresh cut oak leaked through the flooring. Each cut, each detail made by the people of Ophidian Cove. Nothing left to error, or otiosity. The roof thatched strand by strand, every piece of water reed and flowers from their neighbouring plains.

Each door, illustrated with colour, shapes, and styles. Stories and art poured through their people's craft. Imprinting their history into their buildings. The front door opened, revealing the elder stepping through the door's frame. "You like our homes?"

"It's beautiful." Astrid's eyes ran through the stories on the doors.

Elder Noxolo walked towards the chairs in the living space, planting herself down with a slight groan. "You're from Moonsong. I gather from your presence with my son's partner."

Astrid placed himself in the chair adjacent, lowering his form to Noxolo's level. "Yes. He took me in. I was abandoned many years ago. He let me into their ways. Gave me purpose." He stated.

Noxolo groaned slightly, rubbing her foot. Astrid looked deep into her mature features, the deep indents upon her eyes, the darkened rings. He smiled, hoping he would age exquisitely like Elder Noxolo. "Could I?" He spoke softly, pointing to her foot with a warm glance.

"My granddaughter's in good company, if you're this charitable." Her words spread out as Astrid pulled her shoe from her foot, rubbing it gently.

"I've got to leave when Ambe's healed. Save Pazima from capture." Horror reflected from his features.

"He should be able to fly in two weeks. What of Sevar?" Elder Noxolo raised a brow.

"Truth is, I only just met him, saving him from King Alonn's officials and legion soldiers. Astrid stopped rubbing her feet, placing her shoe back softly.

"More surprises from the whisperer. Don't leave him alone. He'll need support." She winked vaguely.

"What if I told you..." His lips sparked. "I can help you with the officials while I'm here."

Elder Noxolo shot up. "We do not permit violence unless the mythic lives, in the cove, and the mythic isles are in peril. We farm, give over our materials, our minerals. Keeping our stories, our culture alive, it's worth more than some—revenge." Elder Noxolo coughed.

She pulled closer, almost whispering with a clear lingering fear. "You must follow our way, as our visitor. Now if something unfortunate occurs..." Her expression remained plain. "Outside our borders. What may we do but accept it?"

Astrid placed his hand in hers, like a promise of comfort. "I'll follow The Ophidian way. No blood will be spilt on your land. I believe in the old ones. All cultures, all our ways, should be accepted—" A jolt of realisation slapped Astrid, not believing his raw emotion was now laid down to Elder Noxolo, as if he trusted her with his life, with Moonsong's safety. He breathed in slowly. "Living together in peace".

Elder Noxolo smiled cunningly. "I see why my son and my granddaughter would love you, Golden Warrior." She walked, placing her hand on the door. "No rush. You have time while they heal. May the mythics guide you."

—

Sea winds crashed against his bedroom window, letting in a slight breeze through the finest crack. Astrid huffed, pulling the thin blanket over his broad chest. His eyes welled with tears long overdue, burdened by Pazima's safety being unknown. The royals had her in their venomous grasp. No Moonsinger captured had ever come back to tell the tale. Astrid brought his hands up to his bruised, sharp face, breathing in short bursts.

As the wind crashed in violent storms, rain smashed against the thin, colourful windowpanes, covering his screams of anger. Astrid couldn't stop it bubbling over, alone in the darkness. Pazima, Caelan, Daj, the kids of Charr. How could he save them all? He couldn't, failing to keep his own partner by his side.

The thoughts fogged till the sun breached the cove's silhouette. The raw emotion drained with nothing left, clearing the fog in his mind. Astrid was left holding his knees in a bedroom, smashed entirely, as if the storm had ripped it apart.

# Chapter 22

Toxic Feelings
*Pazima*

Pazima's skin burned against the tightening ropes, pulling at her arm hairs, slowly ripping one by one. "Seeing a fellow shifter die, what a moment." The blonde woman hissed into Pazima's ear.

"Such rage over one man. How sad." She threw her head forward, smashing it into the mercenary's angelic features, coating her "You'll die with me," Pazima spat, allowing a grin to pierce through.

The room spun, her mind waved, crashed around her skull, seeing the wet stone melding into the flooring. The corners of the room warped, curling the light around hee. Her hairs stood up against the brisk breeze. Pazima's senses decaying, resigning their fate to the ever-pushing poison coursing through her veins.

"Lorstorm will see nothing but blood, same as your friend." The blonde's brow twitched. This vendetta ran deep, laying its course through her captor's nerves. Pazima jumped to that small hope, to clasp to her one clear insecurity.

Pazima pushed. "Who are you? What do you want with him?"

"Jaera." She spoke bluntly. "Trained to kill traitors of the crown. Your companion now fits the criteria.". Jaera grabbed her cheeks. The toxin bobbed in Pazima's veins, burning like the sun had taken her body as its new home. Her teeth gritted, cutting up her gripped cheeks, sending drops of blood onto Jaera's pale-white skin. Pazima hissed. The rope continued to tighten, humming the runic song of torture. A gritting noise of metal upon bone, scraping away charred skin. Tighter it went, the louder it hummed, scraping, ripping at her ear. Tears and screams bellowed beyond the cell walls. The sound of grief, complete shards of sorrow, echoed. Maybe it was the humming, gripping ropes, but it felt real, as if the stone and ice foundations carried men's sorrow as a message to all within. No one leaves alive.

Jaera pulled closer, pressing her knee into Pazima's stomach. "Where is he?" Her tongue twirled, spitting her words. The door pushed open, stopping her movements. "Princess, the King sent a message." Her head spun, turning to the Offical's guards.

"Princess?— Aww—" Jaera's knuckles launched into Pazima's ribs, "Don't leave daddy waiting." Pazima choked vaguely upon the pain.

The murmurs of commands tossed around the hallways, behind the closed doors. The words twirled through the air, vibrating against the ice. "This order can't be true." Jaera's voice was layered in venom, completely taken by evident annoyance.

The door swung open, slamming the door handle into the wall's indent. The soldiers stomped, tossing her roped joints free. Her charred ankles throbbed, pushing for strength. Nothing came, crumbling to her knees. Groans passed from the soldiers, holding her withered limbs around them. Jaera stormed ahead, hurdling commands, cursing anything in her path.

Pazima's vision blurred; the shadows of the halls grew. Ribboning around her, creeping, pulling at her strength. Withered and cold, but all that consumed her mind was Astrid and his possible safety. The pain blazed, swelling her senses. Her eyes burned, throwing her out of consciousness.

# Chapter 23

## Bed of Darkness

### *Raven*

Raven's fingers soaked in a puddle of grey water. His breath wheezed out, straining with hollow intake. Each breath flicked his greasy curly strands out of his eyeline. His tunic's scent leaked through, punching his nostrils with every short breath. Tears throughout every piece of fabric, pigments and quality, flaking away.

His stomach bobbed. Stomach acid bellowed, begging for any form of energy. The metal door swung open. A soldier with a rustic tray placed on the uneven, rocky floor. The soldier's face glanced down, looking into his withering features. His frosted lips muttered, careless and sharp. Raven glanced up but could not sift through the soup of letters on the soldier's lips.

-

Each rotation blurred, his mind counted every dawn and dusk, losing count of how many bland meals he struggled to chew. The scent of the unwanted slops attacked his nostrils, hard bread, scraps of beans absent of any herb, or spice. Nothing to flare a scrap of hope, apart from his short, adventurous memories of Sevar. A spoonful after another, slowly piling, sending hope to a suffocating death.

Each dusk, guards traced the halls, stomping against the cracked, icy stone, teasing every cell door with a harsh jolt. Sleep never came easy, each hour slams, screams and darkness. Complete gloom. The never-ending abyss stared, clamping to his shoulder as he turned, facing the wall. A moist voice spat into his ear, whispering, licking his dry skin. The darkness wrapped around his neck, dragging each thought through the cracks, moulding his weakening core, accepting his fate. Accept your death, it called upon his tearing features.

Death by execution. For the freezing little girl, the rebel woman. For the prophecy, he came to unfold. Tears dropped, accompanied by a vague smile. Raven would be with Sevar again. The warmth of looming death held him tight.

-

Dawn soaked into his flaking cheek, letting icy blue light tease through the cracks. Silence. The halls were empty, no keys jiggling at the soldier's belt, no barking orders, no lingers of stale foods. Raven pressed his right shoulder against the west wall, leaning on the smoothest stone he could spot. A new location to sit within his miniature cell, one slight crack in the ice where a fresh cold breeze snuck through. His fingers danced around the cracks, tracing the thick ice foundations.

"Don't touch the ice." A voice whispered through the ancient ice.

# Chapter 24

## Snakeflowers & Frostcups

### *Astrid*

Astrid's toes softly pressed into the cove's sandy edge, watching the sun climb over the mythic islands ahead. The massive trees were so dense, leaving some islands without light. The smell of mythic magic rode the ocean's smooth current.

He flicked his dagger, planting it into the sand. The waves rippled softly up the shore, teasing the cove's stone barriers by his far left. Guilt burned, building a pressure against his heart. Controlling this raw anger must transpire, he knew that as a complete certainty. Astrid grabbed the sand, letting happiness peer through his regretful thoughts, remembering the night in his quarters. A night of tears, Pazima comforted him, showed him what was right. He laughed into his tunic, the thought of her teaching him how to braid her kinky hair in front of the flickering embers.

Children's whispers snuck in the wind, layering down on the grains of sand. Their fingers tracing shapes and symbols with pure innocence. Their ivy green irises reflected upon the water, tinting their drawings. Their hands pulled at their pockets, placing a small pouch at their sides. Dipping their fingers, highlighting their fingertips in powdered snakeflower. Running their fingers through their drawings, the peaceful earthy green colouring calmed him, green as the vines in Moonsong.

Giggles and whispers slipped from the children's expressions, slowly moving to Astrid. "This is for you, outsider." The eldest child spoke, cupping a hand-crafted symbol from twigs, string and nearby flowers.

The child pointed, showing his drawing. "What does it mean?" Astrid asked, keeping an upbeat tone.

He beamed a smile, sitting back down on vibrant cushions. "It's the symbol for our loving warrior, Lerato." The symbol tinted, its shape grew in different reflective angles, affected by sunlight, a warrior spanning fresh wings, absent from any scales. Free, unmasked. Completely out, ready to be smashed by his foes.

"It's beautiful."

The children sang softly into their symbols. He listened to their songs, to Pazima's history and to their culture. She never mentioned this place and their people, their peace and creativity. His brow weighed, wondering if she knew any of her own history. Did the Commander's hidden past deny his daughter her truth?

Their words whirled around them, whispering the story of the broken warrior. "He laid his heart," they sang, grinning at him. Each warming interaction, inviting him in as their cloaked ally. "Two lands divided, hoping to save it all."

Astrid brushed the sand from his knees, stepping away carefully. He slid his hood up, grinning. The plan to support her people brewed in his mind. Astrid knew he would enjoy it.

-

The book of untold hovered at his palms. He knelt in the grass below the dusted window. The hill line hid his body away from the upper layer of homes. He peered up, wiping the condensation from the panes.

His sight jumped from body to body. Counting the size of the group. The ranks stood clear, with symbols of their hierarchy sewed into their tunics. The oldest man sat at the painted oak table. His muddy boots planted, slapping the mud into the drawings. The disrespect of their culture. Astrid's fingers tensed, cutting into his palms.

The soldiers stood upright against the western wall, facing him. Their words vibrated against the panes, slipping through, touching his ears. "The status of the Ophidian Cove remains stable, Commander."

"Stable?" The Commander raised from his chair. "I find it difficult to believe it's stable. Children sing on the cove's edge. Stomp it out." He strode closer. "King Alonn, and The Four will not stand for this—difference." Difference, a word of celebration, manipulated across the realm by tyrants for their own mysterious gain. Wealth? Power? Astrid's lip raised slightly.

A murmur left one soldier; his knees quivered. He looked up, struggling to keep the hollow expression towards his Commander.

The Commander stared through his brow. "Speak up, Soldier."

The soldier stepped back. "I... Why do we need to stop their singing? It does our king no harm."

Quickly, the Commander's small side dagger teased against the soldier's throat, pressing on his pulsing vein. "These people." He spat out. "Their stories, their grotesque drawings. The children, dancing and singing into the seas." All the soldiers froze, almost ignoring the knife against their fellow soldier's throat. "It sparks hope." He pushed away, walking back to his desk, throwing down his dagger into the drawings. "The Four connected us and made us one. The legion is for peace." The Commander played with his dagger, flicking painted wood chips into the air. "You want peace, Official Stroke?"

"Yes, Commander." Stroke replied, emotionless.

Their eyes sparked a sharp violet. Their hands raised, moving their fingers, forging the symbol of the Four on their chests.

Astrid's anger bubbled up like an uncontrollable acid. Spiralling, commanding to see their blood filling the cove's drains. He shook softly, pushing his senses back into focus. He had to follow the Ophidian way, follow their wishes as rules. No blood on their lands. The purple glow beamed onto Astrid's face, *The Book of Untold.* He flicked the pages carefully again, hoping it would hold a spell, leaving no harm yet rendering the Official's futile.

The group of soldiers and their Commander walked through the cove, entering the community's eating place, the gathering. Where the Ophidian people came every morning, as the sun rose over the Mythic Isles. Astrid followed behind, keeping behind the groups of Ophidians with rustic fishing rods, clearly ready for their rotation of labour.

Hums and vague singing slammed to a sudden halt as the Official's glanced across the gathering's population. "The next to sing loses their tongue." The commander threatened with a casting, briskly tone.

Astrid walked to the side, pushing himself next to the Officials as they picked their morning meal from the gathering's tables. Fellow their way, he reminded himself as he purposely fell into the youngest Official. The group whipped their heads over, glaring at Astrid. No longer looking at their own plates. His palms launched open, spraying crystallised dust into their meals, one by one, sinking without any lingering runic smell. "Apologies, sir."

"Get up, fool." The youngest Official scoffed, wiped his trousers.

Astrid walked away, observing the soldiers as they consumed their meals, unknowing of what lingers inside.

"This tastes different—" One called out, querying the chef next to the gathering table. "What have you done?"

"Nothing, Sir! Nothing!"

"Liar." The commander scoffed, struggling to his feet, but without a click remaining, they dropped one by one into the wooden flooring.

"What's happening?" Questions flung across the gathering room, as Elder Noxolo cast her voice, forcing the frightened queries to pause.

"Whisperer Talo, from Moonsong has agreed to support us in our freedom of The Four's rein over our land." Her cane stomped across the wooden floor, walking to the centre of the long structure. "Don't be afraid. We will be as we once were, soon enough. With faith by our side." Elder Noxolo turned to Astrid, nodding for him to do as he planned.

Astrid scanned the gathering room, calling over an Ophidian young one. "Could you get me a loading wagon, please?" Astrid's smile beamed, sliding a thick vogue strand of hair back to its middle parting.

The bodies bounced, slipping around the wagon's wooden structure. His arms pushed, burning upon the steep plains. Sweat dripped from his brow, leaking to his red-hot cheeks. The brightening had come in the free lands, no seasonal control, only nature radiated through the blooming plains. The winds carried the brightening's warmth through the oceans to Jinos, while the Fellow's Mounts naturally held itself as the biggest natural boundary from the brightening's warmth for his home – Hlinos.

Astrid pushed the wagon for what felt like hours, up meadows and rocky paths, pushing across thin rivers and thick flower beds. To outside the Ophidan borders. The blooming flowers of Dualia filled the air with its pollen. The plains transition between the beds of snakeflowers, and the land of frostcups naturally forged the divide between the lands. Nature displaying the history of old through a blooming lens.

He needed to respect the Ophidians' way, pushing the soldier's unconscious body across the borders of their lands. His mind felt clouded, the strain of holding onto six Eyldian's unconscious weight with small breaks. It knotted around his waist, weighing down upon his naturally built strength.

The frostcups brushed his knees. The flower of Dualia's second island, forming its continent. Each frostcup bloomed in their organic growth pattern, branching into the curling cupping petals. Their hue beamed a bright sapphire, contrasting the olive grassy plains.

He let out a small smile through his strains, letting the taste of frostcups leak onto his lips. The lingering smell of berries reminded him of home. The taste, the texture of the mountain's berries, they grew at its peaks. Consuming the monstrous winds, producing the juiciest tang.

His fingers dropped, letting himself follow, resting his throbbing joints in the grass meadow. His breath pulsed through him, racing to catch up. Astrid had to be ready. One whisper to slice the sleeping rune's force. They'll wake, fuelled by rage. He knew what he got into, the sleeping rune from *the Book of Untold.*

A small, painful laugh slipped through his lips, thinking of Pazima's shocked expression, if she saw him study the book in tall blades of grass. He read about its power, and its balance. It drained the user's strength rapidly. The knotting of strength and emotion. His mind traced each word between his breaths.

Power was everything to a rune whisper, to the magic in their veins. Yet a new power flared through his veins. Burning like an illness, yet pure like a true connection to something more, something divine. A battle of powers and emotions burdened his mind. Astrid couldn't allow that in this moment, not now the sleeping rune had a hold on him.

*The sleeper forced into unconsciousness shall be gifted with the caster's emotion. A wave of their deepest desires and fears, an echo through the forced connection.* The Book of Untold had been written in hues of purple rune powder, mixed with black ink.

Astrid's lips pressed together, groaning, pushing himself up from the long-bladed grass. Each word graced the plains. He dipped his fingers into his small pouch, using the purple powder, drawing onto his palm, slicing the spell completely apart with a mere whisper.

# Chapter 25

The Ice Lady

*Raven*

The shocking wave of words pulsed through the ice, sending a sharp shiver down his spine. Raven's feet pressed, moving him from the wall, his muscles tensed, being consumed by pure instinct.

"Hello." He whispered, crawling across the cold stones, dragging his brittle skin against the stone's rough surface. Cutting at his knees. His ear pressed up close, hovering at the crack.

"The ice. It'll feel your touch. The runes will shock you." She spoke with layers of caution.

Raven placed his back up the wall, sitting aside of the crack. "Who are you?"

"No one." Her voice sounded hollow of hope. The frosty dimmed light creeped back, slipping back through the cracks. Leaving him alone in his darkness.

Words lingered on his tongue, but nothing came.

His muscles hardened, clamping at his bones. The pain bitten down at his meatless frame, begging for energy, for minerals. It cried, radiating through his trembling body.

Each rotation, his limited mass shrunk, pulling at his sanity. He would be lucky to hear the rattle of the metal meal trays grace his cell door. Rotations at a time, they stopped serving him meals, teasing their shadows under the door's framing. The brute's joyful laughs thrusted at his heart, punching him constantly. He cried, folding his thin arms around his torso. Raven's mind ran into every dark corner, thoughts never to be told. One stood tall, glowing proudly, the image of King Alonn's blood pooling at his toes, moisturising his flaking skin. He smiled, giggling into his ripped tunic.

-

His fingers ran down the crack. *"Alignment..."*

Words speared through the ice. "Where did you hear that?" The woman's voice branched out, laced in a commanding tone.

The darkness bit his cheek. Scratching its nails down his forehead. "The bodies, all dead." Raven lowered his head, placing his forehead on his bony knees. "Bones, skin, blood, the metallic smell." He whispered.

"Listen, " she commanded. "Don't let them break you. "I'm Lassea, what's your name?"

"Covered in blood," He spat out.

"Focus." She sniped.

His head pulled up, turning to the ice. "Raven." Guards stomped by, jingling their keys. Her voice vanished, leaving no reply.

-

Raven paced around the cell, pressing against the stone walls. He had to keep his mind from breaking entirely, shaking his mind, pinching his pale skin, anything to stop the darkness from consuming him completely. Again and again, he counted each stone, waving his finger through its details, every indent, every memory imprinted by prisoners gone before.

The darkness would not get him. The voice of another. It anchored Raven when he desired it. "Hello, Lassea." He spoke into the crack, waiting for the voice to slip through. "How long have you been here?"

"Many years." Lassea paused. "I've lost count."

His slight smile dropped. "How have you survived?" Panic laced his words, painting over his withering frame.

Lassea stuttered against the ice, lingering for a moment. "You'll be okay."

-

He laid, eating, savouring every little bite of old bread. His tongue watered, leaking the limited water he had left in his system.

The door slammed open, kicking the metal meal tray across the cell floor. "Up." A soldier commanded.

Raven pushed, scraping his hands on the floor, struggling upon his knee muscle. King Alonn stepped into the cell, gliding his chalky-white cloak behind him, pulling out a paper, tossing it to the wet floor in-front of Raven's feet.

"You are found guilty of treason against the royal families of The Four. You are to be publicly executed in fourteen rotations. By the Bell's third ring. I'll have your head."

Every word punctured his skin, but he wouldn't let the King see his emotion, see what he had done to him. The shell of bone and skin that struggled to stand before the King of Dualia. Raven stamped a simple smile between his cheeks.

King Alonn's pale lips popped, grinning through his crystal-white teeth. Raven kept his simple expression high, not daring to move. He didn't let a word slip through. Be smart, like Sevar would've been.

King Alonn's lip curled, rising red into his light cheeks. Flicking his thick fabric, the King turned, spitting into the cell. The door slammed behind him, quaking the stone foundation slightly. No words came that night. Nothing but him and the words written on paper.

Fear didn't come, he whirled the words from the paper into his mind. Playing with everything the King said to him. If he had killed Sevar, King Alonn would have tossed Sevar's decaying head into his cell as another way to wither him, to break everything he had, everything he loved. Raven smiled, looking into the cracks, to the ice foundations. Hope leaked through, warming his heart.

-

Raven's sleep within the stone walls and ice foundations never felt full. Comfort came sparingly, his thoughts of the adventures travelling through the beautiful plains covered in unique flowers and powders, roaming in the approaching brightening air. The comfort of Sevar's muscular warmth wrapping him like a thick market fleece. Raven wrapped his arms around his ribs. If only for a moment, Sevar's arms wrapped around his torso in a warm embrace.

The door swung open, revealing an emotionless stance, the soldier glared down. Raven couldn't stop his eyes from glancing at his clean attire. The freshly shined leather boots lanced in a royal detailing. Each boot reflected the sun's blinding rays, peeling his sight into the royal embossing. The brute's sleeves rolled up, held by his thick biceps. His uniform traced nothing of emotion, no desire or personality. The black tunic and trousers both had simple sewing details of the royal colour hue of blue, of King Alonn. His hand placed down from the door handle, revealing the Four's symbol, charred into his skin. "Come." The deep voice commanded.

A mop and an old, chipped oak bucket were dropped in front of him. Raven pushed the bucket across the floor, straining his withered energy. The thin rope handle dangled from its wooden bucket, threatening to snap at any moment.

A voice whispered, teasing his neck hairs. "You didn't give up." The woman from the crack in his wall. She stood at his side, washing the walls. "Keep your eyes on your task. Don't give them any reason to punish you."

Raven gripped the mop, sliding it against the smooth hallways. The difference between the stone's textures, the ice framed the halls, waving through the sculpted stone, arching the halls, framing each cell door.

His head lifted, staring at the section where his cell door stood. The ice cased walls bordering the metal door. Numbers carved out above each door frame. "0439" His lips traced. His life, Raven Whitewood of Elcoo, beaten, starved, trivialised into a series of numbers.

Lassea's force pulled at his shoulder, directing him back to his job. "Raven, eyes down." She darted her head down both sides of the halls. "How did they get you?" She questioned with care.

Raven kept his head down, facing the mops' strokes. "Me and my friend." His voice cracked. "We were looking for his mother. We got caught, labelled as rebellions to the Four. A woman came for him. I don't know why."

She smiled, "The rebellion will win, mark the day." Lassea scanned the halls once more.

"Where are you from?" Raven asked.

"Quarria, in Engoria. I lived in the Queen's palace."

He turned, looking into her features. Her structure, her cheekbones, her thick brows with a slight gap between each other. Lassea's knotted black long hair, locking her slight curls. Raven's head pulsed, throbbing through his brows. Trembling against the mop handle, dropping to the polished stone floor.

"Get up." Lassea struggled to push him up, folding her arms around his torso.

He lifted his head, rubbing his eyes faintly. "Not possible." Her eyes widened, jolting back a couple steps, as if something came back to haunt her.

"What?" He asked, worried an infection plagued his features.

"Alignment power." She placed her hand on his cheek, scanning, darting from eye to eye. . "You need to escape now. If they see your power, they'll test on you, torture you in every way imaginable." The worry written clearly over Lassea's shaking body.

"What is it? It burns, but I can't control it. Why?" He pushed.

"I was locked up for protecting a friend with the same power you had. They killed her. They'll do worse to you." Her words raced out as time became their enemy, mere clicks before a soldier crossed through their halls.

Lassea pulled Raven up to his feet, moaning sharply. "Listen, we all know magic lives in our bloodlines. Your mother or father possessed the gift, but my research into the power was limited by the Four's law on civilian magic knowledge. I only got to see one book in Dreaka. It's an ancient power gifted to a group of people long ago. No one knows what happened to them after the Four's siege."

"My childhood is a void. I retain no memory from before I arrived in Elcoo, in Drossor. It's like an empty echo of who I used to be, drawing to who I am." Sadness ripped through his heart. "If I find out who my parents are, could they help me with this power?"

"Escape this place, find answers and hide. Hide the best you can. They won't stop, if they find out what you possess." Lassea cast her warning firm, darting back to her cleaning.

Raven sat next to the crack, waiting for her voice to slip through. The night came, light extinguished by nature's cycle. His hands circled around the cracks, keeping himself grounded to the cell's damp walls. Hours passed, the soldiers circled the halls, groaning, throwing small conversations with each other. Just the soothing sound of idle words waving in the darkness.

A prophecy, a feeling that pulsed through every sense he knew. It called for him to leave, to adventure out for answers. No regrets. It was more than a simple dream. Raven saw the Four, the foundations they planted into their realms, brutally forged their law upon the land. Letting the settlements rot, imploding on their unstable bases. But his heart desired to learn, teach, and love. Kept far from the fight ahead.

Lassea's voice slid through the crack. "Raven, are you okay?"

"I haven't got strength for this, the fighting."

"You are gifted to bring the realm back to balance, to peace. Have you not seen people die, held under their boot?" She paused. "They took me from my son. I don't know if he's alive. what he's done to survive." Lassea's voice cracked.

His mind raced, the similarities...

Her long black hair, her bruised cheeks. Raven understood the dreams are always blending, bending, melding to infinite realities and possibilities. Quarria, it couldn't be a mistake. Captured, thrown away, given a crack between the stones for a slither of hope.

"Sevar?" His voice trembled through the crack.

A longing sob slid through the crack. "How is he? How do you know my son?"

Raven's mind poured out the short time they had together, the truth of Sevar's life being uncertain. He didn't know if he escaped, if he sat in a cell in this maze of stone and ice. "That's a long story. At first, he held a dagger to my throat..." He smiled. He told her about each rotation, every detail of his kindness, of his bravery. "He slaughtered many officials to save me and other women. We travelled across Drossor. We saw so much sorrow, yet so much joy." His grin washed away. "He never left my side...till a royal mercenary attacked." He kept his voice low, close to the ice.

"You're fond of him." She stated as a fact. "Did he mention his upbringing?" Her voice echoed in a low tone.

"He didn't mention much. He stated he was born in Quarria. Ran from the city after your arrest and became a member of Clockwork. I don't know the details; he kept that information close to his heart." Raven remained completely truthful.

Her quiet sobs rolled through the ice, absorbing all the stories he had of their adventures through Drossor's landscape.

"He loves you dearly. He never stopped looking for you." He whispered.

# Chapter 26

Respect, Love & Conflict!
*Astrid*

The blades of grass waved, following the calm gushes of wind. The smell of frostcups swirled, lingering at their noses, teasing their lips with the taste, sweetness of lush oil. Astrid's feet crossed, sidestepping across the plains, keeping his guard and his stable positioning firm ahead of the awoken soldiers.

"You'll die for this treason." The Commander spoke with a bitter sharpness.

The six soldiers spread out, circling the plains. Space closed in; trapping the air between them, each step squeezing the pressure against Astrid's heart.

Astrid stepped back, lunging out of the circling strike. "Leave the Ophidian people, and I'll spare your lives." His voice echoed cast upon the grass. Avoiding being surrounded was essential for his survival. It wasn't the sparing floor anymore. Now six soldiers circled like hungry, primal animals.

The soldier's hands scanned their belts, their thigh holsters. Every hidden weapon had been removed. He grinned, watching their hands panic, brushing their holsters. His hand teased his sword, glaring at the Commander's brief moment of hesitation. The soldiers nodded, signalling their commands silently through the air. Each circled him like a snake between the blades of grass. Their breaths slowed, forcing the air in Astrid's lungs to follow.

"One last chance." Astrid stated. Sparking the gold in his veins, branching through his cells, his blood gleaming, rushing through his skin. He knew he couldn't control the divine power, but it could be essential to his survival.

"The lonely child, left in the snow. Do you think your love for her will fill that loneliness?" Boots crunched the long grass, stepping slowly across the plains.

Astrid stopped the force of his gleaming energy. "Place her name on your lips again. You'll lose your tongue."

The Commander lunged, throwing himself against Astrid. "You used outlawed runes; Astrid Talo..." He knew him, his name. A last name he chose on himself as he entered his new home. A name that stuck in his mind.

Astrid gripped the Commander's ink-black tunic, surging gleams of power out of his palm, burning upon his runes. One massive force thrusted the Commander, rolling across the ground. "Outlawed? That makes it better." Astrid grinned at the Commander and his soldiers.

The soldiers all lunged forward, throwing their whispers into ribboning energy, twirling with striking force towards him. Astrid whispered, pressing the powder onto his palm in a panicked haste, looking at the soil. A call, a beacon in the soil, he threw his hand into the air, blasting energy through the blooming meadow, tossing soil and small rocks into the air, blinding walls beamed at his front.

His worry weighed on his brows, aching, pulling down at his senses. The love for Pazima beamed through his features. Guiding his movements, collecting his rogue thoughts. Protect her family, their history, protect the difference.

The soldiers pulled at the beaming walls, cracking it apart. Their groans flew through the cracking boundary, punching their fury through his energy.

The plains filled with their groans. Breathing dazedly, struggling to grasp the fresh, brightening winds. A soldier to his left wiped his cut lip, spitting clumps of red. The soldiers on his right glided, lifting their Commander. They collected as one, planting their feet. They whispered, piling their runic power together. Their runes radiated towards him, a cold feeling he had never felt before with any rune. A connection between the runes and their users. Whispers and ribboning energy twirled at their arms. The energy scorched the grass around their footing.

"I call your death." The Commander spoke, emotionless. The beam surged, rocketing through the plains, into Astrid.

-

He forced his eyelids open, wiping the dirt off his face. His body laid in a small crater, littered with dirt and grass. Frostcup petals twirled, floating through the air, landing on him slowly, one by one.

Moans and murmurs bashed against his ear, yet he heard nothing but an overbearing ring. Astrid grabbed his side, supporting the throbbing pain. Grabbing the dirt, pushing up to the edge of the hole.

A soldier laid, moaning, grasping the soil for aid. "How?" The Commander choked.

His neck tightened, grasping at his words. His veins blazed, roaring fiery gold. Astrid felt it rush through his veins. Replacing, evolving his blood into pure gleaming compounds. Blood that ran bright, gilded, and ancient...

He looked down, offering a quivering hand to the Commander. "It manifested recently."

The Commander accepted his hand, pulling himself up to his feet. "I've heard whispers of people with the flaming power of gold. I didn't believe it to be true." His neck bobbed. "They lied to me. To us all." He murmured, darting his eyes to his people. All five were in ripped uniforms, detailed in gold and yellow lines, leading to the Four's symbol upon their chest.

The other soldiers climbed to their feet, closing in on their Commander. They stood cold, ready to attack. "Commander?"

"The Four lied to us about their rule!" He bellowed to his soldiers, shaking his head with a rogue mutter, rubbing his patchy stubble.

They stood frozen in the soil. The silence was attacked by a quick, jolting thrust. Astrid looked up, shocked by a splashing sensation, his tongue layered in a sharp metallic tang. Blood pooling, but it wasn't his own. The Commander's blood sprayed, coating his face, dripping into his mouth.

The tang of death, the taste of the Commander's last moment weaving through his warm blood. The brute Commander, rough black hair, now stained red, dying knowing the Four's rein was built on false stories. Twisting the difference in Eyldia into its ultimate weapon.

Astrid lunged over the Commander's body, punching the smirking brunette soldier in his gut. The soldier's grip on his dragger loosened, dropping Astrid's bloodied dagger. Astrid didn't allow it to grace the dirt, grabbing it mid-air. Lunging it into the soldier's heart swiftly, spitting upon the choking brunette's pointy ear. "You could've seen it like your Commander." He kept his blazing stare into the soldier's blackened irises. The soldier choked, spitting his blood at Astrid's dirty tunic.

Astrid's heart, his fury. It controlled him entirely, fogging his view. The Commander had knowledge, the ability to change. A tear slid down his blood-soaked cheek as he slit through each soldier, allowing his scream to echo across the plains, climbing the far hillsides.

One by one, lunging through the plains. A small blonde, petite but full of fury, a broad man with a scar slicing through his left eye. He pierced his dagger into the soldier's necks, cutting their ankles, pushing his sharp metal through layers of skin and muscle. One last soldier dropped to her knees, into the grass. "Don't please." The plea waved through the red grass. She hunched over, holding her rib.

Astrid clenched the soldier's wet chin, lifting her face up. The uncontrollable rage roared, sending pulses of heat through his skin. Truly consumed by red. Blood dripped through his hair. Every inch of his body was coated in dirt and blood. His nail beds, his pores. Astrid's control was absent. No purple vibrance, no golden gleams. His eyes were completely hollow.

Astrid's dagger shone in the sunlight, the deathly red vibrance, gleaming into his features.

"Please." She begged, unable to control her streaming tears.

He plunged his dagger into the nearby dirt. "You serve the Ophidian people now. You'll fake the ongoing Legion takeover, like nothing ever happened." Astrid panned the field of dead soldiers, grinning as the sun kissed his blood-stained face. Astrid sighed, wiping away the dipping blood from his forehead, combing the rogue hair strands back into place. "You'll serve the mythics and live the Ophidian way, if you desire to live—" Astrid stepped close, grabbing her tunic's collar, scanning over her rank and name. "Nina, rank – Second Commander." He loosened his hold, stepping away.

-

Five graves, some didn't deserve it. Astrid wanted to leave their bodies out, let them rot through time. Left to be forgotten, like the Four did to the Old Ones, and the Aligners.

The Aligners. The wondering question of who they were roamed his mind as he pulled the bloodied bodies into their graves.

Astrid laid the Commander's body into the last grave, placing a hand over his eyes, sliding the lids to rest. He groaned against the withering pain upon his chest. The beam of energy pushed his body to the edge, protected by rogue gold gleams. A soft grunt glided across the field, Nina. Astrid glanced over, watching her place the other bodies into their unmatched resting places.

Astrid walked, hauling the empty wagon. Silence. He had let it absorb his travels. He wanted to support these people, and he had been successful, removing the brutes from their land. A plan to manipulate protection for Pazima's history, their culture. With Second in command - Nina in place. He was successful.

The city waved calmly, in a peaceful silence. His feet began to ache, rubbing the leathers with uncomfortable warmth. Astrid couldn't rest. He had to check on the rebel and Ambe's recovery.

Astrid passed humming children, singing one of many stories they crafted into many forms for their young. They glanced looking at his blood-stained hands, dropping the wagon back into the cobblestone side wall, close to the cove's small dock. "Tell Elder Noxolo her visitor has returned. I have a gift."

Astrid placed his hands in the calm waves. Rubbing them together, interlocking his fingers, rubbing, itching at his stained hands. His ocean-warped reflection. The blood coated him completely. Unable to see who he was anymore. The reflection of a murderer with uncontrolled rage.

"Control yourself." He cursed at his wavey reflection.

"Don't punish yourself. You supported people you didn't know today. You don't walk our path, yet you honoured it." Elder Noxolo placed a hand on his shoulder, offering her support. "Without question, without sharp remarks. All in hope of a better world." She smiled.

"What I did out there, all I saw was darkness." A tear dropped into the waves. "I've been so angry without her. We'd never parted since we were young. Without her to keep me on track, I completely lose control."

"You can't let someone else be the anchor to your control, to your emotions. Take back control. A man with mercy and strength makes a good soldier, but a man with knowledge, honour, and trust in one's self, now that is true power." She stopped, letting it soak into his mind. "Meet me at dinner. We can discuss the details." She walked away, greeting young ones, singing, dancing on the shore.

Ambe's wing struggled to branch to complete expansion. Astrid scanned him and his healing wounds. A couple more rotations and he'd be ready. He spent a moment running his fingers through Ambe's head, telling the groaning mythic he'd be fully healed soon.

Astrid stepped away, chatting to the mythic healer, directing him to the other healing bays. He glided down the halls, admiring the drawings of doctors, the mythical creatures in many variants of hues and sizes. The hall opened, expanding into a main bay, rows of clean beds with many drawers of tonics, minerals, and powders. Dividers made of stained glass held firmly by thick ropes.

He scanned the beds, searching for Sevar, the man they had saved. His sight froze, spotting his broad frame. "Sevar?" Astrid called out.

"Astrid. Why did you save me?"

"We wanted to support the rebellion." He let out a slight frown.

Sevar glanced over at his stained hands. "Been busy?"

"This settlement, the Four had been stomping on its neck since they gained power. I had to do something right." Astrid planted himself next to Sevar.

"We need to leave. I need to save my friend." Sevar's voice cracked, highlighted by pain.

"So do I, and we will. When Ambe and you are healthy enough."

"We need to go now." Sevar commanded, struggling to his feet, forcing an unstable push against Astrid.

Astrid held him by his shoulder, placing him back onto the bed. "We can't. I need you ready to fight." He planted his glare into Sevar's. "We both need to save our people. They'll be on alert; we don't know if they remain in Jinos. We'll go when you're ready. Understood? Astrid pulled back. "You're fortunate Pazima forgives the likes of Clockwork. Or your arse would've been rotting on the shores, or in Jinos' dungeon."

"Expect a thanks?" Sevar struggled up to his feet. "Your people aren't much better. Hiding away. From the words in Hlinos, you're just common thieves."

"We do so to survive. Helping people where we can. At least when they don't set mercenaries on us." He focused his breath, slowing them down between his sentences. "Sevar, tell me, what about the slaughter of Mistwood? Were you involved in the murder of those families, for the Four?"

"King Alonn hired some of the best Clockwork mercenaries to kill your group long ago, and unless my eyes are deceiving me, you and Moonsong are alive and protected." Sevar's words let out a sense of sass. "Don't tell me you haven't done things you're not proud of for the ones you love." Sevar calmed his voice. "Clockwork kept me paid; I didn't have a choice." Sevar struggled to his feet. "Mistwood wasn't me."

"There's more than having counts in your pocket." Astrid spat out, giving Sevar a supportive staff, crafted by the children to help him keep the weight off his wounds. Sevar's face dropped, absorbing his words.

"We both did regrettable things; we agree the Four must be stopped." Sevar whispered.

Astrid nodded, hovering around Sevar's struggling moments. "Elder Noxolo wants to meet us."

They opened the medic building door, welcomed to a calming warmth. The noise clustered together, yet it felt comforting. Candles burned on every stone guarding the cove's edge. The whole of the cove glowed; a warming happiness radiated through the community. The hills had posts of stone, carved as candle holders for their cove boundaries. All lit, coating the hills of grass and snakeflowers in a dim orange glow.

The stone cove walkway reformed into a community eating area. All their doors opened, placing their tables into the cove's stone barrier edge. Young ones sang, dancing around their tables. Hand in hand, they laughed, chanting. "Moonsinger supports."

The Elder Noxolo pulled her face up from his conversations, walking along the curling cove. "Feeling better?"

He graced her with a smile. "I'll figure it out. Thank you for housing us." He helped Sevar down to a comfortable wooden chair.

"Elder, this is Sevar."

She offered a smile. "Welcome to Ophidian Cove, Sevar."

They all sat, talking of the beautiful coves, how the waves graced the old stone barries in a calming manner. Astrid looked over the Ophidian Cove, glancing at its homes. Each had their doors wide open to all. Each home placed their meals at their tables, offering anyone a warming meal. Not one stomach left empty.

"Have you seen what's in the isle, Elder?" Astrid peered up from his bowl.

Elder Noxolo shot him a glance. "I have. When I was a young one, I travelled all over and saw the rip in the realm... Only once before the Elder at the time decided to close the gateway isle from visitors. Even now we choose to respect the closed door between realms."

"Will it open again?"

A clear flicker of worry sprayed over her features. "I hope we aren't alive to see it if it does." She paused. "Many mythical creatures came out of that gateway between realms. Some of pure fury and bloodlust." Silence filled the table. "What's your advice on our new situation?"

"You and your people should be okay for a while, with Nina keeping their people away, keeping the cloak up as long as you can. I can't promise you permanent safety, but it should last for some time. If they come, send for me and I'll come. No questions asked." He spoke with a warrior's voice.

"What of Nina? Can we trust her?" Elder Noxolo twirled her spoon between her fingers, moving around her meal.

"Trust that she wants to live. I have a feeling she'll learn something from you." Astrid's smile grew wide and proud.

"Thank you, Astrid. You're welcome back here at Ophidian Cove. If we can support you in any way." Elder Noxolo placed her hand on his.

Quiet roars filled the skies, the Quetzalcoatls.

They soared, gliding down, above the home's rooflines. Planting their serpent bodies across the hills. The visual connection between the mythic creatures and the Ophidian people. Love radiated through the air, layering in it an undeniable happiness and understanding.

Astrid's sight bounced between the landing Quetzalcoatls. Some spanned their wings, branching the size of three Ophidian homes. An old mythic scanned the cove. A sense burned within, bright and completely raw, pushing Astrid to lock into a shared glance. His scales were ancient with variants of red, from an inner dim coat to the outer sides covered in bright ruby red hues. It sniffed, broadcasting a groan into the air, spreading his wingspan, launching itself into the thin clouds.

Many Quetzalcoatls propelled into the sky, following the massive red mythic. Some with waves of greens, some had scales in splashed blues, highlighted by a white stomach. The hues, the colours, all unique. Astrid's heart let in a soft ache. He loved the warmth, wanting Pazima to see her heritage, her history.

To see her smile again.

-

The sun dropped, reflecting its vibrant orange across the unstable waves. He tossed little stones, bouncing his anger across the current. A faded figure flew over the mythic isles, broadcasting its roars across to shore, flicking a wave at his boots.

A voice behind him bounced. "Warrior!" The young one jumped, placing a beaded necklace into his palm. "A gift from us." The joy beamed on her face, smiling for a click before running back to her group of friends.

Beads of handcrafted colours and shapes. A mix of red and white. He smiled. "Thank you."

-

Astrid found himself teaching a couple of parents in self-defence, enough for them to practise, learn and adapt to protect the mythic isles and their cove. Astrid kept the teaching to simple self-defence, dodging and using their environment for physical advantages. While violence wasn't their path, knowledge of protection wasn't mistaken as anything but important in such unstable times.

Astrid and Sevar walked out of the stone cove, waving farewells to Elder Noxolo and the gathering young ones.

Ambe spread his wings, feeling the wind through his feathers and scales. He let out a roar, playfully pushing him and Sevar into the grass outside of the Ophidian Cove.

"Ready?" Astrid nodded to Sevar.

"Lead the way, Moonsinger."

# Chapter 27

## Poison, Toxic, Burned

### Pazima

"She's clean, Your Royal Highness." A woman's warm, high-pitched voice rolled against her right ear.

The room stirred, the walls patterns twirled, interlocking their details, slowly clearing to a stable image. Pazima waited patiently, listening to the voices, completely idle and limp, as if she remained deeply asleep. The door latched into the wood framing.

Pazima rocketed up silently, pressing her hands around her body, searching, panicking, from the icy dungeons to a warm bedroom, full of colours and rich fabrics. A sigh escaped, touching her boots, her needle pins gone. Every strap taken away, the feeling of her weapon impressions upon her frame withered. Every touch at her empty skin, leaving her the most nude she'd ever felt. Her breathing raced, scanning the room.

The blankets tossed, lying at her feet. She kicked them, revealing the ruby patterns in the rug below. Every inch brushed and washed to perfection, layering the air coated in scents of strawberry tangs. Blackwood boards trimming the walls. Panels over, carved with twirling vines and thorns. The stone arching foundations, painted over by pure white, leaving no space for dust or time to stamp its own expression into the stone. Pazima's foot stepped, heading for the door. She clamped her hand on the nearest chair, jamming it against the door handle.

She cursed against her lips, heading towards the long, narrow clear panes. The sea. She pushed, grasping the metal framing. Her hands pushed, jolting the window to ajar. The fierce wind punched into her, staining her nose with its sea-salt. The shock ate through her features, weighing against her brow.

Pain stabbed at her stomach, crumbling into the rug. Her braids flicked, covering her groans. The door pushed, catching on the makeshift lock. The chair groaned at the pressure.

Her hands grasped at the burning sense. Her nose scrunched, filling with the consuming metallic smell. A scent foreign to her knowledge. Pazima lifted the burned combat shirt. Her eyes widened, looking into the long, narrow mirror to her stomach. A black symbol, burned and raw, still smouldering on the left side of her stomach.

A charred rune. Forbidden ancient magic, once used long ago as a torture rune around Eyldian necks. Panic pulsed, causing her to swear, dripping from her forehead. She had seen this rune only once, back when she was a young one, travelling with Moonsong before the temple. The eldest healer was tortured by magic till his last rotation, burdened by his past.

The door jolted accompanied by commands. "Open the door." A monotone voice broadcasted.

She rolled her shirt down, jumping to her feet. Her mind calmed. She calmed her breathing, controlling her body in a mere click. She now stood in a place she didn't know, with no knowledge, but she wasn't dead. Pazima forced an angelic smile, pulling the chair away, back to its original position. She laid her hands at her front, folding them in an innocent grace.

Guards towered over her, peering with empty expressions. "King Dreaka has ordered your presence in the throne room, now." The command barked. She hid her discomfort, pushing it down into her stomach.

The King of Dreaka ordered... The question roamed, piling possible answers to her temples. Why did he want her alive? She needed to know every minor detail, anything that could help in the fight against the royals. She'd do it for her people. For a better future, even if it destined her to be branded forever.

Pazima headed down the halls, placing a frightened facade over her features. She had to be something else, for she wouldn't survive this castle without a role to play.

"Guard? Why am I here?" She peered up with her sparkling eyes. No words came, just a simple grunt and a push against her right shoulder.

Walking down halls of murmuring men and women, all with loose robes, partly covering their clean white tunics and silk trousers. The rich colours imported from the other cities, gifted, or taken from the rest of the realm. They glared, looking down at her, slowly sliding their eyes up and down her like a second-hand object thrown away.

The castle's women had carefully twirled hair, layered with fabric gracefully on top of their heads, whilst the men kept their hair short, cut above the ears. All with the same length. Rules upon their personal features. She wanted to scoff, but remained with a shy, clean mask upon her frame. Pazima truly desired to punch their sharp dismissals. She shook it off, turning her face straight into the halls ahead. Smooth movements and no weaknesses, she repeated in her mind, coating over her thoughts of Astrid, of Moonsong. He'd be alright, with Ambe by his side.

They headed down a staircase. Carves, statues of each royal and their heirs spaced out, descending the staircase.

*Queen Atula, of Engoria. No heirs.* She stuck to this for a moment. Noting it into her memory. She knew the importance of heirs to crowns and their strength.

*King Dreaka, of Dreaka. Princess Jaera as his heir.* Pazima's eyes widened. Jaera was royalty.

*King Plu Kan, of Drossor, with two sons, Prince Kjan, and Prince Keuan. Sharing most of their facial features yet born years apart.*

*King Alonn, of Dualia, no heirs.*

All the people that choked Eyldians if they didn't rise to their status. How they wanted to live, coated in gold.

The staircase opened to three directions, to the left and the right stood custom made sittings, a place to observe out-goings. Skilled artisans crafted the chairs out of blackwood, giving them a smooth, rich ink black colour with twirling dark brown waves running through the wood. She looked through the corner of her right eye, catching Jaera sprawling her legs on the stone railing. She shot a sharp brisk glare, teasing her dagger between her gloved fingers. Jaera was dangerous being a mercenary, but being royal, the daughter of Dreaka, it made her unstable and completely unpredictable.

The front descending steps opened to the long wide-open hall, following the rich carpets, leaving room for the circular pillars, holding the towering roof. The stone floor spanned, polished, and detailed with carved thorns, connecting the rugs with the stone. Interior walls painted in white, slowly ascend-ing to a washed-out, dimmed white stone, showing the age of the castle's structure. Both sides of the rugs had glass domes protecting ancient relics, shining weapons of times before the Old Ones. A wide broadsword held by golden supports. The hilt carved from a story: Nova, the conqueror's New Dawn. The rising sun drawn into its centre, shining its new stars and its new beginning. Ancient writing casting a story of a conqueror before magic, before the crack in the realm.

The room expanded, leading to the thrones. Two on each side, leaving a space in the middle for the coloured panes to reflect, shine down upon their crowns. Presenting their wealth upon their requested visitors.

Footsteps echoed through the side archway leading to the thrones. Guards covered in black leather armour, layered in black metal, detailed in golden thorns at its edges. Their shoulders were branded with the symbol of the Four's Legion: the Nova Star. White streaks carved down the armour's angles, highlighting their waists, abdomen, and their biceps. The leather weaved, creating a tough, robust suit of protection against their foes.

A long, thick cape waved across the rug, flowing behind the tall, robust royal. His silky light-brunette hair shone, absorbing the coloured panes' reflections. Pazima's eyes drew up, noticing his sprouting pearl-white roots. The colour fading away, draining from his wavy silky strands.

"Kneel." King Dreaka's gravelly voice commanded.

Pazima knelt, gifting a smile towards the broad framed royal. King Dreaka smirked, launching himself to his foot. He walked with a powerful stride, placing his glare down at her lowered head. "My Princess says you're a rebel."

Pazima raised her head, connecting their eyelines. "Just a simple woman, caring for their friend." A dark sparkle twirled in his eyes. Testing for a daring glance.

She pushed herself up, little by little. "May I? Your royal rugs aren't that comfortable." A test. She knew the ever-ending list of risks she had hanging over her neck like a sharpened guillotine, but the fire in her gut wouldn't allow such a royal coward to tower over her.

"Brave. For Moonsong. My legions will find your home soon enough." He teased with a tut between his pale lips. He turned,

stepping back to his throne. "Tell me, what shall I do to such..."
He paused, scanning her features. "An alluring soldier." He
smirked once more, glancing at the guards at her sides. "Don't
you think? Hmm? Saying you wouldn't want to bed her?" He
directed his stare, burning into the guard's leathers.

She could feel their struggling, fighting against their panicking trembles. They murmured under their breath. The King's
laugh cast out, vibrating against the stone pillars and the
colourful panes behind his towering throne.

Steps echoed through from behind her, sending a freezing
chill down her spine. A woman walked with a strong pride,
flicking her cloak across her as she pressed Pazima. While the
other royal man walked with no displayed emotion with his
short light brunette hair, just like the other men within the
castle.

The woman softly sat down upon her throne, allowing the
coloured panes to cast light pink and blue hues across her
curvaceous figure and the silks that framed her softly. She
stared at Pazima. "Playing with your food, King Dreaka?" Her
words were coarse as thorns.

King Dreaka's chuckle rattled. "Welcome back, Queen Atula,
King Plu Kan."

Queen Atula's throne was made of blackwood, highlighted
by quartz detailing. Carvings of thorns and cream roses
throughout, showing her city's status. Their rich quartz mining
stations held firm with her crown. Her throne remained rooted
to the ground as its original placement in the aftermath of the
siege, planted far right to King Alonn's throne.

King Plu Kan nodded to King Dreaka, sitting on his throne
at King Dreaka's left.

The King continued, looking back at his prisoner. "Pazima."
His voice, confident, leaving chilling gushes against her neck.
"You are now placed under our legion. You will do as I com-
mand. A soldier of the Four, at my will." King Dreaka rose from

his throne. Queen Atula and King Plu Kan hooked their gaze to King Dreaka. "Disobey me, show even the smallest twirl of mist. I'll kill you, part your head from your body where you stand." His voice lashed like a rope to her pulsing neck. "If you have any intent to kill me or any crowned royal, you'll burn from the inside. Each organ knotting, engulfed by flames and unimaginable pain. Courtesy of the little rune charred into your skin." He smirked. Pazima's blood raged, bubbling, rushing through her burning veins. King Dreaka's slight smirk coated her thoughts in thick red.

Pazima closed her eyes, blocking her senses, temporarily holding her breath, keeping it from exiting her throat. sustaining it, controlling it. She had to play this game, opening her eyes to King Dreaka. Her lips lifted, fixing a smile of elegance, balancing her form, her thoughts, her mission. Two thoughts grounded her. Getting back to her family. Forging a new Eyldian realm, using the royals' charred bones as its foundation. The Old Ones' deaths wouldn't be in vain.

Pazima tossed the bed's pillow onto the window's alcove, letting the storm's salty gust thrust against her coils. She sat undoing each braid as the sun partly dropped past the ocean's waves. Quartzrose oil had been left for her by the maids. The western continent's rare oils, sold at soaring high count rates, leaving it impossible for outer towns and settlements to gain the wealth needed for pushase, like most products in Eyldia. She sighed, pushing it away.

The thunder crashed, ricocheting against the island's stone sharp cliff faces. The raging waves ate away at the ruff stones, creating stone spikes piercing along the rocky shoreline. She pulled herself off the alcove, roaming through the room. Pazima smiled, praising herself as she launched to the forgotten breakfast tray. Her fingers wrapped around the metal bowl, taking it back to the alcove. She grinned, cursing the

Quartzrose oil under her breath, dipping her fingers in honey, coating each coil.

Her hair was a symbol of her strength. Her discipline. How Pazima controlled her hair like she did her mist, transforming it into symbols of strength upon her body. She pulled her shirt, scanning over the wicked, cold rune burned into the bruised skin. Royal deaths forced out of her grasp. A new plan brewed, staring into the fierce downpour.

# Chapter 28

## The Crow's Last Rotation

### *Raven*

The cell became his last home. Four walls of stone and ice, slowly closing in the darkness. Lassea's voice fought off the shadows that clawed at his skin. Her warmth, her knowledge. It held his essence in balance. She anchored him until his last rotation.

"Raven." She called through the crack. "The guards are restless."

"I die today." Raven replied, void of emotion, refusing to accept the possibility of death, of the prophecy bringing him to this brisk ending. Three rings of the Jinos' keep, bellowing a sharp, high-pitched chime. The ice foundations cried upon the first chime, ringing from the sharp pressure, a hiss of death. Time folded, footsteps slowing, pulsing through the freezing stone floors, clawing its way to his frost-bitten toes. A second ring pulled, a chime pulsed forcefully, as if the bell accompanied his meatless body within his cell.

One last chime. Raven didn't comprehend how much time moved ahead, allowing his head to slip to an uncomfortable angle, leaning against his bony left shoulder.

The last chime bellowed. It felt mighty and violent, completely unyielding.

The metal bashed against the stone wall, quaking the door's foundations, allowing the sun's rays into his pale features, blurring the moving figures. "Get up." A rough, dead voice spat out. The figures came into focus, highlighted by the sun's cast. Their built arms folded under his arms. Their force dragged Raven's withered mass across the wet stone.

"Raven Whitewood. Your death shall be fruitful." King Alonn stepped close, with an obvious grin upon his thin lips.

"What's your problem?" His demanding tone slashed the King's smirk.

King Alonn's cheek brightened, accompanied by his darting eyes. "Leave us." He commanded his guards. The King's stance towered over him, kneeling down into the wet, sharp rocks. "He wants you and him. Why should I give him that?"

"Who wants me and Sevar?"

His laugh echoed against the cracks. A dim purple glow lit through his tunic. "That mercenary was irrelevant." His stare clawed, piling an unworldly pressure on Raven's heart. "You and your twin brother. The two heirs of Dreaka."

His lips loosened; each breath begged for words to lace them. "What?" Raven forced out.

"I've said enough. Your head on my throne shall do well." His whistle rang through the dungeon, inviting the guards back into the cell.

"Alonn, I need to know more." He shouted through the cell, clamping his hands on each frame, gripping the cold, sharp metal door edges, connecting each stone along the wall. "I have a brother?" Raven's nails ripped, bleeding down his hand. "Alonn!" He cawed against the guard's brawny force.

Raven cried, pleading against the harsh sunlight. Only long strands of his greasy brunette curls shielded his bony features, washed out of all definitions. His paper white body hung from the guards' arms, dragging through his last moments. King Alonn knew what he was doing, planting that one thread of information into his palms to consume his final thoughts. It did. A brother, memories of a family he couldn't remember.

His bare feet cut and bled, leaving a trail of his dripping blood down the icy corridors. Through each corridor, pathway and staircase, guards stationed in each corner. Their swords drawn, pointing its steel into the stone foundations. With every trembling step, the sound rippled, slashing at his ears and engulfing his skin in an invisible, burning itch.

Noise bellowed and roared, everything burrowed through him like an unearthly spectre. Bellows forced his ears into focus, forced to hear, to absorb every expression of rage. Men, women and their young, roaring his name in sheer loathing.

"Slaughter the coward!" The crowd roared.

The cold bit at his feet, dragging through the crowds of sullen Eyldians. Every sentence slammed against him, punching his knotted, empty stomach. Eyldians of cities high above their own houses of mud, wheat and odd, abandoned stones. Did they understand this world? He thought as every hair spiked, raised from his snowy skin.

"Traitor to our crowns!" A short man lunged, covered in vibrant fabrics, twisting Raven's arm, his shoulder blade scrapped against his backbone, moaning at the pressure. The pain flamed through his body, flaring into a tortured outcry. The guard launched the men to the side, tossing him to the icy gravel floor.

"Treason!" A young girl spoke on his left side. She stared; her expression coloured with thick hatred, taught by generations of division.

"Make him scream!"

Raven looked up, darting his view around at the wooden stage crafted in front of him. The wet, icy wooden planks, placed together in haste. The stairs uneven, the wood chippings stabbed at his toes, one last slash upon his wilted body.

"Down." The guard commanded.

The word braced upon his ear, but he didn't want to hear it. He couldn't let it pass, taking everything he had seen cut short. The unearthly roars of the crowd filled his ears. The guard's frosted hand clamped around his head, pressing down against his hair, tossing him into the blood-soaked wooden stump. Raven's ear slammed against the surface, rippling a deathening chime. His eyes stuck upon the crowd, their roars silent, nothing but a high unearthly drone to keep him company in his final clicks.

A last tear slid down his nose, dropping, soaking into the bloodied wood. One tear. He left one last mark, his death branded into the stump.

What would he choose to be his final thought? He already knew that. He was always thinking about it, since he entered that damned ice tomb.

*I love you, Sevar.*

Love. A feeling he never let himself have, the emptiness within him, his forgotten memories. A lost life haunted him, tortured him in each corner, in every ale he poured. He could love for one moment.

The murmur dimmed, consumed by a whisper, Vague and completely deafening. twirling, tickling against his ear. *"finally back together."*

Raven's eyes sparked gold, rushing through his tortured body, lifting his glare from the crowd, looking upon the castle walls. Two figures dashed across, one with eyes consumed by mirrored sparking gold.

*"Brother."*

His words unlocked a shining light, filling every corner, battling every shadow. Twirling ribbons of flaming gold bursting entirely, opening an ancient, rustic door in his mind. A connection hidden and locked away, two minds linked by blood and power, two golden ribbons threading and burning. A divine link between forgotten souls found by an interlocking glance.

The axe slammed, slashing through the thick tension. Nothing but the brisk wind brushing against his neck. Raven's eyes burning, erupting in flames of blinding gold. The figure's golden power twirled through the crowd, dancing through the maze of shocked civilians, flinging through the gravel. Its scorching power hummed quietly, like a divine calling. It raised to the platform, tackling the metal axe into the wooden foundations.

*"Brother?"* The man whispered through the unlocked door.

# Chapter 29

## Forgotten Brother

*Astrid*

Astrid's feet forced him to a sudden halt, placing his hands on the stone wall's edge. The crowd sat silent. Their glare shot down to the guards, choking on strings of gold. The air rubbed against the ice towers, whistling its lone song across every cold stone. The singing wind accompanied his power. It felt overwhelming, a growth of power and love through an old door. The figure ever lurking in his mind greeted the rustic door, opening it in ease, smiling, yet showing no face, but it beamed. Its harsh outline faded into the door's blinding light.

Astrid felt the man's withering strength, his cracking thoughts echoing through his magic. Their emotions weaved through each other, their essences intertwining, listening, communicating through the rustic door frame.

*"Get up, get a dagger from the guard."* He yelled. *"Now."*

"How's that possible?" Sevar spoke as they ran through the ice tower staircase.

"Your friend, he is my brother." They lunged through the hallways, jumping out of the exterior guard wall.

"And you didn't know?" Sevar questioned as they both whispered, lighting their runes.

"Our memories are still gone, but we can feel it through our power. Our blood." The sentence laced in rage.

They nodded to each other, launching their runic blasts through the locked spruce door. The door split, splintering into the crowd. Screams blew into the panicked group, sending the crowd into sheer panic, trampling over guards towards the castle gate. The only exit on the southern side of the castle's compound, into the circular street of ice and stone.

Guards gathered, charging through the castle's entrances. Their yells echoed to the ice towers, guards with bows readying their footing. The arrows flew, following their weaving movements. Astrid and Sevar lunged across the gravel, their sight glued to Raven's withered strikes, to fight against the launching legion backup.

"To your left!" Sevar broadcasted, his fingers twirled across his thigh holster, launching his small knife into the guard's neck. The blood sprayed over him as he blocked his movements.

"Who trained you?" Astrid's question shot to Sevar as he whispered, twirling his runic power into an interlocking force laced in burning gold. His groan pushed as he flung his arms into the twirling action, holding the entanglement of power with a tremendous strain on his footing. Astrid's fingers quaked, threatening to crack under the pressure. He pushed, launching it at a group of soldiers.

"Raven!" Sevar yelled, jumping up onto the wooden execution platform.

The arrows rained once more, littering its shots into the field of dead. Sevar pulled his arm up, whispering into his skin. A shield cast through his arm, shielding them from the moment of raining arrows.

Astrid's glance shot down to the arrows. They melted slowly into the frozen soil. A green mist... A poison. Laced in moon-wolf's toxin. The last memory of Pazima crying out in pain from the toxic bites pulled. Flashing memories of his failure into his mind, to keep her safe, the arrows continued to slam against Sevar's shield.

A hand placed upon his shoulder, yet no one stood behind Astrid. *"We'll find her."* Raven cast. He pushed the memories away; his brother was right. He'd save his love, but first he had to save his brother.

The soldier's energy shot, bouncing off Sevar's shield. He groaned at each shot. Every arrow thinned the shield's energy. Sweat dripped from Sevar's forehead, dropping to the blood-stained oak foundations.

"Sevar, drop the shield and blast the ice tower when I say." He returned his gaze to the figure that so long plagued his sight, like a ghost. "Hello, brother. Ready to play with gold?" They smiled at one another. Raven nodded, struggling to hold in a longing breath.

"We need to get to the dungeon." Raven breathed. "Your mother, she's here. I've seen her." Sevar didn't let go of his focus. All he let out was a quick nod in reply.

*"Together, we'll blast the group of guards' formation at the castle's entrance."* He cast. Raven nodded. Their eyes flickered like a mirror, tracing one another's twirls of power within them. Their veins were filled by flaming gold.

"Now." His command directed towards Sevar.

A smile pasted on Sevar's face as he collected the shield's energy, melding it into a blast of energy. The energy quaked the ice, creating a tremendous crack ripping through the left tower's magical foundations.

Their blinding gold ribboned together, beaming into the metal shields of the soldier's formation, hot enough to burn the shield's craftsmanship as if it was bound with sticks and mud. The guards tossed their melting weapons across the field, abandoning the scorching irons in haste. Some roared in pain, crying out for any gracing coldness, while some ran in fear.

They ran, pushing each nearing soldier. Swords swung towards Raven's head, Sevar's hand forced Raven to dodge as he sliced the soldier with his broadsword. His head rolled, soaking the gravel in blood.

The castle's ancient ice foundations hummed a noise deadening to any Eyldian. An embedded runic spell roaring for revenge on their attackers as a magical failsafe.

The stairs, the halls all covered in soldiers, Raven led the way, keeping Sevar and Astrid to his sides. They lunged through every doorway, scanning the environments of each room. They ran through dinner halls, kicking the chairs out of their paths. Raven's mind struggled; he felt it, the exhaustion weighing on his body. Every click it climbed, fighting against the burning power. The only power that kept Raven stable and conscious.

Sevar wrapped his arm around Raven, hooking it under his shoulder, supporting Raven's body with his strength. Sevar held his sword on his right and Raven on his left. Together, they descended from the halls to the staircase.

Astrid moved in front with daggers in both hands, protecting Sevar and Raven. The staircase descended further, with each step damper than the previous.

"Which section? Cell number?" Astrid shot the questions out, blocking the guard's slashes and lunging back, opening their stomachs with one long gash.

"The door. I'll show you." Raven breathed.

A connection of shadows and burning fury, of history unknown. Astrid closed his eyes, pulling himself back into the darkness, completely willing to drag himself through the maze of his mind. The door, ancient, rustic and ungodly, something they couldn't begin to decipher.

Astrid touched the rustic door frame, allowing his mind to touch Raven's withering thoughts. *"Show me."*

*"0439"* Raven stared upon the cell door and its number carvings. Astrid felt everything, completely exposed, falling through sadness and freezing torture.

"Raven are you—" Astrid breathed.

Raven lifted his hand, shaking his head. "I will when we save her."

—

The hum cast louder, stronger, and more deadening as they ran down the dungeon's labyrinth of corridors. Halls, archways and door frames of ice and dripping stone. The brisk cold waved through the air, forcing their arm hairs to stand firm.

The door numbers raised slowly, one hundred, one hundred and fifty...

Soldiers charged through every hallway as their stomps echoed against the ice pillars and the stone walls. Astrid's hope faded slowly down his face with every drop of cold sweat. Dripping down his temples, running to his jawline, descending to the cracked stone floor. Too many people, even for him and Sevar. A Moonsong warrior and a Clockwork mercenary.

Soldiers closed every direction. "We are outnumbered." Sevar shot towards him.

"I know." Panic wrapped Astrid's thoughts. Possibilities, most ending in their brisk death.

They wouldn't use runic magic this low into the castle. They wouldn't be idiotic enough to risk killing themselves and all their prisoners. The ice foundations couldn't save them from the weight of a crumbling castle.

"Surrender and we'll make your deaths swift." A soldier commanded down the hall.

His nostrils flared, his breath quickened. "Get out of our way and you won't die a long and tasteful death." Astrid's words remained playful, hiding his panic.

Mutters of words lingered, too far for them to hear complete sentences. The soldiers grated their feet into the stone flooring, readying their position. Screams and echoes smashed into their backs. Astrid turned rapidly, looking into a group of people slashing with fury against the soldiers. The group, branded with a symbol of rustic orange outlines encompassing clock arrows.

"They with you?" He questioned Sevar.

"They owed me one." Sevar stated, pushing Raven up further.

"Of course they did." His words added to their friction.

The soldiers roared. Running to tackle against the group of Clockwork mercenaries. Swords smashed, grating their metals against one another. Blades slashed from side to side, catching the stone walls. Halls narrowed, filling with bodies. Blood puddled the floor, filling every little crack. Sevar slammed a soldier's head into the wall, one mighty blow, cracking his bald skull, sending their deathly scream across the sharp stones. Astrid knew Sevar would protect Raven with his life, blocking, dodging, attacking between each quick breath.

A dance of metal and fury. Astrid's boot launched down, smashing his force into a broad soldier's spine. "This way, it can't be far." Astrid yelled, scanning the cells numbers – four hundred.

Ice blue archways ran red, sprayed with blood. The thinning cold air stained by the metallic blood leaking onto his taste buds.

He scanned the number's above. "Here!" Astrid shouted to Sevar.

"Grab the nearest guard." Sevar said.

Astrid shot down to the hall, looking for their guard uniform. All the different uniforms of the Four all had their symbols and black fabrics, but the guards had a special detail: a symbol of an axe sewed into their biceps, a symbol for execution, of their justice.

He raced, angling his arm around a guard's neck. The guard struggled, pushing back into the stone wall. Astrid's grip tightened. His biceps flexed against the guard's throat, cutting off his windpipe entirely. The guard's adam's apple bobbed under the pressure, begging to pop out from his tightening grip. The power to take countless lives. It held a pressure over Astrid's mind, yet he pressed harder, feeling the growing pressure above his throbbing biceps. He had no choice but to take them all, for him, for Pazima, for his new blood, for his damned forgotten memories. Astrid tossed him across the hall, dropping the guard at Sevar's side. He walked back over, passing the soldier's hand against the door.

Sevar handed Raven over to Astrid. The metal hummed, swinging open to a meditating woman. Sevar's mother.

"Mother." Sevar forced out the word. His eyes swelled, dropping full tears into his bloodied beard.

"You came for me." She smiled, jumping to a stable footing, folding her arms around her son for the overdue embrace.

"Let's go, you can hug when we survive this." Astrid spoke into the cell.

Astrid handed over an abandoned sword to Lassea. She grinned. "I'm a little rusty."

"Another pair of hands will do." Astrid nodded to her.

Astrid, Sevar, Raven, Lassea and the remains of Clockwork mercenaries ran together, forming a circle of metal and fury. They traced their paths back up through the blood-soaked dungeons, passing halls full of dead. Up the stairs, through the castle's main rooms.

Blood partly frozen by the cold temperatures, cracking upon their footsteps. Screams and yells from the city echoed through the closed gates. Soldiers ran, forming a line on both sides of the gate, no way out.

"The legion has us closed in!" A Clockwork member bellowed.

Astrid smirked. "Don't worry. We'll sort that out." Letting out a loud whistle, using his thumb and a finger upon his lips.

A mythic roared through the wind. Ambe's silhouette cast down upon the castle walls as his serpent body twirled through the air.

"What the fuck?" Raven spat out, glaring with half-opened eyelids, fighting against the sun's rays.

"Don't worry. You'll learn to love them." Astrid calmly spoke.

He whispered against Ambe's scales. The order remained brief, using only three words. Ambe launched, roping his serpent body around the gate's metal. The mythic's brute strength cracked the stone connections, hurling the gate to the side. Soldier's bodies rammed, squeezed under the gate's weight.

"There you go, Clockwork." Astrid said, twirling to a half bow.

Sevar nodded in their direction. They nodded back, running through the gate.

"Quick jump on." Astrid commanded. He and Sevar guided Raven and Lassea up onto Ambe's saddle.

"Thank you, for everything." He whispered to Ambe's wide green eyes.

The soldiers threw their energy, readying their arrows. "Kill the mythic." They roared.

"To the skies!" He yelled to Ambe. Ambe roared in excitement, launching them into the skies. Ambe's serpent body twirled, dodging the runic energy blasts.

# Chapter 30

## The Calm After the Breakout

### *Raven*

Their feet planted onto the dirt path, heading up into the Fellow's Mountains with its peaks as a natural compass. The moon always fell behind the mountain's summit. Sleeping, living, and thriving in the brisk winds of the rocky ridges and its river valleys, full of wildlife.

"The King said he killed you, placing your head on a pike." Raven looked up through the supportive hold. "I believed it for a while." The words hesitated on his lips.

"I have three lives like a vinepixie." Sevar tightened his arm around Raven's torso, pulling him into his burly build. "Your new—sibling saved me with his Quetzalcoatl."

Ambe flew above, cutting through the clouds, roaring with joy. "I've only seen them in my dreams. Seeing them with my own eyes, it's astonishing." Raven said.

"The most beautiful and intelligent creatures to enter our realm," Astrid spoke from a comfortable distance.

"Enter?" He spat out.

"I don't know much of our history. What I do know is all the creatures we have are from the mythic realm. They passed through a threshold of sorts. The Ophidians had stories about it painted over their walls. Like a crack in the mythic isle, a gateway between realms."

Astrid turned his head. "The Four were planning something with the mythic isles. I need to find Pazima first. Travel through each city's dungeons, if I must."

"I'll help you." Raven replied, wheezing vaguely.

Sevar's head peered down. "Raven, you barely survived Jinos. You can't."

"Don't tell him what he can't do" Astrid stopped in his tracks, facing Sevar.

"And you know him now? You don't even know where he lived his whole life. What's his favourite food?" Sevar's voice raised, pushing Astrid. "It's eggs with sliced cherries."

"You don't understand it unless you feel it." Astrid spat out.

"Okay, stop measuring your masculinity. I'll be fine after some rest." Raven peered up to Sevar. A silent facial expression beamed from Raven.

*"It's true. We are strangers with access to each other's emotions. King Alonn told me I had a brother. What if he's lying to reach his own goals?"* He spoke calmly through the door.

*"You're my twin brother. Alonn could lie about many things, but not about this. You feel it too. Our lives have become threaded together".* Astrid replied as he pushed on ahead.

*"We need our memories back."* Raven paused, thinking of what words could speak a thousand meanings to lost blood, to a stranger. *"That feeling of emptiness. I thought I was broken. Not allowed to connect to anyone because of it."*

*"We'll find out what happened. We'll fill the empty gaps together."* Astrid said.

"Thank you for saving me. For being with my boy." Lassea walked from Raven's the left, placing a kiss on his sweaty forehead.

Sevar looked down at him. "I'm coming with you. You saved my mother. I owe you my life."

Astrid looked back, smiling.

"You don't owe me anything. Either of you." Raven fought against a frown.

"Do you know what hurts more than being stabbed?" Sevar placed his hand on his cheek, pulling it to face him. "The fear of never seeing you again. It made my heart shatter. I would have let her kill me if it meant you never got caught." The words rolled off Sevar's tongue, admiring his exhaustion.

"You don't know me, not really. I don't know me." Raven whispered.

"I know enough, Raven Whitewood." Sevar smiled, as Raven mirrored Sevar's expression, staring into his autumn eyes. His eyes rolled, consumed by the exhaustion. Nothing but the drips of wet stone echoed through his skull.

-

"You bastard. You lost my daughter to them." Groans filled his darkness. "Why shouldn't I slit your throat right here? Leaving your young. Caelan and Daj. Your responsibilities to Moonsong, Astrid!" The man's deep voice quaked.

Light burst through as he pulled his lids open. "What is happening?" The green of the vines caught his eye. The clean polished archways with the ancient symbol drawn into them.

"This is the Commander of Moonsong, Sakhile." Astrid looked at him. "Commander, meet my twin brother, Raven."

The gold sparked through his neck, pushing against the dagger. The Commander stepped back, darting his eyes between the two. "Impossible." The Commander whispered.

"We are Aligners." Astrid fixed his tunic.

"I..." The Commander shook his head. "Astrid—This changes everything."

"What do you know, Commander?" Astrid stood firm, holding his head up high. "How does this power change anything?"

Commander Sakhile's face seemed troubled, holding onto information, burdened by a puzzle within his head. "Nothing, stay here. That's an order."

"We are going to find Pazima, get our memories back. Make a better world." Astrid's rage boiled in his veins, racing through his body. The unfiltered rage bellowed through the ribboning connection.

"You've done enough. You already lost my daughter." Commander Sakhile yelled.

"With respect, Commander. The rebellion has already started. It's been going on for a long time now." Astrid's tone froze, ice cold. Pointing towards the exit. "Outside these walls, I supported the Ophidian people, your mother. I will find Pazima, and we will fight. It's what she wanted from the start." Astrid stood up close to the Commander.

*"Breathe."* He whispered through the connection.

Commander Sakhile's face remained frozen and emotionless. "My study, now." Astrid walked through the healing arc's doorway, turning out of view alongside Commander Sakhile.

All the beds were vacant except for his. All the stones were cleaned, absent of cold drips of water running down every stone. The smell of nature and freshness filled his lungs. He could finally let go, and breathe. The cold, sharp air of the dungeons lurked on the back of his neck like a phantom, scratching a deep chill down his spine. "I'm not there." Raven murmured under his breath.

Sevar ran into the room. "You're awake." His relief pushed the pressure from his shoulders. Sevar wrapped his arms around him, his rapid heartbeats pressed against his aching skin.

"Don't do that again," Sevar whispers into Raven's greasy curls.

"But you love to play hero." His laugh muffled into Sevar's neck.

Lassea peered around the arc. Her voice echoed down the hallway as she queried Elder Rose about Raven's healing progress.

"Has Lassea been checked out?" He lifted his face from Sevar's bulky shoulders.

He ran his hand down Sevar's stubble, watching his lips move as he spoke. "The healer said she is malnutritioned, and needs to regain her strength with enrichment tonics and rest." Sevar grabbed his hand, placing it down onto the bed. "Like you should be doing."

"Nothing's going to stop me from going after my memories." The cold brushed against his back.

"Are you okay?" He breathed.

"The cell, the coldness. It stuck to my skin like a fungus spreading down my spine." His words trembled.

Sevar's blinked, accepting his tear to drop into the warm stones, grabbing Raven into a tight embrace. "You'll never experience that again. We'll train you to fight so you can defend yourself." He whispered into his shoulder.

"Better than you?" Amusement filled his puffy cheeks.

"You damn wish, Crow."

He let out a mocking crow noise into Sevar's ear. He laughed, hiding in the painful groan from the jolting movement. "—let's get you cleaned up." Sevar cupped Raven, holding firmly to his petite ribs, step by step, across the warm polished stones. His bare feet, absent of the freezing pain. Raven groaned, placing his hand on each nearby bed for extra support.

"Nearly there." Sevar spoke softly, hooking his hand around him tightly, placing him on the edge of the healer arc's bubbling bath, carved out by hand. The bath's stone moulded to the wall's structure as the moss grew down its stone's indents, allowing flowers to blossom at the bath's edge. Sevar and Raven accepted the quiet, no voices, no drips from cold water. Just vague footsteps and ember flickering. Sevar pulled Raven's shirt slowly over his dirt-filled curls, helping him down to his undergarments. The board mercenary stared down, helping Raven into the stone bath.

Raven's back, covered in deep wounds. Some healed, some still bleeding, completely fresh from his last night in the cold cells. "The wounds, did they—"

"Sometimes." His voice forced out a whisper. "Thank you, Sev." Raven smiled, yet tears dropped into the warm, bubbling bath. "Thank you, Sev."

"It's okay. Crow." Sevar wrapped his arms around his torso, placing his head onto Raven's shoulder. "I'll always be here for you."

# Chapter 31

Oh, brother...

*Astrid*

"How did you meet my mother?" Commander Sakhile sat in his chair behind his thick spruce desk, displaying shock on his features, which Astrid found humourful. A rare moment for the Commander's expression being raw and unstable.

"I have used Ambe to travel to Hlinos..." He kept to the other side of the room, sitting at a small, round meeting table. "The power makes us able to listen to the creatures, like a rider. After the mission, Ambe saved us and crashed into the Ophidian Cove shores." He stepped up and turned, browsing the bookshelves to make sure he kept his sight away from his Commander.

"You lost my daughter and used my partner?" Sakhile slammed his right hand into the messy desk. "Never touch Ambe again. You may be new to the connection between us and our Quetzalcoatl's, but that doesn't allow you to touch him. Do you understand?"

"Yes, sir." He turned to the bookshelves as the air filled with silence. "Commander, why did you leave the Ophidian way?"

"The Four kept coming, kept building their aggression." He stood, walking to the round table. "Saving my wife and children became paramount. My mother wouldn't leave but I couldn't stay to follow their way, so we took a boat and went east, to the Fellow's Mountains." Commander Sakhile walked over to his side, running his fingers across the book's spines. He grabbed a book, flicking it open a couple of pages. "Here." He pointed to the page.

"The First Moon?" Astrid's right brow lifted slightly.

"The Moonsong origins. Time before the Four when the Moonsingers would sleep in the Moonlight, using nature and the mountains' landscape as their homes. When we travelled into the valleys, we found a group of Moonsong." Sakhile placed the book down on the table. "I helped them change, come together to live in the temple permanently so they could be safe. I showed them how to keep history safe within the libraries."

"You always said Moonsong was born between the temple walls." Astrid slid into the thick, brown pillows.

"That's the truth for most. I forgot what we stood for, for a long time." Commander Sakhile walked over to the bookshelf, pulling up a collection of old folded papers. He carefully placed them, unfolding each crease. A map of Eyldia. "I'll send word to our spy in Hlinos. She'll ready you a ship in their docks." Sakhile pressed his finger down upon Dreaka's north border. "Avoid going into Drossor and the Red Marsh lands by sea. If King Dreaka ordered Pazima's move from Jinos then she'll be in one of the main cities." His finger glided over to the royal's shared castle home. "Sailing to Kullur Island is near impossible because of Storm's way and their navy legions guarding most of its territories."

"Storm's way?" Astrid's brow lifted.

"You never were academic. It's the never-ending storm boundary that cuts between most of the north and south.

"Who would have the power?" Astrid's mind bounced around the idea of the never-ending storm. It's impossible, holding an immeasurable amount of mass, of chaotic power surging for hundreds of years. Another question, another detail of history and its puzzle remaining in the shadows.

Commander Sakhile's shoulders raised slightly. "It's rumoured to be cast by the Old Ones as their last act in the Four's siege." Sakhile placed his hand on Astrid's shoulder. "I can't leave our people, find Pazima. I can't lose another daughter."

"What happened to your other daughter? You said I lost your daughters. Not just Pazima." Astrid remained sat, allowing space to collect between them.

Commander Sakhile tensed his fist, hovering over the Eyldian map. "You must be mistaken."

"I'm not, tell me, Commander."

Commander Sakhile's face displayed a weighed emotion, like something held him down for many years. A burdened frown. "The night you were found in the forest, a note was left in your pocket by my eldest daughter, Tauriea."

"Your daughter—she brought me here?" Astrid's face flamed a bright red, punched by emotion. Rage? No, it was sorrow. It gripped his heart, causing him to choke on his breath vaguely. "Why not tell me years ago."

"I'm sorry, Astrid. I did it to protect you."

"How does that protect me?"

"The note Astrid, Tauriea wrote that you are to be protected, that you were special. I didn't begin to understand how much, till now, Astrid." Commander Sakhile turned, facing Astrid, glancing into his eyes. "Her mission was to be in Kullur Castle and keep a note of travel routes, trade points, legion training posts, so we can keep hidden. No one's seen her since Dreaka. Till that note and you were found close to our home.

" Commander Sakhile had a growing sadness peering over his mature features, a frown his thick beard couldn't mask. "You and Raven have the alignment power from a bloodline thought to be extinguished. Together, your power could change the realm." Commander Sakhile's voice cracked. "Please save her, son."

"I will get her back and find out what happened to Tauriea. My lost memories, too." A nod mirrored from one another, filling the study with a bubbling respect.

"Ride Ambe again and I'll make him drop you off Fellow's cliffs." They placed small grins over their faces, existing the study with their next move.

The sparring circle filled with people peering down through every observing ring. Commander Sakhile and Fee leaned over the top railing. Many young of Moonsong sat, whispering to each other, struggling to muffle their laughter. Their giggles twirled up into the stalactite ceiling. Within that group stood his and Pazima's young ones. All glued to the movements in the sparring circle. Caelan and Daj stood against the ground, observing the ring. Caelan signed to Daj, erupting a smile from ear to ear.

Raven and Sevar stood a couple of paces away from him. Sevar placed his sword at his side, leaning on his hilt.

"Are you sure you're up to it?"

"I know you care for me, but please don't overstate the monitoring. We both know I need to learn this." Raven smiled up at Sevar. "I'll be okay."

"you'll kill it."

Sevar looked at him, giving him a nod. "So, what do you know, brother?" Astrid directed his voice to Raven.

Sevar walked over to Caelan and Daj, leaning against the polished stone railings. "I can block and do basic attacks,"

Raven replied, choking on a thrusting doubt. Astrid could feel it all, every splash of guilt, of self-doubt, Raven's worry.

"That's okay, you'll learn quickly." Astrid grabbed out two wooden swords from the young one's training chest. "Now parrying is blocking your enemies' upcoming position. How they attack you. You must think fast." He flicked one of the wooden swords in Raven's hands. "Because it means life or death." The last word spat off Astrid's tongue as he swung to a middle position, slamming Raven's sword to the ground.

"Fuck Astrid, that hurt." Raven tumbled to get the sword off the dusty floor.

"This is the guarding position, keeping your torso, neck and head safe from attacks. Ready to calculate, jump into another position if you must." Astrid placed his sword closed to his torso, holding it firm.

Raven copied each position Astrid displayed. For two hours, he stared at each unique position, how they worked and how they could be defeated by their enemies.

"Hanging position now." He yelled.

Raven launched into the hanging position at his right side. He launched against him, aiming towards his left. Raven's eyes darted, calculating Astrid's movements. Blocking his advances, Raven swung into the back left position. His knees buckled under the straining changes.

"Well done, brother. Again!" He jumped to another position.

Raven placed the wooden sword on the ground. "I need to rest before we leave." Raven sat at the side of the circle.

"I'll pack you some clothes from the spare piles in the cleaning arc." Astrid smiled, wiping his pooling sweat from his side-parting.

*"Thank you."* Raven whispered through the divine doorway.

-

He walked along the vibrant grass, kicking the little stones under his boots. The streams laid peacefully, letting the air take its flowing direction. The place where time stood still, a filtered sense of life between his ears, the purring of the Moonfoxes, their grey ears pointing up to the sky, the grey ran down their fur, twirling till their white twin tails. He adored the wild. How they covered their homes next to the river for each freezing season, moving up into the snowy Fellow's Ridges for the warmer seasons. Maybe he adored them for keeping him company as a lone young one in the brisk forests, perhaps because they didn't hold hatred, didn't allow emotions to anchor them.

The rocks bounced, clicking off the other rocks on the stream's edge.

*"Are you okay, Astrid?"* Raven called.

*"Fuck, don't do that. Yes, I'm okay."* He jumped, stopping his movements.

*"This whole talking through our connection situation feels so unworldly. I can feel your unrest slipping through."*

*"Pazima, she has always looked out for me. What if she's—"* The words fell off his tongue like they begged to be released.

*"—From what I've heard from Caelan and Dej, she sounds like the strongest warrior in Eyldia. She'll be okay. We'll find her."* The feeling of warmth passed through the door. A calming sense of understanding slid through him, coating his bloodstream.

*"Where did you live before all this?"* Astrid let his laugh echo through their connection, casting a grin on his face as he sat up against an ancient oak.

*"Elcoo, a settlement in the south of Drossor. I was raised and worked in a tavern. A kind man took me in, and a baker always cared for me."*

*"Sounds peaceful. Perhaps you can show me after all this."* An offering from a connected stranger.

-

The sun cast the tree's shadow's down upon him, accompanied by the shadows of approaching feet. His face glanced up from the river. "Sevar?"

"Astrid." His words were emotionless to the ear. Sevar walked over, avoiding the tree branch's sways.

Astrid placed his focus back on his small knife, sliding the green apple laid in his palm. "Need anything?"

"Fee said I would find you here." Sevar sat next to him, leaning against the ancient oak.

"That didn't answer my query." Astrid shot with lingering annoyance.

"I'm here to ask you for a promise." Astrid's eyes glued to Sevar's, confirming him to carry on with his proposal.

Sevar turned to face him "For you and me to put our lives at risk before Raven's. I know we both don't see eye to eye. But we both know he won't have anywhere near enough training to fight off soldiers or the royal legion. We fight as a solid team like we did before. If it goes south, if the time comes, we place our heads before the oncoming blades."

He reached his arm out, placing it into Sevar's. "I swear it to be."

"I swear it to be." Sevar replies.

He didn't agree with the clockwork way. Their lack of morality with whom they contract with for payment, but Astrid saw it, the sparkle in Sevar's eye, looking at Raven when he talks. How Sevar places himself in the fury of death, desiring no grace, no power, just Raven.

"I have something to show you." Astrid whispered into his palms. The purple glow coated them and the old tree bark, casting their silhouettes into the forest behind. "I found it in a high magistrate's office. They have stronger runes, so must we."

"Looks like I'll tolerate you better now." Sevar gave a slight smirk.

"Agreed." They grinned at one another. Sevar eyes widened at the sight of the banished rune book. "How did that come into your possession?" His fingers branched out. Hovering over the handwritten words, turning the pages, looking and adoring its craft. Rune of bravery, rune of the silence, a hidden selection of runes for a range of unworldly knowledge.

Each rune had its own description, the wording and pronunciation activation. The spell's originality and, most importantly, the cost of its uses were written in a thick warning below its symbol.

The book laid on the lush, sprouting blades of grass. Its shadows of deep purple slowly twirled around the green blades at its page's edges. Sevar pulled his small paunch out from his belt, pouring its powder into his palm.

"Are you sure?" Sevar looked back up from the bold purple glow.

"Yes, we need some new tricks. Give us the element of surprise." Astrid dipped his finger into Sevar's powder patch.

"How did you get so much rune powder?" His gut knew the answer, but he needed it out of his mouth.

"I worked for them once." He paused. "Only once. For Queen Atula. She wanted someone to sort out a rebel assassin coming for her head. She hired me through the clockwork network. I couldn't say no. She gifted me this full pouch of rune powder from her personal gardens, with many counts included." Sevar dipped his finger into the powder. "After that moment, ending that assassin's life. I knew I couldn't be a part of their legions, their movements."

"And Mistwood?"

Sevar choked vaguely on his saliva. "Mistwood, the second legion was tasked with seeing if a rebellion was growing in the settlement. King Dreaka used clockwork, hiring me to keep it contained." Sevar let out a big breath. "I saw them go into their homes, slaughtering all the men and the women.

Without question, without a click of remorse, all in the name of the Four." Sevar rubbed his beard. "The royals must have spread lies about me killing everyone, including the civilians, to manipulate perspectives against the rebellion."

"You stopped supporting them, trying to correct your path. That is faintly admirable." He investigated the book, drawing the symbol onto his biceps. "This rune should give us a boost." They looked down onto the rune of bravery. A rune for a burst of pure strength. Sevar copied his fingers into twirls as the powder burned through their hairs, their skin. Charring their smooth skin with old runic magic. They sat till dusk, reading through possible runes they could burn into their skin. How different runes' abilities could blend together, supporting their plans.

Astrid looked over to Sevar's raised sleeve. Half of a rune he didn't know peered out, showing a four-pointed star protected by swirls and sparks. "I've never seen that one before. It's not in this book either." He flicked through the pages again.

"It won't be. This rune was from Quarria. My mother gifted it as a family rune before she left years ago. Passed down to the whisperers in our bloodline. It's a rune of invisibility."

"Could that be used to get us in and out of the cities undetected?" Astrid's mind ran with possibilities for helping Pazima.

"Me and Raven tried, that's how he ended up in a cell. The invisibility takes you from our realm like a spirit between two breaths. With that great gift, it rips away at your sight."

He sighed quietly. "Damn, that sounds horrific." He looked back down at the runic book. "We have theses, at least."

They both stood up as Astrid whispered the book away. "The cost of this is going to hurt."

"Back up to the temple?" Sevar's neck strained upon his skyward glance, scanning over every crack on the cliff side.

"Let's go." Astrid replied, flicking a stone into the water stream.

# Chapter 32

### The Fifth Legion

### *Pazima*

Soldiers from the Royal Legion came knocking at Pazima's door the very next dawn, rushing her out of the castle by the order of King Dreaka. Everything she had on her packed into a worn backpack given to her by the kind maids. She didn't want anything from any of these people. The people that lounged on counts, spitting down at the lesser Eyldians.

She threw the uniform that was placed at her door that night into the backpack, alongside some rubbing paste, cleaning paste and anything else she made from the materials she snuck from the maids when they weren't looking.

Two royal legion officials traced her footsteps a couple paces behind her. Their freshly crafted leather boots squeaked against their steps, planting on the ruby red rugs.

Step after step, walking in silence through the never-ending hallways. The continuous patterns of red and white paints, their symbols slapped, carved into every archway, and self-righteous statues in each corner. King Dreak's soulless egoistic grin plastered over the entire castle, spying down on his people. His stamp of ownership over the ancient castle was like an animal marking its territory.

A hand gripped her shoulder tightly, forcing her to a stand-still. The left soldier pushed forward as he whispered into the stone gateway. Each rune lit up in a purple light. The power hummed, radiating, swirling into an image of Sun's Peak. The ancient granite bricks shined a dim red, displaying its age proudly throughout its structures.

The power pulsed a gush of energy, teasing her dark brunette coils. "Go." The soldier grunted. A command useless to her, as a forceful push accompanied the soldier's grunt. The hums completely urging her last night's meal to bob upon her throat. Every small strand of hair on her body stood firmly, pulled by the thrusting power.

Sun's Peak, a city of granite covering every piece of land, its foundations hung over the cliff's edge. Overseeing the deathly plunge into the stone spikes of Sun's Sea. The soldiers glanced, emotionless, watching her plant her feet into the staircase. Stepping down hundreds of steps, burning her feet into her leathers.

The grand descent to the city of Sun. The people dressed in floral patterned silk dresses, laughing and chatting between themselves. They flicked their counts with a pasted smile. Nothing but shadowing bliss.

Pazima turned her head, scanning back up the mountainous staircase. The Peak's Tower. An ancient building gripping to the cliff's stone. The foundations merging into the realm's natural materials. Building's spiralling up, envisioned and constructed by Nova the Conqueror over fourteen hundred years ago. The details of the conqueror's life were forged into the coloured shapes in the structure's panes and its pillars. The tower's archer points were coated in fresh orange copper plating. Workers built their temporary structures around the tower, replacing the plating at any evidence of corrosion.

She turned back to the cliff city. They narrow sideways across all the cliff edges, connecting to the towering structures. Many clung to the cliff's side, using the open space as their lounging balconies. All held by metal and stone, melding into the cliff's ancient foundations.

The entire city utilised the washed granite bricks. Buildings raised tall, housing the thousands of wealthy Eyldians. All basking in the sun's direct rays. She kept her shoulders up, directing her firm stance towards the walking lines of cadets, aspiring soldiers coming into training. Fuck. Worry climbed up her chest, begging to be seen. No, Pazima couldn't observe the urging emotion, she wouldn't. The information of the Four and its legions couldn't be the breaking point between loose and great victory. She would do anything, for the rebellion, for Moonsong, for her love.

Murmurs and side glances came from all sides of the streets. People holding their Young's hand, swinging a basket of fresh fruit in their other. A gentle push came from behind, shooting her head back into line. A tall woman with her hair tied up firmly stomped up beside Pazima, piercing her emotionless, hollow glance towards her. She refused to look back. Pazima shot her a glance to her side as the woman passed, observing the badges and symbols upon her uniform. She had to be important.

"You're welcome." The soldier behind whispered.

She didn't reply, rolling her eyes faintly.

-

The city of dense blocks of buildings. The ancient granite, washed by time, by the generations and the thousand years of change. People's love and grief frozen in stone. The noise of businesses, market roars, soldiers ordering their legions into line, and praying chants of the Nova. Eyldians dressed in dark ruby-red tunics, coated by long, smooth red robes. Shooting stars drawn and stained into the off-white cloaks.

"Nova is the divine one!"

"In him we trust!" They yelled.

-

The main cliff islands connected by ancient stone bridges, arching over the narrow Sun's Seas. Trade's Peak, Lonsai City, The Legion's Quarter, all attached, forming the first city of Eyldia. The ancient supporting building structures from the builders over a thousand years ago rotted and faded into the stone. Leaving eroded metals in the cliff, pointing to one of the seabed. Dried brown vines crusted into the creases between the side's stone indents.

They walked across the bridges, listening to their footsteps marching across the stone structure. They come to a small intersection island. A security point between the sections. The security soldiers scanned the new cadets, giving a respectful, understanding nod. They marched onwards onto the bridge to The Legion's Quarter. The Commanders kept to their sides, pushing people in line, forcing their stances into sync.

The smell of the horse stables attacked Pazima's nostrils, accompanying their groans. Dried shit left on the floor, radiating its horrid scent into the warm, gentle breeze.

The soldier from behind gasped. "That's disturbing."

"Indeed." She spoke quietly. They stopped suddenly, parting them into groups.

"You are the new Nova Fifth Legion." The woman yelled into the group.

"Now. Place your belongings in your new group homes. Return at the seventh bell." A Commander said with a calm, yet with filtered fury lingering in his throat.

-

They split the cadets into groups of fifteen Eyldians. She tossed her backpack onto the nearby bed, scanning the exits and how far each was from her position. Each step or attack she may utilise for many outcomes.

"Excited to get started?" The voice of the soldier that kept behind her now sat on the bed to her right.

"Oh, I'm elated." She calmed, holding her sarcastic tone deep in her throat.

"What's your name?" A young man, kissed with hues of orange, layering his ginger curls in beautiful hues of copper. He wore legion black with gold trim outlines, yet a green silk ribbon interlocked with his belt.

"I'm Pazima. And yours?" She peered up, looking into the young man's features. He looked so pure, an essence clean of brutality or bribery.

"Chip." He smiled. He laid his travel pack down, sliding it under his bed. "What made you choose to be in the legion?"

"I wanted to help our Majesties." She took a long breath, casting her voice across their group's home. "Be in the royal legion." Pazima lied through her teeth, crafting together a new backstory for her uses. How could she forge herself into their legion, spotting and pushing at their weak spots? "How about you?"

Chip smiled as he flopped onto his bed. The gush of wind flicked to Pazima. "I didn't really get a choice."

"Why?" she said.

He scanned the room, dialling his voice to be quiet enough the other cadets wouldn't hear him. "It's what's expected of me."

"Trying to make someone proud?" She pushed her question across with a sweet tone.

"Something like that." Chip's glance pulled away, cutting his reply short.

-

She held herself high, gleaming her unquestionable shiny presence to all the other trainees in her quarters. She had suggested talking as a group. Pulling the situation into her palms, faking a way to connect as a group with its new legion. They gathered, murmuring as they made their way through the far side archway into the common area. Two red tight back sofas patterned with four-pointed stars on its arms. The trainees sat, piling into the sofas, pushing the chairs around the wooden floor. The planks mixed by replacement pieces, mixing a range of shades of oak and whitewood planks.

"Where are you all from?" She started off.

Chip twirled one of the wooden chairs, sitting down, laying his arms onto the chair's back. She placed herself on the left of the fireplace, leaning with her arms folded comfortably. They spoke one by one, trying not to overlap their replies. Many locations were told with passion, Kresa, Lonsai, Drossor, Sreset, Rale.

"Quarria." Chip spoke.

She scanned Chip's expression. His lip pulled, forced to be natural. His eye contact peered to stay for moments at a time. Nothing more than a fleeting glance at each person around the common area.

"I'm from Hlinos." She spoke with confidence. "What do you think we'll do in training?" She spoke again. Their mumbles filled the lounge, some questioning the skills needed for them to pass through their cadet program.

Excitement gleamed through their faces. Some shot to their feet, praising their royal's names. Playful pushes branched the seated cadets, tossing their desires for Commandership, for the royal guard legion status, and for Nova.

"Nova shall see us take out the rebel filth." A cadet chanted out. His shaved short hair reflected the ember's light. "The outer settlements do nothing but plague our lands with violence and illness."

"Have you taken down any rebels?" She forged an expression of pure excitement.

"I've slaughtered many." The cadet grinned, running his hand through his short, shaved ink-black hair. "I saw two men, laughing, cuddling, planning their rebel movements outside of Drossor. Their blood soaked that camp by dusk." He spoke with pride, grinning proudly from ear to ear.

She looked across the sofas, examining each expression. Chip's head turned slightly, pulling his look to the fireplace. Pazima's gut burned at the horrific comments crashing against her ear, but she remained calm.

The room froze as the seventh bell rang through the Quarters.

-

Each group lined up in formation, tucking their arms behind their backs.

"First session. Partner up, Time to have your fellow soldier's sixth." A Commander yelled. His face was framed by his wrinkles.

Chip placed his hand on her shoulder, pushing to her eye line. "Partner?"

She flicked his arm off his shoulder. "Touch me and you'll lose a testicle." She pasted a mocking grin.

He copied her mocking grin. "My dearest apologies, captain."

The Commander stomped against the granite floor. "Shut your fucking mouth, cadet." He breathed down into Chip's dirty ginger curls. His words bellowed, spraying his saliva onto his brow.

She stood, freezing each muscle. She caught Chip's glance, warning him with a slight nod.

He smiled. "Yes, Commander." The legion stared at Chip.

The Commander curled his hand into a fist. "Are you mocking me, cadet?"

"No, Commander." Chip replied. The Commander stepped a pace away, laughing. The laugh echoed, dropping to a sudden halt. His knuckles launched, connecting to Chip's cheek, crumbling him into the polished granite. Punches of unfiltered rage launched, stamping onto Chip's skin.

Gasps layered the air. "Anyone else desires to disrespect me? Disrespect Nova's desires?" He walked away from Chip's groaning, folding his arms behind his back. "Nova formed the first Nova Legion to forge a better Eyldia. Will you do the same?"

"Yes, Commander Yorc!" The legion bellowed, including her.

"Partner up now." Commander Yorc's gritty voice echoed.

She Pulled at Chip's arm. "Come on, get up."

Chip climbed to a stable balance. Cuts and blood layered over his bruising face. His hand held his stomach, removing it with a painful groan. "Why are you helping me?"

"I thought you're my training partner?" She mocked.

"You're not my type. I have a thing for lone scholars. Man, woman, doesn't matter to me" He laughed away the pain, removing her supporting hand as they walked to the training arena.

"Please, I already have love." She smiled, thinking of her Astrid. The thoughts of him, she held it tight. She hoped he's surviving, desiring his safety as she hunted what they needed and fought her way home.

# Chapter 33

## Warning From Within

### *Raven*

Astrid, Sevar and Raven collected their minimal supplies together, calculating their food and their pack's weight. The sprouting vines grew down upon the sparring circle, swinging in the dawn's calm breeze. The blooming Moondwells weaved from the stalactites, pushing their small vibrant sea-blue petals, and releasing its delicate fresh tang of oranges into the temple.

Their pack's laid upon the obversion stone railing. "The blooming." Astrid picked a Moondwell from the side of the nearby pillar. "Pazima loves this season, the flowers coating the roofs, the fields, the valleys. She and I ran together through the Fellow's fields, chasing Moonfoxes and each other with sticks, pretending they were deadly weapons."

"Do you think you'll be okay? If she's in a cell" The icy breeze scratched his neck.

"She's very persuasive. If I was to barter, I would say she'll be putting herself deep into the mess." Astrid smiled for an instant. "Let's go."

They all threw their packs over their shoulders. Raven pulled his pack, trying not to drop it from the brute weight of his supplies. He had to pack extra healing tonics to support his progress. He also snuck some bandages and snacks he had never seen before.

His knees began to shake. "Let me please." Sevar pulled out a hand.

"Thank you." Raven looked up at Sevar's grin, placing his heavy pack strap into his palm.

Sevar pulled a dagger from his side. "I forgot to give you this."

His eyes swelled. "I lost the other when I was caught." Sevar placed the crow dagger into his palm. "It's yours. We'll find a replacement for the other."

He looked down at the crow's wing crossguard, feeling the scratches. The memories of fighting indented into his first weapon. "Thanks again."

Steps echoed against the stone staircase, luring him to turn. Lassea smiled, greeting him with a warming embrace, wrapping her arms around his torso. "Have this. From me." a black cloak enriched by a blue, rich fabric layering its interior. "I heard you gifted yours. Now I'm giving this to you."

A tear collected at the edge of his lid, gripping at his long eyelashes. He looked at her smile, thanking nature open to him. He didn't know what to say. Lassea helped him in the darkest time, keeping the cell walls from swallowing him whole.

She brushed her clean black curls from her shoulder. "You don't need to say anything. We helped each other." She hugged him again, whispered into his ear. "Keep your kindness, your empathy. It's rare." Lassea released her embrace.

She walked over to Sevar, hugging him in a motherly force. Her voice lowered, talking into her son's side. Nothing he could make out. "I will. I love you, mother." Sevar replied with blushed cheeks.

"I love you too. Now I'm going to make this Commander listen to my ideas" She walked back up the staircase.

Astrid laughed from the stone bench. "Goodluck, Lassea."

Raven wrapped the cloak around his body, flicking the hood over his messy, loose curls. Loose strands pop out, curling upon his left brow. "How does it look?" He asked.

"Looking alluringly mysterious." Sevar laughed to himself, raising his hand to his hair. Sevar's hand wiped the strands away with a layering glow in his eyes.

Raven dipped his hood, casting a shadow over his face. "Why thank you," He spoke, attempting the deepest voice he could muster.

He explored Sevar's sharp structure, his thick brows left with multiple little scars throughout. Sevar's dark brown eyes were solemn yet filled with a warm light. Sevar wrapped his right hand softly around his waist. "Does this scare you?"

He grinned. Sevar smiled back, cupping Raven's body into his. Raven wriggled out of Sevar's grip slightly. "We have work to do." He whispered upward.

-

The stones grated apart, letting the sun climb the temple walls. "Astrid." A woman called out from behind. They all turned, facing the robed woman. "Goodluck with finding her. Remember to keep calm." Her face turned faintly, facing him, scanning over his body with her vibrant dreamer-orange iris'. "The crow is here."

"Fuck, that's creepy." Raven murmured to Sevar.

"Damn right." Sevar whispered from behind.

"Could I have a chat with your brother?" She queried towards Astrid. Shook waved over Astrid, enlarging his glare.

"Raven, this is Fee. She's our strongest dreamer, she cared for me when I was a Young."

"Okay." Raven answered Fee.

They walked out through the temple's entrance, stepping onto the grass. Small stones placed on the ground led them up into the Moonsong's main campsite. A point of reflection for its people. Raven and Fee sat at the wooden stumps as Sevar and Astrid waited down the pathway.

"Young dreamer, how well are you with your abilities?" She asked.

His instincts tackled through his mind, but if Astrid trusted her, he could, too. "I struggle to control any of it. All the death and birth. All the possibilities. It all fades together most of the time. It's like I'm completely blind."

"Dreamers must ground themselves to our existence and understand what's true. Understanding the little things seen and unseen. Infinite possibilities within time, we must grip on what we love and who we are. Spot the errors within probabilities. Many are ripples of broken moments. Spot something that wouldn't belong in that moment, like a drop of snow in the brightening season."

"I'll try my best. Thank you, Fee. It's warming to share with a fellow dreamer." He smiled as he raised from the stump.

Her face refused to display emotion. "Raven, I must warn you. There's no turning back from this moment. Go and save Pazima, and it'll come with great sacrifice."

"What Sacrifice?" He walked closer to Fee. "I got a prophecy of a 'Crow's scream.' Is that what you've foreseen?"

"Many possibilities cloud over you. The crow that loses it all to gain his power upon the royal thrones."

"I don't desire the throne or its power. That is what I want to stop." Anger bubbled up in his throat.

"Be careful with your choices. A prophecy throughout dreamers is never what it seems. Listen to it." She walked ahead. "Good Luck, Crow. Take care of your twin." Her face slipped a slight raise of her top lip, walking back to the temple's path.

"What did Fee want?" Astrid and Sevar waited for answers.

"Oh, she gave me advice on my dreaming abilities. Tell me some ways to learn how to control it." He hated lying to them, but he knew nothing would stop Astrid, and if Sevar knew a warning waved over his life, the stress would've consumed him.

Sevar threw the travelling packs back over his broad shoulder. "You have a lot of training to do then. Let's get going."

Astrid looked at him, like he could see through his half-truths. "Are you certain that's all?"

He breathed slowly, forcing on his emotion, pulling it down as far as he could. Into the deepest shadows of his essence. "Yes. She's just very intense." Astrid's glare stayed for a moment, scanning over the intertwined emotions. They walked down the Fellow's edge, strolling through the pathways towards Hlinos and its separated seaport, Storm's Edge Port.

# Chapter 34

## Rocking The Boat

### *Astrid*

Astrid ran across the narrow walkways, kneeling, hidden by empty wooden barrels. Sevar nodded to him, giving the signal to copy Astrid. Raven glided silently across the docking's cobblestone path, as if his leather boots were coated in thick mythic feathers. They struggled through the narrow alleys between the storage buildings. They peered their eyes into Storm's Edge Port, their stripped oak foundations and painted shop fronts, supporting their old cobble second floors. Embers radiated into each room, coating the panes in a warm orange tint. The ships docked, yelling as they dropped their anchors, tossing their ropes to the dockers. Eyldian's dressed in brown trousers, coated in a range of drying mud and dirt. The ends flared by time, lacking any sewing repairs to the loose wet strands. Astrid looked over to the happy celebrations at his far right. People tumbled out of a petite red painted building front; a sign swung slightly in the calm breeze upon their heads. A bolt of lightning amateurly painted onto a sheet of metal.

"May the storm drop for us!" The cheering echoed across the wet docks.

Raven turned to the group. "The storm?"

"The never-ending storm. The Commander said the old ones cast a spell to split the north from the south. One last attempt to stop the siege." He whispered.

He turned his head from the cheering groups of Eyldian's. Shook waved over his face as two figures creeped through the alleyway behind them. Astrid looked back, pulling out a dagger from his thigh holster. Their features appeared slowly as the shadows slid down their figures.

He sighed, shock and worry waved. "Caelan, Daj, go back to Moonsong now." Astrid bit his tongue, gritting upon his command.

"We want to help you find Pazima." Caelan spoke as Daj signed to him in agreement, mirroring Caelan's words.

Sevar looked over Daj, scanning each sign she formed. "We could use a shifter."

"How did you know she's a shifter?" He spat out.

Sevar raised his hand, pointing over to Daj. "She just said she'll be a good support in the skies. That Pazima trained her specially in Spikehawk form."

"You know the signs?" Annoyance climbed his sharp features, tilting his head slightly at Sevar.

"My mother made me have a tutor when I was Young." Sevar replied, pulling away from the situation. Astrid forced his eyes not to roll at Sevar's knowledge of visual language, the useless bubbling anger, knowledge he doesn't know once more.

Caelan moved forward. "And you're my mentor. Where you go, I go." Caelan looked at Raven. "Now you're running off with an untrained stranger." He kept still, refusing to let the comment in.

"He is my blood." Astrid raised his voice slightly.

"We are more trained than him." Caelan flung his arms up, pointing to Raven. "A dreamer with no training. You may as well bring the Charr Young."

"Calm down, Caelan." Astrid weaved past Sevar. His thoughts of what to say flew over his mind, roaring commands into his face, yelling empty threats through his trainee's ears, yet the biggest thought in his mind was a memory. Pazima supported him as he cried, leaning against the healing arc's halls. She told him to understand. He placed his hands on Caelan's and Daj's shoulders. "You can come, but if I sense you're going to be in danger, I'll pull you out. I need you to listen to me and I'll listen to you too."

Caelan signed his words as he spoke. Daj nodded, signing a reply. "She said thank you"

"Caelan, I need to apologise for being an absent mentor. That'll change." Astrid's words dropped to a whisper, consumed with regret.

"Could you teach me your dagger throw?" Caelan's face faded back to his fair taupe skin, revealing his sapphire undertones.

Astrid choked on his laugh. "If you promise not to aim it at me."

One by one they weaved through the crowds of drunken sways, sticking their eyes to the wet cobbles, tracing their footsteps, carefully placing their bodies through the tumbling conversations. Scents of spiced ale lingered through the collecting groups of people, swirling the mix of clove, ginger, and frostcup extract into their noses. He licked his lip, tasting the layers of sweet and spicy flavourings. The frostcup extract lingered through the warmth of the orange flaring embers, the taste of sweetness running rich and soft like the rushing waters of Verglas Forest.

The cracks in the wooden foundations strained under the pressure, kneeling behind the supply crates on the edge of the docks. The sound of oceans current smacked their earlobes as they focused on the surrounding environment. Caelan angled his neck to the left, sending a visual note. Left of them. He peered his sight to the simmering chatter of the dock workers, three men in trousers moist at its fraying bottom hem and a hanging holster filled with tools and rope. Sat upon the timber frames shipment tied together by thick white ropes, wiping their muddied hands over the railings.

Daj pulled her eyes to the side with utter distaste, observing the docker's poor hygiene. Astrid laughed, knowing her dislike mirrored Pazima's. An old lingering feeling of shame punched his heart. He knew their relationship was strong, training every dawn, but he didn't notice how much she nurtured her students. He lifted his hand for Daj, pointing to the dock workers, followed by his hand falling in dramatic fashion, displaying an attempt to show a plan. She blinked slowly, grinning at the visual attempts.

Raven and Sevar climbed the boat's left side as commanded, following his unhinged plan. Daj and Caelan walked out from behind the barrels, swaying and mumbling across the narrow dock. He choked on his laugh, placing his hand over his mouth.

"Oh, to the stars, Nova is our one!" Caelan yelled in a mumbling manner. The dock workers squinted their brows, peering over to their unstable movements.

"Need assistance?" The dockers called out, placing their feet onto the dock.

"Oh, that's so sweet of you." Caelan replied. Daj closed her eyes, slumping into Caelan's shoulder.

The docker's walked over, cursing silently into the salty breeze.

"Thank you, Thank you." Caelan pleaded as he placed Daj into the tallest docker's hairy arms. Daj grinned as she placed herself between the docker's feet. Before they could notice the snaking movements, she pulled with full force. They fell backwards over the short railings. Caelan followed, throwing the other two dockers in haste. The splash engulfed their bellows, sucking them under the short and sharp ripples of water. The sound of merrymaking and slurping of the carless flock coated the echoing splashes.

Astrid looked over to Sevar, passing one nod, a signal to go. Raven and Sevar climbed the boat's side, slipping over onto the boat's deck. Surprised voice muffled, followed by brief thuds. He dashed over the docking. Daj and Caelan followed with their Moonsong formation training, keeping space behind Astrid, yet able to aid him in any assault.

"I told you the plan was definitely going to work." Astrid gloated, amused with a growing smile as he stepped upon the temporary boarding steps. He jumped down onto the deck, scanning the surroundings. The boat's sailings folded away; its rope tied around a metal point. Astrid placed his hand on Caelan's shoulder. "Caelan, the sails." The dockers yell from the waters below. Raven and Sevar lunged through the ship's lounge. The noises of dockers bellowed, following the crack of shattering glass.

Daj followed with a swagger in her step. Her mist slithered out of her nose, mouth and earlobes in small threads, ribboning, thickening into aquatic scales. Colours of red, green, and cyan, like the Fellow's gap, coated the mist's sprouting tentacle form. The struggle painted over her face as sweat dripped, swallowed by her pale red thick mist. The moulding oars' wood strained under her formidable grip. Scales faded, fluctuating through the mist, its hue consumed by the swirling clouds of red.

He knew she couldn't hold on to this form for long. Astrid had to get this boat going for the wind to take them upon its wing. He sprinted down the staircase, meeting Raven and Sevar as they all collected on deck. Caelan jumped, flinging the rope into the air.

"The dock workers have called the guards from their stations. We have minutes." Sevar spoke, looking out to the docking town.

"Caelan, support Daj." Astrid commanded.

Caelan ran out of sight. Astrid scanned the boat, guessing the time Daj would need to move the ship's brute weight. He and Sevar launched back to the dock's foundations, drawing their blades against the oncoming figures.

"King Alonn will have your head. "the guards claimed. A cloaked figure moved between the guards as their cloak overshadowed their features. The docks' floating embers shone down upon them, its light climbed over the figure, teasing their rosy-pink lips. A grin grew as they drew their blade. Sevar's face filled with anger, burning a boiling red.

"It's Raven's second crow dagger." Sevar spoke low towards Astrid. "Tauriea." Sevar's voice raised.

"I would love to have the other for my new collection." She pulled down her hood, brushing her smooth blonde hair to her back. "Is your frail little man aboard?"

"You'll never get to him." Sevar spat.

"Oh, but it was so fun last time." She raised the crow dagger into the air, aiming it towards Astrid. "Your brother." She looked back at Sevar, waving the dagger through the air. "Your lover." Her eyes sparkled. "His blade shall end your lives." She rubbed her boot into the dock's wood. "How poetic." Her last words hissed like a sudden attack, clamping their throats.

*"Stay up there. Support Daj and Caelan."* Astrid bellowed through the connection.

Tauriea launched at him, driving the dagger towards his torso. He swerved to the right, gripping her wrist, twisting and clamping his strength into her bone.

Teuriea groaned in pain. "Now, this is the introduction I was looking forward to." She smirked.

"What are you talking about?" He added more pressure to his grip, forcing her to drop the dagger.

"I'm the daughter of King Dreaka. You two are my brothers." She punched him in the gut in a swift jolt.

"Why are you after us?" He questioned while assisting Sevar in his lunges.

"Father has plans for this realm. I'm tasked with killing you for murdering my mother." The rage bellowed through her as she groaned and yelled into the air. Rain poured down, slapping their cheeks, filling every crease between their hilts, greasing their grips.

Whispers circled them; purple hues climbed the guards' swords. Sparks of energy, imbuement of power, magic twirling through their weaponry. Sevar whispered into his arm, shooting out a shield for them both. He pushed with pain-filled groans, causing the group of guards to tumble to the dock's floor.

"Aww." She teased. "Someone's been in the forbidden runes." She sliced against the shield in a screaming rage. "Naughty." She smashed again. "Naughty." Her bellowing through the nose of the splashing rain and the monstrous waves. "Boy!" She launched down with both hands around her sword, launching them across the dock. Their heads dangled over the edge of the dock's foundation.

"Daj says now!" Raven roared at him. Astrid looked at Sevar, nodding. Sevar could read him like a clean, open book. A story in simple words, the words of a warrior. The language they have in common. Follow his every move.

Sevar smiled, launching to his feet. He twirled his sword in his palm, slicing from right to left. Mist twirled suddenly through the rain's might, ribboning around the boat's base. The boat moved with haste, pushing out of the dock backwards.

Tauriea's face sunk, consumed by her fury, as she burst her mist towards him, wrapping around his ribs. The pressure, the pain burned, stabbing through every suggestion of escape.

Sevar lunged, throwing a dagger towards her heart. The mist reseeded, tying around the dagger. A moment of escape. They turned, running towards the bashing waves. The storming water clashed against the thick oak docks.

"I'll kill Pazima!" She screamed.

He didn't turn back, pushing his instinctive reaction of rage and fury down. He couldn't let her win by forcing the rage up from his depths. They dashed with the most speed they could, water splashing up from their mighty stomps.

She ran, screaming and cursing. "Do they know you worked for us!" She bellowed. They launched off the dock in one final push. Branching out their arms in a hopeful grace.

Their fingers gripped the edge of the turning boat, slipping against the wet wood as the water ran down their pores. Caelan flung his arm down, reaching for Sevar. Raven offered his hand, pushing his fingers to its limits. His stretching accompanied by groans. "You haven't got the strength." Astrid pleaded.

"I don't, but we have." Raven claimed. His arm reached out again. Astrid smiled, pushing his feet upon the wood, launching himself up, pulling off the side of the boat. Their fingers touched for a moment, but that's all they needed, a moment of gracing touch. The golden might flared out, wrapping around their arms. A boost of energy ran through them, tossing him upon the deck.

# Chapter 35

## Plain Sailing & Bashful Storms

### *Astrid*

Storm's Way rippled at the boat's side, an endless storm beaming through the seabed, breaking through the clouds. The storm's lightning crackled, filling the air with charred corals and scents of earth from the seabed's ancient minerals. The boat travelled in the wind's directions, keeping a compass in his right hand to keep due south-west.

The plan to travel with guidance from the rogue isles' shore-lines and make it to Rale. Dreaka's major seaport, the closest point to Sun's Peak.

Sevar climbed the stairs, meeting with him at the helm. "Why Rale? Wouldn't it be wise to stop in a village on the shore, outside of Rale?"

"You heard my murderous sister." The word sister, he choked upon the realisation. "She's seen Pazima, how she could kill her. She was also tasked with killing us—."

"So Pazima will be kept close." Sevar cut in.

"That's my theory." Astrid agreed. "How's Raven?"

"He's doing okay. He doesn't let much slip." He let out a low sigh.

Astrid looked to his side, looking to see Sevar's defeated expression. "He does seem caged since we left the temple. Maybe his mind hasn't left Jinos' torture, which would make anyone crack."

"Indeed." Sevar left the helm, stepping back into the warm quarters below.

–

Astrid's expression narrowed, watching Daj go through basic signs. He scribbled away, fighting against the sea's jolts upon the boat. She signed the same signal again, covering the answer on the old scrap paper.

"Night?" Astrid answered, narrowing his glance on Daj's signing. She smiled as she moved her hand away. She threw her thumbs up on a happy impulse.

Astrid signed back, mirroring the words he spoke. "I'm sorry."

She angled her head slightly, confusion pasted over her narrowing brows. Daj grabbed the paper in one swoop, writing – *You're Sorry?*

His smile slowly dropped as he grabbed the nearby quill. *Yes, I didn't take time to learn the only way you communicate with others. I should be setting an example for the rest of our people. Like Pazima does, and for that, I'm dearly sorry.*

Her eyes swelled as she read, letting the paper float to the old brown oak floor. She launched her arms around Astrid, tightening her lasting embrace. Astrid let the happiness paste over him as the stars flew in the sky's shades of blue, layered in hints of violet rippling through the realm.

He stared up, hoping Pazima was doing the same. Looking into the bright moon that binds them, through their path, their song, and their love.

–

Two rotations passed as they neared Drossor's northern border. He pondered about his brother's Young life, how he survived, and what he loved. The desire to learn more waved over him, watching the sun's edge dropped behind the sea's current, kissing the hues of blue and purple. Astrid knew the errors he made in Caelan's training, about how his problems overshadowed his responsibilities. To the moon, he promised, He'll do anything to fix his mistakes.

The moon's bright casting light shone upon the boat, casting the ship's silhouette onto the erupting waves. He walked down the deck, peering from the peak, breathing the salty air slowly, pausing his racing mind for a single breath.

Yelling raised through the lower level, peaking his worry, turning to the staircase. Astrid turned, jolted by a sudden crash to the left side of the ship, slamming him into the wet wood decking. The noise of commands erupted through the lower level, rising above the cracking and groans of the moist wood planks.

*"Are you all okay?"* Astrid shouted down through the rustic door.

*"There's a hole in the left wall, water's flooding in! we're coming up!"* Raven casted back, his voice choking on panic. The connection between them, tightened by the emotions, wrapping the pressure around their rustic, divine doorway.

Astrid jumped back onto his feet, placing his hand on his hilt, scanning the left side of the ship. A cold, monstrous roar echoed through the sea's crashing waves. An enormous wave peered at their side, ghostly like a creature of pure mist. The wave. It wasn't a wave, standing still in the storming waves. Breaking through the waves as if it was a mere pond. The moonlight gleamed down upon its large claws, as its hands could cup the boat in one mighty grip. Some ancient songs called it the Sea Phantom, remaining unseen and untold in most Eyldian stories.

"Fuck." Astrid muttered.

It was a sea mythic of godly proportions, towering, bigger than most ships, folding its scaly fingers over their ship. A mythic scream rippled across the sea's current, throwing Astrid off his feet, dropping to the ship's edge, holding upon the railing once more. The Sea Phantom's claws, raised into the air, slamming down in one mighty cry, slicing the ship into two, as if the wood had been a blade of fresh grass.

The screams of his friends, his trainee, his brother. All engulfed by the water's current.

# Chapter 36

You Have a Chip on Your Shoulder

*Pazima*

The strings tightened by her calm strength, letting the arrow glide through the air, slicing the idle breeze. The sharp tip of the arrow cut through the wheat and the yellow fabric bullseye.

Chip held in his laugh as the Commander of the Fifth legion glared down from the observing platform on their left, dipping his dry quill into a small container of ink. Writing away, darting his piercing glare from each soldier and their display of their archery abilities.

"Damn, how are you a cadet?" Chip tried to whisper.

"From bad luck." She replied as her last arrow sliced through her previous shot.

The other cadet's bottom lips dropped slightly, looking over at her professional aim.

"Not possible. You're a fraud." A cadet grunted at her right side.

"Have a long walk off the Trade's Peak cliff, Kelee." Chip tensed, flinging his eye to the side.

Kelee walked to Chip, towering over him. His thin lip curled. "Your father's fortune won't protect you here." His words laced in a venomous tone.

She turned, grabbing Kelee by his lower arm, twisting it to his back. He choked on the pain. "Don't be an arse." She whispered.

Kelee pushed his arm out of her grip, rapidly hooking his right fist into her stomach. "I hear the Commanders whisper about you. King Dreaka sent you here. You won't take my spot in the royal legion. Dirty Moonsinger."

"Back to your spots!" The Commander yelled. Pazima pulled herself straight, pushing down the tender pain that waved through her ribs, drawing her lips in, forcing a smile. "Yes, Commander."

-

"Is it correct, you're a Moonsinger?" Chip spoke quietly as they walked into the lounge area. No other trainee in sight.

"Yes, I am. Kelee must have noticed my moon mark somehow." She stated as she lifted her thick coils, revealing the small moon inked behind her left ear. Pazima scanned the room as they sat. They knew they could meet in the common area at mealtime, keeping in mind the other trainees would stalk around the higher ranks, displaying their knowledge and abilities as their assets, pleading to get referenced for the other four legion ranks. Most official soldier's dream of building up to the First Legion, to serve close to the wealth, and their power. To hold status upon their Nova blades.

"What are you really doing here?" Chip's voice slid into a serious tone, one that was rare for the overzealous man.

"What are you doing here?" She copied his question, scanning over his widened expression.

Chip murmured, coughing out his words. "To be a soldier."

"You're lying, you hate it here" Pazima raised to her feet, followed by her stone-cold tone. "The loathing for these people. It's written over your face in bold vibrance, Chip."

He shook his head. Pazima raised her right brow, staring through his bright-red expressions. "I do hate it here." Chip spat out quietly.

"I know. Here for your father. To make him proud?" She asked calmly.

"No. He forced me. I pleaded not to" Chip wiped a tear from his burning-red cheek. "I wanted to be a writer. He said his legacy won't be stained by an idle pixie's way. Said I had to be strong, brutal and haste to the mark."

"You don't need to do what he says. Be who you are." She questioned for a moment, weighing the undeniable risks of placing her plans into another's grip. "I'm the next leader of Moonsong. The rebellion is coming from every corner of the realm. Join me. You won't need to fight if you wish. You can work as a man of knowledge, a tutor, a writer. It doesn't matter if you follow a different path. We all must have peace from the Nova's path and the Four."

Chip smiled with the same innocence, the same hope he had spread over him when they met many rotations ago. "I don't know what way I walk." He told her, ripping any mask he had left. "Why help me?"

"Because you're kind and full of hope. We need plenty of that for the horrors that will follow." She smiled back, placing her hand on Chip's shoulder. "And you're my friend now. I look out for my friends."

"Thank you." His words turned to mere whispers.

She raised to her feet, checking the room and its doorways once more. She knew anyone could lurk in the shadows of these steads. "Why is that bastard Kelee on our backs? Do you know anything about him?" She asked.

"I heard about him and another woman from a different group quarter. It's not good." Chip swallowed. "He thinks anything he wants must be owed to him."

She paced the common room as Chip spoke what he knew. The whispers of his brutally. "The Commanders don't care about his actions."

"What are we looking for?" He raised from the sofa. "What's the plan, cap?" He flicked a loose ginger curl from his thin nose.

Pazima smirked, roping an idea in her mind. "Have any experience being a thief?"

# Chapter 37

## Crashed, Smashed & Bruised

### *Raven*

The deep, vast blue hue bashed against Raven's skull. Wave after wave, its current pulled him with little resistance. Nothing but the hues of deep blue and cyan washing over his mind. No messages bounced between the alignment, Absent of words, alone with water flooding through the ancient rustic doorway. The feeling of sorrow and a soaring pain washed through like a message written into stone with nails and animalistic strength. A thread of hope carved into the stone's structure.

The currents slowed; his body burned from within, dropping into a sea of orange hues, swirling, choking him. Raven's lungs stained, leaving go of his final breath. His vision blurred, spotting the figures of his friends dropping through the sea of orange, like a void of never-ending fire. Burning, filled with screams, of love's death. His ember of life, bursting

The piercing cold soaked in through every pore, the feeling of emptiness creeping through, clinging on. He thought the resolution of blood would keep the darkness caged, but it remained. He hadn't accepted the truth, the gift and the prophecy that tied around his thin neck.

A silent scream bellowed through the water, from the golden power under his skin, remembering the last conversation he had aboard the ship.

An argument, his last regret.

---

*"Are you okay?" Sevar knocked, opening the ajar door.*

*"Yes. I'm okay." Raven pulled at his travel pack.*

*"I can tell you're lying. You look to your right when you lie."*

*"The feeling, the never-ending chill. It keeps brushing against me. Reminding me of what I felt." Raven struggled to look at his shirtless body as he changed into clean clothing.*

*"The training should help you." Sevar stood behind him, softly reaching out.*

*"Why do you and Astrid think training will be the catalyst?" He turned around, facing Sevar, lowering Sevar's inviting gesture. "I only desire to train, so I'm no longer physically disadvantaged. It won't help my mind. I tried in that cell. The feeling never left. Always bashing upon me."*

*"I'm trying to help in the only way I know." He raised his hand, trying to cup his cheek.*

*Raven held it away. "How can you desire this?" He looked down at his bony torso. The withering of his horrific experiences still weighed, scarring his mass.*

*Sevar opened his mouth to talk, stopped by the sudden smash against the left side of the ship.*

*"Are you all okay?" Astrid shouted down through the rustic door.*

*"There's a hole in the left wall, water's flooding in! we're coming up!" Raven casted back, his voice choking on panic. The connection between them drowned by the emotions, wrapping the pressure around their rustic, divine doorway.*

*Sevar grabbed him, pulling against the rushing water. "Listen to me, Crow, you're bea—" All words cut thin by water and screams, slamming Raven to the abyss of the dark sea.*

The blues consumed by the abyss of black, empty of light or hope. A sudden grip pulled at him, pinching his skin. Divine whistles unknown to his knowledge waved through the currents. Communication through their soft voices. A pressure pushed against his ribs, pulling the water out of his system, drop by drop the whistles laced each droplet, dragging it up his throat.

Light crashed through the darkness, begging him to wake. His eyes-lids struggled to peel open, dragging his view upon unfamiliar lands. Fading reds and browns, swaying in the elements.

Coldness clawed, pulling from his lower half, submerged. Water crashed up his tunic, washing away any blood from the crashing impact. Mud and seaweeds spread over his pale, bony body. Raven shook from the bitter cold, hoping the warm, brightening season would grace his shivering frame.

Little handprints pressed into his bruised skin. The whistling kept creeping in the corners of his view. Sparkling hues of blue and red flying through the blooming trees.

Raven glared over the limited dry land, nothing except the water reflecting the red trees' sways. He clawed his way to a stable footing. A sharp pain shot through him from his thigh. A small, sharp piece of splintered wood pointing through his torn trousers.

"Astrid—Daj!" a worried voice echoed through the marshland.

A similar voice, a Young, lanced in worry. – Caelan.

Raven peered to his left. "Caelan, are you hurt?" He called back, struggling his way through the new wet mud. His leather boots sank slowly through each step.

"I'm alive." Caelan yelled. The breeze carried the whistles, swirling around them as they closed the gap between them. "Have you seen anyone else?" Caelan asked.

Raven spoke through his racing breath, "No... No. You?"

"Likewise." Caelan sighed. "They'll be around here."

"The waters, It felt like magic, like something dragged us to land."

"Or someone. It's the Red Marshland." Caelan's voice quivered slightly. Caelan's worried glance forced Raven to focus on his blurring, narrow view. The blue waters merging into smooth pale red.

They supported one another's steps, slowly walking, slipping in the marsh's calm waters. "Pazima had me study with Daj, making us learn about creatures and their locations. The Red Marshland contains many tales." Caelan scanned the waters, watching the rippling movements. "Keep your eyes on everything, even if it's the tiniest and the most insufficient, anything could live in the waters." Caelan pushed Raven up through the mud roughly. "If I let Keep's special brother die, he would never train me." Caelan scoffed, layering into the airs hovering whistles.

-

Whistles gained volume, roaming through the treelines. They walked to the broken, muddy shoreline that tangled into the marshland, scanning over for any washed-up bodies.

"Daj!" Caelan called out. He ran towards her as small balls of light hovered over her body. "Who are you?" Caelan questioned. The whistles flew off into the treeline, jolting with speed behind any nearby bundles of lush, red leaves. Whistling between the balls of light. Caelan held Daj, rocking her back to reality.

"We won't hurt you." Raven called out. He reached out his arm as an inviting gesture. A single ball of light floated down, coming into focus. A figure layering in beautiful, glowing hues, small as a quill. Its skin glowing a vibrant crimson tone. Fine hairs twirled, forming the shape of a small mushroom upon their heads, styled effortlessly. Its greeting smile forced upon its round face. Twirls of blue and red ribboned through its divine crystallised wings. Its pointy toes hovered upon Raven's smooth palm, whistling towards his dripping face. "Is the whistling your way of communication?" Raven asked calmly.

It floated up towards his face, its features filled with purity and innocence yet consumed by worry. "It's okay. You can trust me." Its glowing hand warmed his cheek, its light spread over his face in a moment of red tints, soaking into his skin.

"Hello, Aligner." The creature spoke.

He shook slightly. "How can I understand you?"

Calean peered up, confused by his sudden reply to the whistles. "Raven?"

"We are Pixies. You are connected to us all." The other Pixies floated down towards Caelan and Daj. "Let us support your friends. We are The Overseers. Tasked by Unsa to serve and support." They spoke in unison.

"Caelan, they're friendly. They saved us." Their light twirled through them as one, hovering over Daj, forcing her to jolt to life.

"Aligner. The crack between the planes. It whispers to us all in our dreams. You must stop him. We gift you another chance. Find your friends." They faded away into the treeline.

The whistles carried from his left as a couple of bags floated by pale gold light hovered towards the shore. "This is yours." They pointed to the torn, wet travel bags.

"Thank you." He breathed.

Leaves rustled, steps creeping over in hesitation. Little groans layering the shore. Raven peered over the marshland, pointy muddy hats wandering through the marsh followed by a wave of brassy voices.

# Chapter 38

## Warriors In New Troubled Waters

### *Astrid*

Astrid launched up, pushing against wrapping vines, coughing on the red waters, gasping for fresh air in new lands. His worry weighed upon him as he scanned the area. Thick trees coated in red leaves. Drag marks leading towards him. The water rippled, gliding smooth creases in the tree's reflections.

"Fuck." He muttered towards the water, glaring into his murky reflection.

A sudden force gripped his ankle, piercing its needle-thin fangs into his skin, scraping against his ankle. Astrid forced a sharp inhale. The pain shot through his senses, overwhelming his waterlogged ears. The noise of his groans muffled by the pressure of the muddy, red waters. He struggled to keep his lips clamped, the taste of dirt and sludge slid against his lips, dragging up his features. Roaming lone sticks jerked through the sudden force, prying upon his skin.

The panic followed the pressure of the murky water, pressing its overwhelming grip against his skull. Throbbing at his stretching last thread of air. Astrid slapped his weigh-strapped knifes, struggling to undo its grips. His lungs itched, filling with a burning sensation. He struggled at the thinning quality of his breath, begging for it to last as he gripped his holster, ripping the leather grip from its stitching.

Its force stopped, followed by a hollow chuckle. A gliding force sliced through the water like glowing metal. Its scales jolted a charring pain against his side. The small knife held in his weakened grip, struggling to strike in the right direction. The thick dirt clouded the water's rippling translucence.

The chuckle gained strength, swirled from left to right. Playing, teasing him, taunting their next meal. Its warm breath slid through the gaps in its teeth, highlighting the murky water in a scent of rotting aquatic life. Its teeth rubbed against his cheek, but a sudden groan filled the water. Blood stained the water around him as a force pulled at his tunic.

—

"Can you talk to him through your gold thing?" Sevar pleaded as he wiped the creature's blood off his dagger, dropping them both into the mud, littered with red, thick vines.

"How did you know I was down there?" Astrid grasped for air.

Sevar sighed. "I've been here before. The Red Marshland." He looked through the thick tree lines of red leaves and lurking lights. "Home of most creatures from the mythic realm. At least that's the story. The Four tasked us to trace the borders, ensure the creatures know to keep to the marshland. If they wanted to live." Sevar's lips drawn down slightly. "That creature was a Lashra. Evil thing that only craves blood. Luckily, most of the species aren't hostile."

Astrid pulled his knife from the mud, drawing it upon Sevar's neck. The mud dripping down the small blade, down Sevar's bruised skin. "You would kill innocent creatures without their homeland and sleep comfortably?" He asked.

"No, I didn't sleep, till Raven." Sevar's words laced in a restrained scuff. "Now we have lost them all again." Sevar's deep tone raised, veins popping out, pulsing against Astrid's blade.

"I don't know what path to follow anymore." His voice dropped to a sudden whisper. "I regret more than you know."

Astrid investigated Sevar's strained features. "Good. Anything other royal missions you have in your pocket?"

"No, Astrid, not after Mistwood." Sevar spoke with a clear hatred layering on his tongue.

Astrid lowered his muddied knife. "That's a good start." He climbed to his feet, offering a supportive hand. "Time for us both to be better in this damned realm." Astrid let his smirk peer for a moment.

Sevar accepted his offer, lifting to the lush red treeline.

-

Branches rocking in the warm air as playful groans and whistles swirled through the tree line.

"No reply is coming through. It feels blurred. Like his focused—." He rubbed his forehead. "He's alive, that's a comfort."

"We'll find them. They must have washed up at shore or deeper within like you and I." Sevar replied. Hats of old wore-out leather popped out of the treeline, jumping back into the water.

"Did you see that?" Astrid popped out, jumping back slightly.

Sevar glared over. "No." He replied bluntly.

"Don't lie. It was a floating hat" He spat out, scanning the red water's soft reflections.

"Did that thing impel your skull?" Sevar grinned with amusement.

Murmurs brushed through the warm air, sliding across the puddles of murky waters. Piles of mud left with scaley imprints. The whistles carried through the moist breeze. "I'm not unhinging." Astrid stared through the marsh. "Hear that?" He punched Sevar's arm lightly.

"Fuck off." Sevar spat out, peering through the never-ending lakes and marshland.

"Eyldians" A high pitched voice hesitantly spoke.

"Roam in our home without a swear-by?" Their voices carried on top of the water, growing in mass.

Sevar pulled at his holster, drawing his left dagger. "We don't aim to harm."

Blunt thuds creeped up the trees, following sudden clicks of drawing weaponry. "Crossbows ready!" Another high-pitched voice echoed towards them.

"Don't try it." Astrid warned as his fingertips warmed with wrapping gold twirls. He lowered his bottom lip, readying his whispers. The unknown creatures were seemingly another mythic threat.

The blunt thuds dropped to a stunned low chatter. They circled in the mud in front of them, murmuring, shouting, shushing, and slapping one another.

"Okay I may be crazy." He turned slightly, whispering to Sevar. "are they—"

"Slapping each other? Indeed, Astrid, they are." Sevar muttered back.

"Gold." Their chants grew, forming a line of short humanoid creatures. They let their ears flop slightly upon their sides, fixing their pointy muddied hats made of old abandoned fabrics. The colour, taken by duration and wear, fixed its positioning with an outlandish pride. "Gold" They ran towards them, kicking mud from their thick metal boots.

"Gold is back to save the Kinling!"

"Balance may be restored." A Young Kinling stepped towards her side, circling, sniffing Astrid's ripped leathers from a safe distance. She lifted her large goggles, moving it to support her thick, crimson curls. The hues of pale red and pink mixing throughout her textured features. Budding pink cheeks matching her fingertips, like a natural warm glow.

Astrid kept his hand on his hilt, scanning over her wondering stance.

All the Kinling shared a glowing innocence, like purity itself kissed their blossoming pink cheekbones. Textured, gritty skin with smooth round faces.

"Are you the last?" The Kinling asked while pulling out a glass ball out of a patched satchel. She stared through the glass, spinning it in her palm. "This tells all, shown and un-shown." Gold and purple twirls ribboned together within the glass ball, shining in a bright raging light.

"There are more. There is hope!" She called out to the other Kinling. She turned back, hugging him in a tight, squeezing embrace. Her goggles punched into Astrid's stomach, causing him to jolt, biting his tongue with a painful groan. "I'm Myx, but you can call me Myxi." She jumped to his back, pushing him forward through the sloppy marshland.

"You have supporters." Sevar glared down at Myx. "Myxi, have you seen any other Eyldians along the shore?"

She pushed Astrid forward, glaring to her side, towards Se-var. "It's Myx to you." She pulled up her stained orange sleeves. "The shore is Lashra territory. We only came close enough to their territory because of the rebirthing."

"Rebirthing?" Astrid questioned lightly, while letting Myx guide him forward. The Kinling group pushed forward, chopping away the overgrowing vines and bushes of thick red leaves, forging a new path.

"We Kinling don't birth from our bodies like your species. We bury our dead and Unsa supports our rebirth." The elder Kinling moved slowly, supported by an ancient red staff. Roots wrapped it and the glass ball that laid on top, held together by blends of ropes and scrap metals.

"Who's Unsa?" Sevar asked calmly.

Myxi's sharp glare punched towards Sevar. Astrid held in his chuckle, watching Sevar's struggle for answers. "Magic them-selves. Have you not heard the story of Unsa and their sacrifice to us all? Even you."

Astrid squinted his eyes. "You're saying a divine entity from your realm is all magic itself. All that runs through our veins, in our blood?" He questioned.

"It's the truth!" Myx pleaded from his back.

Deeper into the marshland, the trees grew thicker, blocking the outside glares. The sudden light of warm orange bounced off their skin. "Welcome to the Dwelling." Myx's voice filled with excitement, jumping forward. She shouted down the pathway towards the interconnected buildings.

The Dwelling, full of hollowed out trees, moulded with mud, and stripped redwood, forming natural forming homes. Leaves floated through the air, dropping continuously throughout The Dwelling, followed by whistles of flashing red and blues through the thick tree branches.

All the hollowed tree homes circled the huge central tree, forging paths around its natural root system. Many trees grew up, branching like hills of wood and leaves. This tree stood ancient and proud, supporting the mythical creatures of another land when they needed it most.

"How did you make the marshland into this?" He asked with pure curiosity.

The elder Kinling stood by his side. "Our ancestors collected all the other peaceful creatures to help create this settlement. For all of us to be safe from your royals." He frowned. "We used to live as one before your royals decided we were lesser."

"I didn't know." Astrid spoke with shared emotion.

"There's much that is hidden." The elder walked on, directing himself to Myx. "How is he?"

Realisation slapped over Myx's cheeks. The hue of pink brightening in the warm orange glow. "His at peace, there's not long left."

"Go say your farewells." The elder adviced Myx softly.

Myx waited down the redwood bark steps. Astrid followed her, keeping Sevar to his side with a simple nod of agreement. Stick at each other's sixth. "They don't seem to like you."

Sevar rolled his eyes, letting a small chuckle through his lips. "You're funny."

Myx glared at Sevar. "I guess I'll let you come with us."

"Why thank you." Sevar snuffed.

"Be nice." Astrid choked on a small chuckle, looking to Myx's excited jolts. "We need to find our friends and then get to the Dreaka continent. Could you guide us in the right direction, Myxi?"

Myx pulled out a large map, bigger than her whole body, letting it roll onto the dry mud and bark ground. Myx dropped to her knees, digging her hand into the satchel elbow deep. "I know I have a one somewhere." She groaned, slapping paper and bottles to the other side of her large satchel. She raised a thick stick in pride, her brows tightened. "Oh. Pixies!" She yelled into the dense tree line. Tiny lights of red and blue floated down upon their heads. Their whistles grew louder, replying to Myx's request, circling her in a warm glow.

The light sprinkled a vibrant red dust down onto the stick she held between her fingers. "Thank you." Myx softly smiled.

"Gifting a stick?" Sevar scuffed.

Myx's glare cut to Astrid. "You travel with this, clot?"

Astrid choked on his shock, coughing on his sudden laugther. "No my choice, my brother loves hi—"

"No he doesn't." Sevar spat out, glowing a bold red tint.

"Mhm." Astrid smirked, looking back to Myx. "What's the stick for?"

"The pixies love the sap from trees on Dreaka's border with the Red Marsh, I explore out sometimes to gain favours." She held the stick in the warm air.

A small creature, flapping its mirror-like wings. No words, no whistles. Only greeting him with a welcoming stare. Its little fingers reaching out towards his face. Its fingers placing itself onto Astrid's cheek. "Another."

"You found Raven?" Sevar shot the question.

Astrid held his glare to the hovering pixie. "What of Daj and Caelan?"

"He is here, with your friends." The pixie smiled widely. "Apologies. We told him to take time learning his dreams. While we find you."

"You understand the whistling?" Sevar squinted.

"Yes." He looked down back to Myx and her muddied map. "Which way is safest?"

"You could go back through the Lashra territory or go south along the southern border, which is Howler territory." She shot up to her feet, rolling her map up hastily, ramming it into her large satchel. "I'll take you after the rebirth. Follow, follow." She ran down the roots, jumping through the pathways.

"What's a Howler?" Sevar yelled. She ignored Sevar's question, running through the other Kinling.

They sped up their pace, struggling to keep up with her rogue jolts from the side path to narrow parts between homes. The whole settlement, covered by red and orange light, protected by the thick tree branches and moulded leaves. An ancient tree, tolerant of time and endurance. The bright zooming lights whistling across their ears, darting through the pathways.

Willow trees melded into one, doors and windows left open, letting its fresh scents leak into the trotted paths, crafted by time and redwood bark. Foxes with two long tails spinning, flopping its fur against the dry mud. "Why would they throw all these creatures away?" He spoke in a low tone to Sevar.

"I don't know. No one ever spoke about it." Sevar replied. "Word in Clockwork says King Dreaka forced Queen Atula to let go of all the mythics, pushing them here."

"Other there" Myx came to a sudden stop at an ajar orange door with a small circle window with its red coating slightly flaking away.

Myx entered, slowing her shoulders step by step, entering a living area filled with polished relics placed around the table and sofa. "My grandfather is in there." Astrid ducked, dodging the low door frame.

They walked slowly to an elder's bedroom, struggling to let the air fill his lungs. "Myxi, come." The elder man coughed a thick orange fluid. Myx grabbed a cloth from the bedside draw, gently wiping the elder's pasty red chin.

"Grandfather." Myx's voice quivered. "It's nearly time to go." Astrid looked over to Sevar, communicating through their glances. Sevar stepped out, closing the door softly.

The elder's hand shook, placing it into Myx's. "You'll be okay without this silly old man."

"Shush." Myx wiped his brow. "I love you."

"I love you." He breathed, coughing lightly, closing his eyes softly. His head slanted against his plumbed pillows.

Myx sobbed, lifting the spare blanket over his head, tucking it under his body. "Help me carry him." She mumbled.

# Chapter 39

## The Wonders of Rebirth
*Astrid*

Myx walked behind as he carried her grandfather's body, carefully keeping his balance, step by step up the spiral staircase made of wood, edges wrapped in stripped bark. The Pixies whistled, singing in an ancient language, following and waiting for the wonder of the rebirthing to occur upon them all.

"May he grace the soil and embrace the ancestors." Kinling branched out from their arms, hovering their palms over the leaf tea-stained blanket.

They joined behind Myx, climbing the ascending staircase. Collecting as one in soft silence, holding hands in pairs. Allowing the pixies songs to brace the warm air. "The soil may take; the soil may give." Their words spread out long with unison, respecting their dead, the grandfather, the father, the son. The Kinling that may gift their essence into the realm, to Unsa, so they may gain new life.

Astrid peered up from his concentration, looking through the Kinling, all on both knees on top of personalised, worn-down blankets. All patterned individuality, all with different symbols, colours and sizes.

Myx walked ahead with haste and purpose, struggling to push the fabric out of her satchel. She flapped it out, cleaning the dust off in one strong thrust. Myx looked at Astrid, pointing to her grandfather's rebirth spot. He looked over at her quivering finger, placing his eyes upon a pre-dug grave. A field of dead with cleaned stone placed at their feet.

Astrid placed him down slowly, stepping back without a word.

Two elders came up the spiralling steps, entering the enclosed field of dead. Shadows of black and hues of red coating the fields of marsh. Bushes of branches, leaves, mud, and scraps of sharp metal all piled together to create boundaries to their settlement where the trees' natural root system couldn't protect them. They walked, nodding to each Kinling in their path. "Another rotation blessed with Rebirth!" The Kinling cast their voices, reaching Myx.

Astrid looked up slowly, peering through the groups of Kinling. The golden glow teased through his veins, highlighting a brightening hue in his palm. *"Raven? You here?"*

*"To your east."* Astrid swung his view point east. Raven nodded towards him. He nodded back, thanking him for saving his trainee, Pazima's trainee. Relief surged, layering in guilt. Uncountable number of mythical creatures, abandoned, tortured to a home unknown to them. Astrid scuffed, clenching his fist within his leather jacket.

Myx grabbed a patch out of her satchel and a needle. "This marks the rotation in which Jez, third of his name, now offers himself and his name back into the soil. To Unsa, to give to another." Myx pushed the needle through the blanket, slowly sewing the patch into the blanket, letting out a quivering sob. An elder popped open a vial of blood, pouring it into his hands. "The sign of Unsa. We gift you the blood of whom is now yours." The elder pleaded as he traced a circle around the grave.

"Lower him to Unsa." Myx commanded. Four partners of Kinling came to Myx's side, placing their blood vials in their own ancient wooden case on top of Jez's body.

"May he gift you." Myx whispered to the partners. A line formed naturally, each taking a moment sprinkling dirt in their own respects to Jez.

"May he rest with Unsa." Sevar muttered to his left. Astrid glanced at Sevar. Could he trust him, truthfully, with the Alignment power, with their mission, with everything he did?

All the Kinling dropped to their knees. "May you rest."

"Unsa will keep you safe." Their voices collected, casting through the dense marshland. The words rippling and bouncing across the muddied waters. One last chant.

No words echoed through the marshland, all dropping to their blankets.

Silence.

The whole settlement paused, respecting their dead, to the Rebirthing, to Unsa.

Every Kinling drawn their view to their knees. Muttering words to their divine entity. He followed their movements the best he could, mirroring Myx in her grief. His thoughts ran through his thoughts. The loss, the memories that remain hollow within their connection. Pazima remaining locked in the Four's grasp.

The ground quaked, but the trees refused to shift. The leaves clamped themselves to the branches as the quaking vibrations ran through the soil. Red light broke through the soil, following the cries of Kinling. The cries of hope, for Unsa, ripping through Jez's grave edge.

The elder muttered, "We are gifted once again."

The soil flicked up as hands broke through the blighting red light. The Kinling casted their voices to the hands, pleading for them to climb through the ripping soil. Muffled cries broke through in a sudden thrust. Laying two baby Kinling's in the middle of the blood circle.

"Two are gifted!" Myx spat out in a jolt of joy, climbing to her footing, gripping the soil. The hopeful partners sobbed, following Myx to the babies' cries.

"Thank you. Myx Second, for your support." They sobbed, bringing Myx into their embrace.

Myx's pale red lips layered in her tears. "Welcome to the Dwelling, Jez Fourth and Fifth of the name."

# Chapter 40

## Harsh Marshland & What Lives Within

### *Raven*

The blanket slipped down Sevar's broad torso. His muscles coated in a small layer of sweat, displaying the struggle of the dense marshland this settlement held firm. Raven slipped out, gracing the old redwood floorboards. Even a sudden jolt of his toes would cause the wooden boards to groan.

The tiny rooms made for the Kinling and their smaller structures. He held down his giggle as he glanced at Sevar's feet branching over the bed frame. The curiosity broke through, teasing him to look at every detail. The curving of stripping the marshland's ancient wood. Details drawn into the grooves, creating symbols and tales as one. Of Unsa and their loved ones within each room. The colours of red and gold mimicked over the symbols and their architecture. An odd mix of brown and yellow petals and minerals, mixing to make an earthly gold detailing.

He walked across the small room, sitting at its lone work desk. Humming, absorbing the warm orange embers across his cheek. His gaze caught upon a narrow mirror that leaned against the wardrobe. The reflective glass held tight by sticks and rope withered by time and humidity.

The remains of the meal from the previous dusk dropped through his stomach, glancing at his slender body. A reflection he didn't adore, absent of any bulked definition.

"This is me." He muttered. His words weaved into a slow sigh, followed by a sudden wrapping pressure around his chest. Sevar placed his head on his shoulder, sharing his warmth.

"Being creepy comes with being a mercenary?" He teased through the warming embrace.

"Definitely." Sevar's calm breath spread across his shoulder, teased to his neck. "I'm sorry about upsetting you, on the ship." Sevar spoke, raising up from his shoulder.

"It's okay, it's my issue. I need to own it now." He smiled into the mirror, looking into Sevar's features. "Does it bother you?" He forced out the dreaded query. The fear threatened to buckle his ankles.

A scoffed with a full grin. "You're the Moon and the stars itself." Sevar pulled him in tight, "cunning and full of light." Raven turned in Sevar's arms, facing upward into his sharp beard line. "I'm with you because you're the only guy that would punch and jump me to the floor. That was alluring." Sevar let out a deep laugh.

"I'll do it again." He laughed, raising a tease of gold through his veins. Raven raced, jumping back onto the small bed, wrapping himself with the thin blanket.

Sevar followed, branching his arms to the bed frame, hover- · ing over Raven. "How are you feeling, being an Aligner, having Astrid, Moonsong."

"Astrid's hot tempered, like you. Kind. I'll learn more after we save his partner. She'll tell me all his secrets." He let out a mocking laugh. "Being Aligner. It's challenging. I don't know what's deemed of me or Astrid. All magic demands balance. What'll we give for the rebellion, to the Alignment power."

He knew Sevar couldn't answer the questions he had but his stomach still warmed to the invite for querying, for sharing.

"You won't do it alone. We'll all do it together." Sevar spoke softly yet commanded like a promise.

The front door jolted against a sudden force. "Come on lovers, Pack up!" Calean and Myx tumbled into the small room.

Sevar glared at them as his reply. "Noted. See you in five." Caelan said, grabbing Myx's arm. The door left slightly ajar, their laughs echoed, fading into the narrow rooted paths.

Raven tossed his bag over his shoulder, struggling to keep it at balance. Sevar offered to hold it for him once more, but he refused. He had to hold it. Keeping with the plans, he and Sevar spoke about the morning meal, focusing on growth through their combat training and endurance.

"Morning all." Astrid spoke, letting out a small cough.

Caelan, Daj and Myx came together like glue, chatting in a group. Astrid looked over, glaring at this new dynamic.

"Save us." Sevar muttered under his breath.

"Myx, map please." Astrid asked.

"Oh, of course." She grinned from ear to ear, throwing out the map in a thrust. "So Redtide Sanctum is us, here." Myx pointed into the middle of the dense marshland, circling her finger around its location. "The perimeter is here, which is protected." Her fingers followed multiple routes. "I'll take you around the edge of Howler territory. Guide you and have an adventure." She grinned as she rolled the map up in haste.

"Do you know the Howlers territory well?" Sevar questioned, folding his arms.

Myx stared through her thin brow. "I know it like each scale within my skin, thank you." She scoffed at Sevar.

"Your skin looks like ours." Caelan spoke out Daj's signs.

Myx pulled up her sleeves. "We shift between our Gethl form, and our Eyldian form." Her skin rippled, forming into scale-like thick spikes, all in slight different red hues. Astrid looked up, forcing his shocked expression to freeze. Her face, each white freckle removed, rewritten by small scales.

"You're aquatic?" Raven asked.

"We used to have thicker skin permanently, for protection in Gethl's conditions. From the corruption clouds. At least that's the tale." Myx threw her satchel back over her shoulder. "Time in Eyldia changed our form, bless Unsa." Myx marched on. "Come on!"

"I've felt safer in Clockwork." Sevar muttered to Raven

"Agreed." He grinned.

"Thank you." Astrid cast out to Myx.

-

It became more difficult to keep above the marshy water. Leaping across stones embedded into the ground. Skipping through puddles of moss and leaves. No more dense trees to cover the ground. Nothing but sky and the red marsh. Water soaked up their trousers, filling their leather boots, squelching with each strained step.

Daj jolted to a sudden stop. Signing to Caelan. Her face scrunched, flaming the worry in his stomach.

"She says she can feel something." Caelan translated.

They all came to a halt. Astrid mouthed, ordering them to get low, using the marsh's thick grass to cover them. Myx refused. "We aren't in danger. We are on the border of their territory." A giggle wrapped around her words.

Daj scoffed, moving forward with her worry slapped over her brow.

"Sevar, keep your eye on our left." Astrid commanded quietly. Sevar nodded calmly, keeping to the left of their jagged path.

-

Raven's feet burned, yet its squelches echoed through his legs, shaking his footing. The blades of grass were wild and untamed, flopping slightly as his torso. Moving through the thick grass and algae. All clashing hues of red, fighting for his admiring observations.

Daj dropped to the ground as an echo screamed through the air, passing through the gaps in the thick grass. Claw marks shredding through the blades like threads of cotton, dropping to their feet.

"A Howler?" Caelan asked Myx.

Myx's expression widened, slowing her breathing. "Yes." She muttered.

He could feel Astrid's fear of absence of knowledge, begging, pleading to know each creature's weakness and their desires. The door groaned, pulling the emotions back through to its origin.

"What's its weakness?" Astrid spat out, forcing his voice to a sudden whisper.

Echoes creeped through the swaying red blades on each side of the fading path. Water closing in, leaving nothing but small stones to leap across the marsh.

"I don't know." Myx shook, gripping her satchel close.

Sevar and Astrid spat with frustration. "You said you knew it all." Both of their brow's scrunching, letting out a shared, sharp exhale.

"That may have been an exaggeration." Myx pulled a quivering smile.

Daj placed her hand onto the muddy floor, digging her fingers further into the ground. They all observed her, dragging their daggers out of their holsters. Readying their footing for a sudden attack.

The echoed forged to a tainting voice. Letters pulling, twisting, and manifesting through the blades. "Eyldians." Its echo deepened to a brisk tone.

Daj's head stirred, launching her hand into each direction, towards the echoes jolting movements. North, south, east, north again. Faster than anything within their own borders.

"What will you gift us for your uninvited passage?" The echo laughed, pushing closer, sending a wind down Astrid's neck. "We smell power." It creeped closer.

The blades swayed, creating a gap in the dense grass. Their glare raised, seeing claws as long as broadswords, thorns sprouting through their thin fur. The Howlers.

The wind broke through a sudden jolt, followed by a deathly howl. A Howler jumped through the grass in front of Daj, circling her in an instance. "A girl without her ears, yet she can hear us." The echo laced in annoyance, echoing in punching thrusts against their ear lopes.

Daj looked up with a jerking smile. Her hand slid across her side, throwing a small knife into the Howler's chest.

The echo screamed. "We shall have her for your payment!" It spat. Astrid flung his hand into the air, signalling the others to keep their positions.

Raven froze, watching Astrid race to her side, lowering his knife. "No." Astrid spoke calmly. Sadness quaked through the rustic copper door, knowing the payment Astrid had to give for Daj's safety meant everything to him. "I have something with more value."

Sevar stuck to Caelan's side, protecting the other trainee. Myx fell back behind Raven.

Astrid whispered to his side. A book, ancient and powerful, twirling with runic energy. "This is the Book of Untold. The last book for runic knowledge, found in Dualia. I'm sure you can find a traveller that'll pay well for it." Astrid claimed, completely unsure of his conviction.

The howlers backed up slightly, collecting at Astrid's front. Peering, observing the book's power. They sniffed, raising their long noses upon its purple glow. "You would give away knowledge, for one Eyldian?" The echo calmed. "Very well." They growled, raising their claws to the twirling power, leading the book to their grasp.

An instance later, the blades of grass cover its gaps, leaving the silence in the air to fill with their racing breaths.

Myx walked ahead, leaping stone to stone, refusing to slip on the algae. Astrid and Sevar stuck together in a frowning grunt, keeping in the back, monitoring the grass and the waters for any sudden movements. Always keeping the trainees in sight.

"Caelan, tell Daj she did a good job sensing them." Astrid broke the silence.

Caelan nodded, carrying on his conversation with Daj, adding in Astrid's statement. Daj turned her head, forming a quick thumbs up before turning back to leap from stone to stone.

The sweat dripped down his back, causing his travel pack to slip. He looked back to see Sevar observing him, scanning over his frustration. Raven could tell Sevar could read him like fresh ink on a clean page. He pulled a mocking expression, whipping his face back to his front before he could see Sevar's reaction.

The open sky of thin wispy clouds, shadowing the rays of the brightening sun, filled with a pale façade of Dreaka's mountain range.

"You will be at the border in a moment." Myx claimed, slowing her steps.

"Thank you, Myx." Astrid spoke.

Myx lowered her face. "Don't thank me, I lied to you." She gripped her satchel. "I just wanted to do something fun, with outsiders." Her cheeks went a brighter hue of red.

"It's okay. We understand. Get back safe." Astrid spoke with care.

He stepped closer. "My home is in Elcoo if you ever see yourself on the Drossor border. The rest are from Moonsong in Dualia. Visit some time, when it's safe." He smiled, being her into a hug.

"I owe you all." Myx hugged Calean and Daj. "May Unsa oversee your quest!" She bellowed, running back through the marshland.

"All those species thrown into the marsh like nothing." Astrid muttered.

"How did all this go unseen?" He asked, peering over to Sevar.

A clear clash of shame and frustration written over his sweaty, thick brows. "We'll make everyone see." Sevar told them all with a gritting undertone.

# Chapter 41

## The Hard Way Around the Quarters

### *Pazima*

The bell rung, alerting them to be in their sleeping houses. Chip peered over her shoulder. "Clear?"

"Everyone's in." She looked to each side, checking for any movement. "Clear." She dashed across the polished granite, running through the compound. Using the shadows of the cadet's buildings for cover.

Chip followed, but another silhouette appeared in the shadows ahead. "Where are you two going?" Kelee smirked proudly.

Chip's shoulders raised. "Off into the city, we heard of a party." Chip spoke with confidence. She decided to not pile on, wondering if Chip's confidence is one of a strong façade.

"And I didn't get an invitation. Am I not your friend?" Kelee's smirk grew wider. "Are we not cadets together, soldiers, brothers in the war against the fifth?"

She swung her arm, wrapping it around his neck in a sudden movement. Kelee's breath rapid and wild against his clamped throat. "If we want a rat following us, we'll go into the sewers." She pushed against Kelee's windpipe till his cheeks radiated a bright red, clamping his blood, forming his features into a swelling ripe fruit. "Now fuck off and rest your head. Tell anyone and I'll break your neck." She tossed him against the granite.

Kelee gasped for air, scoffing as he struggled up from the granite foundations, running back to the quarters in a burning rage.

Chip's face stuck in a dropped expression. "What if he tells?"

"We won't be here long enough to care." She declared with a smile.

-

She knelt into the clean polished granite stones. "Well, this must be where all the higher-ranking legions and Commanders live." She scoffed through the information, staring into the nearby tavern. Songs rhyming about the fall of rebellions, all in the name of Nova. She rolled her eyes, glaring back at Chip. "Remember to write about these songs and how shit they are for me?" They both chuckled into the shadows of the alley.

They kept to a crouching position, searching each delivery box with its owner's ranking name at its side. All homes in blocks, some rising to three-level buildings. Every building proudly swayed the symbol of Nova. Built with clean curves and cuts of smooth granite, absent of any tiny imperfections. Yellow tiles placed perfectly against the granite bricks, complimenting the orange hues. Blooming patches of Sunkissers, twirling and gripping to the building's brickwork. Designed and cut, attention given to each yellow stem with aims of complete prestige. Her nostrils raised slightly, like by instinct. The battle of smells, moist socks and sharp vanilla layering through the polished granite stones.

"This one." She whispered while picking the lock to a blue round door, its small window rusted into the painted wood. She and Chip remained silent, listening out for the lock to click softly into her ear, while Chip watched the pathway for any signs of movement. Clicks pulsed through her fingers, teasing, twisting the two metal rods prodded into the lock's old mechanism. Gifting entrance to the Commander of Nova's Fifth Legion's home.

—

Chip launched himself with a wide grin. Thrusting the air from under him, the bed bounced him up. "This is so soft." The surprise on Chip's face made her grin climb slightly. Reminding her of Astrid for a moment. An instance of bliss, of playful enjoyment.

"Check his drawers. Don't steal his undergarments." She smirked, walking out of the Commander's bedroom. Chip's sharp reply was muffled by her beaming focus.

She walked through the greeting room, scanning through the letters on his dusty cabinet. She scrunched her brows, reading through the addressed letters about the counts for the soldier's new weaponry building, some addressed to all Commanders about the rebellion's status within Dreaka. One at the bottom of the pile. A black envelope with a gold ink signature on its back. Addressed to the Commander and his wife. A meeting with the King of Dreaka. Stated to be of great importance to the realm. She folded the letter, pressing it into her left-side pocket. She hurried her search, scrapping the need to leave the home in its original state.

"Found anything?" Chip asked, trying his best to land on his toes as he crept through the halls.

"Letters about counts, meetings. Nothing with any important details." Her spat out in her frustration.

Chip walked slowly to her and knelt position. "I found this file, you need to leave." Chip handed over the thick, loosely tied file of papers, glancing at her reaction.

"Storm's way, Storm's End. They're testing on spells to remove it? Why would they do that?" She tossed the paper to the sofa nearby. "To what result?"

"I'm sorry, you need to go. Now." Chip pushed at her shoulder.

"Breathe, Chip. What's happening?" She asked.

"I didn't think I would befriend. She said she would get me a job in the Tower, to work with the greatest scholars." Chip's face ran crystal-white.

Her breathing thinned, followed by a sharp piercing pain shooting through her ribs, building a swift pressure upon her heart. "What did you do?" Her voice dropped, completely cold.

"The princess, she offered me the world. You got to leave. She'll slaughter you." Chip bellowed.

"Oh Chip, you idiot." Her emotionless tone cracked like a thin veil upon her face. "They won't give you anything." A sob begged to slip through the veil. His innocence, his need for a peaceful life, manipulated, yet she felt completely alone and truly betrayed.

"Seems you don't have any friends." A woman's voice filled the room, cutting at her ears. "Now you know of our plans, we can't allow you to wonder." Lassea's voice spitting with venomous tones. Her twisting glance drawn to Chip, scanning over his shaking footing. "Come here." The princess ordered.

Chip's head dipped, staring at his feet. "I'll make it right." Chip muttered to her side. The wooden planks groaned at his feet's dragging weight.

"To what end would you need to remove Storm's Way?" She questioned once more.

"To bring the realm to our true vision." A hollow, brisk voice echoed through the greeting room, slamming the door. The figure lined up with the Princess. "King Dreaka will love to hear about this." The Commander of the Fifth Legion mocked, glaring up at Princess Lassea.

# Chapter 42

### The Meadows of Wanted Foes
*Raven*

The hill of Dreaka, the sea wind blowing through the peaks and the narrow rocky valleys. All its paths entirely blocked by fallen boulders, blocking off the sharp, sheer drop to the Sun's Sea below. Moss wrapped itself thickly around the stones, refusing to stump its growth. Dense green firmly blocking all ancient routes. All paths leading to the major cities, refusing to turn to older settlements.

They walked through the east of Dreaka. Settlements all bartering for any extra counts. Collections of homes surrounded by fields of grain and meadows unmarred, brightening blues and vibrant green grass dancing at their feet, yet all felt ghoulish. The air was eerie, a feeling of uncomfortable stares upon their backs.

"Break?" He queried to the group, all silent, letting out sharp exhales. "There's a tavern." He pointed in relief.

"How can you tell that from here?" Astrid mocked slightly.

"I lived in one, it's not hard to notice its tavern symbol stained into the glass." He smirked proudly. One thing he could hold high in praise, knowing where a damned old drinking hole is located, by one small indicator. Caelan rolled his eyes, marching up the meadows ahead.

"His resentment for me is clear." He stated.

Sevar fixed his broadsword's grip on his broad shoulder. "I don't see it."

Raven glared up to Sevar, a playful glance, pleading for him to see the same. "He rarely spoke to me on our journey from Redtide Santrum." He looked over to Daj. "Daj, you saw."

Daj raised her head, nothing but a blank expression welcoming them into their conversation. Sevar signed to her. She replied in a tone anyone could see through her mocking hand movements.

"She... she said to keep her the fuck out of it—detail on the Fuck. Also, that Caelan is just as easy to anger as his Keep." Sevar eyes widened vaguely.

"Not wrong." Astrid admitted. "We'll talk to him together, brother." Astrid wrapped his arm around his shoulder softly, pushing Raven up the flowery meadow.

-

He pulled out his cloak from his pack, smiling into its details. A gifted warmth in a brisk cobblestone cell, a source of comfort for a sharp memory.

A tavern, proudly broadcasting its timeless features like the Old Mace. Wore-down stalls gripping to the tacky floorboards. Ale dripping from the tables, no mop could scrub its tang from the wood's creases. Bangs of barrels slamming into the front bar's foundations, roaring their offers on two-count refills. They came to the bar, ordering their refreshments between each other.

He scanned over the small room, tables and stalls clashed for room within the floor space. Songs muttered against the stained panes, teasing its way across the bar's surface.

"Five Ales." Sevar ordered.

Raven and Astrid expressions widened, glaring at Sevar. "Three ales and two cherry brews." Raven spoke loud, coating Sevar's order.

Caelan and Daj sat next to the doorway, cleaning their weaponry and their leathers from any remaining algae of the Red Marshland.

His attention pulled to the walls, its framed painting of stars shooting across the sky in a proud glory. Words, ancient and thick, twirled throughout the edgings. His expression widened, reading from afar.

"Nova the Conquer rose in the dusk of the brightest stars. Declared to be the light to be followed." He muttered it, exposing its words through his body.

"What are you reading?" Astrid asked, opening his mind wide.

"The paints, they all celebrate Nova the Conqueror. Eben would tell me stories of the conqueror if I misbehaved." He tried to stop the worry from plastering over his face.

"Nova is their way. Most believe in the Conqueror, the Four, the right to rule Eyldia under one banner." Astrid replied. He calmly placed his ale down. "for many years."

"Oh fuck." He spat out, looking into papers peeling off the wall, its ink running, yet still legible.

*Sevar Lorstorm.*

*Astrid Talo*

*Raven Whitewood*

*Wanted for capital murder, breaking into royal property, taking royal property, rising to rebel actions, treason against the Four crowns of Eyldia...*

*Reward – one hundred thousand counts.*

"We need to go now." He pleaded.

Caelan and Daj looked up to Astrid, nodding to a visual warning. Sevar followed swiftly, all planting their footing with a warrior stance, opening the hanging door in haste.

He flicked his hood over his weighed brow, raising a thick shadow over his identifiable features.

Voices murmured, layering with confusion behind.

# Chapter 43

## The Regret of Lost Time

### Astrid

"Now you three are wanted because you saved him!" Caelan scoffed. "A man with no talent, bare minimum training and looks like a barebone goblin."

Sevar raised a knife swiftly to Caelan's eye, touching his sweat upon his eyelashes. "Say It again." Sevar's voice dropped, like no sense of morality could hold him back from protecting Raven.

"Stop." Raven ordered Sevar, throwing his bag into the gravel path. "He's a Young, Sev." Raven stepped slowly through the grass, sliding between Sevar and Caelan. The blade pressing against his bony cheek. "Pulling his anger like the ones before him. Exactly what you are showing him now."

Sevar's icy stare flickered, pushing to Raven's guiding words, lowering his blade. Astrid hovered over his hilt, yet no fear brewed, only him, listening into the divine doorway between their minds, knowing Raven's emotions remained collected and sharp.

"No second chances, Young one." Sevar whispered, filling the warm air with a sharp breeze.

Caelan turned in a huff, darting down the meadows.

-

Two rotations passed with minimum chatter, walking through lush valleys and plains of yellow flowers. Crossing through other settlements with their cloaks up, knotted tight at their necks, never stopping, till a plain clearing opened, leaving a packed-down campfire and moss-covered logs. The mountains cut Sun's Peak and its city's noise from the rest of Dreaka's continent, overshadowing the forests below, one they could use for a travelling advantage. A forest, whispering, dense with oaks and shadows creeping through bushes of thorns and mysterious fruits.

"If another golem comes, it's your turn." Sevar declared to Raven, forcing a serious face upon his beaming grin.

"You were unconscious till the last strike." Raven replied sharply.

Sevar smirked. "I remember taking that golem down, easily." A sudden thrust echoed behind Astrid, turning back to see Raven laughing down to Sevar's shocked features, pushed into a nearby bush.

He smiled, the warmth of love twirling through the golden doorway. A warmth he hoped will return to him once more, with Pazima by his side.

He walked alongside Caelan a couple of steps ahead, trolling the close radius of the campsite. "Caelan, I'm sorry I didn't take care of your training as much as I should, but that doesn't give you the right to flare insults."

"It poured out. I couldn't stop." Caelan stated, full of burning frustration.

He scanned Caelan's face, his flushed cheeks, scratches down his jawline. Astrid turned his head lightly, observing the tears upon Caelan's nail beds. Tears aged, layering with fresh red rips. "I didn't realise how much my anger affected you." He paused for a moment, running his fingers through his sweaty middle-parting, breathing in slowly. "Pazima scolded me back in Hlinos, to control my anger, my frustration—" Astrid breached the gap between them, placing his hand on his trainee's shoulder. "My regret, Caelan. Running from my responsibilities, from you will be my biggest regret, but I'll make it better."

Caelan looked at him with a crystal reflection. "I just wanted to be seen."

"I'm truly sorry." Astrid pulled Caelan's swelling emotions, holding his trainee into a tight embrace. A hug, long desired for a Young one without love.

The sun dropped, shining its orange dusk into their dried tears. Caelan sat in the gravel, watching the warming copper hue spread across the calm stream. Fishes bobbing up through the clear water, eating a struggling worm at the stream's edge.

"Fee once told me how focusing on a sense can help you support your emotions; I use the noise of the water's current." He sat down, letting his toes dip into the water. "Normally the river by the cliff behind the temple." Astrid looked to Caelan's face, full of confliction. "An elder Ophidian also told me to anchor to something, not someone. An anchor no one can take away from you."

Caelan didn't reply, slowly closing his eyes.

"What pulls at you?" He asked.

Caelan smiled vaguely. "The foxes. I can hear their barks, calling in the shadows to their partners, to their Young."

"You can hear that?"

"I have good hearing. Daj swears I stole hers to make mine better than most." His smile grew, looking into Astrid's observation expression.

# Chapter 44

## The Settlement Unfortunate, Unseen & Forgotten

### *Raven*

He ran back, laughing from his aching core. Daj playfully punched his arm, signing with a tasteful comment. *Fuck you.* Daj flicked her fingers with a mocking expression.

"I'll teach you how to." He expressed the words with his lips, holding his laughter to a halt. He scanned her clothing, noting how he could patch her favourite leather coat.

"You're learning fast." Sevar added.

"You're an outstanding tutor." Raven grinned at Sevar, smelling the roasting meat slowly rotating over the campfire.

Sevar's eyes flicked over his expression, reading his face. "How are you feeling? It's been a while since you left your home." Sevar teased with a clear and warming tone.

"Overwhelming." He stopped for a moment, juggling through his knotted thoughts. "—But pulling a blind eye isn't an option any longer. The dreams kept dragging me down this path, so I may as well walk." His thoughts rolled onto his tongue without caution. "We don't know anyone in the rebellion. Who leads it? How are we going to help?"

"I have a couple names I'm querying that may be involved. We should focus on supporting Pazima first before we open the possibilities." Sevar stated, all his words clear as the river's water.

"How about you?" He placed his hand onto Sevar's thigh. "It must have been hard to leave your mother right after you got her back. Not being with Clockwork."

"I sleep well knowing she's safe, doing something she'll love." Sevar interlocked his fingers into Raven's hand. "As for Clockwork, it was always a means to live. I forgot that for a long time, but you reminded me, and so did your irritating brother." His cheeks blessing a soft-pale magenta.

Sevar looked over to Daj. *Food?* He signed.

Daj glared to her right. *Is it edible?* She let on a small grin.

Sevar mockingly giggled, passing over a metal container of meat and odd pickings of vegetables from settlements and farmlands they passed throughout the plains of Dreaka.

–

Astrid sprinted smoothly across the gravel. "Do you hear that?"

They all came to a sudden stop, silence began prominent. The birds launched into a flock, refusing to render a singular chirp. A scream ripped through the treeline, bellowing through the wildlife, causing their fur to stand on edge. The foxes whined, darting to their burrows.

"The scream." Astrid's stance stood firm, angling his face into any movements throughout the forest's dense treelines.

Sevar's mixed expression clashed, worry washing over him entirely. Raven touched Sevar's quivering fingers with his own, offering an understanding embrace.

"It's Mistwood." Sevar spoke as the settlement's name hung in the air, refusing to let go of his neck. Sevar glanced at Astrid. A realisation, or an understanding, burning between them.

"What's happening?" Raven asked.

"My past with Clockwork—" Sevar gripped his dragger's hilt. "I ran. I didn't save their people." Sevar's stone expressions, melting to a shaking quiver. "I couldn't. I had to leave." He wiped his tears, shaking his face. "I know what I must do."

Astrid nodded, knowing Sevar's next move. "We'll go to Sun's Peak. Meet us there?" Sevar nodded back, Astrid placed his hand onto Sevar's shoulder. "Fix what you can. Come back to us."

"I'm coming with you." Raven commanded from his core.

"No. You should go with Astrid. You'll be safer." Sevar pleaded through a vague voice crack.

"You promised." Two words, Sevar cursed through his lips, muttering, refusing. Fuck.

Sevar sighed into the air above. "Stay in the treeline, if it gets messy, you're gone." Sevar ordered.

Caelan raised his head. "I'll go with Sevar and Raven. They'll need a Moonsinger's touch. You and Daj can hide better with less bodies." He was right. A shifter and a singular Eyldian would raise the odds of success.

Sevar's face didn't strain, looking into Astrid's. "Granted, give them all you got." Astrid lifted his palm out, offering what laid within.

"Really?" Caelan questioned, lifting his brows. Caelan flicked Astrid's throwing knifes into the air, twirling them with his whispers. "Thank you." Caelan wrapped his arms around Astrid for a quick embrace.

"Raven, I'll tell you where we are when you come to Sun's Peak. Keep the door open." Astrid yelled, walking up the hill's narrow path.

-

Sevar's firm grip quivered as he stared through the treeline. Mistwood, a small settlement enclosed by large, towering ash trees. Its thorny bushes and leaves coating the settlement in a natural boundary, one the Legions abused to their own advantage years ago, and yet again, time repeating like a clock. Each rotation striking twelve, death calls from the shadow's boundary. Soldiers launched out of the forest's thick shadows, aiming towards their prey. The Eyldians' screams echoed into the treeline, bringing brisk shivers down his spine bones.

"It's the same as last time." Sevar's voice spilling out, raw and unfiltered, like the memories held his words with a vengeful force.

"It won't end the same." Caelan spoke as his word was truth, inked into paper. He flicked the throwing knives, twirling its hollow ring at the bottom of the handles. A smile rising vaguely, staring into the knives like it smiled back.

Sevar gave a slight raise of his head. "Caelan, you take the further homes. I'll take the big guys."

"Yes, Commander." Caelan replied swiftly.

They ran through the treeline, shadowing their movements between the tree's silhouettes. Sevar ran in front, followed by Raven with Caelan on his sixth, as commanded. The three moved as one, a squad with one similar need to help the unfortunate, the unseen, the forgotten people enclosed by their brutality.

"Three." Caelan whispered behind him.

Sevar darted his glance to the whispered direction, knowledge Raven hadn't curved into his memory so far. Three soldiers swung their swords with broad grins, smashing into barrels of leaking water. "You got the shipment for us?" One soldier spat out to an elderly woman, white hair trailing down to her hips, knotted, and lacking any moisture.

"Please, you know the land hasn't been fortunate this brightening season." She pleaded with a sharp tongue. Each word felt withered, scared, but not for her own being. For Mistwood and its people. Her expression, the emotion sprayed itself over her quivering lips.

Another soldier laughed, pushing the woman, causing her to tumble into the worn-down barrel stack. A sob filled with utter defeat bellowed through Mistwood, into the treeline.

"Now Commander?" Caelan asked, twirling the throwing knives faster with each click that dragged by.

"Wait." Sevar didn't peel any attention off the ongoing situation. "Raven, stay in the treeline."

The soldiers collected, bellowing into their chatter. A jolt slammed through Mistwood as a strong force pushed through, hurling them off their firm footing.

Raven froze utterly still, like a creature alarmed by a larger creature. His response frosting between his frozen pale lips.

"Rebels." Sevar let the relief wash over his response. "Now!" Sevar called.

Caelan and Sevar pushed through the treeline like birds on their unknowing prey. Sevar launched his broadsword down, slashing a towering soldier's head into two clean parts, coating the nearby cottage panes in a fresh coat of thick red, dripping down into the chipped brown window edges.

Caelan flicked his first throwing knife into a clear line, cutting the wind with a mere grin. The knife landed upon a soldier, filling their throat with metal and their own gushing liquids.

"Now that's great." Caelan said with a beaming smile, scanning the treeline for Raven's safety. Caelan lunged through the mud, darting the metal with smirking whispers.

Raven's eyes locked on Sevar's sharp grunts, blood spraying across his beard, dripping through the thick black coils. Sevar's dagger plunged into the creases of skin and blood-soaked fabrics, their necks gushing, pouring their blood down his hilt. Sevar's eyes sharpened on the brute soldier's smashing through the cottages at his right.

Raven's leg quivered against the bark of towering trees. The wind pushed through his hair, his skin, like a plea to move. "I cant." He replied with a ghostly mutter.

The wind roared against the bark, swinging the leaves in huge thrusts. His glare pulled up, focusing on Sevar. Soldiers circled him, waiting like creatures weaving through the mixes of bark, twigs, and drying leaves. Sevar's focus narrowed.

The wind pushed once again, pushing him from the tree-line. Exposing him, ripping his body from the cover of nature. No time left to ponder, running through the mud. "Behind you!" He ripped out his crow dagger, wrapping his arm around the smaller soldier. His dagger sinked into the soldier's side. The youthful features completely froze, groaning against the blade's pressure. The warmth rippled through the hilt, creeping up through his cold fingertips.

Sevar's eyes widened, gripping Raven's body with one launching thrust. Time felt clouded with one jolting embrace. Breathing in the sharp, punching spice of blood, coating his pale lips. He dropped into the mud aside Caelan.

A mercenary's rage blown through like a mighty storm, utilising a puncturing and swift movement. A force of nature wielding a broadsword, Sevar tossed his weapon with a razor-sharp scoff. "You." He pointed at the remaining soldier. One with a unique symbol sewed into his bloodied uniform.

Raven struggled, freezing to the mud, looking into the man he thought he knew, travelling through the realm's cities, sneaking, experiencing Eyldian cultures. Yet completely knotted with anxiety. Sevar's past, he still knew limited amounts, struggling to lift the grates of the mercenary's guarded mind.

Caelan walked around the bodies, scanning the symbols. "All these have symbols with ones on them. Is that important?" He asked Sevar.

"All Cadets, isn't that right, Commander Anak." Sevar launched Anak to the ground, planting his fist into his nose.

"You find it fun to get inexperienced people killed, some of those could have led good lives." Sevar's rage roared. "Now we killed them..." Sevar's voice cracked vaguely.

"You've gone soft Lorstorm. How's Mommy?" Commander Anak smirked, spitting blood onto Sevar's cheek.

Caelan and Raven muttered to the Eyldian's of Mistwood, asking them to wait in their homes.

Sevar's eyes darted over Anak. "She's safe." He raised, pushing up with his left foot on Anak's ribs. "No thanks to you or your Legion. The power of dreamers." Sevar glanced up for a moment, looking into Raven's blood-coated hair.

Anak struggled to knees, turning to look at Caelan and Raven. "They'll come for you. Power takes power." Commander Anak stared at him, the unfiltered hatred pouring through the piercing eye contact.

"The rebellion will reforge Eyldia into a peaceful realm, one of fair, smart and clear judgement, one of no royalty at its peaks." Sevar spoke clearly. A smirk raised as Commander Anak turned to look up at Sevar. "It's a sheer shame you won't be there to see it." He raised a dagger from his right, embedding the metal into Anok's skull. The cracking of bone rippled through the mud, climbing Raven's feet.

Sevar's face, brimming with flaming chills, brisk to sight. Raven stared into Sevar, into the Commander's cracked skull. Blood swimming through the mud, forging its own river of rage through the settlements' fleeing footprints.

# Chapter 45

## The Price of Love & Intel

### *Pazima*

Her finger twinged at her hilt, following the basic Moon-song training. Be prepared. There's always a way out. Her heart bubbled in raw emotion, feeling the lingering acid in her system, still burning vaguely, like a rotten meal from a previous rotation.

"Don't think about lunging, moon bitch." Lassea's smirk almost glowing through the shadows, only light climbing through the windows from the outside lamps.

She glared through each of them, scanning their bodies for weaknesses, bruises, or cuts, anything she could strike for any extra longing click by her side. "Threatened by my abilities, Princess?"

Lassea sneered loudly. "Threatened? By a moon dweller?" Lassea strutted across the lounge, tracing the cushion's fabric patterns with her finger, flicking into the air against her words. "Never." Lassea smirked. "Taking you away from brother dearest is perfectly poetic, wouldn't you agree?"

"You lie. Your family's plagued blood would never run through his veins." Pazima's calculating power bubbled up,

292

bursting into a consuming, thick cloud, storming over her mind. An emotion kept folded and maintained in an enclosed dome of light within her mind, pushed, knotted by the sharp pulses between her ribs. Her heart, refusing to feel any emotional ache.

"You don't learn, Pazima." Lassea's grip twisted upon her arm, bending and burning against Pazima's pulling jolts.

"You must be mistaking me for someone else." Pazima punched Lassea's lower stomach with bursts of glowing red. Power of transformation in pure form, stringing energy of her being, laying her fury in bright power. The princess crumbled into the rug beneath her. Tension cut wide open by shock, radiating through the lounge. The Commander, completely frozen.

Her vision peeled open, jolting to her hilt. Her dagger slipped in her sweaty palm. "You understand nothing, Princess. You'll never get Astrid on side." Aiming her daggers frantically between the two blurred figures.

"Oh, no, now you're mistaken. I don't want him to join our family, we want him died." Lassea smiled from the rug, flicking her rogue blonde locks from her beaming smile.

Her thoughts shredded and threw between her temples, following the throbbing ache. Why murder newfound blood, removing possible royal overthrow? Pazima kicked at the sofa, pushing it into Lassea's struggling climb. Launching her body through the narrow hallway. The bellows of the Commander clawed behind her.

She aimed her dagger up, thrusting her force through her palms, lunging across the long table, kicking the Commander sharply, dodging his groaning swings, launching herself into the rusting window panes. The shattering of glass vibrated across her skin, consuming her groans as the glass sliced at her forehead, catching into her coils. Her arms reached out, planting into the bushes below.

The pain threatened to consume her entirely. Climbing up her ribs, bobbing at her threat, spitting up her bile like a toxic acid. Burning at her thinning breaths.

She muttered to herself. Her magic burst through her body, bellowing at the bottom of her essence. Its grip forcing its way up to her bruised, hazed silhouette. The pressure built as she climbed to her footing, shaking off the shattered glass. Pazima's power gripped control, peeling open her lips, forcing her to let out a long-lasting exhale. The rage, the tearing, slashing pain twirling with the mist, taken in its forceful grip.

Her eyes pulled to the blurring abyss, opening to the inviting warmth of untouched snow, her cuts screaming out at the sharp gushes of frosting winds. Her vision wrapped in red, pushed and strained to sharpened focus, glaring into the creatures of the frosting Fellow's. Playful spins of three tails, flicking the flaky snow into the air. Their barks wrapped by the snow's clean, thick sheet. She cupped her ears in a sudden pressure, pulling, flicking, the turning of pages, the burning of candles, its embers popping against her senses. The mist called upon the knowledge of the Fellow's exhibitive, with the smell of ink rushing its way up her stained fingertips.

The pages turned, forcing her to mutter each term of the creature's life cycle, its difference in anatomy, its thickening fur pelt wrapping its thick skin, lashing its sharp claws upon their prey, and crystal sea-blue eyes, all-consuming. The three tails, stories passed down from ancient rumours. How the Moonfoxes protected Eyldians in a dear time of need, holding the power of air within their screeching howls.

The wind of the frosting pushed Pazima off her footing, manipulating to her new form. Her mist ripping away, absorbing back into her fur pelt. She was Eyldian no longer, lunging from the polished granite pathways, pushing off her back legs, across clean-cut bushes, holding in her sharp groans as she leaped through the quarters. Her tails twirling, adding to her painful thrusts.

–

Market stalls brimming over with fresh meats, overwhelming spices and layers of clean fabrics. The smells tortured her exposed senses, grating between her sharp fangs. Blood dripped from her back legs, pushing every little primal Moonfox sense. Her back legs pushed her forward, hiding her in the nearby alley.

Springing into focus, she leaped into a window left ajar, running through a building coated in dust and old furniture. The air left caged and abandoned, dust floated, settling into the building foundations. She crept up the stairwells, floor by floor she jumped with the last of her energy. Dust-covered thick fabrics laid upon neglected desks, chairs, sofas and foundations of granite, exposed and kissed by time. Copper lines ran through the building, humming quietly, accompanying her sharp breaths. Pazima's eyelids pressure built, each step weighing down upon her paws. It ached through her pelt, causing her to groan in an empty room. Nothing but her and layers of untouched dust. Time removed, leaving her stiffened on a frayed rug. Even in the shade of an abandoned narrow building, she cried in the burning heat. The Moonfox form, removing thick and ready for the freezing season's might, yet it's the only form Pazima had in mind, with all its knowledge, of its shape and love.

"Run, Pazima." A calm voice muttered into her flopped ear, familiar, but far from reach.

"They're coming." Another crept through.

Chip's voice crawled over, echoing through her covered ears. "I'll make it right."

She forced her eyes to peel, straining at the fatigue. Chip hovering over her Moonfox form. "Move." Chip yelled. His body, moulding into the floating dust, begging for her to move, to live.

She trembled to all fours, looking through the empty rooms. The stairwell door slammed, allowing a crumbling echo to cast against the granite brick foundations. "Moon bitch." The princess of Dreaka strung her words out, her smirk visible through her laced tone.

She looked into the wall, greeted only by floating dust filling the stale, still air. Silence began deafening to her fresh, animalistic senses. Her eyes darting across the narrow stairwell, up, down, a groan crept at her side. A briskly scream filled the air as sharp fangs of another Moonfox leaped at her torso.

"You think you can escape by being in form?" Lassea pressed down her paw into her ribs. "I could smell you from a block away."

She groaned, forcing her claws to branch through her paws, slashing down Lassea's smirking features. Her whiskers ripped and flung into the layers of floating dust. The dimmed cast of sunlight glared down upon the dust, casting the pale yellow across the empty room. Pazima's stomach burned, like her blood transformed into scorching flames. She screamed, pushing the Princess into the stairwell.

"The gift from my father, remember?" She teased while her mist twirled out of her paws. Lassea's Eyldian form towered over Pazima like a reminder, the Four and its power towering over her.

*If you have any little plans to kill me or any crowned royal, you'll burn from your insides. Each organ knotting, engulfed by flames and unimaginable pain. Courtesy of my little rune charred into your skin.*

"I'm a crowned Princess. I hope it burns." Lassea looked down at Pazima, now in her original form, holding her stomach. The rune...

Its red glow burned through her tunic, charring through each layer of fabric, pressing any slight pressure against it. The rune burned and sung. Her ears, consumed by ancient words unknown. Words she's never heard before, nothing of their language, drowning in mere sorrow.

"No time left, my father's orders. We need you back in the castle."

The pain, the flames burning through each vein under her skin, engulfed her entirely.

# Chapter 46

## Peak's Tower & Its Guards

### *Astrid*

The structures of sun-kissed granite, mixing of many sizes and clean, all polished and curved perfectly. All building's filled with pristine stained panes, absent of sun-staining, leaving nothing but mixes of red and white, centred by stars, so as old as time, some melted and moulded to the ancient buildings, fresh as each dawn's light. Smells of crushed flowers and variations of metallic copper frames, weaving through the market's thick air, partnering up with the grossly increasing tang of warming meat, attacking each balmy breath.

"Fuck, that'll make any mythic turn their nose up entirely." Astrid scoffed through his overhanging cloak hood, lowering it with careful glances around the sweaty market. Stone columns framed the market, along with long fabrics drooping over the cleaned wooden display tables. Each table was seemingly different within its withering, some absorbing the beaming light from above into its oil coating, some left to watch its borrowed time, reaching its last rotation of use.

The towering range buildings of ancient granite stones, refusing to allow the wind to whistle between its creases.

Mazes of narrow staircases teasing through the cliff's peaks. Some buildings dropped to a sudden hang, gripped by ancient stone cliffs.

Daj pulled to his side. Her eyes rolled, passing him with a newfound swagger. Partnered with a smile framing her features, painting an innocent façade, pulling her hands up, flicking and pronouncing within the sun's rays, highlighting her button nose. He let out a playful scoff, leaning into the meat seller's right stone column.

The market seller's posture shot up, revealing a greeting smile, using his hands and his mouth to reply to Daj's signs. "A dungeon? I don't understand, young girl." The bearded man twirled his fingers, ending his sentence with a slight flick against his white rogue strands. "Nothing of such gore would stand in Sun's Peak" The seller's features glared across the markets with an ever-growing, beaming grin.

Astrid stared into Daj's hasteful signs. His brows arched; the struggle painted over his sweating forehead.

The seller's glare sharpened at Astrid. "You don't know the visual language."

"Many know of it?" Her head shifted to an acute slant, focusing her view on the market seller's lips.

"Dearest Queen Atula passed a law to carry her grandmother's wishes for all to learn the visual language." The seller lifted his hand, wiping at his forehead. "All in her continent must be fluent. Many in Dreaka follow that favour." The seller's glare cut towards Astrid for a brisk instant. He lingered at the seller's arching brows, highlighting his confusion.

Her expression hollowed, like a cracking mirror. No response came.

A sudden bell rang through the Peaks. Each strike vibrated the tiny, cracked pebbles against the granite city streets. He hooked his hand into Daj's, guiding them into the gathering crowd. Blend in, it's the only option.

His feet throbbed by the pressurising heat, guiding their steps carefully between the wandering paths of muttering upper Eyldians. All casting their smiles, flicking their long dresses within the thick air. Hues of red painting across the crowds. Men loosening their knotted tunics slightly, letting their torsos breathe. Their thin fabric trousers waved in the calm breeze, rising from the sea below.

The bells rang each minute. Youngers dashed at his side, bashing against his hip, singing through the muttering crowds. Young gathered at the lower glass panes outside the cathedral's staircase. Pressing their hands, gliding wet white powder against the clean panes. He glared over with caution. The shapes were drawn clumpy and unconnected, yet still visible as a blinding star beaming its light across the night's skies.

"They truly don't understand what happens outside their walls." Astrid muttered to Daj.

Daj looked up at Astrid's blazing expression. She signed one of the limited visuals he knew.

*Breathe.*

His exhales followed the bell's vibrations, forcing his sight to the gathering outgoings. The enormous doors, crafted of clean, shining copper, trimmed in small quartz and varnished oak symbols encased by its copper framing. The doors banged, sliding open with a casting hollow ring, sending a warm gush through the crowd. Silhouettes of wide, thick fabric folding onto the stone foundations became apparent. One silhouette remained in its centre with spikes piercing at the top of the figure's sharp outline.

"Kneel to our grace. King Dreaka of Dreaka." An elderly man, absorbing the harsh sun's rays into his rough bald head. His plain off-white fabrics refused to frame his body. His arms covered with hanging fabric, lifting a long scroll. "He offers his presence, therefore, his precious time to this rotation's prayers." Row by row, they knelt, raising their heads to the skies.

"To Nova, to the shining stars." Each row spoke as one.

Astrid and Daj knelt, focusing on a long inhale. He glanced up to the King as he scoped each row. King Dreaka's eyes piercing and cunning, a sense of unfiltered purpose flowing around with his icy stare upon his crowd.

His mind felt as he knew this place, the stones familiar but blurred by a never-ending storm within their mind.

*"Are you three okay?"* He casted down.

*"Sevar killed the Commander. He seemed to have known him from before."* A prolonged pause bridged through. The feeling of Raven's worrisome strains crept through, hooking to the divine rustic door. *"Something feels unsettling. Before he killed him, the Commander looked at me like no one has before. Like he knew something, knew me."*

He focused his glare on the proud King, as the crowned man prayed. *"I'm getting the same feeling. There's a connection between father dearest Dreaka, the Four and our missing memories. Nothing of Pazima yet. Come to Sun's Peak with haste. I could use Sevar's skillset."*

A wave of mutters rode through the large square like a pack of wild Moonfoxes, scoffs and shocked expressions drawn over many Eyldian's faces. Astrid looked up, scanning the officials and the King. The long-robed man cast his words, echoing against the ancient granite. "The King gifts his people with an offering, to show their promise to a safe, long and fruitful royal rule." Groans completely vague, cutting between the chattering and prays. "He gifts you a woman, one on a dark path down to rebel actions. One that hopes to bring Eyldia back to chaotic, to plague of illness and hunger."

A woman. Overshadowed by the cathedral's shadows, she spat, struggling against glowing metal wrapping around her arms. She threw herself in front, raising her head to the sun. The white-robed man shouted out. "The Four will bring the rebellion to its knees, one by one. Its leaders pulled out like a sprouting infection within our harvests."

*Pazima.*

His instincts jolted him forward into a cupping pressure. Daj struggled to keep him glued to the sun-kissed granite and its ancient drawing on its foundations. She held on, gripping at his arm, shaking her head, pleading for him to stop. Astrid knew he shouldn't. The training he and Pazima had as Young ones curved their learnings into their beings. To never risk the many for just one soul, even if it's one of much love. He pushed it away, every lesson, every connecton but his friend, his love, his entire heart. Astrid sobbed, slamming it behind the divine door.

The gold beamed from his palms, twirling in a primal force. Raw, limited as one, it beamed with his uncontrollable groans. "Till death, we said." He pushed Daj's arm to her side. Dashing, pushing, and weaving through the crowd.

"Pazima!" He called out, scratching against his throat. All he had gone into his screams, pleading for her to hear him.

The King turned with a sharp smile. "Restrain him." His voice filtered with mere calmness.

He lunged to the long steps, reaching for his right dagger. He pressed at his hilt. Nothing but straps. He focused a hasteful inhale, absorbing his shock. A child's laugh bridged to him, flicking his dagger into the cobbles in the crowd.

Astrid turned to branch his arm out for his sword, but the King's guards lunged, tackling him down the steps. His head bashing against the granite, the bells rings rushed through him, slamming against the rustic door, begging to open once more. His vision blurred with each pulsing ring.

Astrid launched his knee into the tackling guard, pressing his hand against his wide veiny neck, the echoing of cracking bone cast through his skin, through the very stone beneath them. The King's scoff crashed at his left ear, causing him to cringe, biting at his bleeding gums.

Darting his punching towards the two lunging guards. His gold grew, twirling around the two guards, cutting at their skin like thin paper. The gold burning, beaming, and thrusting into what is in his way, completely raw and almost uncontrollable.

"Let me." A woman's voice cast down the wide staircase. Lassea jumped, aiming towards him, looking to the King. The King grunted, whispering into the air as he glared at Pazima.

Pazima screamed through her knotted coils, dragging her palms across the smooth stone. Her lips open, spatting out, pleading within her screams.

He jolted. Her screams buckled his knees, freezing him like he was many years ago, left and abandoned. The peak of frost and snow, innocent and young with nothing but the thin fabrics wrapping his shaking body. Found by a girl with richness in her features, absorbing the freezing season's reflections with mere grace. That grace remained fractured under royal hold, screaming into the ancient granite.

"Stop!" Astrid screamed out, trying to grip at his pouring sobs. He tossed his sword down the steps, allowing it to drop into the open square. Everyone was gone, hiding away. The floor without kneeling Eyldians, revealing a four-pointed star, their Nova, constructed by quartz and chiselled granite and washed-white cobblestones.

The King knelt, grabbing Astrid's cheek, pulling his sobbing face up into the sun's harsh beams. "Where is the other?" The question spat out calmly, brimming with venom.

Screams echoed through the crowd, forcing the Eyldians to cradle in the building's shadows.

# Chapter 47

## The Worry of Closed Doors

### *Raven*

Raven pulled himself to a stable footing, looking between Sevar's frozen, sharp glare and Caelan's loose lip. "Who was he to you?" His heart pulsed as he felt Sevar raise from the smashed skull, mixing in blood and mud. A sense knotted around his ribs, pushing and pleading. He shook it away, holding his rib.

Sevar briskly long breaths crept through the mud. "No one, anymore."

"I thought I knew who you were while travelling with you, sleeping next to you." Caelan walked to Raven's side, supporting his quivering posture. "You just split that man's head into two, without remorse." His words struggled to connect. "I--"

Sevar lunged, supporting Raven's sudden drop. "This comes with war, little crow." Sevar guided his fingers across Raven's blood-stained rogue curls. "Don't be afraid. I'm still me, the one you travelled with." Sevar's words crumbled slowly to a mild whisper. "Anak used me, controlled me. He—abused me and many others but wasn't the top rank. There are many others

304

still abusing people." Sevar's face cringed slightly. "You don't need to come. I can take you back home."

"The possibilities all pull to you, to this. We need to help my brother." He whispered back.

–

Caelan pushed Raven down swiftly, blocking their sight behind the narrow stone bridges. The wind, whistling through the stone railings, ancient and filled with tales of old, curved in roughly, like the old ones utilised their fingernails for their craft. Figures peered over the bridge's walls, looking into the Sun's Sea. Hues of light blue crashing the rocky cliffs. Time wiping and cutting away at the stone, curving into the depths, sharpening the blunt stones into natural weapons.

Sevar whispered into the gushes, twirling his runic power silently. Purple ribboning echoes refusing to glow brightly, purposefully hiding its presence. He waved his hands like it wrapped around each bone. Tethering his broad structure to his magic core with a visible strain.

"Does it ever get easier to use?" Raven's curiosity peered upon the runic power.

"Never, it'll always strain and take. It's a formidable force." Sevar paused, twisting his hand slightly. "That's why weaponry and combat training are paramount for most."

Caelan supported Sevar's strain, adding his own muttering words, simply mirroring Sevar's runic words.

The soldier's unaware, arched carelessly over the bridge, spitting over like an odd competition for the longest salvia launch. Their differences in hues of purple ribboned, knotting around the soldier's arms in a swift and painful grip. The soldier's groans masked by the waves of power wrapping around their rough faces, burning their pointy noses and thin lips. Sevar flicked his fingers up, pulling them together with a quick grunt. They pulled up from behind the boulders, forcing their footing firm into the bridge's ancient cobbled stone foundations.

"Over the edge, Caelan." Sevar sniped.

They pulled their runic whispers together, pulling the soldier's muffled groans to a silenced scream, scraping their thighs against the wall's thick, stone railing, nothing but the runes' pulsing power and the rogue gushes of wind keeping the soldier's firm in the air.

Caelan glanced over to Sevar, nodding in agreement. They snapped their fingers, cutting the runic connection in one brutal click. The soldier's screams consumed by the currents crashing waves, dropping to a long, knowing plummet to a swift death.

–

Raven pulled his hood over his head swiftly, as demanded by his travelling partner. He muttered in a stale agreement. He knew Sevar desires to protect and care for his well being, but he needs to learn about his environment.

They dashed into Lonsai city, covering their arrival with the cast shadows of narrow homes made of stained stones and sandstone-coloured coverings. Their titles stained yellow and claimed by time and unkept conditions. The city's people lurked and muttered closely between them, glaring at any uncertainty. Lonsai held most of the city's population, connected to Trade's Peak and the Legion's quarters through their ancient stone bridges, dropping its pillars into the Sun's Sea deep below.

Sevar pulled forward, heading their way, curving through the jigsaw of lurking citizens.

Raven grabbed Caelan's focused glance. "I look into his eyes sometimes and think he's still a mere stranger. What that Commander must have done, what he must have endorsed. How do I get him to open that wound?" He spoke low towards Caelan.

"All anyone can do is try. And when that isn't successful. You try again. Let him know you won't leave." Caelan gripped his sword, keeping his eye on the lurking, wondering concerns.

"Wise for a Young." He smiled.

"I'm seventeen." Caelan replied in haste. "I'm sorry for my anger against you, it wasn't ever about you."

"I know, Caelan, I understand." Raven pushed his shoulder to Caelan's.

Running, never-ending seas of Eyldian's forming a natural wave of fear and mere confusion. Dashing throughout each city, across the narrow bridges, into their homes to wait out the lurking rumours of chaos and war within their boundaries.

"The rebels!" A woman bellowed, holding her firm and rounded stomach. The wave of force and footsteps pushed under her footing, tossing her into the smooth stone foundations. They kept to the edge, pushing with all their strength, whispering for any protection they could muster.

Sevar glanced for a swift instance, launching to the stone. "Ma'am. Are you okay." He held her up, pushing through the bridge.

"Thank Nova, thank you!" She pleaded out with a full sob.

They pushed through the final steps, launching themselves into the creases of an Inn's structure. Sevar pulled into the Inn's door with a mighty thrust. "Stay in here till it calms out there," Sevar ordered softly, offering some fabrics from the nearby sofa.

Caelan kept to the doors, peering out to keep sight on the ongoing situation.

"It must be important to be visiting our lovely city?" She hinted.

"We have an audience with the King. Important import of weaponry for the First Legion." Sevar lied through his cast smile.

"If you're looking for an entrance to the castle, the King arrives through the Peak's Tower. No one can pass except officials and scholars. But you'll need to wait for the scum to be snuffed out."

"Thank you. We'll see if we can help." He turned, nodding vaguely to others.

# Chapter 48

### The Peak of Rebellion

Sevar sighed. "Sun's Peak is a fucking maze." Existing the Trade's peak's southern bridge.

"She said the Peak's Tower, which must be quite a tall structure." Raven muttered.

Sevar's face dropped. "Really?" Sevar's eyes sliced through him. "You know, I didn't think of that, sweetie."

Caelan spat out a swift laugh, forcing it to stop within a click, cupping his lips with his sweaty fingers.

He angled his face slightly, puzzled, questioning if to be offended or highly amused. The broad brute had quite a sarcastic side. "Big brute needs to control his temper." He blew a kiss, walking across the smooth stone, clenching his heart under his cloak.

-

He and Sevar walked closely. "What if we run into the King—"

"Your father?" Caelan highlighted from behind.

Sevar's head turned swiftly, followed by muttering grunts. Raven smiled vaguely, knowing the high possibility of Sevar's emotive protectiveness towards Caelan and himself.

Hooded figures stepped out, placing their boots softly. Their trousers and boots coated in dried blood. The smell still lingering, teasing their noses. "I knew you wanted to fuck him." A voice echoed, familiar to the ear like a fading memory of their travels.

"Bastian?" Sevar angled his head, focusing on the cloaks shadowing.

Their hoods flew, flicking a smile onto their features. Blood dashed over their grins. The hues of red coating their sweating rosy cheeks. "Indeed, brother."

"How? When did you get involved? The last time we spoke about that, your ideals weren't... well, ideal."

Bastian ran his hand through his sweaty, short, oak-brown hair. "Wasn't sure I could trust you till he came along." His glance peered to Raven.

"What about him?" Sevar said.

"It's like you were dead, without a heart or drive. Seems the crow gifted you both." Bastian kept his gaze to Raven. "You know what you must do, don't you?"

"How many know?" Raven muttered low.

"As many that will listen, it all calls to you. Dreamers whisper of your sacrifice, as Sun's Peak mourns." Bastian claimed, placing a hand upon Raven's.

"Dreams can mislead us all." He replied sharply, pushing through while holding a silent tear. His heart pulsed, racing, sending panic through every vein. Raven pushed Bastian's hand, weaving through the groups of rebels, banding together in union and blood.

He choked on his sob. "Why must I?" He called out into his hands. "I've just begun seeing the most beautiful things, experiencing the wonders of our world." He sobbed into his arms, rolling down the building's rocky textures. "Snow, cold, and beautiful sunlight, mythics of old."

"Raven." Sevar called softly. "I won't let you die."

"Even you can't promise, everyone, the dreamers all speak of it like its mere truth ribboned into the fabric of the realm. Demanding it." His breathing raced like the air became unusable. "I can't. I can't—" He gasped. "I can't do it, Sev."

Sevar dropped to his side, wrapping him in one smooth glide. "I won't allow it, even if any of the gods themselves demand it. I won't." He whispered, lifting him into a supportive hold. "You have so much more to keep hold, to keep safe."

"It's so much blood, I've seen what it could become, the meadows of blood." Raven's raised from his

Sevar pushed open the nearest door, placing him into an old study building. "If war is to come, I won't let any prophecy take your life." Sevar looked at Raven like time was unforgiving. "Sorry, my sweet crow. I'll finish what we started." He whispered, slamming the door, knotting his magic around its bolts.

"Wait!" Raven bellowed, bashing his shoulder into the slammed door.

"If you go, they'll kill you. I'm sorry." Sevar pleaded, looking into Raven's tearful eyes.

"Sev, please" He screamed. Emotion erupted, scared, completely frozen into place. Screaming, punching against the door's thick panes. He knew the prophecy could end him, but if his here, who would take his place, and scream for a better world.

# Chapter 49

## Blood That Runs Through the Cobbles

### *Sevar*

Slicing through the thick, warm air in swift and direct moments, Bastian whipped his head to him. "Where is he?" Bastian's blonde brows rise, covered in blood. His eyes widening with each second passing.

"He's gone another way." He spoke bluntly, folding the piercing pain out from between his ribs.

Bastian scanned him. "Don't fuck this up for us, Sev—"

"Let's carry on, we have a rebellion to support, and I have friends to find." Annoyance breezed through, tackling the warm air.

"Is he safe?" Caelan ran up to his side.

Sevar looked to the left, giving Caelan a vague nod.

Bastian raised his arm with force, collecting the rebels from the city's streets. Calling out, chanting for the first act of rebellion, together.

-

Bastian's commands bellowed through the inclining streets and their mountainous grand steps. The soldier's whispers roared down the sides, launching to quake their chaotic footings. The cobbles threatening to loosen under their boot's piling pressures, Sevar looked down to his palm, and the new rune that itched through his skin, teasing a flickering ember through his umber skin.

Purple radiated from his palm, following his whispers. His mind battling between the words of the newly learnt runic ability and the pain stabbing at his heart. Raven's sobs cracking through his trained, narrow focus. He grunted, forcing his whispers to pile onto his overwhelming emotion, forming chains connected through links of purple thick ribbons, knotting, and melding together with each word spilling into the cobbles.

"Sev, to your right!" Bastian bellowed as Caelan climbed up the stone walls, launching himself and his throwing knives into the blockade of soldiers.

Sevar's whispers were clean of regret and sorrow, coughing out into the chains that lay in his glowing palm. His dark-brown skin soaking in the purple hues, casting it out in a pure light, filling the steps with his unknown rune.

Soldiers began to scoff and spit down upon him. "Going against the law of runic possessions, act One and Two. Sevar Lorstorm." They yelled.

"Sorry, got it from a friend." small poisonous smirk grew, lifting his cheeks, letting the sun glare upon his white teeth. He left no time lingering between each strike, whipping the humming chains into clashing rings quaking through every stone. The chains, waving through the air, slicing through the warmth and their flesh in ease, wrapping around a soldier's arm, tossing him down the stairs in one mighty thrust, burning and charring through layers of skin, the runic essence scratching at the soldier's bones, radiating up to Sevar's ever-tightening grip.

The soldiers, all labelled differently through their sewed patches on their right sides. Many taken down through their limited whispers, or swiftly by Caelan's deadly projectiles. The soldier's own whispers cut short, throwing off their forming words, spitting and stomping on their tangling focus.

Sevar's mind spun, following his runic power dwindling through with every metallic thrust through the air. Latching on the soldier's broad arms, tossing them into the ancient stone walls, through the thin sun-stained panes. Shattering the hues of translucent orange across the ascending staircase.

Sevar and Bastian caught each other's eye, nodding. Their Clockwork training together, roaming through their thoughts. Swift deaths to be gifted, till wronged.

The legion's numbers dropped, littering the floor in layers of warming flesh and blood-soaked uniforms. The screams of revenge and grunts, noting their legion's next wave of unknowing deaths.

One lone young man struggled through the layers of dead. Sobbing, begging for his life to pause, he begged to anyone, anything that lived within the very air they breathe each rotation. "Please, Nora" The man coughed, spat out small amounts of his own clouting blood. "The Moon, the stars, Anyone." He pleaded.

Sevar pulled the chain, in one long breath, his rune burned, pulling and ripping the chain. The metal shattering into purple hues of bright dust. He grunted, holding his burning palm. "Fuck." He spat. He knew the price of summoning the chain's power, the grip it'll take on the user's body for many rotations.

*Their magic weakened, severely weighed by the summoner's costly bargain.*

Sevar's knees threatening to buckle. He gripped his broadsword, latching onto the limited power remaining, withering, pleading for it to keep him together. His thoughts barrelling around in his skull. The pain of leaving Raven grew, fuelling him. He brought up his broadsword, walking to the trembling man. The man threw his hands over his face, dropping into another body. Sevar paused, looking into his quaking hands, his highlights of browns and reds like a symbol to the Crackling.

Bastian reached Sevar's side, reaching for his sword. "What are you doing, kill him."

"Stand away, Bas" He looked through Bastian's steaming grunts. "What's your name?"

The young man peeled two fingers away, letting his eyes breach through his blood-stained hands. "B--Beni."

"Why did you join your legion?" He choked on his fatigue.

"My parents were promised a new life. The legion picked me up from the farm, raised me to serve—" Beni spat out the words, but his lips quivered, holding his left side. Sevar glanced down sharply, launching his hands to force pressure on Beni's gushing wound. "I'm sorry." He whispered.

Sevar whipped his head to the right, facing Caelan. "Take him to the nearest rebel camp, keep him safe."

Caelan's brows narrowed sharply. "Help a legion soldier? You abandon Raven, now wish to save this?" Caelan's cheeks burned bright red.

"What's the point in this rebellion, if we don't save the good?" He spat, venously. He glanced at Bastian. His face ran pale, nodding to Sevar.

"Take him, now." Bastian glued his stare to Caelan.

Caelan pushed forward, leaning next to Sevar, vaguely scoffing at his task. "I'll do it. Swear you'll bring them home to the temple?" His voice dropped, exposing his straining features.

"I will, I'll bring them all home." He smiled at Caelan, placing Beni into Caelan's arms.

-

"The Tower is their last known spotting?" Sevar questioned.

"Yes, on the city's edge, where their people gather, just down that path. It's chaos." Groups of rebels ran into the square, screaming and pleading. The sound of clashing metal, cutting through the air.

He raised his sword, running through the streets with Ba-stian on his sixth. "I need to reach the gateway."

"Good luck." Bastian sharply replied, glancing at a worrying expression.

He launched through the cobbles, lunging across unstable stalls, Sevar's broadsword straining, begging to use any runic power left, yet no energy poured from his palm. His body left drained. He let out a primal grunt, breathing rapidly as he sliced through three soldiers' lower stomachs in one long casting swipe. Their guts spilled out like a rotten old vegetable soup, dropping chunks of potato onto the scorching granite floor.

Sevar refused to look back to the other rebels, their pleas for assistance. Bastian's orders barked across the square, ringing like a blunt golden bell. Even with his taxing exhaustion, he promised many to bring their loved one's home. One thought rang through him, making him feel utterly exposed to the warm elements. How does the prophecy fit? As a rebellion starts, how will the crow scream out...

A low, venomous voice called out. "Lorstorm, I've read about your quests across Eyldia, to save mother. Sad it'll be in vain" Sevar cut through the soldiers and the cowering civilians. Their screams cracked at his umber skin, turning the air to a sharp blade.

He pulled up his sword, lunging to the left as far as he could. His breathing strained and thinned. "Where are they?" A mighty sword of gold, wrapped in sharp copper, slammed down, cracking the granite stone at his feet. King Dreaka. The man who started it all, the Four, their siege. The plague upon their peace. Sevar lunged for his broadsword, swinging his position up against King Dreaka's sword, the royal's strength radiating down his golden blade, pushing his black hairs to stand firm.

"You'll be with them soon." The King grinned, full of light.

"I'll kill a royal if need be," Sevar spat.

They launched their swords, grating their metals against one another, sparks spitting into the thick air. The screams blurred into the background as time slowed between strikes.

"Oh, you humour me." King Dreaka laughed. Soldiers ran to his side, the King sliced the ground, like a warning. His commands were calm yet rendering utter fear upon their features. "This has grown tiresome." King Dreaka's potent loathing knotted the air around their stances and their readied blades.

Sevar whispered, wrapping his tongue with runic pleads. He never would offer his words to any gods, but the racing sharp pulses ripped at his ribcage, clawing to his heart. The weight of his sword became unwieldable, like ancient stones forged to its hilt.

"You see, now this is clear evidence why we don't use illegal runes." The King's grin grew, moving his sword from his right, cutting at Sevar's arm. Sevar ankles twisted, letting go of the last drops of energy that ran through his veins. Nothing but the thought of Raven accompanied the darkness.

# Chapter 50

### The Crow's Last Vision

*Raven*

The walls of stone, caked in dust, and memories of old times. Abandoned. Passed by, folded into a crease of the busy streets, hidden by flickering oil lamps and covered red panes.

The door's rung, stinging his ears. Left with only his unfiltered thoughts and unhinging emotions. "I'll smash his beautiful face into the cobbles." He muttered into the floating layers of dust and dead skin.

"Why do this? I'm scared, but I know I must go." He groaned, wiping his eyes. "Did he know what Fee said? No. They weren't close enough. He can't be stupid enough." His breathing raced.

Gold tint began to flow, ribboning the layers of unmarred dust. "Oh, alignment." His vision completely filtered in hues of gold. Like a cave of old ores, some exposed to the elements, some with a beaming shine at its purest form. Its hue flashed, highlighting between its gold and brightening orange.

"Focus on you." a voice fresh to his ears, coating his skin in an all-knowing warmth. "Who are you, One from a lonely life in an old cottage?" The voice questioned.

Hues of orange and gold twisted at his irises, forcing his vision to blur.

The study of dust, odd books and papers spun into an infinite black abyss, colours warping space, turning, twirling. Drums bashed, clocks ticked, bells rang, crashing upon his temple. The orange tint pushing back through his unfiltered power.

Focusing, pushing back into reality became impossible. He lifted his head, looking back at the old unstable bedside table, with its draws left ajar, with undergarments unfolded, peeking through the draw's opening.

His cottage. His home.

Abandoned by time and his own choices, time refused to lay its force upon it. Raven climbed to his feet, shocked by a shocking sharp noise. Ringing, growing as he pulled through the cottage's narrow hallway, bashing against the old cloak hangers. A never-ending ring, like a calm song of warnings for times to come.

Raven held onto the kitchen's countertop, rubbing his scorching eyes. The kitchen's panes shook, cracking by smashing black feathers, some roughed by the mud and winds of Elcoo. The shapes of crows forming and moulding across the glass panes. Gold dots grew to sharp circles of gold. "Aligners, gifted to help us win in this brutal, brisk war. A war birthed by the crack connecting our realms." The crows angled their heads. "Raven Whitewood, this is the start to the end. Will you help us?" The voice echoed, all-consuming. Toned and crafted with utter care and understanding.

"I'm not strong enough. I tried." He looked into the crow with rage. "I've barely lived." Raven yelled out, launching his nearby bowl of rotten oats into the window panes.

His focus pushed and cracked once more, pushing him into the dark hues of gold and orange. "Do you disrespect the sacrifice of Unsa? To form into a divine source of power for this realm's mortal beings?"

His vision fractured yet fixed to a focus of screams and sobs. His friends. All left in a line in a darkening hall of royal statues. Rope tying around their necks, tightening without remorse. "Without you next to your brother together, they will all be damned. Connect and dig to the depth of what you've been gifted."

Their necks filled with air. Gasping to their skin, their groans replacing their pleads to life. "Stop the Four. For what they plan will break this realm. They bargain with power they do not understand."

The voice became strained. "You and Astrid are chosen by blood, by Unsa. Don't let me down." It almost pleaded, with a lingering fear. If a divine entity, a god could fear. What stood behind the crack.

He groaned through the golden hue that grew through his veins, the blast of gold pushing, splitting the crowding crows. Scorching gold filled his iris with power, godly and completely overwhelming. Raven screamed with hollow lungs.

Dust flew, hiding away from the power that soared through his veins. The runic power burned at the door, peeling away as it fought against the gold ribbons, tightening at its core.

"I'll do it." He spoke with promise. Pushing through the shards of old wood, with the purest glint of gold filling the edge of his vision.

# Chapter 51

The Gateway to many possibilities

Blood and bodies filled the cobbles and smooth, polished streets. All styles covered by the pain of death, lingering in the air. The smell of burning skin replaced the dust in his nose. The tinting of gold and orange, interlocking through his veins, syncing as if they spoke through his skin, each hair, every inconsistency, all seen and recorded. Moulding his power to work together in a calming harmony.

He breathed slowly, racing up the mountainous staircases. "No more hiding." He kept muttering, pushing the words to clean formations.

A voice echoed from the left side, an echo calling to him. "Raven!" A familiar voice. Caelan ran to his side. "Where were you? Sevar ran into the square with the rebels."

"Alone?" His stomach dropped like an endless pit into utter darkness, threatening to be consumed with anxiety.

Caelan nodded with a stiff shake, like his fatigue piled on his shoulders. "He had me saving someone, bringing them to the healers." Caelan's glare strained to the bodies lying on the cobbles.

"Let's find our people." Raven spoke, holding his longing breath. His grip ever tightening upon his golden veins, folding through his palm's bruised skin.

-

Caelan and Raven walked as one as Caelan sorted his weapons at his sides.

Raven reached down, taking out the lone dagger left in his weaponry. The dried blood of his first kill, the blood of a life taken by his hand. He wiped it, wishing the lost soul well.

Caelan moved forward, pushing himself into the groups of wounded soldiers. "Your King shows no care for your lives." Caelan roared out.

Their heads, straining and stirring. As if their minds had experienced the true brutality of the Four.

"We serve. It's the only way." A soldier held his right arm, holding his pain between his gritting teeth. The soldier's shaven hair, completely dyed by hues of red, by spilled blood.

A young soldier to his right climbed to his feet, keeping his hand on his hilt. "I need this to feed my family." The young soldier's hand quivered, hovering below his mouth.

"Join the rebellion. They will help anyone who needs it." Caelan claimed.

The soldier in the middle climbed hastily. "I will cut my name with treason." The man slid across the smooth stone, gripping a lone sword left on the ground.

Caelan ripped his sword off his side. "Don't!"

The soldier's face pasted with an unreadable expression, his sword swinging in the warm, dense air. Caelan's left hand flicked up, slicing the soldier's neck in one smooth strike. "I'm sorry." Caelan dropped to the smooth stone next to the choking soldier. He held the blooding official's neck. "You could've been more" The soldier's eyes glistened like the Nova stars filled his view.

"Stay and help the wounded. Collect at the Peak's exit." Caelan's tone simmered to a low base.

Raven came to his side as they walked to the Peak's tower, pushing their legs to a quick sprint before any willing soldiers came to guard their pathway.

The stairs of death, he thought to himself. Too many stairs to count, all narrowing to the entrance to the vast tower. Breathes thinned as they reached the double doors. Pushing with mere relief.

He glanced again quickly, keeping his hand to his hilt as Astrid and Sevar taught him. Their steps remained close, stepping through the rooms that seemed frozen to time. Eyldia's history and its cultures hung on the walls, planted into pots on the sides of the thick sofas. Cultures, time forgot, perfectly placed and framed, but coated in dust and old fabrics.

"The portal is normally found connected to the natural stone. At least that's how it looked in Sreset." Raven ran his finger softly against the table. "The Fours seem to discard theses cultural historical items."

"It doesn't fit their story." Caelan muttered. "Stairs down here." He filled the empty silence.

Raven pulled up, walking with him. The wood, fading away, step by step. Time removing the wood foundations. All stones and metal holding the structure together.

The tints of purple and white swirled as they entered the long, narrow hall. One room full of portals to the other cities. The carpets were clean, smelling of vanilla, like it's fresh off the market.

"You used these before?" Caelan whispered.

"Once. When me and Sevar were running from Sreset." His framed lips dropped to a frown.

"We just step through?"

"It's open, so yes." He replied hesitantly.

Caelan stepped in front, nodding in silent agreement. They stepped into the infinite twirls of runic ribbons. The tang of ancient runes pushing through his nostrils, filling his taste buds in bursts of acid.

–

Raven's vision peeled open to pure symmetry. Pillars on both sides running down the hall, supporting the reflective white stone. The contrasting colours of the black wood wall detailing and the white paint coating the ancient structure caught his focus.

"They must be in their royal dungeon. Let's look for a way downwards." Calean whispered.

"Agreed." He replied, looking into the painted over symbols. Paint clumped and layered, covering a sentence. A statement. Raven ran his finger over the lettering, asking for it to speak to him as his orange tint raised across the painted wall.

*Amidst the tapestry of difference, a longing understanding of love and peace peaks above all Eyldians.*

A tear dropped from his cheek, falling to the carpets below.

"Raven?" Caelan placed his hand on Raven's shoulder.

"Sorry, these words. It must have been here originally. Their mark on understanding, on peace. It needs to be spoken."

Caelan's eyes scanned over it, tracing his fingers across the words. "Indeed. It does. We need to go before someone spots us."

Raven nodded, walking down the halls of endless polished white.

–

"Down here?" Caelan stopped the silence. A staircase with statues on both sides, all the Kings, Queen, and their heirs. The carpet, vibrant and fresh with the smell of fresh baked vanilla hovering through the staircase.

"It's the only descending staircase we have come across at this level." He replied, holding his breath slightly. Each step felt like a pause in time. The air slammed to a sudden stop. Thin and warm, tickling his throat.

His palm clammed, running his fingers across his trousers. Accepting another warm, long breath in, filling his lungs. The view of the room edged into their eye line. Glass squares holding ancient items at the sides of the carpet. The final longing steps pushed against his heart like a blade against his spine.

"Welcome." A gravelly voice echoed against the white stone.

His heart clenched, choking on the raw anxiety burning entirely through his lungs.

No tears ran. Everything froze from within. His thoughts racing, yet utterly frozen into place. Like a corpse in the peak of the freezing season.

Caelan launched across the carpet. "Astrid, Pazima!" He cried out, straining against the guard's angled blade at his neck.

The guards pushed Raven further across the room, forcing him to focus upon the figures kneeling below the thrones with a mere lunge away.

"If you ever thought you were in control, Raven, then you are as stupid as I thought." King Dreaka's grin beamed, reflecting the white embers.

# Chapter 52

## The Kings, The Queen & The People

"Kneel, son." King Dreaka grinned, glancing at his fellow royals, King Alonn, King Plu Kan and Queen Atula. All sat in varying positions. King Dreaka kept back, tapping his throne's thick armrest. King Alonn and Plu Kan sat firm, almost completely stiff. Scared? Of what, Raven thought to himself, juggling the racing thoughts. His focus pulled to Queen Atula, sitting at a slight angle, facing the exterior wall, looking seemingly uncomfortable.

Astrid grunted as a guard held him with whispers creeping behind them. Rope coated in runes tying around each of their hands. The smell of burning skin lingered between the royals and themselves.

All in a line like animals to slaughter. Waiting for the Four's final act upon their lives.

King Dreaka gripped his staff, rising to his feet. He glanced to his left. King Plu Kan reflected Dreaka's piercing grin. "I'm going to enjoy this, after the mess you caused in Sreset." King Plu Kan hissed.

"Indeed, they caused quite a storm." King Alonn called out. The disdain poured out from their expressions.

Raven looked at the woman's struggling posture. All of his friends knelt, this woman had to be her. "Paz—" He tried to mutter, but King Dreaka brought down his staff, striking its end against his left cheek. A rageful grunt broke through the air as he dropped into the carpet.

Astrid launched to Dreaka's throne. "You bastard." The guards lunged, pulling against the burning runic rope, launching Astrid back onto the cold carpet.

"Stop!" Sevar roared out.

Raven scanned the line of the group, noticing the absence of one of their own. He pushed against the closed door, roaring against the mental lock. *"Astrid, open the door. You closed it, only you can open it now. Your power. You need to control our power and your emotion, now"* He stared at his brother for a longing moment. The plea noted in his expression.

Astrid's face widened, refusing to turn to Raven, knowing not to pull attention to their connective doorway. The door clicked, following the sweat building on Astrid's brow. *"Sorry, controlling the power and the rage, I closed the door without knowledge."*

*"It's okay. We need a way out."* Raven pleaded.

*"We are outmatched in every way."* Astrid's face looked up to the Four.

*"We just need to get close enough, the alignment. We got it for a reason. Trust me."*

"Where are our memories?" Astrid spat at King Dreaka.

King Plu Kan raised in haste, reaching for his croaked dagger. "Don't ask the King—"

"You want to know?" King Dreaka smiled.

King Plu Kan and Alonn's faces pulled back, yet Queen Atula looked vaguely absent between the eyes. No stars sparkling in her features, such beauty in her pale skin, but nothing but a neutral glance peered down to Raven, with her lips closed.

King Dreaka chuckled to himself. "Me and your mother were dearly in love many years ago. We were happy ruling this land together. We planned to have children, you dear children." He looked to his sides, glancing at the other royals. "But then Alonn decided to destroy that—" He signalled to the guards with a single mere glance.

"What are you doing?" King Alonn questioned as the guards lunged the rope around his hands.

"You see my friend. I knew." King Dreaka placed his hand on Alonn's cheek, teased across his pale features. "I always knew."

"I—We didn't mean for this," King Alonn began to plead out.

"You didn't? You didn't fuck my Queen?"

"We were in love. Don't disrespect her name." Alonn looked into Raven's glance. The man he once tortured for mere entertainment. "Why bring them here?"

"Use your knowledge, Alonn." King Dreaka's eyes went a shade darker. "You are their father."

# Chapter 53

## The Father, The Mother & Their Blood

*Astrid*

King Plu Kan's jaw hung with shock, while Queen Atula remained absent of any mere expression, like she had been frozen in stone.

"It was entertaining to see how it would unfold. Difficult at first, as for the location of Raven, but we had our resources for that minor issue." King began to whisper towards the left side entrance, causing the doorframe to slam open.

"Welcome back." An Eyldian with red fabric wrapping around her silhouette. A thin belt hanging from her hips. Her hair dropped like silk; ink black yet absorbing the embers light with grace.

"Fee—" He choked and struggled upon the burning rope.

"She's been working for me for many years, countless rotations, never-ending reports of your movements and your developing skills." King Dreaka glanced at Pazima with a solid stone's grin. "Your relationships."

"You raised me!" He screamed out, letting the rage consume him from his core, burning any reason, or sense, scorching like a fire had poured through his veins. Every inch filling and soaring. "You knew everything, I loved you."

"Astrid—" Fee's lip quivered.

"Enough." King Dreaka commanded silence. "I will get what I'm owed. Bring these two forward, now." He raised his sword, pointing it at Pazima and Sevar.

"Why do this? Because your wife loved another?" Raven spat out.

Dreaka placed his sword to the side, walking to kneel in front of Raven. He cupped his chin softly. "Even for a dreamer, you don't open your eyes and see."

"What are your plans for Storm's way?" Pazima spoke coldly.

"Clever girl! See this is why I kept her around. She is smarter than most. It'll be a shame if I need to kill you." He winked to Pazima, walking back up the small step to his throne.

"Touch her and I'll chase you to each corner of the realm till you piss your royal pants, thinking of my name." Astrid pushed himself to his legs, ignoring the burning that sung through his skin. Guards wrapped their arms around his biceps, keeping him anchored to the floor.

"You see, Alonn, you took her away and what she had promised me." Dreaka's face ran pale, as if a monster rose to the surface. "You took the twins—my right to their power by birth and blood." He swung his sword carelessly through the air, forcing Astrid to weave his head to the side. "Now theses overgrown bastards threat our reign." King Dreaka sighed, sitting back on his throne, rubbing his chin.

"We won't rest till you all rot in the ice dungeons of Jinos." Raven looked to Alonn, scanning over his scared expressions.

"You took my wife away from me!" King Dreaka launched from his throne, laying his sword to Raven's side. "Now I'll take who you love." He raised his sword, pressing it against Sevar's beard. "Don't you know her, Lorstorm?" His mocking grin grew. "One night when the moon was shining brightly, in the forest of Rale. A dreamer gave you purpose." The King's voice dropped to a whisper. "A prophecy."

"Not impossible—" Sevar's throat bobbed.

"A fool who believed a crafted prophecy but my own hands. Now your love for the crow will be your end." The King raised his sword with a firm grip. "Hold his head." He commanded the nearby guard, exposing Sevar's neck to his hovering blade.

"Stop, please." Raven sobbed.

"I didn't get the chance to plead, well it wouldn't have made a difference. Would it Alonn?" Dreaka turned his head.

Alonn kept utterly still, forced to kneel at the foot of his own throne.

"This isn't your fault." Sevar spoke quietly.

Raven's sob echoed through the room as he waited for any signal for movement. He pushed slowly against the rope. "Caelan, look at me." He whispered to his trainee, wishing for him not to be a witness.

King Plu Kan launched off his throne, full of venom, grabbing Caelan by his cheek, holding his view to Sevar's ordered execution. "Look at what happens when you come against us!"

"He's only a Young!" He roared out, pushing, dropping to his face, filling his view in the old red fabric. Astrid cried out, breathing in the old fibres of the Four, where countless Eyldians, old, young, all unfortunate to be knelt at their feet.

"Lucky for you Astrid, I'll keep Pazima alive. Just for my enjoyment."

"Keep me alive and I'll poison you in your sleep." Pazima spat at King Dreaka's thick leather boots.

Dreaka scoffed. "Call the maids, we'll need a deep clean of the throne room at dusk" The broad royal laughed, dropping his blade with brutal force, slicing through the air of borrowed time.

# Chapter 54

## The Crow's Last Stand

### *Raven*

Time felt old and rustic to the eye. His hand shaking like he remained in the brisk environments of Jinos. The moments he would live in endlessly to keep his love from being cut. The only person who understood him, yet it was forged. Crafted by revenge.

The love he held tight, the first time he truly felt seen within his skin. Without memories or purpose, without connection or understanding of the outside world. Sevar gifted him more than he could have imagined.

Without another longing thought, his gold power burst like a boiling cauldron. Ribbons of gold burning the guards' eyes, wrapping its burning temperature around their throats.

He launched without thought, without warning, without question. The prophecy may have been crafted, but he smiled. Pushing up with burning power, launching across to Sevar. He smiled.

He now understood who he was, as a dreamer, as an Eyldian.

He was the Crow that will cry for his realm, to lose for all to win, and do so without rage or question, for his love, for his family.

Raven pushed Sevar with one longing, ungodly thrust, the gold ribboning, focusing on Sevar's roll to the coloured panes.

The blade of Dreaka landed, cutting Raven's flesh and bone in a clean strike. The pain radiated through his skull, the blood pouring, puddling upon the polished stones, and soaking into his clothing. He sobbed, looking down at the severed right leg. His right knee left to go cold, ripped, left on the red carpet.

# Chapter 55

## For His Brother, For His life!

### *Astrid*

"Raven!" Astrid and Sevar called out. He tensed against the rope, bursting with boiling golden rage.

He whispered, launching ancient metal into existence, whistling the noises of old through the clashing metal chains. "We end this now." He commanded into the room, knowing his people would follow. Astrid whipped his chain against his friend's runic ropes, sending runic sparks jolting into the ancient glass cases.

Pazima slid, jumping onto the nearby guard. Calean kept to his side, circling his throwing knife. Caelan launched it to the oncoming guard that charged down the staircase.

The chaos. Noises of commands roared across the throne room, King's ordering for soldiers, struggling to pull at their throne's sword holders.

"Impressive." Astrid smiled.

Sevar dipped to the ground, pulling his way to Raven's side. "His blooding out." Sevar's voice cracked. He looked down to Raven, whispering softly. A sudden scream breached their ear drums as Sevar groaned against a soaring beam of energy from his palm.

The smell of melted skin stained the air of the throne room. Lingering up the walls and the tapestries. Raven's eyes flickered.

He looked to his front as King Dreaka launched his sword into the air. A clean strike towards his neck. Screams crashed, slamming against the panes behind the thrones. Shards of red and white shattered into the warm air, cutting at anyone in its path. The creature spanned its wings, slamming into King Dreaka, forcing him to bash down into the long throne room. A Spikehawk's wide wingspan twisted and twirled, shifting into a thick pale red mist.

"Daj?" He called out.

Her disapproving expression escaped the thin mist, throwing blades with unfamiliar hilts.

"I know! I know! I'm stupid. You can say it when we get out of this." The growing knowledge of her vivid expressions jumped into action.

Pazima ran across the room, diving for a sword from Daj, twirling to slice into the guards budging shin muscles.

He turned to face King Dreaka, as King Plu Kan charged from the thrones. Daggers in both hands, he faced him. Astrid readied his stance, but Plu Kan beamed a mocking grin. Lunging to the left.

A blink, a moment of motion, of uncertainty, for one life to be ripped from this realm. Their energy and blood left to pour into the stones below. Left with only memories and regrets.

"Take someone they love." King Plu Kan smirked, full of pride. "I did it, King Dreaka." Plu Kan's blade dripped, overflowing with blood.

Astrid's focus whipped to the side—Caelan.

"No—" He choked. Every sense froze and burned, bobbing bile at his throat. Time felt forged, raw and completely fucked. A click, one to the next, a life brimming with possibility, taken.

Anguish now held Astrid's blade, wrapping it's metal in scorching gold, throwing his blade like a sharp, long arrow into King Plu Kan's ribs.

"Caelan!" Pazima cried out, shooting out a stream of thick red mist, wrapping around King Dreaka's torso.

Only then did they notice the Queen of Engoria had abandoned the castle as blood poured.

"Astrid." Raven called out softly. He raised his palm, bursting with the last of his withering energy. Astrid and Raven's energy interlocking, intertwining like an ancient song whistling upon Eyldian soil.

King Alonn kept to the corner of the room, folding himself into the shadows.

The mist and gold ribbons of blinding energy roared, gathering like partners between the fabric of their realm.

Magic as one. Dreamer, whisper, shifter, aligner. Power sourced together apart from one. Astrid sobbed, screaming into their aligning power, hoping it would be enough.

King Dreaka's Body held in the air, choking on his blood. The gold reflected like a soaring sun, tinting against the King's cheek. "Fee!" King Dreaka pleaded.

Her eyes were full of orange hues, yet her expression was completely hollow. "Don't do it, Fee." Astrid stared. "Please."

"I'm sorry." Fee muttered. She lunged from the side doorway, clamping her arm around King Dreaka. Her orange ribbons strained his vision. Their power jolted, beaming into nothing but shattered glass. King Dreaka, gone.

He dropped to the floor, cupping his hand around Caelan's coils. "Shh, It's okay."

"Ast—" Caelan choked. "You are the best Keep," Caelan struggled to glance up at Daj and Pazima. "I—I love you all". His chest deflated, letting go of his final breath with a small smile upon his young features.

Astrid raised from the shattered glass, with each step entirely numb. The crashes of Sun's Sea's current climbed through the smashed window, accompanying their loss. Pazima and Daj hook their arms around Astrid, dropping their embrace down to Raven and Sevar.

Anguish and love - What's loss without treasured memories of ones passed?

# Chapter 56

## Loss and Love Bares No Limits

### *Pazima*

"Raven, stay awake." Sevar pleaded upon his lone tear.

"Let me." She placed her hand on Astrid's shoulder, softly pushing up to Sevar cradling Raven. Looking up, Sevar nodded as he climbed to his footing. His hands were covered in Raven's blood. She glanced at them deeply. Sparks of gold glimmers slowly faded through Raven's lowing blood.

She held Raven with care, filling her, accompanied by the worry lining her stomach. Her mist consumed them. Holding his body, wrapping in her wingspan as her lungs filled with the salt of the Sun's Sea.

# Chapter 57

## Prophecy Came Upon His Body

### *Raven*

"What's the current status?" A familiar voice echoed, pressing against his eyes.

"We remain in control of Lonsai, but the legions keep the Quarters and Trade's peak chained down. No reports of King Dreaka."

"Is it trouble—Raven?" The light soared at his iris, burning yet warming. The gift of mere exposure to sunlight, to touch the hairs that stand upon his lover's skin. To wave his fingers through his beard as the moon lights their intertwining bodies.

"I love you." He whispered.

Sevar crumbled to Raven's side. "Our love sets us free. I love you." Sevar whispered back.

-

"Healer? What's going to happen?" He choked, looking down to where a stall propped the remaining leg up.

The healer pulled their grey rich locks into a rough bun. "I won't twist it, Whitewood. This will be the hardest experience of your life. If you plan to walk once more. You'll need to learn how to bend your power to a hand-crafted prosthetic leg" She carried on measuring each crease of skin to the tiniest imperfection. ". Hopefully, Lorstorm and his people can find a way to get resources or people in and out of Lonsai City."

"How long was I asleep?" He asked, glancing around the clean copper framing, circling the bay's boundaries.

"Four rotations. You lost a lot of blood." She answered sharply.

"Thank you."

She smiled, walking off to other tasks without another word.

# Chapter 58

## The End of a Life Marks Us All.

### *Astrid*

The snow of the Fellow's mountains popped into view like a shock to the system, causing his stomach to bob slightly. He wanted to talk as they flew across the wide-open seas, but nothing of meaning brewed. Not rage, nor the hunger for revenge.

Sadness of a love lost to the soil. He had to bury the one he swore to protect, to train, but he failed him, to show his care, like Pazima had warned. He gagged, swallowing hastily, Pleading Daj didn't hear from behind.

Pazima's shifting twirled away by one glance, revealing an unmarked wooden box. One to bring their family home in speed.

"Astrid—What happened." The Commander choked. "The royals? They did this?" Sakhile and groups of Moonsong raced out through the sliding stones.

"Yes, Commander." Astrid forced his words to flow, offering the little sadness he had left to gift.

Commander Sakhile branched out, inviting Astrid, Pazima and Daj into a tightening, warm embrace. "I'm so sorry."

-

The wind whistled in a song of sorrow. You couldn't tell if you listened, but the birds knew, as they crafted their nests for the next upcoming cold seasons. They felt the shift deep within ancient stone. The invite of a new soul ribboning throughout the soil. Offering their final essence in hope of mere peace.

"I didn't look out for him like I should've. I could've taught him more. He was more than a trainee, he was family. When all came to, he loved and cared for us all." Astrid flicked dirt upon Caelan's grave. "May the moonlight guide you, Caelan." His expression, struggling to keep frozen in place.

Pazima hooked her arm into his. "We will make it right, my love." Her words were laced with promise. "I swear it to be."

-

The sharp wind cut through his hair, brushing the tears off his cheek, dripping every lone droplet into the river.

He stared, as time forgot, planting himself on the river's edge, staring into his golden irises upon the smooth ripples of the fresh river water. Ever-twirling like the suns above, threatening to set the world aflame.

*"I'm sorry I couldn't get to the temple."* Even through the mental framing between their minds, he could feel Raven cough upon his words. *"—For Caelan."*

*"You lost your leg, brother."* He spoke softly, with a mere mutter. *"I know you wanted to come."*

*"I swear to you, they'll get what they deserve."*

Astrid pushed an emotion through the fresh golden door, replied with what words couldn't express. An ever-flowing connection between brothers, a love between people.

The ache in the lining of each Eyldian's stomach as a loved one leaves their life, as he flicked small stones across the river's edge. He wished for one thing, closing his eyes with a longing breath, hoping any unknowing gods would stalk his thoughts, creeping in the corners of his eye.

Astrid wished for more time.

Milton Keynes UK
Ingram Content Group UK Ltd.
UKHW040611030624
443648UK00003B/11/J